CHRISTINE
FEEHAN

Bound Together

A SEA HAVEN NOVEL

piatkus

PIATKUS

First published in the US in 2017 by The Berkley Publishing Group
An imprint of Penguin Random House LLC
First published in Great Britain in 2017 by Piatkus

1 3 5 7 9 10 8 6 4 2

A CIP catalogue record for this book
is available from the British Library.

ISBN 978-0-349-41645-8

Printed and bound in Great Britain by Clays Ltd, St Ives plc

Papers used by Piatkus are from well-managed forests
and other responsible sources.

MIX
Paper from
responsible sources
FSC
www.fsc.org
FSC® C104740

Piatkus
An imprint of
Little, Brown Book Group
Carmelite House
50 Victoria Embankment
London EC4Y 0DZ

An Hachette UK Company
www.hachette.co.uk

www.littlebrown.co.uk

For Leslee Huber, thanks for all the love and support.
I can't tell you how much it means to me.

FOR MY READERS

Be sure to go to christinefeehan.com/members/ to sign up for my PRIVATE book announcement list and download the FREE ebook of *Dark Desserts*. Join my community and get firsthand news, enter the book discussions, ask your questions and chat with me. Please feel free to email me at Christine@christinefeehan.com. I would love to hear from you.

ACKNOWLEDGMENTS

With any book there are many people to thank. Leslee Huber
took me on a great adventure, going up and down the logging
roads at the Egg Taking Station to plan my battle. It was fun,
and I learned a lot! Her husband, Skye, answered tons of questions about the area for me. Thanks to Ed for his help with the
motorcycle club questions, of which there were many.

Thanks to Domini for her research and help with editing.
And to Brian Feehan, who I can call anytime and brainstorm
with so I don't lose a single hour.

TORPEDO INK CHARTER MEMBERS

Viktor Prakenskii aka **Czar** President
Lyov Russak aka **Steele** Vice President
Savva Pajari aka **Reaper** Sergeant at Arms
Savin Pajari aka **Savage** Sergeant at Arms
Isaak Koval aka **Ice** Secretary
Dmitry Koval aka **Storm**
Alena Koval aka **Torch**
Luca Litvin aka **Code** Treasurer
Maksimos Korsak aka **Ink**
Kashmir Popov aka **Preacher**
Lana Popov aka **Widow**
Nikolaos Bolotan aka **Mechanic**
Pytor Bolotan aka **Transporter**
Andrii Federoff aka **Maestro**
Gedeon Lazaroff aka **Player**
Kir Vasiliev aka **Master**
Lazar Alexeev aka **Keys**
Aleksei Solokov aka **Absinthe**

Bound Together

1

IF they were going to get out of this alive, they were going to have to be ghosts. Viktor "Czar" Prakenskii faced his men and their disapproving faces. He detested arguments, especially, like now, when they had very little time.

"Let me clear the way," Savva "Reaper" Pajari said. His eyes were flat and cold. Ice-cold. There was no emotion whatsoever in his voice.

Viktor knew he was the cause of that emotionless voice. He had that on his soul forever. There was no taking back their childhood or the things they'd had to do to survive—things that Viktor had conceived—just like this job. It was all on him, and he wasn't going to allow them to surround him like they all preferred, keeping him safe. This was his mess. He had never been able to put the brakes on, to say *enough*. For him, it was never enough, and where he went, the others followed.

"Not happening," he said, his voice low, terse. He was angry, but not at any of his brothers. At himself. He'd chosen a path and one by one they had followed him. His path had led straight to hell. "We don't have time to argue. We knew walking into this it was a trap. Nothing has changed."

Dmitry "Storm" Koval sighed heavily. "We all voted,

Czar, just like always. Stop trying to carry us on your shoulders. We chose this life. All of us."

Viktor clenched his teeth. That was a blatant lie. None of them had chosen their life. Not a single one. They all shared a common beginning. Each of them had parents murdered by a man named Kostya Sorbacov, because their parents hadn't agreed with Sorbacov's politics. He had taken the children to the most brutal orphanage/school ever conceived in the hopes of shaping them into assets for his country—at least that's what they all thought at first.

"That's bullshit, but we don't have time to debate right now. The longer we wait, the more men they'll have guarding this place."

The thought of what he was going to find turned his stomach, but then, it always did and he kept doing the same thing over and over. Five years of his life had been given to this mission. Evan Shackler-Gratsos was the number-one human trafficker in the world. Viktor knew he couldn't stop everyone, but he was determined to take the man down. That decision had cost him five years of his life, possibly his marriage and the knowledge that the men he called brothers had made the choice to follow him into hell, just as they always had.

He refused to argue with them any longer. He simply gave them a small salute and pushed through the wall to find his entry point. The warehouse where a chapter of the infamous Sword motorcycle club had set up shop, already renting out the young girls they'd acquired only a scant two to three weeks earlier, was in the industrial district. They moved the girls often in order to stay one step ahead of the cops.

This time, they had more new girls, most between the ages of eleven and sixteen, just the age Evan preferred to add to his stable. They lasted longer. Right now, they were "training" the new girls, which meant beatings and rape to get them to the point where they felt hopeless and so afraid they would do anything they were told.

Viktor knew what that was like. They all knew, and yet for five long years they'd ridden with the scum, wore their colors and defended them when they went to war. For this. For these moments. To take some of it back, and hopefully draw Evan out into the open where they could get to him. So *Viktor* could get to him. Evan Shackler-Gratsos represented every one of those pedophiles and sadistic monsters that had run the school. The rage that burned so hot in Viktor's belly night and day had come to demand the death of the human trafficker.

They'd wreaked enough havoc over the years to keep every Swords chapter on alert, especially when they brought in new girls. Viktor ran two teams, and often they hit two chapters simultaneously, but lately it had become more difficult. Evan demanded the girls bring in money day and night, seven days a week, so even when baiting a trap, they kept the women working and the lines long. It was no different in spite of the storm brewing.

There were guards hidden in the brush surrounding the warehouse on all sides. The roof connected with a second warehouse housing mostly heavy equipment for a local contractor. Viktor chose that building to make the penetration into the Swords' makeshift brothel. There were at least two guards between him and the building.

The chapter was spread thin trying to surround the building as well as keep the work going. They had to have guards inside to make certain the women were doing as they were told and that the customers didn't abuse their privileges without paying. They needed men guarding the outside line in order to keep it moving properly. All the while they feared the mystery crew that freed their slaves and killed the members of their chapter would strike.

Viktor and his men had spread fear throughout the Swords club and there was some satisfaction in that, but Evan, although seriously angry, hadn't personally made an appearance. The man was secretive now, and very paranoid. He had inherited billions from his brother, a Greek shipping magnate, and he had the money to stay hidden for as long as he wanted.

Viktor had been patient, moving up through the ranks of

the Swords. He was a huge asset, with his background. There wasn't a weapon he didn't know how to use. The club found him very useful. He didn't mind carrying out the assignments as enforcer because anyone doing business with them was covered in as much slime as they were. One by one, his men had joined after him, over a period of two years until all of them were in the Swords with him. All had come out of the shadows to take his back.

He waited in the darkness until one of the guards grew restless enough to give his position away. Very slowly he began to move from shadow to shadow, always cognizant of the fact that the Swords liked to lay elaborate traps and always used night vision goggles. He came up behind the man and killed him swiftly, a knife shoved hard into the base of the skull, severing the spinal cord. It was a signature kill for his crew.

To his left, a radio crackled. The noise was muffled. A voice spoke. The guard answered, his voice bored. The moment he stopped speaking, a dull thud followed. Viktor worked his way toward the sound. A body lay on the ground, someone pulling the boots to take it farther into the shadows just against the wall of the warehouse. He recognized Reaper.

Shaking his head, Viktor watched as Reaper removed the radio from the dead guard's ear and put it in his own. He should have known. Reaper had had his back in every situation for longer than either cared to remember.

"You don't follow orders."

Reaper straightened. "You didn't give any worth listening to."

Viktor narrowed his eyes at his enforcer. The man was a law unto himself when it came to protecting Viktor. He was ruthless, relentless and a pain in Viktor's ass. "Damn it, you take too many risks. You should have stayed out while you had the chance. All of you. Instead you follow me into this mess. Five years of our lives have been given to these scum. This mission. Who knows if we're really going to get our shot at taking the fucker out?"

Reaper glanced up toward the roof and then sighed. "You don't have the slightest clue why we all followed you, do you?"

Viktor looked at his friend. There was no evidence of the boy he knew, the young toddler brought to the school a year after Viktor had been ripped from his family. What had he done to Savva Pajari? There was nothing left of him at all. He was Reaper in every way. Slowly he shook his head, his eyes on the man who always had his back, whom he loved as family.

"You were free. As free as you could be with Sorbacov alive. You got out and you should have stayed out."

Reaper shook his head. "We'll never be free. Alive or dead, that man branded us, turned us into killers. You changed that, and gave us purpose."

"We did it together."

"We were animals in there, Viktor, and every one of us would be dead, just like the others, but you made us human again. You gave us a way out."

There had been a cost. A huge cost. The evidence stood before him in the form of a man, but what was left of Reaper, he wasn't certain anymore. He shook his head. "You were *out*. Sorbacov could have sent an army after all of you, but he never would have found you. He *didn't* find you, even after you came back out of the shadows to ride with me. None of you should have done that."

"You give us life. You make us believe. Look around you, Czar. This is where we belong, where we're always going to belong. We aren't like the rest of the people. We'll never be. What they did to us . . ." He trailed off, shaking his head again.

Viktor wished he could see one small hint of emotion, hear one small inflection in Reaper's voice, but there wasn't anything. Just an ice-cold, expressionless mask that became colder with each kill. Viktor detested that for him. Detested the fact that he had set the killing in motion. It might have saved all of their lives, but it didn't do anything good for Reaper.

"We can get out of this life."

"Don't kid yourself. You know better. You want us to be different because you found a woman to love. You want her in your life, and you don't think she'll accept you as you are. Just so you know, that isn't love, my friend. She either takes you like you are, with us, with what we have to do, or she isn't worth it."

Reaper rarely talked, and he never gave anything resembling advice to anyone. Viktor wanted to tell him to go to hell. He didn't want to think that his woman wasn't waiting for him. Wouldn't accept him. Worse, he knew Reaper was right. They had been trained as assassins and worked for their government from the time they were teens, sent out on the most dangerous and ugliest, most vile cases. They were expendable assets, nothing more, not even considered human beings. He knew no other life.

Life had to have purpose. He'd been an unwilling participant for so many years, blackmailed emotionally into doing service for Sorbacov. The deal was simple enough. He had six younger blood brothers, all in different schools and, at the time, working for Sorbacov as well. If Viktor didn't cooperate, one of his brothers would be tortured and killed.

Viktor had taken the dirtiest jobs, survived them, and continued working until the moment he knew it was safe to disappear. Like the others he'd stashed plenty of money and had multiple identities. He'd met the woman of his dreams and planned to spend the rest of his life with her. But Sorbacov had demanded he take the job to kill Evan Shackler-Gratsos, or his youngest brother, working for Interpol, would be killed, and he couldn't stop himself.

Reaper held up his hand and then replied into the radio, his voice a perfect mimic for the guard's, "All clear here. Very quiet. Yeah, the wind is picking up."

Viktor flashed him an appreciative grin. He admired the various gifts his brethren had, talents Sorbacov never knew about. Combined, they were unstoppable. They'd survived by banding together and using those gifts.

He glanced up the side of the building. The wind was coming from the west, powerful gusts, but so far, the rain wasn't pouring down. He could feel drops in the air, and the clouds spun in dark threads overhead, but climbing wasn't going to be that difficult.

"Your woman knows what you do?" Reaper asked.

He nodded, still looking the side of the building over, determining the best way up. "I told her everything. I had to. She was my 'in' to get close to her stepfather. He was a notorious pedophile. He traveled all over the world, and set up a network for others like him. They bought and sold young boys. I fell hard for her, knew right away she was the one. It sucked being undercover, but I married her legitimately. So I had to tell her everything. I had to leave, but I told her I'd be coming back for her."

"What did she say, after you'd just killed her stepfather?"

"I explained who he was and why he couldn't be prosecuted." Viktor had already figured out the route he'd use scaling the wall to the roof.

"What did she say?" Reaper repeated.

"I wrote it all out for her, and left the letter on our bed. I haven't talked to her since. I didn't dare get in touch with her—it would have put her in too much danger—but I sent her hundreds of messages assuring her I'd be coming home. She lives in Sea Haven, the small village where the Prez sent us to get things ready for his arrival."

Reaper shook his head. "Czar, you're the smartest man I know, and I respect you in every way, but that's the dumbest thing I ever heard. You leave your girl a note pinned to the bed, and you're gone for five years."

Viktor scowled at him. "Not a girl. My old lady. That makes a difference."

"You're so fucked. Get up the wall and give us our orders so we can get this done and head for Sea Haven. I can't wait to meet this woman who has stood by your ass for five long years without one real word from you."

Reaper was just saying what Viktor already knew. He was fucked. He'd run into Blythe's sister a few weeks earlier and she'd all but intimated that Blythe was moving on with her life.

"With Evan finally coming out of his hiding place to ride with the Swords to Sea Haven, this thing will be over and I can straighten everything out with her." But he was afraid it wasn't going to be that easy. "She lives there with the others."

Of course Reaper had that information. All seventeen club members knew exactly where Blythe Daniels lived. They'd sworn to look after her if he died. She lived on a farm in Sea Haven with five other women.

The "all clear" signal he'd been waiting for came and he reached up to use his fingertips to pull his body up until he could find a purchase with his toes. He went up fast. He was a big man, incredibly strong, and had good climbing skills. Like all the others, he stayed in the best shape possible and trained continuously.

Once on the roof, he ran across the flat surface, making certain to stay crouched low. He made it to the huge industrial fan churning around and around in the heat of the evening and went still, so still he disappeared into the shadows of the night. He waited a heartbeat or two and then moved his head cautiously to pinpoint the exact location of the three men sitting across on the adjoining rooftop with automatic weapons and goggles.

Three men on the roof. They're expecting us, he told his team, speaking telepathically. *Night vision. They've got the building surrounded. Reaper, you're up. Ice, you and Storm take the two to the west. We need a clear path if we're going to do this.* From his vantage point on the roof, Viktor directed the action.

The wind had picked up, tearing at his clothes, whipping at him with swirling debris. The clouds hung dark and heavy, swirling above them angrily, threatening that all hell was going to break loose soon—and it was.

Below him, Isaak "Ice" Koval slipped through the dark to come up behind one of the two guards at the outer edge of the building. Reaper would have to climb up the side of the other building, just as Viktor had, before he could dispense with the three guards on the roof. Not actually guards—they were there specifically to kill Viktor's team. Both men had to deal with the Swords surrounding the building to the west.

One down, Ice reported.

Two down, Dmitry "Storm" Koval added.

Transporter, you go to the east, the front of the building with Alena. Stay in position. We don't want anyone to know anything is happening until it's too late. Alena Koval was little sister to Isaak and Dmitry, one of only two female survivors from the school. Needless to say, the men were extremely protective of the two women and, although part of the team and gifted with their own rare talents, both women were guarded as carefully as possible in every situation. Pytor "Transporter" Bolotan knew his job was one of the most important to all of them.

Moving into position, Czar, Transporter acknowledged.

Viktor had done this so many times in the past, orchestrating and carrying out dangerous missions, putting his brothers in the line of fire over and over again. What made it so bad every time now was the knowledge that every single one of the others had been free and clear and they'd joined the Swords to take his back. Reaper might try to explain it to him, and on some level he understood, but it didn't take away the guilt or the knowledge that if any of them were killed this night, that death was squarely on his shoulders.

His brothers were hitting two chapters at the same time. His vice president, Lyov "Steele" Russak, was running his own team of eight men and one woman, attempting to do exactly as Viktor was doing here. They were hitting another Swords chapter two hundred miles away as they'd been doing for the last three years. Living a double-edged sword, undercover, always one step ahead of death, was commonplace to them, but it took its toll.

Storm and Ice, follow Reaper up and wait for his go-ahead. He tasted something close to fear in his mouth for his brothers.

The three men would take out the guards on the back side of the warehouse where the Swords chapter held the girls. Reaper would go up first and kill the three men sitting with night vision goggles and scopes and then call in the rest of the team. Once again, Reaper would be in the most dangerous position. He'd been taking that position from the time he was five years old.

Savage and Absinthe, you take the wall to the north. One man is in the driver's seat of a van parked on the street, pretending to be asleep, and there are two more concealed in the long hedge about twenty feet from the building. Savin "Savage" Pajari was Reaper's younger brother. Like Reaper he was a very scary man. He shaved his head, had more tats than most of them, which was saying a lot, and sometimes, the way he looked at Viktor with those empty eyes shook him—and it was very difficult to shake Czar.

Absinthe was more laid-back, but not less lethal. Aleksei "Absinthe" Solokov could have been a great statesman, a man who could have done a lot for his country. Sorbacov hadn't even bothered to find out about the sons and daughters of his political enemies; he'd simply determined which ones he was going to use as assets and which he would experiment on and torture just because he despised their parents. Absinthe had no business being in the occupation of killing, but he'd learned, and because he was extraordinary at everything he did, he was good at it.

You'll have to take out the two in the hedge to get the one in the van before he can raise an alarm. Viktor continued to search the area to the north. He knew from experience that each chapter had only so many members. As it was, he and his team had been ruthless in killing off the members of the Swords club whenever they took back girls. Each time he heard of a fresh shipment, he and Steele strategized to find a way to free the girls and get rid of as many members as possible at the lowest risk to themselves. As the years had passed and the club had been hit hard, security had tightened and the risks had become greater.

He kept his gaze sweeping along the north, while first Savage and then Absinthe each killed one of the two Swords in the hedge and laid them out gently behind the bushes. It was Savage who slipped into position, waiting for Viktor's signal to give him the go-ahead to cross the open area to the van. Of course he would take the most dangerous position.

Viktor had to ensure the three snipers on the rooftop on the adjacent building weren't looking to the north and the enemy hiding in the car wasn't paying attention to what was in front of him. The driver seemed nervous, continually looking behind him and around the van, rather than in front. Viktor almost gave the all clear and then something about the way the man cocked his head toward the backseat made every hair on his body stand up.

It's a trap, Savage, they've got more than the driver in the van.

Acknowledge.

Instantly there was movement, a shadowy figure sliding from hedge to bush, Reaper coming to back up his brother and Absinthe. Naturally it would be Reaper. Viktor had hesitated this time bringing both Reaper and Savage along. For the last few months, he'd been worried about both of the men he'd grown up with. Reaper and Savage had always been different, even as children, but they were growing apart from the brotherhood. They were quieter, colder, eyes like ice. Neither ever smiled. Never. Not even for Lana or Alena, women they considered younger sisters. Lana made all of them smile with her soft, compelling voice as she broke into song at the tensest times.

This was his fault. If something happened to Reaper or Savage, the blame would be squarely on his shoulders. The brotherhood had made a pact to disappear, and one by one the others had. They'd changed names, become chameleons, blending into the world like they'd been taught practically since birth. Not Viktor. He'd taken one last job because

Evan Shackler-Gratsos made him sick to his stomach and he
needed to protect his blood brothers. Monsters like Evan
shouldn't be allowed to live. Viktor couldn't get Sorbacov,
the man who had murdered his parents and taken his brothers from him, but he had a chance of bringing down Evan.

Loyalty was a strange emotion, a characteristic he looked
for in others, and he'd found it at the school where Sorbacov
had placed him. Two hundred and eighty-seven students
had attended the school. Only eighteen survived the training there—through loyalty. The eighteen had banded together under Viktor and worked as a whole to survive. They
became brothers and sisters, not of blood, but through survival. Torture. Training. Kill or be killed. And it had been
Reaper and Savage who had done most of the killing so the
others could live.

Although all of the others had been in the wind, impossible for Sorbacov to find, they had one by one followed him
on his assignment to rid the world of Evan Shackler-Gratsos,
the international president of the most feared motorcycle
club in the world, the Swords. Evan had built up a multi-
billion dollar business in human trafficking. Young women,
girls, boys. Lives meant nothing to him, only power and
dollar signs.

Viktor had put away his Torpedo Ink colors—those of
the brotherhood—and worn the hated Sword colors, doing
whatever it took to get inside the club and move up fast.
What it took turned his stomach—and it took a lot to do
that—but he kept his eye on the prize even as he disrupted
as many of the trafficking chapters as possible without
jeopardizing his own mission.

What's the plan, Czar? Reaper asked.

You have a silencer on those guns? Viktor knew the answer. Of course they did. Just about every kill the two brothers made was done in silence. Silence surrounded them.

That's affirmative.

*When Absinthe makes the kill with the driver, you two
take the back of the van. It has to be fast and thorough. Not
a sound. Simultaneous with Absinthe.*

No problem, Savage acknowledged.

Viktor watched from his vantage point, his heart pounding in spite of his ability to control all organs. The best he could give them was cover from the roof, and he made certain to do that, although he had to keep his eyes on the guards, to ensure they weren't seen.

Need a little commotion, Transporter, you and Alena need to provide that, but make certain you don't draw any attention to yourselves.

Transporter was a human computer. His hand-eye coordination was astonishing, but more, he could read a book and absorb the entire thing in minutes. It was the same with languages. He figured prominently in all their plans to settle once this was over. He would do the custom work along with a couple of others for their cars and motorcycles.

No problem, Czar. One distraction coming up.

Two minutes later, a fight erupted at the tail end of the line of waiting johns. All three guards hastened over to get a better look, rifles ready.

That should buy us some time, Transporter said.

Now. Now. Viktor gave the go-ahead.

He shifted the rifle to his shoulder. This was a telling moment. If the guards on the roof went back to their sweeps before Absinthe, Reaper and Savage took out the enemy hiding in the van, while Viktor's back was to them, everything would be lost and there would be a hell of a firefight.

His three brothers moved into position. He heard the whisper as Reaper gave the order. Reaper and Savage stepped up to the van doors and flung them open, firing rapidly. Viktor knew from long experience, every bullet fired hit a target. Absinthe stepped up simultaneously to the driver's window and shot the man in the head. Reaper and Savage closed the van doors quietly and melted back into the hedges alongside the warehouse. Absinthe joined them, and then Reaper broke off to go back to his point of entry.

Viktor moved into his original position so he could watch the guards. *Go, Reaper,* he ordered.

Reaper climbed up the side of the wall like a spider. He

was strong. Incredibly strong. He moved fast, but when he went still, like Viktor, he disappeared. One had a much more difficult time disappearing when the enemy wore night-vision goggles.

Night vision, Viktor reminded, willing Reaper to be careful.

On the roof, Reaper reported.

It was impossible to see him, but kills had to be silent or they would tip off those inside holding the latest crop of young girls to be violently trained for their new lives. Reaper could move in absolute silence. If he said he was on the roof, he was.

Ice, Storm, make the climb but hold back until I give you the all clear.

Two more of his Torpedo Ink brothers began the laborious climb up the building to follow Reaper. Ice and his twin brother, Storm, moved rapidly to get into position. Once Reaper took out the guards, they would use the roof to gain entrance into the rooms below.

Ice had tattoos of three tears on his face. He hadn't cried since he was three years old and the hideous instructors had taken him, kicking and screaming, from Viktor. He'd come back silent and bloody, his eyes wide with shock and his mind traumatized. He could bring down the temperature in a room fast, or heat it up at the same speed. Viktor suspected that something wild and uncontrolled in Storm had been let loose when the instructors had taken him, and now, when he was raging with the need for revenge, that wild broke loose and fed the outside storms.

Reaper was a wraith coming up behind the first guard. The enemy actually turned his head and looked right at Reaper with his night vision goggles. Viktor had his weapon out and aimed, only just stopping himself from pulling the trigger when the guard looked away. How did Reaper do that? He didn't talk much so it was impossible to understand how he could get away with the things he did.

Viktor silently cursed in his native language, wishing he

could take back the orders he'd given that morning. Everyone had voted, as they always did, but he should have pulled the plug when they knew it was a trap. It wasn't that he thought Reaper would be careless—he was never careless. If anything, he was sharper and more aware than ever. He just grew more remote and cold. Reaper couldn't afford to get any colder.

Reaper stepped up behind the guard in plain sight of the other two, if only they turned their heads. One sound, one slip and it would be over. Viktor knew Reaper would never make a mistake. He'd always taken Viktor's back. Always stood for his brothers and sisters. He was quiet about it, but he'd made his first kill to protect a younger boy who later betrayed him. That had been the beginning of Reaper's slow withdrawal from the others.

Now there were eighteen of them left. Reaper and Savage still protected them. Still killed for them, but they did so slightly set apart from the others. Viktor understood why it had to be that way, he just didn't have to like it. Reaper and Savage always understood that if any other betrayal took place, they would have to be the ones to do the killing. They couldn't afford to hesitate, not if they wanted to keep the others safe.

Reaper killed by simply shoving his knife through the base of the enemy's skull, severing the spinal cord. He caught the gun and the body and slowly lowered both to the roof of the building. Viktor couldn't help but think it was a thing of beauty. Reaper killed with maximum efficiency and minimum fuss. He didn't threaten. He didn't posture. Men were afraid of him because he gave off a dangerous, don't-fuck-with-me vibe. Most of the time he wasn't even seen until he wanted to be seen. He stayed in the background at Viktor's back until, like now, he went to work.

Viktor watched the other two guards carefully. Ice and Storm stayed on the wall, just at the top out of sight, waiting for Reaper's all clear. *Mechanic, once you deal with the fan, you take the guard position. We need a clear path coming out.* Nikolaos "Mechanic" Bolotan was Transporter's older blood brother.

Affirmative.

Absinthe and Savage, Mechanic, start your climb.

The three came up fast and joined him on the roof, staying low to keep the two remaining guards from spotting them.

Reaper was on the second guard, slowly lowering him to the rooftop. Still the last guard didn't turn his head. Was Reaper able to will the guard to look in the other direction? If he could, he'd never told any of them of his ability. He moved like the wraith he was, a specter of death, rising up behind the third guard and performing the same ritual, slamming the knife deep into the base of the skull and severing the spinal cord.

Viktor cursed again as Reaper looked out over the rooftop and called a perfect mimicking cry of an owl missing prey. It was a sound heard at night, not often, but occasionally. The sound was chilling. Ominous. A perfect replica, and yet to Viktor it represented death. Reaper called in the team after he made his kills. He could mimic anything or anyone, just as his brother, Savage, could do.

The moment the last note died away, the two brothers, Ice and Storm, were over the thick wall and onto the roof with Reaper. Viktor was already in motion, moving fast, running from one roof to the other, Mechanic, Savage and Absinthe right with him. They gained the other roof, staying low to avoid being seen by the men hidden on the ground, waiting for just such a move against the shipment of young girls being brought in from around the country. Ohio. Arizona. California.

Ice and Storm, crouching low, joined them just above the entry point. The large heavy-bladed fan rotated in fast cycles behind the screen. On the other side of the fan was the same webbing of metal that had to come down before the men could enter the building.

Mechanic was already there, crouched beside the industrial fan, working on the problem. There was a reason he'd earned the name Mechanic, and it wasn't the custom bikes and cars he engineered and built. It was his ability to control any kind of metal or electronics. He had been a big part of their survival in the school and even more of a help as he'd learned to control and strengthen his talent.

Storm had one hand on his brother's back as he waited for the huge fan to slow and then stop rotating. They had to be fast in order to keep those below from knowing what was happening. To do that, the sound of the fan had to continue. Like a refrigerator running in the background, no one would notice the noise until it stopped. While Mechanic worked to slow and eventually stop the fan, Storm reproduced the sound and projected it throughout the building below them.

Viktor watched them working together flawlessly, something his brothers had done from the time most of them were young. That ability to seamlessly blend their talents had allowed them to survive the insanity they'd grown up in. The gifts each of them had always astonished him.

The fan slowed and finally stopped altogether. By that time, Ice already had the screen peeled back and Storm was through, Ice right behind him. He had to get the next screen down as quickly as possible while Mechanic kept the fan from moving. It wasn't easy and the strain showed. Small beads of sweat trickled down his face, but he stayed locked in place while Ice and Storm dispensed with the second screen.

The other men went through fast, Viktor bringing up the rear, waiting to ensure Reaper, the last man, made it through safely as well. Mechanic would stay behind and guard the roof, making certain they had a way to retreat if needed. The moment Viktor stepped into the long attic, behind him, the fan began rotating again.

2

MASKS. *Make certain sleeves are down to cover all identifying marks. Keep gloves on, you know the drill.* Viktor gave the order. They didn't bother to slick over their fingers for jobs like this; gloves sufficed. The idea was to get in and get out fast. A lightning strike and then they became phantoms.

He waited while the others moved like silent wraiths along the beams above the dirty rooms housing the women. They'd done this often enough that it was a pattern they knew well and performed efficiently. They always took the individual cubicles first. They had to be quiet and trust that the girls would remain silent. Then they wiped out the hall monitors. The training room was next and after that, they took out as many of the johns waiting in line before they slipped away.

He used hand signals and his men spread out. Each took one of the small rooms. They weren't really rooms, just makeshift cubicles with four walls and an open ceiling. The Swords club carried the guts of the cubicles in a large truck that went from site to site. They could put up and take down the flimsy walls in a matter of an hour. Their operation was moved nightly, the word going out on the Internet, or if the customers were regular, through texts, just an address.

He gave the signal, and each man disappeared into one of the small, rectangular rooms. He dropped down behind his target, slamming his knife deep into the base of the skull and wrenching the body off the girl almost simultaneously. Her eyes went wide and her mouth opened. He put his hand over it and shook his head. "We're going to get you out of here."

He waited until that sank in. For a moment hope dawned, and then she shook her head. "They have men waiting for you to show up. They talk about it all the time." She kept her voice low. "We never thought you'd come."

So the word had spread even to the women. That made his job easier. Sometimes it was difficult to persuade the girls they were free. Of course, he always called the police anonymously, but that was always a crapshoot. The Swords had money, more money than any club out there, including his, although his genius treasurer had been siphoning money into the Torpedo Ink accounts for the last four years and by the time this was done, they would have Evan's money.

"Stay quiet. I'll come get you when it's over." He waited for her nod before leaping up to grasp the edge of the thin boards forming the wall so he could pull himself up into the rafters.

Walking along the beam, he saw that his team had been busy. He dropped a second time and then a third before they had succeeded in freeing the women in the cubicles. The hallway was always the most dangerous point. They'd wiped out the enemy in under two minutes inside the cubicles, but at any moment, one of the men guarding the halls could check on the women. They had to work even faster.

Each team member indicated which of the guards they would take in the halls. They were two men down, with Transporter guarding the front entrance and Mechanic their way out. Two men were left. Reaper and Savage indicated they would take the extra men. Viktor wasn't surprised. They were lightning fast. He also wasn't in the least shocked that the men they chose were close to the target he had chosen. Reaper always had his back.

Viktor ran lightly along the beam, waited, poised and ready right over his target. He gave the signal when they were all in place and as one single unit they dropped down behind the enemy, knives severing spinal columns right at the base of the neck. Viktor spun toward the two extra men Reaper and Savage had taken, but both were already falling, almost in slow motion.

Crouching low, Viktor jumped for the edge of the wall, drew himself up and ran along the beam back toward the training room, his stomach in tight, hard knots. The rage slowly burning in his belly began to churn and roil. He loathed seeing the young women so beat down they didn't move when man after man was brought in, but the training, the rapes and beatings, always threw him back to his childhood. If he could have, he would have wiped every member of the Swords from the face of the earth.

Viktor. Absinthe touched his arm, stopping him. *Let us this time. You always take the training room.*

Viktor didn't respond. He couldn't. There was no way he would stay behind while the others risked their lives to do the very thing he had vowed to do—stop Evan Shackler-Gratsos from selling women and children. Reaper and Savage took up positions on either side of him.

Viktor peered down at the scene taking place in the room below. In spite of the fact that the Swords were expecting trouble, they were still training the new girls. Training equaled beating, raping and intimidating them over and over. He had seen the scenario played out again and again, and by now he felt he should be immune to all emotion, or at the very least numb to it, but he wasn't. The sight not only made him sick to his stomach, but that slow, burning rage in his belly blossomed into a churning storm.

Viktor couldn't stand to see the bruised, swollen faces of the young girls, or the hopeless, vacant look in their eyes as they lay waiting for the next faceless man to use them and then leave them to their fate. For a moment he closed his eyes against the sight, and immediately he was flooded with images from his childhood, that same hopeless look on so many faces. The rage went from a fiery inferno to a full-blown volcanic fury.

He didn't look at the men with him. He couldn't. Like him, they would have nightmares. Like him, he knew somewhere inside of them was the same fury toward the kind of human beings who could commit these types of violent acts against children, and young men and women.

Seven young girls somewhere between the ages of eleven and fifteen lay on dirty mattresses in the corner, crying softly, trying to muffle the sounds while a four-man team assaulted an eighth girl. That girl looked like a baby to him, a girl no more than eleven or younger. She had fought, but there was no fight left in her. None. Still, that didn't save her; the men surrounding her didn't let up.

All of the girls showed signs of beatings and rape. There was shock in their eyes, on their faces, and most looked hopeless already. Three were fighters, and one in particular looked as if she'd tried several times to stop the assault on the girl they were "training." Even as he watched, she tried again and was beaten back with fists. When she went down, one man kicked her hard in the stomach and Viktor winced for her, his gaze narrowing on the man as he went back to join the others raping the youngest girl.

Viktor, Reaper, Savage and Absinthe dropped fast, directly behind the enemy, while Ice and Storm covered them from above. The man Viktor had selected as his target must have seen the flare of hope or shock in the eyes of his victim, because he started to turn. His jeans were down around his ankles and he tripped, falling into the man next to him. Before he could make a sound, Viktor slammed his knife right through the man's throat and then withdrew the blade and slashed the jugular on either side. Savage put his finger to his lips, facing the girls. Still, two of the younger ones cried out. One girl, the fighter, hastily crawled to them and put a hand over their mouths.

"We'll get you out of here," Viktor assured. "We have to get rid of the ones guarding the place. Keep them quiet and wait for someone to give you the all clear. You understand?"

His hands were gentle as he pulled the young girl out from under the four dead men and carried her to the girl who had fight left in her.

"Zoe," the fighter whispered, tears in her eyes. She cradled the young girl to her, rocking her gently back and forth. Zoe didn't respond. Clearly she'd withdrawn in her mind to another place. Viktor had seen it happen too many times.

"Take care of her. All of you stay very quiet and try not to look at the dead men."

The little fighter nodded. Viktor made a mental note to check on her later, just to make certain she'd made it out. "What's your name?"

She lifted her chin, knowing what he saw, knowing he knew what these men had done to all of them. "Darby. Darby Henessy."

"Hang in there, we'll get you out." He hated leaving them, he always did. But he couldn't save the world, he could only do his best. He'd freed them and it was up to them to put their lives back together. It wouldn't be easy. He knew that better than most.

Once more they took to the rafters, easily running along them back toward their entry point. *It's done*, he informed both Mechanic and Transporter.

Mechanic immediately slowed the fan until it halted, this time not bothering to mimic the noise. Anyone inside who would have been a problem was already dead. They had taken out the entire operation in just under five minutes. Mechanic had their rifles and he tossed them to each team member as they came through. They ran along the rooftop, positioning themselves for the best coverage, tearing off their masks for better vision as they did so.

They opened fire, each selecting a target, going for the remaining Sword members first and then any of the men waiting in line stupid enough to stay. Each shot was a kill shot. They didn't waste bullets. As far as Viktor and the others were concerned, the men buying the young girls were as guilty as those selling them. They saw the condition of the girls, their ages, the bruising and lacerations, and yet they did nothing to help them.

Now they had only minutes to get the girls free and clear of the area. In spite of the dead bodies, or maybe because of them, any survivors managing to run and get away never called the police, but Viktor didn't take chances with his men.

Alena, you're up. Wear a mask and make certain you're covered completely.

He saw Alena striding fast toward the warehouse doors, stepping over dead bodies as she went. She was tall and curvy, and as a rule, her hair was a glossy mess of thick platinum waves, wild just like her brothers'. Alena was one of their greatest assets and rode with the Sword club as his old lady. Ice and Storm watched over her like a hawk, although the other Torpedo Ink club members, Viktor included, were almost as bad. She shrugged off their protection, but took their respect and admiration as her due.

The moment Alena stepped out into the open, they all went hyperalert, scanning every possible place of concealment for a stray Swords member who might take it in his head to shoot her. Transporter followed her, his back to hers, in perfect sync with her in spite of walking backward. An automatic was cradled in his arms. His body was wider and taller than Alena's, blocking her from any attack from the back.

She pushed a body aside with the toe of her boot and stepped inside. It would only take minutes for her to calm the girls and lead them out. She would caution them not to talk about their rescuers and insist they didn't see them. They could say they wore hoods, but there was nothing else to be said. When the girls came out, wading through the dead bodies, it was Darby helping to lead and calm them. She did so carrying the youngest girl, Zoe. Viktor made the call to the police and they disappeared quickly, leaving the area fast before any Swords member or the police might get there.

They were playing poker in the motel room where Viktor was staying when their chapter president burst in with two other Swords members. They wore their cuts, the dripping sword across the center of the back and the name of their club on the top rocker. The bottom rocker proclaimed they were from a chapter in New Orleans, Louisiana. Viktor had made certain to join the chapter Evan had originally been part of.

"Have you heard, Czar?" Habit demanded.

Viktor turned his head slowly. He'd built up his reputation, a man not upset by much. He was casual until he wasn't, and then no one wanted in his way. "Heard what?"

"Two more of our chapters got hit and half the men are dead."

Viktor sat back in his chair. "It has to be another club, Habit. Someone wants to take over the trafficking business. Who would step into the Swords' shoes if we were weakened?"

Habit toed a chair around and straddled it. "I hate being away from our clubhouse and our own territory. I don't know why Evan couldn't have asked one of the other chapters closer to home to do his work for him."

Viktor shrugged, keeping it very casual, as if the entire conversation bored him and he didn't have a preference one way or the other. "Seems to me, I can understand it. He started in the Louisiana chapter, and that's where the feud with Jackson Deveau started. He wants to end it himself with us, not some other chapter."

Habit nodded several times, glanced at the others in the room, and Viktor immediately jerked his head toward the door. The others seated around the table put the cards down without a word and left the room, closing the door behind them.

Habit smiled and shook his head. "You do that so easily, as if you were born to take command. I should feel threatened by you, but I don't. You never seem to want to move up from where you are right now."

Viktor had been careful to study Evan and in doing so he realized the man would want revenge on Jackson Deveau, not because the man had ever done anything to him, but because Evan, as a teenager, had made the young

Deveau and his mother the monsters in the closet. In Evan's mind, the two had kept Jackson Deveau Sr. from loving his mother and him. From choosing them.

Jackson Deveau Sr. rode with the Swords way back. He had a wife and son he loved, but then his wife became ill with cancer. He couldn't stand watching her fade away, so he rode with his club and eventually Evan's mother and Evan rode with him as if they were his. It was that simple. Nothing huge. No one big event had started Evan on his path to such hatred that he rotted from the inside out with it. Deveau Sr. continued to visit his wife and child in the bayous, and never divorced her, never fully committed to Evan and his mother. Evan believed Deveau Sr. had chosen the other two over him.

"Never wanted to be the president," Viktor said. "Not my thing." He'd been "Czar," the president of his club, Torpedo Ink, almost from the time he was ten. Back then, they hadn't known they would ride motorcycles to feel the wind on their faces, in order just to feel alive—to feel free for one small moment in time. He would always be the president to his men, the man they followed, whether he wanted it or not.

Evan would feel in competition with any chapter president and he would feel as if he had to prove he was in charge. Viktor was an enforcer, high enough that Evan would take notice, but not in a position to threaten him. He had worked his way up through the ranks from prospect to enforcer in record time for the Swords club, making himself indispensable to Habit without threatening his position either. He'd brought fifteen other prospects in, good men who aided the chapter in everything from gun running to carrying out assassinations, but all steadfastly refused to participate in human trafficking. They were too valuable at other things, so Habit let it go.

Habit rubbed his jaw. "Evan is paranoid. Stark, raving mad." He glanced around as if someone might overhear him. "He detests women, and he always wants everyone around him to agree with him. I've seen him take out a gun and shoot a trusted lieutenant because the man didn't say yes fast enough. I'm talking someone he's known for years. The more money and power he got, the worse he got. When he moved up to international president, something in him snapped. He got so paranoid, he got rid of his most trusted men, and by that I mean he put them in the ground because they knew his secrets. He told everyone he'd uncovered a conspiracy against him, but we all knew he was full of shit."

Viktor didn't say a word. He knew all that. He'd studied everything there was to know about Evan before he ever joined the Louisiana chapter.

"I'm telling you this because you're the kind of man who's going to draw his attention, and, Czar, you don't want his attention. You have a thing about your old lady. Alena's beautiful, and he'll want her. He wants a woman in the club, she's his. He doesn't care if she's an old lady or one of the club whores. He'll take her, and he's rough. Mean. The women don't come back the same. Sometimes they don't come back at all. He's been in Europe, so we haven't had the problem here, but if he's coming for real, and it looks as if he is, Alena will be on his radar."

Viktor stared at Habit without blinking. "Man tries to take my woman, he's dead, Habit. You know that. I made that perfectly clear. Same goes for Lana. Not that either of them need protection. You haven't seen them in action, but they're good old ladies. They don't talk about club business, and they can and will defend us."

"That won't matter to Evan." Habit looked agitated, sweeping a hand through his salt-and-pepper hair. "I'm telling you, you can't reason with him. He uses the women for drug running and sex. That's it. Period. As far as he's concerned, they don't have very many other uses. As your friend, I'm telling you to stash the two women somewhere, just until he's gone. He won't stay long. He's already asked for our club to scout this Deveau character out, not touch him, but find a place the club can hole up until Evan shows. He wants to kill the fucker himself, and then he'll disappear again. He's never around more than a day or two."

Viktor almost felt sorry for the man. Almost. Habit ran the chapter by the rules Evan laid down, and that meant they enslaved young girls and even some boys. Viktor had hit their own chapter once, but couldn't do it more than that or it would draw suspicion on his crew. He'd waited until he had been sent on a particularly dangerous mission and he'd taken several of his crew with him. They'd carried out the assassinations in record time and hit the mobile whorehouse hard, taking out as many of the men as they could and freeing the women.

Habit had gone crazy, roaring with rage at the loss of his men and demanding Viktor and the others help him build up the stables fast so Evan wouldn't turn his spotlight on them. Viktor had just looked at him with cool eyes and slowly shaken his head. He would do any other kind of work for Habit, but not that. Habit had stormed out, but he left Viktor and the others alone because they were too valuable to him, especially when a good number of his members had died.

"Why don't you just kill him?" Viktor asked, as if it were normal to kill anyone you didn't like—and for him, it was. Killing had become too easy. Too routine. That should bother him. It didn't.

"He's got some kind of weird . . ." Habit trailed off and looked around again as if Evan might have eyes and ears on them right there in the motel room.

Viktor didn't change expression but he felt the way the adrenaline tried to rush through his veins. At last. The one thing he couldn't find out about. Evan Shackler-Gratsos had some kind of psychic talent. His brother, Stavros Gratsos, the deceased shipping magnate, certainly had a strong psychic talent. Viktor believed most people did, they just weren't really aware of it or didn't believe in it. They paid no attention to the fact that they were aware the phone was going to ring, or they had a bad feeling a child was in trouble.

People didn't believe in psychic talent, so it didn't exist. He knew it did. Each of his fellow students at the school he'd attended in Russia had possessed a talent in some form, large or small. They'd worked on those talents night and day to strengthen them, not where the school's vicious instructors could see, but when they were locked up in the dark basement and would have gone mad without keeping their minds occupied and strong.

Viktor waited patiently, not tipping his hand or appearing eager. Habit wanted to share. He was afraid of Evan, and even more afraid that he might lose Viktor to Evan. Viktor had become important to him.

"He's scary with the things he can do. I've seen him make people do things they wouldn't ever do, just by staring at them. He can do things to people, make them believe things. One of the men made him angry and the next thing, the poor fucker was tearing off his own skin thinking spiders were crawling all over him. They weren't, but he wouldn't believe it. In the end, Evan just shot him, laughing the entire time."

"What's he got against Deveau? Why come all the way to the United States for a sheriff's deputy? Just hire a hit. Hell. I could do it myself."

"He's had a hard-on for Deveau for years. He got drunk once and ranted and raved about him and his old man. How the old man didn't want Evan and his whore of a mother. I swear, that's what he called her. A whore. Said she was worthless, just wanted Deveau and wouldn't even stay clean for her son when Deveau wouldn't keep her. He hated her. I wouldn't be surprised if someone told me he'd killed her. I think she drowned. Maybe she threw herself in the lake to get away from him. For all I know he was whoring her out for the club and then blamed her. I wouldn't put it past him. He's sick, Czar, seriously, certifiably insane. His half brother died and left him a shit ton of money, more than most countries have, so he's untouchable."

Viktor shrugged casually. "No one's untouchable. Still, you say stash my woman, I will, and I'll give Ice the heads-up as well. He wouldn't appreciate anyone touching his old lady any more than I would."

"I have to admit, when we have a blowout, those two can cook."

The two women could do a lot more than cook, but Viktor wasn't about to clue Habit in. If Evan managed to get his hands on either of them, he'd be in for the shock of his life.

"Evan asked me to pick seven of my best men to scout out Sea Haven and find a place to stay. He wants all the details on Deveau and his wife, Elle."

Viktor managed to look bored because he was. "We went over that. I chose seven men to ride with me. I was careful not to take anyone involved in our main business. I know you need them." Human trafficking. Sometimes the rage welled up so strong he wanted to burn the club to the ground. The problem was, it was so big, cutting off the head only meant it would grow another one. That didn't mean he wasn't ambitious enough to try to take it all down. He was doing that, just using another means.

He'd made a few mistakes in the beginning, thinking to get close to Evan, kill him and get back to his wife. It hadn't been that easy. Evan was so paranoid, it was impossible to track him. Investigating him showed no law enforcement agency had gone untouched by him. He owned far too many cops, everyone from Interpol to officers in various countries. Evan Shackler-Gratsos the shipping magnate did, not Evan Shackler-Gratsos the international president of the notorious and feared Swords motorcycle club.

He couldn't bring down the shipping magnate, but there was a very good possibility that he could get the international president of the club. The chapters, all over the world, brought in tremendous amounts of money. Each kept their own books, but they answered to Evan. That meant he had books.

Evan had enough money to have the best in software to keep out hackers, but most hackers weren't Luca "Code" Litvin, another one of his schoolmates, a brother whose skills were extremely important. He had a little psychic ability of his own. Data flowed from machines to his mind. Code was always low-key and stayed off the radar, but he was the Torpedo Ink treasurer for a reason. For the last four years he had been on the trail of the Swords' money, going from computer to computer. They needed irrefutable evidence, so much so that no law enforcement agency could ignore it. Viktor would kill Evan, and Code would bring down his private army—the Swords.

Code was close. He was moving through the Swords club, chapter by chapter, getting information from the real books, not the ones given to the feds every time they tried to take the club down. He had compiled a great deal of information, concentrating on the human trafficking component, but encompassing all of their activities.

"Thanks, Czar," Habit said. "We're nowhere near bringing in what Evan insists on. The club is giving up its take just to satisfy him. He doesn't care about the trouble just so long as the money keeps pouring in. I've stepped up the drug trade to bankroll us again. He pulled us out of Louisiana, how the hell does he think I can build the business back up again? I got men there, overseeing things, but they can't exactly go recruit."

Recruiting was a joke of a word. They used every means possible to get young girls. Luring them on the Internet, at bus stations and airports, kidnapping them from malls and using drugs and any other scheme they could think of. It wasn't that difficult. If any member had teenage daughters, they set up friends to be brought in, and some of the daughters themselves had been used.

"Things will get back to normal fast when we're done with this," Viktor assured. "You said yourself he never stays in one place more than a couple of days. I'll scope things out, make my report, back his play when he takes out the cop, and we'll be free to go home."

He'd be free to go home. His wife was home. Blythe Daniels Prakenskii. He missed her with every breath he drew. She'd been so unexpected. He couldn't think of a better word. He had been tracking a notorious pedophile, a man who had set up an international organization for other pedophiles to post pictures, share children and buy and sell.

The man used women as cover, was charming, rich, and moved in social circles. He had targeted Blythe's mother for his cover in the United States. He'd courted and married her, as he often did. He was a widower for a reason.

Blythe was Viktor's in. He'd arranged a casual meeting and swept her off her feet. He was good with women. He knew exactly how to read them and what they wanted and needed. He was good at providing. Blythe turned the tables on him. She was genuine. Sweet. Protective. Nurturing. Everything he'd never had and didn't know he needed or wanted. It was impossible not to love her.

He hadn't known that kind of love existed. Not that fierce, driving need that was so deep, so intense, it shook him every time he looked at her. There was no stepping out of his role, he had a job to do and it was an important one, so he gave her as much of the real man as he could. Every second in her company was sheer paradise.

He'd taken her one night to a Russian Orthodox church where a friend of his was visiting. He'd married her, using his real name, Viktor Prakenskii, not the one she knew him as. He had deliberately given her a glimpse of the paperwork, although it was in Russian, but his name was there. He had put his mark on her, the one Prakenskii men had been branding their women with for centuries.

Her name was branded on him. His chest, right over his heart. He had insisted they both get tattoos. She'd been reluctant. His little innocent. He had loved corrupting her, teaching her wicked, sinful things, watching her eyes go wide with shock as her body came apart for him. He thought of her night and day. Dreamed of her when he wasn't having nightmares. She gave him respite from the horrors of his memories. He touched his chest, the spot right over his heart where he'd tattooed the lock. She had the key, and she always would.

"When we join you in a few days, Czar, keep a low profile. You always do, but I don't want him noticing you. Right now he thinks he's funny sending my enforcer on a shit detail. Finding us a camp? Following Jackson for a few

days to get his routine? We could send a prospect for that.
He's jacking with me."

Viktor shrugged. "It won't matter."

"He's showing he has no respect for me—or for you."

"You can't take things personally, Habit. If he's as loony
as you say he is, you just get through it, hope he goes back
to whatever hole he crawled out of fast and get back to
business."

Grinning, Habit clapped him on the back. "You always
put things in perspective. I've never seen you shaken up.
Not ever. We've got some business we have to do right now.
Right here. The chapter that just got hit has product coming
in and no one to receive it, guard it or get it moving along
the pipeline. They've asked for our help. That's your spe-
cialty, so you pick your brothers and get it done. You'll have
to get the details from Speed."

Viktor shook his head. "What are you doing, man? We
can't run product here. This territory is taken by another
club. We're riding naked, without our colors, in order to get
to Sea Haven without war with them. And we wouldn't win.
They're strong here, we're not. Even with two chapters on
the move, we don't have enough manpower to win in a
fight."

Habit nodded. "I know that. Their club is nearly as strong
as ours is."

"Or stronger. They were the first international club. You
don't want to fuck with them or disrespect them. War isn't
fun. We're already losing too many members to whoever is
after our whore business."

"It's not my call. Their chapter president had some product coming through this route and his men were going to
make certain it made its way out back east. I don't know
why they're using this route or how often they do it, but
they have men down and they've asked for help."

Viktor knew that tone. Habit lived by their laws. You
helped your brothers. You didn't turn your back on them no
matter how nasty or dangerous the job. Viktor respected
that. He lived by the same code, but his loyalty and his

brothers were those members of Torpedo Ink, not the Swords.

He cursed silently even as he kept his features expressionless. He had no choice. If he was going to cut off the head of the snake, bring down the man responsible for the biggest human trafficking ring in the world, then he was going to have to see this through—and so were his men.

They detested drugs nearly as much as they did pedophiles and with good reason. He couldn't save the world and he couldn't stop the rage burning inside his brothers any more than he could stop it in his own belly. It was always there, coloring their lives, keeping them apart from every other human being.

Reaper was right. Viktor hated that he was right. He wanted to fit into normal like his birth brothers had. They lived with their women on a huge farm in Sea Haven. He supposed it was all relative. Their *normal* probably wasn't exactly the normal others lived in their homes. Behind their fences. Comfortable in their jobs and with their neighbors.

"Czar?"

"I'll get their product through, Habit."

Habit grinned at him again, but this time it was strained. He didn't want to lose his number-one enforcer. Viktor had brought too much to the table. He was efficient at killing. When he did a job it got done, and fast. More and more over the last five years, Habit had relied heavily on him. In addition, Viktor had brought in the others, men he'd called friends. He'd vouched for them and they'd turned out to be equally as lethal and every bit as ruthless and reliable as the man Habit knew as Czar. If their loyalty leaned a little toward Viktor, Habit overlooked it—or didn't see it. Viktor found that Habit saw what he wanted to see.

Habit, now that he thought they were in sync, grabbed a handful of peanuts out of the can sitting on the table. "You leaving first thing in the morning for the coast?"

"Yeah. I figure it will take a few days to find us a good camp and to scout out Deveau. If Evan is really going to make an appearance, I'll want to be able to ensure his safety. We have to get in and get out before the other club knows we're in the area."

Habit nodded. "That makes sense. And Evan isn't going to ride with us." There was a sneer in his voice. "He's too good for that now. He'll come in a helicopter or private plane."

That was good. He'd have to use the Little River Airport if he didn't want a three-hour drive from one of the main airports—San Francisco or Oakland. It might not be a bad place to hit him. Viktor tucked that thought away. For now, he had to meet whoever was bringing product into another club's territory. Product or not, it was so damn disrespectful he could barely tolerate the thought. If a man lived free by a certain code, he kept to the code as much as possible. Even undercover, he was part of a brotherhood, and you just didn't screw with that.

Viktor gave his famous casual shrug. "It doesn't much matter. He'll wear the colors when he makes the kill and we'll watch his back. He'll leave and we can all go home. Just another couple of weeks, Habit, and you'll see your old lady."

Now he knew why Habit hadn't brought his woman with him. Of course, he hadn't said anything to Viktor about Alena, or Ice about Lana. Now they'd have to worry again about the two women. Lana could be left with the rest of the boys. She was a little spitfire. They affectionately called her "Widow," not because she was one, but because she made them so frequently.

He debated about taking Alena or leaving her behind. She had certain skills that could be useful, and if they all were going to stay alive, they might need them.

"Seriously, Czar, I'm sorry about the product thing. I had no idea the other chapter might route something through this territory. We wouldn't have known, probably ever, but they got hit hard and they're too many men down."

"They shouldn't have tried bringing the women with them."

"It was business as usual. Evan made that very clear. He made their entire chapter ride. We only had about half come."

And most of those were Viktor's Torpedo Ink brothers. That had worked out nicely. Habit had left the men running their trafficking business home. That suited Viktor just fine; in fact, he'd counted on it. Habit's chapter had only been hit once, and they hadn't lost as many members. That had been a calculated move on Viktor's part. They had to get hit, or it would look suspicious, but they couldn't lose too many men or Habit would insist that Viktor and the others help with the whore business. That was never going to happen. He could stomach only so much for a job.

Viktor glanced at his watch. "I'll go get the details from Speed and take care of this so we can get moving. My crew will be riding early tomorrow morning."

3

THERE was nothing in the world Viktor loved more than riding his Harley for hours on the open road. It was the only time he ever felt truly free. For a man like him, caged and shackled most of his life, freedom was everything. The wind in his face, the roar of his bike, his brothers at his back—all of it made life good. Worth living.

He'd taken this assignment and in some ways, it turned out to be one of the best and yet the worst he'd ever taken. He'd spent five years with men who were mostly scum. In his world, he would have cut them down, one by one, and in fact, he was actually doing just that. There were few men he'd met in the Swords club who were worthwhile. Drugs, gun running, using their own women as prostitutes and drug runners. The worst was human trafficking. It was the club's biggest moneymaker, and no one seemed to object.

It wasn't that he hadn't done his share of fucked-up, illegal things, but a man had to have a code to live by. The Swords' only code was to wreak as much havoc in the world as possible. Sometimes, when he put on their colors, he felt filthy. Covered in shit. He wanted this over so he could wear his own colors with pride. He'd be truly free when that happened. At least, after five very long years, he could see the end coming.

He lifted his face to feel the full onslaught of the wind. The sensation made him feel clean when he wasn't. He didn't have the right to judge, not when he'd killed more people than probably the entire Swords club put together. Not him alone, of course. He glanced to his left, and Reaper was there. To his right was Savage. Ice, Storm, Mechanic, Transporter and Absinthe rode at his back. Alena had her arms wrapped tightly around him. Twice she'd thrown her arms in the air for sheer joy. The action had made him smile.

For the first time in years, they were close to finishing their task. They would be able to strip off the stench of the Swords and wear their own colors. Once they were back in them, none of his brothers would ever take them off again. They were done with being someone's puppets. Word had gotten to them that their greatest enemy was dead—taken down by Viktor's brother Casimir and his woman.

Viktor honestly didn't know how to think about the death of Uri Sorbacov and his father, Kostya. The men deserved death ten times over, but he'd been dancing to their tune for so long, he almost didn't know how to exist without them threatening his family to force him to carry out the dirtiest, most dangerous jobs they had. Like this one. He could walk away clean right now if he wanted. Start his life free with his brothers, wear his own colors, go to his wife without fear she'd be killed, but if he did that, he'd be letting the lowest scum of the earth crawl away free as well. That was against his code.

For now, riding for hours in the sun with the wind on his face and his brothers at his back, he felt alive again. He knew the others were feeling it too. They might not be wearing their colors, but they had the ink on their backs, and it felt as if they were living life free, if only for a short period of time.

They'd been traveling along Highway 1 for a few hours

now. The ocean was mellow, looking like blue-green glass shining on the surface. The farther north they went, the darker the water, as if something lurked beneath the surface, ready to erupt at any time. He liked that. It made him feel he belonged. The air was perfect. So far, they hadn't run into a single cop, at least not one that paid attention to them.

He was eager to see his birth brothers, to meet their women, see their homes. It had been a long time coming, a long hard road, but now that it was nearing the end, it was all worth it, knowing they were alive and safe. They'd gotten out alive, intact, able to have normal relationships. His Torpedo Ink brothers knew all about his younger birth brothers. He knew they would protect them and their families just as he would.

And then there was Blythe. He let his mind turn to his woman. Five years was a long time for any woman to be alone, let alone one like Blythe. She was beautiful and nurturing, the kind of woman who would make a good mother, or a dynamite old lady. She'd look out for the members of his club, take them under her wing and help them find a way to live.

He knew their club would continue doing what they did best, and it wasn't legal. It would never be legal. Others would view it as taking the law into their own hands. Before, they'd been sanctioned by their government, weapons let loose on enemies of the state, or criminals impossible to bring to justice any other way. Now, they would continue on their own. They were good at hunting criminals, the kind the law couldn't get to. They used the kind of force the law couldn't use. It was in their blood. He thought long and hard over the "it." Killing. Fighting. Life and death. It was how they lived and they knew no other way.

Blythe had to understand how important this assignment was. She couldn't view it that she wasn't every bit as important to him—she was more. He'd just have to make her understand that she was his life. His hope. His reason for getting up in the morning. This . . . this was something he did because he *had* to do it. He had no choice. There was something in him that just couldn't allow Evan and his club to ruin the lives of so many young boys and girls. Girls like Darby Henessy. Again he put it in the back of his mind to check on her, to make certain she had a home and a family watching out for her.

Alena's hands gripped his shirt tight and twisted. That was her signal that they needed to stop. She never admitted she had to pee. She didn't ask. They'd developed a system after he found her in tears. The rage burning in his belly, always so close, flared into a hot bright ball of burning knots. She wasn't the only one. They'd managed to live through their past, but it left a lot of scars, some of them uglier than others.

He raised his hand, fist closed, giving the signal that they'd stop at the first available place. Granted, there weren't too many on this road, at least not close together. What there was were parks, several of them. All of them had restrooms, most nothing more than upgraded outhouses, but they worked. After their beginning, outhouses were fashionable.

Alena nuzzled his back, and he patted her hand. She was gorgeous. Sweet. Strangely vulnerable and yet lethal as hell. He thought of her as Torch, rather than Alena. They all did. Earlier on they'd established names for themselves. He was ten and he'd come up with the idea to give the others things to think about. What kinds of talents they might have, what each thought of the other. It was a way to pass the time and to bond closely with one another when they were locked down in the dark "dungeon."

The school had a dungeon, a real one, where they were often taken to be tortured for some mythical infraction, but the confinement area was without windows and always kept dark. Mostly, they were kept down there without clothes, treated like animals. He gathered the youngest close and told stories and made up games. Eventually, the other boys just under his age helped him to distract the younger ones. Over the years, as children died, the instructors brought in younger and younger ones. Being toddlers didn't prevent the instructors from using them for their own evil purposes.

He spotted a sign ahead. Another park, this one larger than some. He signaled and they all turned onto the winding drive. A small wooden hut separated those driving in from those driving out. A park ranger stuck her head out of the booth, eyeing them warily. Viktor didn't bother to smile. It never helped.

"We're here just for an hour or two." He pulled out the money for all eight of them, even though he considered making her take money from all the others. If she thought he looked intimidating, she should get a good look at Reaper and Savage.

She handed him a map and told him where the bathrooms were before waving him through with the stickers to put on their bikes. Like that would happen. He shoved them in his jacket and glanced back. The ranger had stepped out of her booth and was looking after them as if they disgusted her.

"I hate that," Alena said as she slipped off the bike so he could park it right in front of the bathrooms.

"What?" But he knew.

"The way she looked at me. At us."

"Fuck her, Alena," he snapped. He caught her chin. "She isn't better than us."

But he knew that wasn't true. The woman looked down on them for riding motorcycles, for their tattoos, guessing at their lifestyle, but they were killers. Every single one of them. Learning to kill had shaped their lives from young ages. There was no getting around that and maybe, because it was stamped into their bones, it was there in their faces for everyone to see. Bringing them all home to Blythe maybe wasn't such a good idea after all. If she looked at them the same way, with such distaste and disdain, he didn't know what he'd do. Then again, his woman would never do that. Never. It wouldn't happen. Blythe was the best the world had to offer. He didn't understand why fate had given her to him, but he absolutely knew she was the one, and nothing could shake his faith in her.

"Alena is having too many nightmares again," Ice said, looking after his sister as she made her way to the bathroom. "I don't like it."

"None of us do," Viktor acknowledged. "She had been sleeping in the bed with me, and that helped some. She was with Lana when Lana and the others got into camp last night."

Storm was on the other side of Viktor, scowling after his sister. "Scared the hell out of us. You were gone most of the night with Reaper and Savage so you didn't hear. It was that horrible sound that she makes when she's asleep and you know if you touch her you'll just be part of her nightmare. I thought knowing Sorbacov was dead would stop them, or slow them down, but they're getting worse."

Viktor knew exactly what they were talking about. Alena's nightmares were becoming worse. All of them knew it, but no one knew what to do. He rubbed the bridge of his nose, although hitting something instead would have made him feel a whole hell of a lot better. Still, there was Blythe. He was counting on Blythe. She lived in a world apart from them, and she was smart. She knew things about that other world that they were closed off from.

"My woman will figure it out."

Ice and Storm exchanged a long look that annoyed Viktor. "What the hell is that supposed to mean?"

Ice tried to look innocent, but Storm shook his head as if Viktor was to be pitied. "I don't think this woman exists, Czar. If she did, she'd have to be a fuckin' saint, and since she married you, that can't be."

"Or," Ice chimed in, nudging his twin, "Czar made her up so he could get himself off at night. He has such a problem with the skanky women hanging around the Swords clubhouse all the time."

Storm nodded. "That could be, he has a Madonna complex."

"A what?" Ice demanded.

"You know, the mother of his child has to be a saint."

"That's not what a Madonna complex is, you moron," Viktor snapped. "It would mean I couldn't maintain sexual arousal in a committed relationship. Believe me, I had no problem, and thinking about her gets me hard as a fucking rock, so shut the hell up."

Both men burst out laughing and sauntered toward the path leading down to the ocean. Viktor glared after them.

"Trouble, Czar?" Absinthe asked as he pulled off his gloves.

Viktor couldn't help but stare at the tattoos on his fingers, the ones sleeving his arms, going up his neck and disappearing into his shirt. They all had tattoos. Ones that told stories if you knew how to read them. Every single one of them wore the Torpedo Ink tat on their backs—and they wore it with pride.

The cypress tree spread out with seventeen branches. Roots tangled at the bottom with piles of skulls buried among them. Crows flying away from the tree or picking through the skulls at the roots. Each skull represented a kill. Reaper's tat was alarmingly full. The others were quickly catching up with this last assignment. He hoped to slow them all down. To find reasons not to do what they did, but Reaper was so right when he said they'd never be able to stop. *He'd* never be able to stop.

What would Blythe think about their inability to stop what they did best? Could he get away with not telling her? Women, as a rule, didn't know club business. That was the way it was. They didn't sit in on the meetings, and they were expected to do what their old men told them to do.

Blythe wasn't going to like that. She was all about women's rights and women being strong. He liked strong women, especially her, but he wanted her to trust him enough to follow his lead. He was a leader. He'd been put in that position at age ten and he was still in that position. He couldn't be anything else. He glanced over at Reaper, who was still sitting on his bike, taking a careful look around. The man was right. Either she loved him for who he really was, or she didn't.

"Your woman knows how to deal with trauma?" Absinthe prompted.

His woman walked on water. "She can do just about anything. She'll love Alena and Lana, and they need a little love."

"They have us," Absinthe reminded quietly. "We love them, and they still aren't better."

Viktor raised his head and looked his brother in the eye. "Are you?"

Because none of them were. Not a single one, especially him. Viktor was as screwed up as the rest of them. He suffered the same nightmares and had all kinds of issues he didn't want to talk about—especially with someone as sweet and innocent as Blythe. He sighed and shoved his hand through his hair. "You're right, Absinthe, they aren't better."

Alena came out of the women's room walking toward them with her long, confident strides, her glossy platinum hair flowing around her. She always wrapped her hair in some kind of intricate knot when she was riding, but took it down the moment she was off the bike. He knew that was a leftover from when one of the instructors had beat her senseless and shaved her head. She'd been six and it had taken all of them to console her. But then, she'd never really gotten over it.

"What is it?" Reaper asked.

The man was creepy silent even in motorcycle boots. Viktor heard everything, but he never heard Reaper or Savage. The two were a force to be reckoned with. He didn't know which was worse: Reaper, the older brother, or Savage, the younger. Most likely Reaper. Had any of Viktor's birth brothers been in that place of horror, he would have lost his mind.

"We're all pretty fucked-up, aren't we, Reaper?" What if Blythe didn't take him back? That question had haunted him for too long now. He woke up in the middle of the night numerous times, sweat pouring off of him, his heart pounding at the possibility. He had never once considered she wouldn't want him, not in the first year or two, but then as time stretched out and he couldn't see or hear from her, that fear had begun to take hold.

"Some of us more than others. You, not so much. You were older than the rest of us and figured out a way to fight back. You kept us human when we would have all been animals." Reaper gazed out at the shimmering water. "You gave us a life, Czar. Stop beating yourself up. I've never seen you like this. She's either the one or she's not."

Viktor pressed his thumb to the center of his left palm and held it there. Prakenskiis didn't make mistakes when it came to choosing their women. Blythe was the one. She was his wife. His partner. His only. He touched his chest, the lock tattooed over his heart. She had the key tattooed on her body. "She's the one." He turned toward the ocean, and strode away from Reaper. The man saw too much.

Alena waited for him on the small, beaten-down trail leading to the beach. "Who did you leave with the bikes?"

He ruffled her shiny head of hair. Her brothers had the same color, a throwback to some Nordic ancestor. "I didn't have to leave anyone. Savage is sitting there, scaring the hell out of people."

Alena laughed. "He does like to do that."

That wasn't true. Savage just didn't give a damn what people thought. He wanted them to leave him alone. Viktor worried about him almost more than he did about Reaper. Savage was one year younger than Reaper; he'd been only three when he'd been brought to the school. He rarely showed feeling, even with Alena and Lana.

Viktor lowered his shoulder and hit Alena in the belly with it, lifting her and running toward the cold water. She screamed and pounded his back, laughing as she did so. Ice and Storm moved to intercept him, running to cut him off before he would throw their younger sister into the sea. He wouldn't, but he believed in living in every moment. That was a gift from Blythe. He wanted the others to learn laughter. It was so rare in them, and they needed it.

Blythe had taught him to play. She'd been his mark. He'd studied her and become everything she needed, inserting himself into her life until she was lost in him. Except that—he'd found himself lost in her. He'd delayed killing the stepfather in order to spend time with her. He found laughter, something he had never known, and he wanted to give that to his brothers and sisters.

Ice came at him from the side at a dead run, leaning low to catch him around the waist. Storm caught his sister as if she were a sack of potatoes rather than a human being. Ice tackled Viktor, taking him to the ground. They rolled in the sand, like two little kids, yet there was no laughter, not even a glint of it on Ice's face. Viktor's heart sank. Where was the feeling they all needed to remain human? He couldn't find it, and he'd pinned all his hopes on Blythe—not just to save him—but to save all of them.

Before Ice could get up, Transporter was on him, a dive that took him several feet across the beach, landing hard. The two rolled several times and came to a halt at Alena's feet. She caught both by an arm. "Get up, you two clowns."

Transporter jumped to his feet. "You're afraid of clowns."

"I'm not afraid of clowns, you dope," Alena protested. "But you are."

Transporter caught her around the neck in a headlock and rubbed the top of her head with his knuckles. Alena dug her fingers into his pressure points at his elbow and back of his knee. His knee collapsed and he staggered. She took him down by planting her shoulder in his belly.

Mechanic caught her around the waist and lifted her off Transporter. "I can't have you beating up the younger brother, Alena."

Absinthe dove on top of Transporter the moment Alena was clear. "I've been waiting for this moment. You owe me seventy-two cents. I'm taking it out of your worthless hide."

All of them knew Transporter had lightning-fast reflexes. It was one thing for Alena to attack him; anyone else was taking a chance. He rolled out from under Absinthe before their bodies touched. Somehow he managed to turn the tables on Absinthe. Ice and Storm instantly went to Absinthe's aid, racing to get into the fray, wrestling Transporter. Mechanic let out a roar and dove in to help his younger brother.

Alena laughed, the sound like music, drawing Viktor's attention. She looked beautiful with the sun shining down on her sleek hair. She *was* beautiful; she just didn't believe it. Viktor sat in the sand, watching his brothers play. Ice and Storm wrestled with Transporter, Mechanic and Absinthe, yet he didn't hear the sound of their laughter. There was an occasional grin, but no real laughter. How had Blythe managed to teach him? He couldn't remember the first time he'd smiled with her, and that bothered him.

He rubbed his chin on his knees. He was putting too much on her. He knew that. He hadn't been able to stop the insidious spread of the need for violence through his brothers and sisters. How could he expect her to save them all? Him included? Yet he did. She had to. If she didn't, if she couldn't, they would all eventually be lost.

He was certain they knew it. They needed violence. Craved it. If they went too long without action, they got restless and moody. Some were worse than others, but they all had those symptoms, along with a million other various issues. They were one fucked-up club, but what the hell, they were alive and on their way to their new home.

Reaper sat at the highest point, not paying attention to the antics of Transporter, Mechanic, Absinthe, Ice and Storm. His gaze moved restlessly around him, checking out the few others on the beach and watching their backs. Savage hadn't moved from the motorcycles.

It wasn't long before a low whistle warned him. A car nudged its way slowly through the parking lot, *California Department of Parks and Recreation* on its side. The men kept up their wrestling, but all were very aware of the official vehicle coming to check them out. The low whistle had warned them. It didn't matter what they were doing, when the alert sounded, they all paid attention. It was ingrained in them. It was also a very bad thing to have Savage be closest to the vehicle. There was no doubt in Viktor's mind that the rangers had also called the sheriff for backup. He didn't kid himself about how they looked. They looked like exactly what they were—killers.

He sauntered over, intercepting the ranger as he got out of his SUV. Reaper was on his feet, looking anything but casual. Savage was off the bike as well. They were a distance away, but they definitely were intimidating, two tall men with roped muscles, scars and covered in tattoos.

"Afternoon," Viktor greeted. "You need to see our day passes?" He didn't pretend to smile. Frankly, he was sick of this shit, always getting hassled just because of the way they looked.

At the back of his mind that red flag wouldn't stop waving. They would always be different. They were different. *He* was. Blythe was either going to take him as he was, or he was royally screwed. He'd been counting on her for the last five years. Every minute of every day she'd been with him. He closed his fingers tight around the center of his palm, holding her to him, holding that mark that had faded right through his skin to his very bones, branding him hers.

The ranger nodded curtly and looked expectant. His gaze behind his glasses kept shifting back toward the main road. Clearly he was expecting company. He'd definitely called the sheriff for reinforcements. That rage, always held so deep in Viktor's gut, began to bubble toward the surface. The need to feel his fists hitting something. The need, through physical violence, to get rid of the rage that was always present, stamped every bit as deep in his bones as his connection to Blythe, rose like a wave.

"Baby?" Alena slipped her hand on his arm and smiled at the ranger, all charm, when he could feel the same anger simmering in her. She turned the full beauty of her smile on the ranger. "Is something wrong?" Her voice sang with innocence. The voice of an angel. She'd always had that.

The ranger couldn't help but respond. Viktor had never seen anyone resist Alena. The man smiled at her. She came up to the ranger's shoulder, all curves and wide, blue eyes. He actually took off his glasses to get a better look.

"Did we miss one of the bikes when we were paying?" That was directed at Viktor, but she kept smiling at the ranger. "It's such a beautiful day. I love the ocean. And the sand. You must love working here." She made it sound as if she admired the man and thought his job was the absolute best in the world. That was another of Alena's gifts. She focused completely on the person and they focused completely on her.

Viktor knew at that moment, every single one of his brothers could surround the ranger and he wouldn't see anyone but Alena. She had been very useful as a child growing up in an environment where it was important to disappear right in plain sight.

Viktor pulled the passes out of his pocket and handed them to Alena. She didn't even glance at him, keeping her entire attention on the man already eating out of her hand. "Here they are. I hope everything's in order. I just couldn't resist stopping and soaking up the sun." She stretched her arms toward the sky as if she was offering herself to the universe.

Viktor couldn't help but admire her. He shifted his gaze to take in the others. Ice and Storm were close. Alena was their baby sister and they watched over her like two predatory hawks. They'd seen child after child killed in that school of horrors, and they had determined it wouldn't happen to Alena—and it hadn't. They hadn't been alone in that fierce determination: the others had been just as watchful over her and one another.

Transporter and Mechanic flanked the ranger, two brooding men with death in their eyes and deceptive smiles on their faces. Absinthe was to their right and Reaper was at their left. Savage remained by the bikes, but he was the one Viktor worried most about. It was impossible to predict his actions. Reaper and Savage had lost two sisters in that dungeon of horrors and they watched over Alena and Lana to make certain they didn't lose them.

If for any reason the ranger threatened Alena, he would be dead, and they would be gone before his body hit the asphalt—and it would be Viktor who would do the killing. He was close enough, although Alena was crowding him. He'd have to reprimand her later. She knew better, but she was doing it deliberately.

"Everything looks in order. Paula must have counted the bikes wrong as they came through, ma'am," the ranger said. "You staying long?"

Alena shook her head regretfully. "We're heading up the coast."

The sheriff's car made its way slowly up the drive to the parking lot. He parked his vehicle at an angle, not in a space, partially cutting off the bikes. Viktor watched as the driver got out of the car and walked toward them. There was no show of strength, no blustering. This was a man with confidence in his abilities. He looked of Cajun descent, roped arms, a powerful deep chest, shrewd, cool eyes that looked a little like black obsidian. He had faint scars on his face that only made him look more rugged. It was impossible to read his expression, but his gaze took all of them in, their positions and the fact that the ranger was surrounded and didn't even know it.

Viktor recognized trauma when he saw it; not just trauma—this was a very dangerous man. He also recognized Jackson Deveau. Deveau didn't make a show of looking at Savage, but he certainly clocked him and noted him as potential trouble. Same with Reaper. Alena's voice wasn't going to enthrall this man; nothing was. Deveau's gaze touched on each man and then came to rest on him. Further evidence he was a man to be careful of. He recognized Viktor as the leader. They weren't wearing colors, there were no identifying markers, but in two seconds, Deveau had read all he needed to know.

"Bronson," Jackson greeted the ranger. "Everything all right here?"

"Why wouldn't it be?" Viktor challenged. He knew it was a dick move, but they'd been having a good day. A fucking *great* day. This was the man costing him five years of his life, probably his marriage and worse, and his birth brothers possibly their homes. Now his good day? It was enough.

Jackson's eyes rested on him. Flat. Cold. Eyes like Reaper's. Maybe not as intense, or as gone, but definitely close to it. "Just checking, sir."

"Their passes are in order, Jackson," Bronson said hastily. "You know Paula, she's dramatic. Sorry to call you out for nothing."

Viktor wanted to smile when the man partially shielded Alena from the newcomer. Clearly he was a little uneasy in the presence of the deputy. Jackson noticed everything, even the way the ranger protected Alena. His expression didn't change.

"Nice bikes. Where you heading?"

Some devil in Viktor wouldn't let sleeping dogs lie. "Heard about some prime real estate just north of Sea Haven, in Caspar. We decided to take a look at it. Want to set up a couple of businesses and looking for the right place to do it."

He kept his tone mild, no challenge, but he wanted it clear that he wasn't going to be pushed around.

"Nice area. There's a big part of the Caspar area for sale right now, including the roadhouse, inn and quite a few homes. Most of the residences overlooking the ocean are occupied or vacation homes, but there's a good deal of property for sale in that area."

Informative. Non-judgmental. No hint of wanting them to move on. Still, the man was looking at him. Studying him. Seeing too much. Seeing what Viktor needed him to see even if it was too early. He knew the exact moment when recognition hit. It was his eyes. Viktor had the eyes of a Prakenskii. He was older, harder, scarred and tattooed, but there was no mistaking his eyes. His six birth brothers resided in Sea Haven with their women. Deveau knew Ilya, the youngest Prakenskii, and there was no doubt that he'd soon be visiting the others.

"Nice to know. Thanks for the information."

Viktor kept it short. There was no point in further engagement; he'd seen all he needed to. The short encounter backed up the information he had on the target. This was the man Evan Shackler-Gratsos wanted dead more than any other. He wanted it so badly he was willing to come out of hiding in order to kill him personally.

Viktor had studied Deveau. He was recently married to Elle Drake, and just back from his honeymoon. The man was quiet, but well-liked. He had been in the Army Rangers, did a brief stint with the CIA, and had at one time been captured and held in the Congo for several weeks where it was reputed he'd been tortured. Seeing him in person, Viktor knew those speculations were true.

Deveau inclined his head and tapped Bronson on the arm. "We've both got things to do. We'd better get to them and leave these folks to their day." A not-so-subtle hint to take off. He wasn't leaving Bronson behind, although he gave no indication he thought Viktor or the others were threats. He had seen them surrounding the ranger, wolves circling the lamb. Viktor forced himself to step back, taking Alena with him.

Bronson followed, reluctant to give her up. "Caspar is right up the road from where I live. You'll like the area."

Deliberately Viktor put his arm around Alena and pulled her to him possessively. "If she does, she'll like it with me," he said, staring the man down.

Bronson flushed and let Jackson pull him away. Alena smiled demurely and waved her fingers. "See you later." She even injected a bit of a hopeful note in her voice. That was Alena, wanting the same thing he did, a little violence to take away the fire burning inside. They didn't call her Torch for nothing. She ignited fires both physically as well as emotionally. She could get men to fight by batting her lashes.

"I know what you're doing," Viktor said, just letting her know. He kept his eyes on the deputy. The man was a definite threat. He hadn't even put his hand near a weapon, but Viktor had the feeling it wouldn't have mattered.

Alena shrugged. "Why do you think I came over here? I kept that poor ranger from getting a beating and us from having to fight our way out of here."

That might have been the truth. Viktor had wanted to smash his baby face when the man made his power play. And Paula, the female ranger, he might have to pay her a visit in the middle of the night and mess with her head just for payback. He hated that they couldn't ride for a single day without getting hassled.

"Let's get out of here," he said.

Alena gave him one emotion-laden look. "After you say thank you."

"Thank you, Alena. I appreciate the fact that you kept me from doing something stupid."

She inclined her head regally. "You're very welcome. Glad to help. And just for your information, that deputy was good-looking. Did you notice he didn't really look at me? He's the real deal. Hard-core."

Viktor nodded. "Yes he is. He wouldn't have been easy to kill. He would have taken several of us with him."

"I had him in my sights," Reaper said from behind him.

Viktor felt a chill creep up his spine to his neck. Reaper could do that to him. He never heard him. Not even here where there was sand and rock and the man was wearing motorcycle boots.

"He knew it too," Savage added. "He was aware of both of us, and he walked right in the middle of that trap to get his friend out."

"I didn't have the feeling they were all that good of friends," Ice said. "More like acquaintances. But Alena is right, he didn't even look her way."

"That, brothers, was Jackson Deveau." Viktor dropped the bomb.

Reaper and Savage kept looking at him. Neither blinked. Alena gasped. Ice and Storm exchanged a long look with each other, as did Mechanic and Transporter. Absinthe simply shrugged. They knew they were between a rock and a hard place when they'd agreed to take the job.

Deveau was the bait, plain and simple. The biggest problem as Viktor saw it was he actually respected the man. He knew Jackson had grown up in the world of bikers. How he'd gotten into law enforcement was anyone's guess, but at one time, his father had been in Viktor's exact position—an enforcer for the same chapter of the Swords. In another world, Viktor might have liked Jackson, maybe even been friends, but that world was far away and this one was his reality.

Viktor wanted a home, a wife and a family. He wanted the same for his birth brothers and for his brothers and sisters in Torpedo Ink. They'd come up with the name when they were kids, teens, because in Russian, *torpedo* was *assassin*, *hit man*, and they thought it was funny to use the term in reference to themselves. By that time, Sorbacov was already sending them out on hits.

Originally INC was used, but because Ink was so good at tattoos, they thought it would be a great idea to use INK instead of the other so if they ever had a tattoo shop they could call it Torpedo Ink. Over the years, after they'd learned to ride, they formed their own club with their own colors. They kept the names they'd called one another as teens and used Torpedo Ink for the name of their club.

"We've got to do it," Viktor said. "If we can keep the man alive, we will. The main objective is to kill Evan. We can't lose sight of that. We cut off that head, and Code gets to the Swords' real books, we've destroyed the empire. That's our goal, and we stay on course no matter what."

The others nodded, and with his arm around Alena, Viktor walked back to the bikes.

4

VIKTOR didn't really acknowledge fear. When you lived and breathed it every minute of your existence as a child, you learned to accept fate. What you couldn't control you just had to accept. He knew that, so why was his heart pounding out of control? Why couldn't he keep his fingers relaxed instead of gripping the bike so hard he thought he'd leave indentations?

He was going to see his wife for the first time in five years. They were minutes outside of Sea Haven, and the first thing he intended to do was break off from the others—he would leave them at one of the bars—and he'd go find her house. The taste of her had never faded. Not in the least. The moment he thought of her, she was there against his skin.

It wasn't fair to put so much on her, but over the last five years, seeing the things he'd seen, doing the things he'd had to do, he had slowly been losing himself. He couldn't afford to do that. He had to stay strong for the others. He was the one that kept them all together. Without him, he knew both Reaper and Savage would be lost, and probably several if not all of the others.

He was bringing all of them home to Blythe, certain that she could work her magic on them the way she did him. She had to. The burden was becoming too much. Not the burden of his brothers and sisters, but the burden of being Viktor Prakenskii. Like the others, he had leftover childhood trauma issues, and they were catching up with him. Being in the Swords club and carrying out the insanity of his chapter president's orders day in and day out, watching the vile way the men treated women, had only brought his past roaring back, threatening to consume him.

He had already been hardened into something not fit for society, believing himself lost until he met her. Blythe. His wife. Her laughter and soft skin had saved him at a time when he was certain nothing could. He would have that back. A few more minutes, that was all.

They turned off the highway, taking the exit to Sea Haven. It was a very small town, overlooking the sea, unique in its historical beauty. They took the main road that led straight into downtown, the ocean across the street from the small shops beckoning tourists. The bar where he was hoping to leave the others was located on the main street between two shops. They nudged the bikes up to the curb right in front.

Viktor looked around him, inhaling the sea air. A breeze came off the ocean, but it felt good on his skin. The sound of laughter caught his attention. He knew that laugh. That musical sound. Alert, he swung his leg over his bike and turned toward the sound. A tall man with a short beard stood just outside a shop, leaning one hand against the side of the building, positioned just to the right of a blond woman's head.

Blythe. She looked up at the man, laughing softly. His breath caught in his throat. She was more beautiful than he remembered. The sound of her voice struck him like an arrow piercing his chest. For one terrible moment his vision clouded until the man was nothing but a target, and a dozen ways to kill him flashed through Viktor's mind.

Damn her to hell for betraying him. He was moving before he could think. He didn't want to think. His mind refused to do anything but insist he get the enemy away from his woman. He could deal with her treachery later. He *would* deal with her later. Ground-eating strides had him on the sidewalk and practically on top of them before his wife—his *wife*—realized she was caught.

The smile faded from her curved lips. He loved her lips. Worshipped them. He remembered them under his, soft and so inviting. He remembered them wrapped around his cock, sexy as hell. He was definitely killing the fucker if she'd sucked his cock. He was going to kill him anyway, but that would seal his fate.

Blythe put a hand on the man's chest just as he got to them. The male turned toward him, but it was already too late. Viktor had Blythe's arm and yanked her hard to him. "Get the hell away from my wife," he snapped.

The man paled. "Your wife?"

"Yeah. My fucking wife. You come near her again and you're a dead man." That was stupid. When the man turned up dead he'd be the first one they looked at. He'd have to make certain no one ever found the body.

"Viktor."

"Yeah. Viktor. Nice that you remember who you're married to." He started to walk back toward the bikes, taking her with him. He wanted to shake the life out of her, and at the same time, he wanted to kiss her senseless, remind her just who she belonged to. The scent of her filled his lungs, a scent he remembered all too well. Sometimes while she slept, he'd just inhaled her, putting his head beside hers on the pillow so he could breathe her in.

She planted her feet stubbornly as if she could pit her strength against his. "Let go of me," she hissed. "I mean it. Let go right now."

He didn't; instead, his fingers tightened until they were a shackle around her upper arm. "Not happening, babe. Did you fuck him?"

Her mouth opened and closed twice. There was a kind of horror in her eyes as if she looked at a monster—or she was shocked that she got caught. "After five years of *noth-*

ing, that's the first thing out of your mouth?" She kept her voice low.

"You must have forgotten. I go for the important things and keep the bullshit to a minimum." She struggled more, and he tightened his grip warningly.

"*I'm* giving you bullshit?"

Her eyes narrowed, and the dark chocolate washed through him like a heat wave. His blood turned to molten lava. He'd forgotten that reaction to her little flares of temper. Whenever she got annoyed with him and gave him that look, his cock reacted, going hard with urgent demand. It took control not to drop his hand and feel that honest reaction, something that didn't happen as a rule, another thing beat out of him in his childhood.

He did drag her close, tight against him, her hips against his, so she could feel that hard length imprinted on her soft skin. "Yeah, you're giving me bullshit."

"I'm not the one who *murdered* my stepfather and then disappeared without a word. A single word. Just left the dead body and my grieving drunk of a mother."

He noticed she didn't say she'd been grieving. No matter how much her stepfather had tried to con her, she had never liked him. "I left you a long, *detailed* letter. Get on the back of my bike. I'm not discussing this with you in the street, especially after waiting for five fucking years and I find my wife with another man."

She put both hands against his chest and tried to shove him. "Stop saying I'm your wife. I'm *not*, and unless you want every sheriff in a hundred-mile range running here fast, let go right now."

"You *are* my wife, legally and in every other way, so that gives me the right to know whether or not you're fucking that coward."

She glanced back at the man who had slunk away. He had his cell phone out so they were going to get a visit by the cops soon. "No. Not that you deserve an answer. And stop saying *fuck*. I hate that and you know it."

She had always hated that word. He was going to have to clean up his language, and he'd catch hell from the others letting a woman dictate to him, but the one thing about Blythe he couldn't imagine changed was the fact that she didn't lie. He could see it in her eyes. Not only was she telling the truth—she *hadn't* slept with the coward—her body wanted Viktor and was glad to see him, whether her brain and heart did or not. That was something.

"Clearly you're a Prakenskii, and from what I understand that means you were working for your government. When we found out who my stepfather was, a notorious pedophile, I realized, rather recently, that you had been assigned to kill him. You did your job and used me to do it. I get that, so I'm not calling the cops and turning you in for murder, but stop saying I'm your wife, because I'm not and you have no right to act all self-righteous."

"You *are* my wife. In case you don't remember, we got married. In a church. I remember. Too bad you so easily can forget." He couldn't help the snarl in his voice. She could piss him off like no one else. He liked being her husband. He wanted her to like it as well, but mostly he wanted her to admit they were married.

A low whistle warned him the sheriff must have showed up. He glanced over his shoulder. Reaper and Savage flanked him; the others sat on their bikes, watching.

"Get on the bike, Blythe." He heard a car door shut. Two men were striding toward them. He recognized Jackson Deveau immediately and guessed the man with him was Jonas Harrington, the local sheriff. He'd heard of his reputation. "They don't stand a chance against my brothers and me, so don't be stupid and make a scene."

She stiffened at his not-so-veiled threat. "They're law enforcement," she whispered. "Viktor, don't be crazy."

"You know what will happen if you don't just get on the bike. I'm not leaving you again."

Blythe glanced behind her at the two men walking up the sidewalk toward them. "Fine." She bit the word out between clenched teeth, turned away from him and stomped toward the bikes parked in front of the bar.

Viktor took the time to admire the sway of her ass. He'd always liked the way his woman walked. He didn't look at the sheriff, but followed behind Blythe, ready to catch her if she tried changing her mind. Reaper and Savage had his back.

Blythe halted so abruptly he nearly ran her down. He caught her shoulders, his body crowding hers, in order to force her forward, but she only took two small steps and then stopped again.

"Just which bike is yours?" she demanded, staring straight ahead.

He followed her gaze to his bike. Alena sat on the back, looking relaxed, as if she belonged there. There was no explaining Alena there on the street with the cops coming right up on them and a small crowd watching the drama.

"You bastard." Blythe's voice was low, a whisper of sound, but he caught the note of hurt. "Nothing coming out of your mouth is the truth. You wouldn't know it if it hit you in the face. I'll have my lawyer check into the marriage. If it was legal, you'll be hearing from him. I won't stay married to you." She spun away from him, her back ramrod stiff.

Viktor cursed and caught her arm. "There's not going to be a divorce."

"Is there a problem here, Blythe?"

It was the taller of the two men who spoke. Jonas Harrington. He and Jackson had spread out a little, giving themselves room if they needed it. Reaper had positioned himself on the side nearest Jackson, perceiving him as the bigger of the two threats. Savage flanked Harrington. The other members of Torpedo Ink slowly stood up, ready to move on his signal.

"No, Jonas," Blythe said brightly. "We were just talking, but we're finished now." She sent Viktor a glare. "*Completely* finished."

Deveau didn't appear to be fazed by being surrounded by the bikers. He walked up to Viktor and held out his hand. "Nice to see you again. I had no idea you knew Blythe."

It was a stab in the dark. He and Blythe had been speaking low to each other. All Deveau had to go on was the way they looked together.

"She's my wife," he said and signaled to the others to get on their bikes. They were leaving. He wasn't going to risk her or Alena getting hurt.

Blythe stepped closer to Deveau, and that pissed him off. She didn't need the man's protection. Not from him. Then again, maybe she did. If he had his way, he'd be taking her somewhere private and they'd be getting down to business fast.

"Is that true, Blythe?" Jonas asked.

Viktor went still. It was one thing to have his woman call him out, but another man? *Hell* no. He'd been spoiling for a fight and the thought of hitting someone really hard was more than tempting. "You calling me a liar?" He spoke low, but his words carried, and there was no mistaking the menace in them.

Blythe turned immediately and put a hand on his arm, stepping squarely between him and the sheriff. "Of course he's not calling you a liar, Viktor. He's just shocked because he's known me practically since birth, and I'm not wearing a ring." She held up her hand with its naked finger. "See?"

He caught her wrist. "Where the hell is your ring?"

Her eyes flashed that startling brown again, a pure flame of dark chocolate. His body, as perverse as it was, reacted a second time, his cock full and aching, no half measures at all. She put both hands on his shoulders and leaned into him, her mouth against his ear. "Your girlfriend is wearing it. I told her she could have it."

Her lips brushed his earlobe, soft and inviting, sending heat spiraling through him. She went to pull away, but he caught the ponytail. All that thick, silky hair she had tied up at the back of her head. Using her hair, he tilted her head and brought his mouth down on hers. She gasped and his tongue swept inside.

Her taste. He remembered that taste. Raw honey. Lust rose sharp and terrible, a need that nearly overwhelmed him. He kissed her like he'd wanted to over the last five years. All those lonely days and nights of hell, gone just like that, swept away by her magic. She'd always been able to do that. Take him somewhere he'd never been or even imagined. It didn't matter that he was angry with her or she was angry with him. The moment his mouth was on hers, his past was gone as if it had never been. She wiped it all out with her taste and the way her mouth moved under his. The stroke of her tongue. The heat and fire.

Deveau cleared his throat. Her fingers curled into fists in his shirt and she pulled away. He let her, only because if he didn't there was going to be an altogether different type of scene right there in the street and Blythe was no exhibition-ist. He wouldn't care; the woman was his and as far as he was concerned, the entire world needed to know it.

She pressed trembling fingers to her lips, her gaze avoid-ing his. She'd kissed him back, and there was no denying that fact. She hadn't been passive at all, but then, she never had been. Blythe was a woman who knew what she wanted, and she matched him fire for fire. She ducked around him to put Jackson between them.

"Your wedding ring, Blythe. Put it on." For some reason he couldn't let that go. It hurt not to see it on her finger.

She raised her chin. "I lost it."

She was lying to him. Totally lying.

"Put it on," he repeated and stalked to his bike. "Ride with Absinthe," he snapped to Alena.

She nodded and sauntered over to Absinthe's bike, swinging one slim leg over to fit herself easily behind Ab-sinthe's back.

Blythe made a sound that had him spinning around. Was she weeping? He couldn't see. She was walking away, her back to him. She was so damned beautiful he wanted to rush after her, throw her over his shoulder and carry her off. They could work out whatever problems they had if they were alone. In bed. Anywhere alone. Instead of doing what every cell in his body demanded, he threw his leg over his bike and started the engine. All the while, his gaze was on his wife. She didn't turn around, didn't look back. She thought it was over. Little did she know, he was back to stay and he was going to be in her life permanently.

Blythe heard the roar as all eight motorcycles started up. She desperately wanted to look at him one more time. Viktor. She thought she'd never see him again. Never. She'd been so in love with him. She'd felt as if she'd come to life, really started living, when she first met him.

She touched her lips, still tingling from his kiss. Her entire body was on fire. From the moment she'd met him, he'd been able to do that when no one else ever had. Tears burned behind her eyes but she refused to cry. Not in front of everyone. Growing up, she'd always been reserved, very private, and she was even more so as an adult.

Her father had died of cancer when she was barely five. Her mother had become a secret binge drinker. Blythe had learned to take care of her, to make grocery lists and even cook at an early age. She didn't confide in anyone, not even her friends or cousins. It felt like a betrayal. The alcohol had changed her mother from sweet and funny to bitter and violent. And then she met Ray Langton.

Jackson fell into step on one side of her, Jonas on the other. They were silent as they went down the sidewalk with her. She walked quickly, not daring to look at either of them, especially Jonas. He was married to her first cousin, Hannah Drake, and she really had known him since she was a child. She hadn't lived in Sea Haven, but they visited often if her mother wasn't drinking. She could feel concern for her pouring off of Jonas, but to his credit, he waited for her to speak.

She made the effort. "He's a Prakenskii."

"I met him earlier in the day at the State Park," Jackson said. "Seems nice enough. Tough, but then Ilya is tough."

She forced herself to look at the deputy. He was married

to another first cousin, Elle, the youngest of the Drake sisters. "I heard you'd gotten home. I hope your honeymoon was wonderful." Hers had been. She still dreamt of it. Days and nights of paradise with Viktor. She hadn't known life could be so good. He made her feel beautiful and intelligent and bold. She had often wondered, over the last few years, how much—if any—of the things he did and said were true.

"We cut it short. Elle needed to get back to Sea Haven. We got home on the weekend, and I had to go right back to work. You should stop in and see her."

She kept walking. She had no idea where she was going, only that she had to keep moving or she'd feel hurt so intense she might drop to the sidewalk in front of everyone.

"I'll do that. Have you had time to meet . . . the others?" How did one delicately put to Jackson that *all* the Prakenskii brothers were living on the farm? All of them, including Lev. He'd been undercover when Elle Drake had been taken by a human trafficking ring. He hadn't saved her.

"No."

Just one word, but then Jackson Deveau was a man of few words.

"Honey, you're going to have to talk to me about this man you claim is your husband. Prakenskii or not, he's a dangerous man. He's not wearing colors, but I'd bet my last dollar he's in a motorcycle club," Jonas said, making it a half question, half statement.

She shook her head. She wasn't going to cry in front of either man, nor would she betray Viktor, as much as she'd like to. No one had ever hurt her the way he had. No one. She'd practically worshipped him. Still, she couldn't bring herself to say one word against him—not to Jonas or Jackson.

"There isn't anything to say."

The two men exchanged a look over her head. She wasn't short and she saw it. The speculation. The interest. In Jonas she saw concern and sympathy. It was impossible to read Jackson. She stopped short. They'd walked all the way to her sister Judith's gift shop. She sold her kaleidoscopes as well as the smaller items of blown glass Lissa,

another sister, made. Lissa was fast becoming famous for
her chandeliers, particularly in Europe where they were
sought after. Judith was famous for her paintings and her
kaleidoscopes. What was she famous for? She choked back
a sob. Screwups. She was world famous for screwups.

"Thanks for walking me here," she managed to whisper,
and yanked open the door to her sister's shop. At once the
soothing scent of orange and vanilla greeted her. She all
but ran into the shop, hoping the two men would take the
hint and go away. She needed to be alone. She needed her
sisters. She needed to cry her eyes out and rebuild her de-
fenses.

She could still feel his mouth on hers. Smell him. His
scent. She practically ran down the aisle, threaded her way
through the tourists examining various items and pushed
her way into the back room. Someone was working behind
the counter, but it wasn't Judith. Judith had to be in the back,
and she needed her desperately.

"Blythe?" Judith straightened from where she was pulling out a roll of Bubble Wrap to secure it onto a spool. Even
her back room was immaculate.

Judith was tall like Blythe, but that was where the re-
semblance ended. Her hair was long and board straight,
black as a raven's wing and extremely shiny. Her eyes were
dark and mysterious, very exotic. She'd inherited her hair
and coloring from her Japanese mother. Her sparkling per-
sonality always drew people to her. Blythe had met her in
group counseling, a closed group for women who had lost
a loved one to a violent crime and for whatever reasons felt
guilty.

Judith frowned and stepped toward her. "Honey, what's
wrong?" There was genuine concern and maybe a hint of
alarm. Blythe couldn't blame her. Blythe had the reputation
of always being calm, very serene.

Blythe threw herself into Judith's arms and gave herself
permission to cry. Once she started, she couldn't stop. It
wasn't a little bit of tears; it was a storm. She hadn't allowed
herself to cry like that since her mother died. She'd even

blamed Viktor for her mother's death, although she knew he wasn't responsible for any of the things that had happened after he'd gone. She wanted to blame him for *everything*.

Judith remained silent. She just held her, letting her cry. Blythe was afraid she'd never stop. Why did Viktor have to look so good? Why did her heart choose him? He'd *left* her. Used her and left her. Without a single word. No phone call. Nothing. She didn't care if he was a Prakenskii and she loved every one of his brothers. She wasn't going to love him or forgive him. And that woman. Who was that woman?

"She was so beautiful." She managed to get the words out, making them semi-intelligible, but then the storm was worse than ever.

Judith handed her several tissues. "All right, honey, you're going to make yourself sick. I'm going to tell them up front that I have to leave, and then I'm driving you home. We'll make a cup of tea and talk there."

Blythe nodded and turned away from her, covering her face with her hands and crouching down on the floor. She was there until Judith came and tugged at her arm. She followed her out the back and slipped into the passenger side of Judith's convertible. Thankfully, she had the top up.

"So tell me, honey," Judith invited as she drove through the village toward Highway 1.

"Look at me. Just look at me, Judith. I'm a mess," Blythe wailed, knowing she was on the verge of hysteria. She was never hysterical. Ask anyone. She was the epitome of calm and cool. "I'm wearing a tank top and ripped jeans. A sweater. I look terrible. I'm not even wearing makeup." She wiped at the tears and clenched the tissue in the middle of her fists. "I want to pound him into the ground."

Judith glanced at her but Blythe turned her face away, ashamed she was out of control. She didn't lose control. Her mother did that. She had promised herself she would never be a shrieking shrew, and yet here she was. Viktor was responsible for that as well. Her left palm itched but she refused to scratch it. She was going to a tattoo place to see if they could laser that mark off of her.

"When a woman sits on the back of a man's bike, do you know what she is, if they're members of a motorcycle club? His old lady, that's what. Especially a *gorgeous* woman. She should have been all windblown, her hair matted and heavy makeup, *something* awful. Just one ugly thing about her, but no, she looked like a million dollars, Judith."

Judith turned from the highway into the private drive leading to their farm. It was several hundred acres now, as the Prakenskii brothers had bought up the adjoining land around the original farm. Each of the women Blythe called a sister of the heart had their own five acres where they built their homes. Everything else was shared land. All of them contributed in some way, whether it was farming or through their small businesses.

"All of you are married or committed with the exception of me. To a Prakenskii." It came out an accusation. "How did that even happen? It's inexcusable."

Judith didn't say a word, which was just as well. Blythe knew she wasn't making any sense, throwing seemingly random comments out, but it all made sense to her. Viktor's brothers were probably in on the conspiracy. Judith parked in front of Blythe's house and they sat in silence just looking up at the two-story structure.

The house suited Blythe. It was too big for one person, but she didn't care. It was completely different from everyone else's and she liked it that way. It was all cool Mediterranean tile, thick walls and banks of inviting windows facing the forest. The views were incredible. The house was in a U-shape, giving her the courtyard she'd always dreamt of having. She'd wanted a houseful of children and a husband she adored. She thought she'd found that in Viktor.

A fresh flood of tears came and she leapt out and all but ran up the wide stairs to the wraparound verandah. The upper story had a surrounding balcony to match the decking on the lower story. Judith followed her in and went right to the kitchen. Blythe loved the kitchen.

"You know why I love the kitchen, Judith?" she asked. "Because he's never been in it, that's why. I love every single room in this house because he's never been in it. And neither has his old lady. She hasn't been in my house either."

"All right, Blythe," Judith said as she filled the kettle with water. "You're not making any sense, and honestly, I don't think you want to, but you're going to have to tell me what's going on with you. Who did you run into today?"

Blythe pressed both hands to her stomach. She'd wanted a child so badly. His child. Viktor's. Now it was too late. She wasn't a young twenty-year-old. She wasn't going to have a baby with anyone, let alone Viktor. He had a young twenty-year-old riding on the back of his bike. She'd give him babies. That gorgeous woman. They'd be gorgeous together. Viktor and his old lady. Dried-up-prune Blythe would be a spinster.

"Can you be a spinster if you're married?"

"*Blythe*. Tell me what happened."

Blythe took a breath. She hurt. Her entire body, as if she'd been beaten with a baseball bat. Just breathing hurt. "I saw him today. He rode in on a motorcycle with another woman on his bike."

Judith glanced up from where she was putting loose leaf tea in a wire basket. "Him? A name would be nice."

"Viktor. Viktor Prakenskii. That's who." She dropped the bomb, knowing it was going to be an explosive one.

Judith gasped and spun around. "No way. Are you sure? Very, very certain it was Viktor?"

"I'm certain."

"We have to tell the others. Stefan is going to lose his mind. He hasn't seen his brother in years. Not since they were children. What did he look like? Did you talk to him?"

Blythe nodded slowly. "We talked. It wasn't pleasant. He claims we're married." That was the second bomb.

Judith spun completely around and leaned against the sink, gaping at her. "Oh. My. God. Are you? Are you married to him?"

Blythe rubbed her palm along her thigh to try to relieve

the terrible itching. Sometimes at night . . . She blushed and shook her head. He was messing with her. Right now, he was making her palm itch. "I don't know. We were married quietly, running away together to Vegas, but a few weeks later, he insisted we marry again in a church."

The kettle whistled and Judith poured water into the teapot before turning back to her. "A church?" she prompted.

Blythe's gaze met Judith's. "In San Francisco. The same church all of you were married in. With the same priest. I recognized it and the priest. It was five years ago, but you don't forget that sort of thing. Everything was in Russian. I couldn't understand a single word. He had me sign a piece of paper that was written in Russian. At the time, I was so in love with him I didn't think to question anything. It was a church ceremony, and I thought maybe his family was religious."

"Why did you think you weren't married if you married him in two ceremonies?"

"He murdered Ray. My stepfather. It was so ugly, the entire thing. He was gone without a word and then Mom . . . It got worse from there." Blythe ducked her head again. "Really, Judith, if I'm going to talk about my past, we should call the others. They need to know Viktor's in town. Everyone is married to or living with one of his brothers. They'll want to know."

Judith nodded. "I agree. You go into the great room and I'll make the calls. Stefan is really going to lose his mind when he finds out his brother is here. They talk about Viktor all the time, but kind of in awe, sort of . . ." She trailed off, at a loss for words.

"Fearful," Blythe supplied. "Like they do with Gavriil." Lexi, the youngest of her "sisters of the heart," was living with Gavriil Prakenskii, a very scary man. He was devoted to Lexi, but anyone else was not so lucky. Gavriil let few people into his world. She liked to think he was becoming fond of all of them living on the farm.

Each had their own homes and five acres, which gave

them privacy and separate lives, but they came together often and worked together to make the farm a success.

"Is Viktor as scary as Gavriil?" Judith asked.

Blythe nodded slowly. "In a different way. Viktor's covered in tats. He looks like the epitome of a very scary biker. The bad kind." Her chin jerked up. "He acts worse."

She turned away from Judith, feeling tears burning behind her eyes. She wasn't going to cry again. She'd given enough tears to Viktor Prakenskii. She couldn't get the sight of the woman on the back of his bike out of her head. "Do you know what he is, Judith? A bigamist, that's what. I know what it means when a man has a woman on the back of his bike like that. His old lady. His *wife* in biker terms. Oh. My. God. He committed bigamy. Why not? He's a freakin' criminal anyway. Bigamy would be just like him. Right up his alley. He's good at seducing women. I ought to know. I should have warned that poor girl."

Judith picked up the phone. "Honey, you might be going off the deep end, just a little. That's not like you. You never judge people before you know the facts. She could have just needed a ride somewhere and he was being kind."

Blythe gave a little sniff of disdain and stomped into the great room. It was massive. She liked it that way. She liked space, lots of it. High ceilings, lots of room. The house had a warm feel to it, very inviting. Her sisters often gathered in her home to visit. She was never going to have children of her own, so she enjoyed mothering all the women she'd come to love.

Recently, one of them, Airiana, had begun the process of adopting four children she'd helped rescue from a human trafficking ring—the same ring that had taken Elle Drake. Blythe spent as much time as possible with them, enjoying just being around them. She liked children and had always envisioned having several of her own.

She pressed a hand to her stomach, listening to Judith calling each of her sisters, telling them to come immediately without their men. Gavriil and Lev wouldn't like it, but they wouldn't protest. They never did. It wasn't that they didn't want their women to have fun without them; it was that they were insanely protective—at least Gavriil was. With Lev, Blythe sometimes thought his wife, Rikki, somehow kept him grounded, which was odd since Rikki was autistic.

The view was gorgeous; she could watch the sunset and see the forest so close, all the trees swaying in the wind. It gave her a sense of freedom. She could see anything coming at her, and she needed that. She needed to be able to know what she faced every single day, good or bad. Inside her home or out of it.

She hadn't seen Viktor coming. She hadn't even had an inkling of danger. Wrapping her arms around her middle, she wandered closer to the window. She'd been so in love with him. She'd never thought she'd ever find a man she wanted to be with. She tasted him in her mouth. Some nights she couldn't lie in bed alone without him and she'd go out running, a practice the other women didn't like, but one she couldn't stop. She'd never been able to stop thinking about him, even after the terrible chain of events he had set in motion.

"Viktor." She whispered his name and pressed her thumb into the center of her palm. She'd loved him with everything in her, and he'd used her and left her without a word. Without one single word. He'd never looked back. She'd never been able to move on. Maybe his coming back was a good thing. Maybe now she'd be able to finally just close that door. She hoped so.

5

LEXI handed Blythe a cup of tea off the gold, polka-dotted tray. She smiled, that sweet Lexi smile that always made them love her all the more. Lexi had green eyes and a little pixie face surrounded by masses of wild auburn hair. She didn't just have a green thumb; her element was earth and it spoke to her. She could grow anything, and the farm thrived because of her.

"You should taste the lemon bars, Blythe," she encouraged. "Lucia made them. She's becoming quite a baker."

Blythe took the bar and placed it on a napkin. "Lucia's already a wonderful chef."

"She rivals Lev," Rikki said, snagging a lemon bar. "And that's saying something."

Blythe raised an eyebrow, shocked that Rikki was eating something other than her beloved peanut butter. "When did you start eating cookies? Other than peanut butter cookies?" She'd tried for years to get her "sister" to eat more foods.

Rikki had dark, almost black eyes and sun-kissed dark hair she wore in a ragged cut that suited her. A sea urchin diver, she was bound to the water. She didn't like to go anywhere other than her boat, and her sisters' homes. She had a difficult time with textures and foods, so Blythe was very happy to see her eat something different, even if it was a cookie.

Rikki shrugged. "Lev and Lucia cook together, and lately they've been baking. Lucia gives me those eyes of hers and I make myself cave and Lev . . ." She blushed, the color creeping up her neck to her face. "He likes games."

The women burst out laughing. Blythe took a sip of tea and found herself relaxing for the first time since she'd seen Viktor Prakenskii. It felt good to be with her sisters in their circle. They were there for her. They'd come immediately at Judith's call, dropping whatever they were doing to be with her.

"That sounds intriguing," Airiana said. An air element, she was small and fragile looking, young to be the mother of teenage Lucia and her three siblings. Still, she seemed to thrive in the role. "Do you want to tell us what that means, hon?"

Rikki made a face at her and bit into the lemon bar. "I've added lemon to my list of good things, especially if it's in the form of this cookie."

Blythe laughed softly. "I guess anything added is an improvement."

"Lev is always cooking now that Lucia comes over," Rikki confided with mock disgust. "I think he got her to enter into a conspiracy with him to get me to eat, although neither will admit it."

Blythe was fairly certain that was not only possible, but probable. Like Blythe, Lev and the others always worried about Rikki's eating habits. She worked hard underwater, collecting sea urchins to sell. It was difficult work with the waves constantly battering her. Before she met Lev, she dove alone, a terrifying thing for Blythe and the others to endure, worrying every single time she went down. Now, Lev dove with her. He was an experienced diver and had learned to harvest the sea urchins nearly as fast as Rikki.

"I met him, Blythe, before, in Italy. He came to the wedding," Lissa confessed. A fire element, Lissa was all flame.

Red hair, small and curvy, she helped support the farm with her glassblowing business.

Blythe swung her gaze to Lissa, feeling a hard punch to her stomach. "You met Viktor and didn't tell us?" Lissa had no way of knowing that Blythe was maybe—okay, probably—married to him, but still, shouldn't she have told them?

"He's been on a very dangerous undercover assignment, and he made it clear to us that we couldn't blow his cover. Any leak, no matter how small, might get him killed."

Intellectually, Blythe understood, but it still hurt. Everything to do with Viktor hurt. He was invading her world again. Last time he had all but destroyed her. This time, she couldn't let that happen.

"Blythe, honey, I didn't mean to hurt you," Lissa whispered, her blue eyes wide with compassion. "Please don't be upset."

Of course she was upset. They were loyal to one another, that was how it worked. Now, Viktor had managed to drive a wedge between them. She felt eyes on her, the others watching her closely. She took a sip of tea, concentrating on keeping her hand steady. She wasn't going to allow anyone to see just how much Lissa's betrayal hurt.

"I'm upset that he's here. He claims we're married." She said it aloud, staring directly at Lissa, watching her face. There was no shock. No surprise at all. Lissa knew because Viktor had to have told her. "How strange that you didn't even tell me that. Don't you think I should have known I was married? What if I'd decided to date someone?"

For the first time Lissa looked uncomfortable. "I would have stopped you. I struggled with this. Casimir said we couldn't tell his brothers, let alone all of you. Viktor made it very clear it was life or death. Is he still undercover?"

That was a good question but . . . "You know something, Lissa? I don't care if he is or isn't. In the morning I'm calling an attorney and immediately filing for divorce. Viktor can carry on with his life, undercover or not, and it won't have a thing to do with me. I don't want to see him again.

Not. Ever." There was a part of her that knew that Lissa made a convenient target, but right then it didn't matter. She felt hurt and betrayed, all the same things she felt when she found Viktor gone and Ray Langton dead.

The knots in her stomach told her she was a liar, but no one else—not even Viktor—ever had to know that. She took another sip of tea to try to remain serene. In the face of a crisis, Blythe was always cool and calm. She couldn't be any different now.

Judith leaned forward. "Tell us what happened, Blythe. All of it."

She pressed her hand deeper into her stomach. Her womb. Her empty womb. "I met him on a Sunday. I was running in the park, and he was running too. He nearly knocked me over, and the next thing I knew we were running together, then lunch and then we were inseparable. He was . . ." *Is.* "Extraordinary. Tall, and I'm tall so that's saying something. Good-looking. His scars only make him rugged. He looks like a man. He had tattoos everywhere." She blushed thinking about all the times she'd traced those tattoos with her tongue. She'd practically devoured him. At the time, nothing they did seemed wrong.

There was silence, her sisters waiting with rapt attention. She took another sip of tea and a bite of the lemon bar. It tasted like dust in her mouth and she pushed the napkin away from her. She felt so empty all the time. Half alive. Just enough to walk through the motions. She'd been getting better, slowly, coming out of that dark place Viktor had left her in.

"I thought we were happy, made for each other. He seemed happy with me." She couldn't keep the hurt out of her voice. "He's a great actor, and he takes his undercover roles very seriously. I certainly believed him. We were married very quickly, after only four weeks. I should have known because he was the one pushing to get married. My mother and Ray lived a good distance from me, but Viktor wanted to meet them. I was . . . reluctant."

"Why?" Judith asked. "You told us Ray was a pedophile, but you didn't know that until he was murdered."

"My mother drank a lot, I told all of you that, but I didn't say how bad it was. When I say a lot, I mean she binged. Sometimes she was sober, but when she drank it was ugly. I thought after she met Ray she'd back off, but instead, they drank together. I didn't like him at all, and my relationship with my mom deteriorated even more than it already had. I tried once going to her sisters to talk to them about it. They hadn't seen her drinking, not since high school and college. She took great care to always appear perfect around them."

Blythe tried to keep the bitterness out of her voice. "I was an only child, and life growing up with an alcoholic parent wasn't a picnic. My mother thought nothing of throwing things or hitting, slapping and even punching me when she was drunk. When she was sober, she 'couldn't remember' ever doing such a thing. She would cry sometimes and beg forgiveness, other times she'd call me a liar."

She didn't look at her sisters. She couldn't. She didn't want to see sympathy; she wasn't telling them for that reason. They had to understand why Viktor had become her world. "I didn't date, because if I did, I'd have to bring my date home and Mom would be awful. Later, I just couldn't trust anyone enough to bring them into my life. I tried taking care of Mom, I even put her in a rehab or two. She walked away from both of them and refused to talk to me for months because I called her an alcoholic."

She drank the last of her tea and put the cup carefully back on the tray. It was impossible not to glance around the room. Each of them had a horrendous story, but this was her own. She'd gotten through it, and she'd thought it had made her stronger. And then she'd met Viktor.

"I thought I was whole again by the time I met Viktor. It's really no wonder that I fell for a man like him." It didn't matter that it wasn't any wonder; she still felt guilty for falling like a ton of bricks, for bringing him into her mother's life. "He was attentive, always careful of my comfort, and he acted as if he would protect me from anything or anyone—and he did. When we finally met my mother and Ray, things didn't go well. Both drank with dinner, and then drank after dinner. Mom grew belligerent with me the way she always did, and Ray followed her example. Viktor told them both to go to hell and took me out of the house. We didn't go back."

She found herself rubbing her thumb into the middle of her palm. When she was anxious she often did that, a bad habit she wished she could break. It was a telling sign in front of her sisters. They all wore the mark of a Prakenskii, two circles intertwined that faded beneath the skin and only came to the surface when one or the other brought it forward. She rubbed her palm on her thigh, forcing herself to stop touching that exact center where it felt as if she were touching Viktor.

"Keep going, Blythe," Lexi encouraged.

Only Lexi could sound so close to tears, so completely compassionate, without upsetting her more. Blythe took the glass of water Judith handed to her, drank most of it and forced a smile at her youngest sister.

"Viktor and I spent several weeks together. That was when he insisted we get married in his church. It was in the dead of night and felt very runaway and exciting. Right after that, though, he began to get quieter and edgy. Not with me—he was always sweet—but he stopped talking so much to me. Mom and Ray decided to come for a visit. I didn't know, but later, Mom told me that Viktor extended an olive branch to them. They needed a loan, and he'd agreed to give them money."

Bile rose and she pressed her hand over her stomach again. She felt empty and lost, very alone right in the midst of the women she loved enough to call sisters. "We were at dinner, and of course they were drinking. Ray was obnoxious, and Mom ended up throwing a plate at me because I told him I didn't want him talking the way he was about my mother at the table. He was disgusting and she just let him carry on. I knew he was doing it on purpose.

"Viktor suddenly stood up and said he'd had enough. He looked straight at Ray, but he was talking to Mom and me. He told us Ray was a notorious pedophile and justice had caught up with him. Very, very calmly, he pulled out a gun—one I didn't even know he owned—and he shot Ray four times. Both eyes, the middle of his forehead and his throat. He threw pictures on the table and then grabbed my hair, pulled my head back and kissed me. *Kissed* me with my stepfather's blood all over the walls and my mother screaming. Then he was just . . . gone. He was gone."

The burn of tears was back. It was so difficult to keep from feeling that shock and horror all over again. "I picked up the pictures, and they made me vomit. Not the blood. Not the death. The pictures of Ray with little boys. I knew instantly why he kept Mom drinking. He didn't have to touch her. Mom went crazy, trying to rip the photographs from me, hitting, kicking and throwing things at me. Viktor had already called the police, and when they got there, they had to restrain her. They called medics, who gave her a sedative, and then they took her up to our bedroom, leaving me to deal with the questions."

She looked around her a little helplessly. "I didn't have any answers. I kept expecting him to come back, to say it was all a mistake. Something. Anything."

"Oh, Blythe," Airiana whispered.

Blythe took a deep breath. She wished the story ended there, but it didn't. "It came out that Ray was this horrific pedophile wanted by Interpol in just about every country in the world. He had set up a huge site on the Internet where children were bought and sold. He was the lowest of the low and my mother had married him. She was humiliated, and somehow I got blamed. If I hadn't brought Viktor into their lives, Ray would have turned over a new leaf with her."

"What?" Rikki was horrified. "Blythe, you know he wouldn't have. Even if he could have, what about all those children he hurt during his lifetime? You know it was a good thing he was gone."

She forced herself to nod. "Mom shut herself in the

house and I was once again taking care of her. A couple of weeks later it was very apparent I was pregnant." Just saying it hurt. It hurt so much she could barely breathe and she had to stop to force air through her lungs.

There was a collective gasp all around, and Airiana covered the small baby mound with both hands protectively. "Blythe." Just her name. The anguish was for both of them.

Blythe stood up and beckoned to the others to follow her. She'd kept this room sacred. No one had ever been in it. At first they'd asked her why she locked it, but when she wouldn't answer, they dropped it out of respect. She unlocked the room, grateful she didn't have to hide it anymore. Still, the agony burned through her until she could barely breathe.

"I was just over six months along when Mom went crazy again. She'd been drinking all day when I came home from work. I went upstairs to change and she followed me up, screaming at me how I'd ruined her life. How I was so smug, but no man wanted me and no man would ever stay with me. I ignored her. I shouldn't have done that. I knew better. It only made her angrier if I didn't answer, but I was so tired and I just couldn't deal with her."

They followed her into the room—her shrine to her child. To Viktor. She'd mourned them both. The room was the smallest in the house, and she'd covered the walls with beautiful paintings of mothers and infants. There was a picture on canvas of Blythe lying on a bed with a tiny infant on her chest. The baby's head was turned to one side and her eyes were closed. She had dark hair, quite a lot of it.

Blythe had to steel herself to tell them the rest. "Mom's voice kept swinging out of control and she said the most vicious things. She hated me, she always had. She never wanted me. No one did. That sort of thing. Her voice was slurred, and I turned to leave the room. She must have picked up a baseball bat because she swung it at me. Hard. The first hit knocked me down. Then she kept hitting me." Bile rose. She pressed her hand to her stomach as if she could protect her unborn child. "She hit me several times right in the stomach. She kept kicking me and hitting me and I passed out."

Her voice broke on a sob and she pressed trembling fingertips to her mouth. She closed her eyes. "I think the neighbors called the cops, or maybe she did when she saw what she'd done. They took me to the hospital but it was too late."

She touched the canvas with gentle fingers. "She lived two days and they let me hold her like this. There wasn't any way to save her. Then she was dead. *His* daughter. All I had left of him. Of our dream. *My* dream. All I had left, period." She lifted her gaze to her sisters. "I wanted her so much."

There was silence with the exception of Airiana's soft weeping. Lexi had tears running down her face, but she was silent. She'd learned to stay silent no matter what and, although she was free of her past now, those hard lessons she'd learned as a child stuck with her.

Blythe sighed. "I may as well tell you the rest of it. It's ugly, but anything to do with my mother is ugly. She claimed in court she'd blacked out and didn't know what she was doing. Her sisters hired the best defense attorney and pleaded with the court to give her rehab. I honestly don't know whether it was the letters, or if they used their gifts to persuade him. I was so numb I couldn't have felt anyone's energy."

"They wouldn't," Judith said, gasping. "That would be so wrong."

"The judge gave her five years because, after all, the baby hadn't been born yet, and I didn't have any real permanent damage. She was remorseful, and if she agreed to go to rehab that time would count toward her sentence. If she did good there, they would put her on probation. Of course she tearfully took the rehab, begging my forgiveness in front of the entire court very dramatically. I got up and walked out. I couldn't forgive her or my aunts. I just couldn't. I still can't. She committed suicide three years ago, but you all know that. Now you know why I didn't cry when I heard and I refused to go to her funeral."

There was more silence. Blythe couldn't look at any of them. She didn't want Airiana and Judith to think she was upset that they were expecting—and both were. Neither was very far along, but enough to show. With the new baby, Airiana would have five children. Judith still had fears about having a child, but she was excited, and Blythe knew she'd make a wonderful mother.

She waved them back out of the room. At the last moment she reached out and caught up a photograph she kept on the end table beside her reading chair. Now that her sisters knew the truth, she was putting it in her great room with her other family photos, the ones of her sisters—the people she loved.

"I'm making more tea," Judith said, all but running out of the room.

Blythe waited until everyone had found a seat again. "I know that your husbands will want to see their brother. I don't know if he's still on an assignment or not," she continued doggedly. She was going to get this out in the open. "I wish him well. I want him to succeed at whatever he's doing, and I don't want any harm to come to him. Ray Langton was a pedophile. He was everything and more than Viktor said that night. I'm not sorry he's dead. I never felt guilt over Ray. I know everyone assumed that, and I let you."

"It's the baby," Airiana said softly. "You aren't in any way responsible, but you look back and there's so many things you tell yourself you could have done differently."

Blythe nodded. "Intellectually I know it wasn't my fault, but night and day, it haunts me. If only I'd given Mom the attention she craved. Let her think her berating me was tearing me down like she needed it to do. Instead, I just stayed silent, knowing that made her crazier. *Wanting* to make her crazy. It was my petty revenge."

She choked back the sob welling up in her throat. She'd

already cried a million tears for her lost daughter. The baby hadn't been real to the judge, but she was alive and real to Blythe.

"His coming back has brought all this back up again," Lissa said.

Blythe shook her head. "I wish I could say that, but it's never gone away. I think of her every day. I miss her every day. I want her back. I wanted to see her born." She looked straight at Lissa, still hurting from her withholding the news of Viktor. "He just makes me feel the way my mother did—like I'm worthless and nothing at all. He didn't even bother to call me or let me know he was alive and well. I can't afford to feel that way. I have a difficult time some days finding a reason to get up and keep going."

Lexi gasped. "Blythe. No."

"I wouldn't." At least she told herself she would never get that depressed. She fought it often, and running was her way to lose herself. When she ran, she didn't think about the past. She didn't think about her daughter or Viktor or how she never forgave her mother and her mother died alone. She should care, but she didn't. She couldn't. And she did feel guilty about that too. She just wasn't going to tell anyone.

"You have us," Rikki said fiercely. "You saved us. All of us. Without you, I have no idea where I'd be. Lev will want to see his brother, but he doesn't have to do it here, on the farm. He can find somewhere else."

"This is Lev's home," Blythe reminded gently. "He should be able to see his brother anytime he wants and to invite him home. I just would appreciate a heads-up from all of you so I don't run into him. I'll either leave the farm until you text me the okay, or I'll lock up my house and stay inside. I think that's being fair. Tomorrow I'm calling an attorney to start divorce proceedings. Please, please talk to your men and make them understand."

The women nodded.

"He saw me on the street on his way into town, and he stopped. He was with a group of bikers. They weren't wearing colors, but they were definitely bikers. He had a woman on the back of his bike, and yet he was angry because I was talking to Derak Metzer. He told me we were married and demanded I go with him."

Judith came back, leaning one slim hip against the archway leading to the kitchen. "Blythe thinks he's a bigamist."

Lissa's breath hissed out, but when Blythe glanced at her, she just shook her head and looked down at her hands.

"Derak must have called 911. Jonas and Jackson showed up. Viktor told them I was his wife. He all but challenged them. I had to admit we were married or Viktor might have done something terrible, and his men had the better positions."

Blythe was certain both Jonas and Jackson would have been killed if there was a fight. Viktor might have been as well, but no way would the two lawmen have gotten away unscathed. Viktor's biker friends were menacing. There was no doubt in her mind they were armed.

"Does he know about the baby?" Judith asked.

Blythe shook her head. "By the time I was certain, he was gone and I had no idea where he went. He called himself Viktor Regent, not Prakenskii. I did check to see if the marriage was legal under Regent, and it wasn't. There was no such person. His identity, which had been all over the Internet, was gone. I didn't know the name Prakenskii then and everything was in Russian, including the priest when he talked to Viktor."

"Did you know when we went to that church to get married?" Judith asked.

"I suspected. My palm always itched and sometimes at night . . ." She trailed off, not wanting to think too much about those nights when her body ached and she had needed Viktor to put out the fire.

"The Prakenskii mark," Lissa said. "Casimir definitely put it on my palm."

Lexi held up her palm. "Gavriil. Right there."

Judith held up her left palm. "Stefan did the same."

"Maxim hit me with it," Airiana added.

Rikki nodded. "Lev totally got me." She rubbed her palm as if it was itching. "He's calling me now."

"That's no surprise, honey," Blythe said. "I'm shocked he's not sitting here with us. I wouldn't put it past him to get a wig and wear it in the hopes we wouldn't notice he's a guy instead of a girl."

Laughter erupted, sweeping some of the tension from the room. They needed that small reprieve. Lev had come to them first. Rikki had literally pulled him out of the sea, saving his life. He was over six feet with wide shoulders, a thick chest, all muscle and covered in scars. It would take a lot for him to pass himself off as a woman. Blythe had come to love him. He was protective over all the women, not just Rikki, but the sun rose and set with his wife. Blythe loved that for her. Rikki was odd, but she was a good person and a hard worker. Lev had succeeded in bringing her a little further out of her comfort zone and lately, little Lucia was helping him do just that.

Rikki got up and paced from one window to the other, looking out. "It would be just like him, and he'd better be home, behaving himself. We have the new puppy. We've decided he's going to be a sea dog. Black Russian Terriers like water, and they have life vests big enough for them. I don't want him at home alone. Gavriil told us they prefer the company of humans all the time."

"That's true," Blythe said, grateful the spotlight was off of her for a few minutes. She needed the reprieve. "But, honey, you do know he doesn't have to be with you every single minute. You need to let him know that it's all right if he's alone a little bit."

Rikki made a face and looked around the house. "Where's your puppy?"

Blythe opened her mouth and closed it. She was caught and there was no getting around it. "Lucia's watching her for me. I had things I had to do in town, and she's a little too young yet. She still needs another vaccination and it wasn't quite time yet."

The room erupted in another round of laughter, this time at her expense. She found she could actually smile and mean it. Her little puppy, Maya, was a small miracle to her, snuggling close and making her feel less lonely. She wasn't going to admit that to her laughing sisters. Unfortunately, she didn't think anything, not even a miracle, could take away the pain she felt right then after seeing Viktor.

Why couldn't she get over him? It was silly. She told herself he was a murderer, and yet she'd never really believed that. She told herself he abandoned her—which he had—but she had been certain it was her fault. He couldn't possibly love a woman like her. Her mother's words echoed through her mind, tearing at her self-esteem, and Viktor had just fed right into that. Today, seeing him with a beautiful woman on the back of his bike only cemented the belief that he had never really loved her, he'd just used her. That alone should make her stop daydreaming about him.

"Blythe." Lissa's voice had her coming out of her reverie to really look at her sister. "If you want Viktor gone from here, from Sea Haven, we'll make that happen."

"How?" Because seeing him tore her apart and made her back into that vulnerable child who had no self-esteem when she'd worked hard to be a woman of self-empowerment.

"Jackson and Jonas could ask him to move along," Judith suggested.

For a moment Blythe wanted to grab at that. They would do it too. They wouldn't like it if he hadn't actually done anything wrong and they wouldn't have cause, but for her family, they'd do it. She shook her head. The Viktor she knew, sweet and caring to her, was still a man who wouldn't be pushed around. If anything, he would become stubborn. The Viktor he was now, probably his true self, would take it as a challenge and he'd never leave.

"That won't work. I think it's best to just let him take care of whatever business he's looking to do here and avoid him as much as possible. If it looks as if he's going to be here awhile, I'll take a little vacation. I haven't gone off by myself in a long while." She hadn't needed to, but she couldn't afford seeing Viktor. Not again. And not with that woman. That had hit her hard. She barely slept now; how was she going to sleep with him in town?

Judith brought in tea, and Blythe gratefully accepted another cup. "You shouldn't have to be the one to leave."

"I don't mind, Judith," Blythe said quickly. She didn't want them all to protest or she'd start crying again. She supposed she was due. She hadn't cried since she'd buried her daughter. Now, it felt as if she couldn't stop.

"*We* mind," Lissa said, leaning forward. "We can have a meeting with the men here and tell them Viktor has to go."

"No. No, you can't do that. He's their brother. I wouldn't want them coming to me and saying one of you couldn't be on the property, let alone in the entire town of Sea Haven. He won't stay long. He's got an agenda."

"What if he doesn't, Blythe?" Lexi ventured. "What if he's come here for you?"

For one moment her heart leapt, but immediately she knew that wasn't possible. Even if it were, she would never take him back. He'd crushed her. He'd left her alone to deal with her mother and the aftermath of Ray's death. That had been bad enough, let alone her mother's drunken outbursts. Finding out the man she married wasn't even real had been a blow. And then the baby. How could she ever get over that? Had Viktor been there it never would have happened.

She shut down that way of thinking. He wasn't responsible. Her mother was. She had to keep the responsibility where it belonged, not on Viktor and not on her. She took a fortifying sip of tea and pushed at the stray strands of pale blond hair escaping her ponytail.

"He had five years to come for me, honey, and he didn't, so the chances of that being his reason is zero to none. He probably came to see his brothers. They're all here, he hasn't seen them in years, so it would be natural for him to want to see them."

"I'm so sorry about your daughter, Blythe," Airiana said. "Why didn't you tell us?"

The pain was too great. "Just thinking about my daughter,

let alone talking about her, hurts too much." She swallowed down the lump threatening to choke her. "I named her Viktoria after him, and buried both of them, father and daughter."

There was a small silence. Blythe could hear her heart beating, telling her she was still alive, when for so long, she didn't want to be. It was these five women who had made her strong again, made her want to live again. She loved them fiercely. Was proud of them and their accomplishments.

Little Lexi, kidnapped at a young age, her family killed in retaliation for her escape. She was more daughter sometimes than sister, although she would never say that. Airiana, a brilliant, sweet woman, her mother had been an alcoholic, but she'd tried to take care of her daughter and been murdered for a project Airiana had been working on.

There was Lissa, whose entire family had been massacred by a ruthless uncle. Her world had turned upside down recently when she'd discovered that the uncle who raised her had been behind the killings of her family. Rikki had been stalked by a mentally unbalanced firestarter, one who killed her parents, and then ultimately burned down fosters' homes. And Judith—sweet, wonderful, talented Judith—whose brother was murdered by a man she thought she could love. All of them understood loss and guilt even if they weren't guilty.

They all nodded, understanding what she couldn't articulate very well, and she was grateful. Just seeing Viktor had been a blow; now talking about the things that had happened in the aftermath of his leaving sickened her. She suddenly wanted to be alone, and yet, at the same time, she was a little afraid. She'd been scary depressed after her daughter died. Those days had been so dark, she feared what she might do from one hour to the next.

"Jonas and Jackson will come here to question me," she said. "There's no stopping them." She glanced at Rikki. It was no secret that her husband, Lev Prakenskii, hadn't saved Elle Drake when he was undercover, trying to stop the same human trafficking ring that she'd been after. Elle's capture and suffering at the hands of Stavros Gratsos had been horrendous. Jackson was furious when he learned Lev hadn't blown his cover in order to save Elle.

Blythe leaned toward her autistic sister. Rikki had established a good life for herself. She loved what she did and felt able to cope. If Jackson and the Drakes made it difficult for Lev, it would mean all of them relocating. Lexi would be uprooted from her farm and Rikki from where she finally felt comfortable. They would do it, of course, all of them had agreed, but no one wanted to go.

"I'll talk to Jackson about Lev, tell him what a good man he is. Ilya will talk to him as well if we ask him to. I don't think there will be a problem." She *hoped* there wouldn't be a problem, but one never knew with Jackson. He was very quiet, but he could be extremely violent. She had no problem imagining him in a biker club rather than law enforcement.

Rikki shook her head. "You have enough on your plate with your husband coming back to town."

Blythe winced. *Husband.* She didn't want anyone referring to Viktor Prakenskii as her husband, not even Rikki. She opened her mouth to protest, but Rikki squared her shoulders and made her announcement.

"I'm going to talk to Jackson and Elle. I've already called Elle and asked to see them. She said I could go over tonight. Lev doesn't know, or he'd never let me go on his behalf. Of course I'll tell him afterward," she explained hastily.

Blythe watched as Rikki twirled her fingers nervously, a habit she couldn't quite break. She could see stark fear on Rikki's face, but also determination. Rikki had a difficult time talking to people she didn't know well and anything out of her comfort zone could throw her into a bad place. She could disappear inside her own head for hours if she was upset.

"I think that's wonderful that you took that initiative, honey," Blythe said quickly. "Maybe I'll just go with you.

It would get my mind off of all of this. Of course, if you prefer to go alone, I'll totally understand."

Rikki looked relieved. "I'd like that." She glanced at her watch. "I'm supposed to be there in an hour. The timing worked out great. Lev wasn't happy with me coming here, so it would have been really difficult to just leave this evening. I can go straight from here with you."

Blythe knew Jackson would never ask her personal questions as long as Rikki or anyone else was around; he was too good of a law enforcement officer. She'd be safe at least until tomorrow morning, and maybe she'd get up early, pack a bag and leave town just for a little while. She owned the local gym, was a personal trainer as well as a physical therapist. It wouldn't be easy to reschedule her clients, but it was doable and in her opinion necessary. She felt better with a plan.

Her sisters kept up small talk, mostly about the puppies. Lexi and Gavriil had the breeding pair. Gavriil had brought them with him from Russia. Each household got one puppy. They had regular puppy playdates scheduled, and the children went from house to house spending time with the puppies so they'd be used to kids. Gavriil was going to help train them, and he'd already given them all valuable advice. Her own little Maya already sat before her meals and was becoming familiar with Blythe's routine. She took the pup to work with her, and she was very good there as well.

Blythe sat back in her chair, allowing the talk to swirl around her while she stared out the window and wondered if Maya was miracle enough to get her through the next few weeks.

6

VIKTOR stood very, very still, afraid if he moved, he might shatter. He'd seen children die. He'd watched them die. Children he'd felt responsible for, but nothing got to him the way this did. Blythe's voice when she told her sisters about his leaving her. About their child. A daughter. He'd had a daughter and she was dead. Murdered by a drunken madwoman.

Bile rose. His legs turned to rubber. He went down on one knee right there at the top of the stairs. Everything said after that was merely a buzzing in his head. Inside his chest, his heart shattered. Her revelation had gutted him. *Gutted him.* His mind went from chaos to red. Rage rose, swift and terrible, a volcanic eruption imminent.

Rage was there to protect him, to keep him from shutting down completely. He knew that, but it didn't help. Nothing helped. For a moment the world narrowed to a place of pain and suffering, where torture was physical, emotional and even sexual. Where he was helpless, a mere child trying to survive, trying to find a way for the younger boys and girls to survive. He'd done that at a great cost to all of them, but he hadn't found a way to save his own child.

A girl. A daughter. Viktoria. He collapsed completely,

sitting down hard, but even that didn't bring him out of it. He was afraid he was going to vomit, and the pain in his throat, in his chest, behind his eyes was so bad he couldn't breathe. There was no air. No way to find air. "This can't be happening." He whispered the plea to Reaper.

Reaper's hand clamped on his shoulder hard, steadying him, or he might have gone all the way down. "We have to go."

He stared up at his best friend without comprehension. Reaper got an arm around him and urged him up. Once his legs were under him, he went with Reaper through the hallway back to the master bedroom. He wasn't certain he could manage getting through the window, so he just collapsed on the bed.

Reaper went down in a crouch in front of the man who had been an absolute rock his entire life. The man who had single-handedly saved seventeen children from certain death. He'd helped, but it had all been Czar's brains, his plans, his calm and steady leadership. For one moment panic welled up. He hadn't felt panic since he was a four-year-old child looking to the ten-year-old to save him.

Czar was the rock. The absolute rock all of them counted on. They were trained to lie with conviction. To con with ease. To seduce as an art. To stalk and kill without feeling. Czar taught them how not to do those things. How to channel rage and resentment, hatred and bitterness into something else. Something good.

Reaper took a breath and let it out. His job was always to watch over Czar whether the man liked it or not. He didn't like it most times, and in the beginning they'd clashed a lot, but over time, Czar realized there was no stopping Reaper. He'd do what he thought best. What he thought best was keeping Czar alive.

"Let's get you out of here," he said softly, afraid Czar was in shock. His skin was almost gray beneath the dark tan from so many years out in the weather.

Viktor shook his head. "Can't leave her again, Reaper. If I go now, I won't come back, and I won't survive without her."

"You can come back." Reaper tried to be reasonable. He

wanted to throw Viktor over his shoulder and haul him out of there. Czar was too shaken to think reasonably. Any moment one of the women could come upstairs. They'd scream bloody murder and call the cops. He hadn't liked the look of either sheriff. They hadn't postured or blustered, and although they were aware they were outnumbered and surrounded, they hadn't so much as flinched. Men like that weren't easy to kill.

Viktor shook his head. It hurt to even move that much. He had to fight not to vomit. "If I leave now, I wouldn't know how to approach her, how to ask her to take me back. How can she forgive me after the loss of our child? She's been through so much. I had all of you, she had no one."

Reaper shook his head. "She can't blame you for what her bitch of a mother did."

"I wasn't there. I didn't even know she was pregnant." Viktor pushed a hand through his hair. "She didn't send for me. She should have sent word to me. I would have come. I would have walked away from the assignment." In a heartbeat, he would have rushed to her side. Had she just once told him she needed him, he would have dropped everything and gone to her, risking his life, risking the lives of everyone he cared for. For her. He would have done that without weighing the consequences, because she was Blythe—his everything. Where the hell were his birth brothers? Why hadn't they told him?

"She didn't even know who you were, Czar," Reaper pointed out.

Viktor lifted his head and looked the man he called brother in the eye. "For her I risked everything, even my younger brothers' lives. For her. We had a system to contact each other in an emergency. Sorbacov would have killed for that information. If he got it, he would have hunted every one of them down and killed them. You know he would have. Still, I left her the code. I needed to know she was safe. I gave her the priest's code in case she needed to get word to me as well. I risked him, my brothers, all of you, just to make certain she was safe, and she didn't use it."

Reaper frowned and stroked his chin with his long fingers. "You know, Czar, it's looking more and more as if she didn't get that letter. She was genuinely shocked to see you, and she had no idea you were married. I was watching her face, watching her closely; she didn't know."

Viktor sucked in air to keep the room from spinning. When he inhaled, the scent of her, peaches and cream, slipped inside, deep into his lungs. She was everywhere in this room. The girly shit she liked was everywhere. He had always loved to watch her as she got ready for an outing. His favorite had been to lie on the bed and just drink her in. She was practical, but she surrounded herself with things women deemed necessary in their lives. Her hairbrush was ornate, a beautiful carved wooden handle, the bristles embedded in a thick rectangle. He'd chased her around the bedroom once threatening to spank her with it when she'd teased him unmercifully about the beard he'd worn back then.

His life was so fucked-up. How could he have made such a mess of the only thing that was going to keep him alive? That mattered to him? He was drowning, and it was Blythe who could give him the air he needed.

"I left the letter right in the middle of our bed." Viktor smoothed the lacy comforter as if he could bring the letter back. Even if she hadn't gotten the letter, why hadn't one of his brothers told him what was going on? That didn't make sense. None of this made sense.

"You heard what she told those women. After you shot her stepfather, her mother went crazy."

"Sharon had been drinking. She was always drunk. Ray just pretended to drink, but he kept her glass full at all times."

"Her mother was given a sedative and taken upstairs to the master bedroom. The bedroom where you left the letter right in the middle of the bed. It didn't sound as if Blythe went up with the medics. She stayed downstairs with the cops."

Viktor closed his eyes briefly. Of course Sharon would have taken the letter. She would have read it and destroyed it out of malice. The woman was so jealous of her daughter, she detested her. She would never want Blythe to know a man wanted her, loved her beyond anything. She'd spent a lifetime jealous of her sisters and then jealous of her daughter. But that didn't tell him why one of his brothers hadn't reached out to him. They must have checked on her.

Downstairs there was a lot of movement. Reaper went to the door of the bedroom to listen. "They're leaving," he reported. "Blythe is going out with the one they call Rikki."

That was so like her. She'd go with Rikki in spite of the fact that she was hurting—and he knew she was. Just that small thing told him she was everything he remembered. She was the one his extended family needed. She was the one *he* needed.

"You don't have to stay, Reaper. I'm going to wait until she comes back, and then I'm going to talk to her. If she needs to yell at me, or hit me, no one will be around and she'll feel like she can."

"And if she wants to shoot you? Women are unpredictable. And lethal. You should know that. Alena and Lana would take you down in a second." Reaper made his way back to stand in front of Viktor.

Viktor allowed a small humorless smile to escape. "They'd try. Blythe might try to hit me, but I doubt it. She's not prone to violence like we are. Get going, Reaper, I'll be fine. It isn't like I'm going to get hurt here." If she wanted to shoot him, he'd let her. It wouldn't happen, but if she needed that, he would oblige. Reaper couldn't be there for that. He'd retaliate.

"Don't be an ass. I'm not leaving. She comes back, I'll sit on the roof and wait for you." He looked around the room. "This is nice. Wide open. I like that."

"My woman always liked space." Which was a good thing. Viktor still didn't like walls surrounding him. The more space, the better.

"They have a pretty piece of land here. Never thought I'd be thinking about buying land for myself or for us. We're nomads. No roots."

"*I'm* staying," Viktor said decisively. "I have no intentions of leaving her again."

"She could come with us."

Viktor shook his head. "I want a home. We need one, Reaper. All of us. We'll ride when we want the open road, but we need a base. We talked about this." He'd made up his mind, told the others and left it up to them whether or not they wanted to come with him. The vote had been unanimous. They wanted to buy land, build a clubhouse and set up their legitimate businesses. Sorbacov was gone, and they were going to live openly, not hide in the shadows anymore.

"So we'll stay here. Nothing's changed, Czar. I've got your back, same as always. Your woman will either accept us or she won't."

Reaper's tone said there wasn't a chance in hell Blythe would accept their club, but Viktor knew he was wrong. Blythe wasn't at all the way Reaper thought she was. She had too much compassion in her. She knew fun and laughter, and she gave that magic to everyone around her. How, with her shrew of a mother, he didn't know, but there really was something magical about Blythe. She shone from the inside out.

Sharon had been eaten up with jealousy that her youngest sister had inherited the Drake estate and that her daughters had carried out the legacy of the Drake family. He didn't know much about it other than they all had very strong psychic gifts. He believed everyone did to some extent, although Sharon's gift seemed to be to make everyone around her miserable.

Ray had researched her carefully. She'd been the perfect cover—a woman who presented one face to the world, and was another behind closed doors. Blythe's records at the hospital made it very clear all the broken bones she'd suffered hadn't been from being clumsy. Viktor knew child abuse firsthand. He'd lived in a secret school with no one to help him but himself. Blythe had lived out in the open. She had an extended family, doctors, teachers, neighbors, and yet she'd still been subjected to abuse. That didn't make sense to him.

Reaper's hand suddenly went to the inside of his jacket, his body already beginning the turn toward the window. Viktor leapt at him, covering his hand with his own, preventing him from drawing the knife he kept there. He could draw and throw in one smooth motion, and he was deadly accurate.

"Keep your hands where I can see them."

"Put down the gun," Viktor said. "Seriously, put it down. I'm your brother. You're not going to shoot me, but I can guarantee you that there's another brother outside somewhere on that roof and he's got you in his crosshairs. Am I right, Reaper? Did Savage follow us?"

"You're right, Czar, and you know my brother. He's unpredictable."

Reaper seemed relaxed beneath Viktor's hand, not a tense muscle, but that didn't matter. His entire being, mind and body, was a weapon. He was fast and deadly and he never hesitated. Savage was arguably worse. Reaper was correct; he was unpredictable and as mean as a snake.

"Which one are you?" Viktor kept his tone casual. He couldn't see the intruder, but he had no doubt Savage could see him.

"Lev."

"You were just a toddler. You don't remember me."

"Not much."

"You're going to have to trust that I would never harm you or yours. Keep your gun and step into the room. Get away from the window." He wasn't a praying man, but nevertheless, he sent up a small prayer that the kid believed him. He raised his voice just to be on the safe side. "Stand down, Savage. He's my brother." Just for safety's sake he kept his hand over Reaper's. Reaper's fist was around the hilt of the knife, but Viktor prevented him from drawing it. They stood that way, waiting.

Lev moved into the room, slipping his gun inside his jacket. Viktor let go of Reaper, but didn't attempt to step around him. It wouldn't do any good. He knew from experience that no matter what he said or did, Reaper would keep his body between Viktor and a perceived threat until it was clear there was no threat. Still, he feasted his eyes on his younger brother.

He looked good. A man. Tall. Broad-shouldered. Confident. He wasn't afraid even knowing there were three against him. Viktor found himself a little shaken. He'd never really believed this day would come.

"Viktor. Everyone calls me Czar."

"Never thought I'd see you," Lev said.

It was impossible to tell what he was thinking; there was no expression on his face or in his eyes.

"You look a bit like our father," Viktor said. What he could remember. He'd tried his best to hold on to those memories. His father had been a good man, and he wouldn't have liked what Viktor had been forced to become. Sometimes Viktor wondered if it would have been better to let the bastards in the school kill him. There might have been more honor in that. Live or die. Even that choice had been taken from him.

"I don't remember him."

"You were too young."

Lev held his hands out from his body to show Reaper he wasn't a threat as he walked to one of the chairs Blythe had in the little sitting area. He sank into it. "What are you doing here?" There was no welcome, but no belligerence.

"I'm working."

There was silence while Lev studied him. He sighed. "Can you tell me what?"

"I'm after Evan Shackler-Gratsos."

Lev blinked. Sat up straighter. "You're kidding. I was after his brother. Spent several years undercover, working my way up to getting next to him. The Drakes and their men took him out. I was nearly killed. That's when Rikki found me."

"Evan inherited the money and ships, but he already had a major human trafficking ring going. Now he's got the money he needs to expand and the ships to dump the dead bodies when the really sick fucks pay him the right price." Viktor sank down onto the edge of the bed again.

Reaper moved to one side, but never took his gaze from Lev.

"He's the one you've been after all these years."

Viktor nodded. "He's the international president of the Sword MC. It's been impossible to get close to him until now. He's always had a burning hatred for Jackson Deveau. It started in Louisiana with his mother and Deveau's father. I joined that chapter in order to ferret out more details. I knew sooner or later he'd go after Deveau. He's the kind that stews on things. He's paranoid as hell and hates everyone. I also figured when he did go after him, he'd use the New Orleans chapter to do it. Deveau's father was the enforcer for that chapter."

"I presume you think he's going to try to kill Jackson now."

"I *know* he is. Jackson Deveau got married. More, he married the woman Evan's brother was keeping as his own personal sex slave. Evan's bragged he had to show his brother how to train her. I don't know what he has in mind for the woman, but he wants Deveau dead. Before he dies he wants to taunt him with the fact that the woman is now in his possession."

Lev was silent again, digesting the information. Again, his expression gave nothing away. Finally he sighed. "You warn Deveau?"

"Not yet. I've been given the job of scouting out an area where we can bring the members of two chapters in a few at a time to camp. Evan plans to show up once we're all in place and we know Deveau's every move. I just got here. When I find the right campsite, I'll send for the others."

"You here with people you can trust?"

Viktor nodded. "My brothers." That said it all. Lev had better understand what he was telling him.

Reaper glanced at him quickly and then his gaze was back on Lev.

"How is that?" Lev asked, his tone mild.

"We survived the school because we had one another's back." He wasn't going to lie. He hadn't seen his birth brothers in years, not since he was ten years old. He kept their memories, and he stayed in the school under Sorbacov's thumb to keep them safe for those memories, but the men and women he'd suffered with, he'd watched tortured, were his family as well. Maybe more so. He'd die for them. More, he'd kill for them.

Lev nodded as if he understood. He'd gone to one of Sorbacov's schools, but even he couldn't possibly understand what it was like in the hellhole Viktor and the others had been in.

"We'll give you whatever help you need. Just tell us."

Viktor had known his blood brothers would back him. Still, to hear him say it without hesitation made something inside him open up a little.

"I'll be bringing the boys by to introduce at some point. We're searching for land right now for ourselves. I've already got a lock on a place that might work to tell the Swords to come in to camp, but need a few days to straighten out my business here first. Also, a lot of civilians use these campsites. I want to make certain no one will get caught in the crosshairs."

"Does your business include Blythe Daniels?"

"Her legal name is Blythe Prakenskii. She's been my wife for the last five years and two months."

Lev shifted in his chair, a frown flitting across his face. "Our Blythe? You certain, Viktor? She's as straight as they come. If she was married, she would never act single."

"What the fuck does that mean? She seeing someone?" If it was that coward all but peeing in his pants while he ran down the street, leaving Blythe alone with Viktor, he was paying the bastard a visit. It wouldn't be a pleasant one—at least not for the coward.

"No, but there's a lot of men who've made it plain they'd like to date her. She's been restless lately. Thinking about dating. I know because the women talk to one another. If she's anywhere near Rikki, then I'm close by."

"Well too bad for the men who want to date her. I'm finishing up my business with Evan, and then she'll be living with her husband."

He made it a decree, ignoring the warning voice that told him there was a lot of really bad water under the bridge and maybe it wouldn't be quite that easy. The other voice said he knew Blythe. He *knew* her. He believed in her. He'd fallen like a ton of bricks because she was the only woman he'd ever run across in all his travels who was genuine. No guile. No lies. She was a woman a man could count on. He'd let her into his narrow world and he'd tried to give her as much of the real man as he could. She'd accepted that man with all his issues and flaws, and he had them in spades.

"You would have known Blythe was mine if you'd bothered to check any of the messages I left for you. For all of you. I wanted her looked after. Even before you took the assignment going after Stavros Gratsos I was leaving messages for you all to keep an eye on her. I wanted her watched over." There was accusation in his voice. Anger. The rage was close to the surface.

He'd *counted* on his birth brothers. He'd lived and survived in that school of hell to save them. To keep them alive. He'd hunted the men who had murdered their father. He'd kept an eye on them over the years, intervening when he could if their safety was in question. "Was it so damned much to ask that someone look out for her?"

"Viktor, we never got any messages at all from you. Not in five years. Half the time we wondered if you were even alive," Lev said.

That pulled him up short. He'd left *dozens* of messages. Risking his life. Needing to hear news of her. Any news at all. He'd assigned a couple of "brothers" from the school to watch over her when they were in the States, but most of their work was done in Europe or Asia.

He shook his head. "That's impossible."

"There was never a single message from you. We wondered how you knew about Casimir and Lissa getting married. Casimir didn't even post the notice on our emergency board."

"The priest told me. Of course I would go to one of my brothers' weddings if I could possibly get there." He kept all expression from his voice. Lev had gotten married without him. So had Stefan, Maxim and Ilya. Gavriil was the only unmarried brother, and he lived with a woman. He'd never do that if the woman wasn't his sun, the center of his universe. Viktor had missed everything significant in the lives of his birth brothers.

Lev shook his head. "I'm telling you, Viktor . . ." He trailed off and shook his head again. "There hasn't been one single communication from you in five years. No one knew where you were."

Viktor raised his gaze to Reaper. He'd been cut off completely from Blythe. Completely. More sins on his soul. She'd needed him and he hadn't known.

"Did you know about my daughter?" He would never forgive his birth brothers if they knew and hadn't turned over every rock in the universe looking for him.

Lev frowned. "Daughter? You have a daughter?"

His breath escaped in a rush of relief. "Blythe and I had a daughter together. She died. Was murdered before she had the chance to live." The words tasted like copper in his mouth. Like blood and death. His gut churned, and he knew if he let himself think about that child and his woman alone, enduring such a brutal attack without him, he wouldn't be able to function. He had to function. It was what he did no matter how bad it got. And in his life, it got bad. Ugly. "It's a long story. I didn't know until now. Just now."

"I'm sorry, Viktor," Lev said. "Really, really sorry." He rubbed the bridge of his nose. "I just don't understand why

Blythe wouldn't tell us about marrying you. She knows we're all Prakenskiis. Why wouldn't she say anything?"

Viktor couldn't blame Lev for pressing him. In their business they lied all the time. Blythe didn't. It was that simple. Lev knew her, and he knew she wouldn't hide the truth from them. She would have told her sisters and his brothers—if she knew. How she could forget their wedding, he didn't know. The memory of that day and night was stamped into his bones.

"I have a feeling Blythe didn't believe any part of our marriage was real. I met her when I was hunting Ray Langton, one of his many aliases. He was a very . . ."

"Infamous pedophile," Lev finished for him. "He had a partner, but no one could ever figure out who it was. Sorbacov wanted Ray taken down. He knew about the schools. At least that was the rumor."

Viktor nodded. "One of the instructors at the school became Ray's mentor. I don't know how old Ray was when he was gotten ahold of, but he knew all the details and was trying to blackmail Sorbacov. It was a particularly stupid move on his part. Sorbacov set me on his trail."

"How was Blythe involved?"

"Ray used women as a cover all the time. He married Blythe's mother. I arranged a casual meeting with Blythe. She went running every day and I 'accidentally' bumped into her. She didn't live with her mother so I had to be in a position to meet her parents, and that meant marriage."

"You would have had an alias," Lev pointed out. "Not a legal marriage."

Viktor didn't like the fact that his brother was eager to keep Blythe from him. He couldn't exactly blame him. He looked rough. He was rough. He did like that Lev was protective of Blythe. It was nice to know someone had her back, but he was her husband and all of them had better come to terms with that fast. He wasn't going anywhere and neither were his "brothers" and "sisters."

"I married her in the church as Viktor Prakenskii. The papers were legal, signed and documented. She might not think it was legal, but I assure you, it was. We've got a lot of things to clear up, but that's between Blythe and me. In the meantime, no one can blow my cover. The Swords play for keeps and they don't mind spilling blood. I have enough of my men with me to make a difference, but make no mistake, Lev, hell's coming."

"No one will jeopardize your cover."

"I go by Czar. In the Swords and out of it. I'm used to the name. Blythe is the only one who calls me Viktor."

"How are you going to protect her from Evan and the rest of his club?"

"They aren't going to know about her. Once they're here, she won't be in the equation. What I'm doing has nothing to do with her."

"If this was an assignment you took when Sorbacov was alive, he's dead. You can walk away."

"I spent five years of my life with these scumbags. This is my one chance to get Evan and shut down his operation. I'm not walking away now." Viktor was decisive. The price he'd paid was far higher than he'd ever imagined. His child. Perhaps Blythe. Five years of protecting utter filth. He was going to complete what he'd started out to do.

Lev nodded his understanding. "I spent a good deal of time with Evan's brother, Stavros, and they both have strong psychic abilities. Stavros was terrified of his brother's talent, so much so that he built an entire grid to keep anyone from using psychic talents. It was the only place he would meet with his brother. Evan was a sick son of a bitch. I mean really sick. He hated women and liked hurting them."

Lev didn't need to tell Viktor that. He'd observed the "training" methods Evan had instituted on the young girls he kidnapped or lured into his international prostitution ring. "Did you get a sense of what talents Evan has?"

"Only that whatever gifts they are, they're strong and he uses them to hurt people."

"Thanks. I appreciate the warning." The fact that Evan had unknown psychic gifts made his task harder, but it also made him more determined. The man was even more dangerous than he'd first thought. He had the manpower and the money, and with strong psychic gifts as well, he could be unstoppable if he was allowed to retreat back into whatever secret fortress he was crawling out of. This was their one chance.

"I have to go. My woman is autistic, and she's looking to protect me from Deveau. They think the Drakes will force us out. Rikki's a sea urchin diver and she's comfortable here. We're not leaving no matter how much they want to freeze us out."

Viktor stirred, nearly made the offer and then stopped himself. It wouldn't be that difficult for Deveau to come to an untimely end, but he had been the one to decree to his brothers in Torpedo Ink that they were going to start a new chapter in their lives. Their first inclination would always be to remove a threat to them or their loved ones permanently, but normal people didn't do that. They might never be normal, but they were going to try to come close.

"I know I don't know the first thing about relationships, Lev, so I'm the last person you should listen to, but I do know something about women."

"Go on." Lev looked him straight in the eye, daring him to give advice.

Viktor didn't care whether or not he took it, or if he didn't like his oldest brother reaching out. "If she's autistic, then she's doing something enormous, going to this man and talking to him. For you. She's doing this for you. It's a gift."

"Hard for a man to swallow, having his woman plead for him."

"I doubt she's going to plead. In any case, she's doing something I respect and admire. If Blythe did that for me, I might want to turn her over my knee when she got home, but I'd be damned happy she loved me enough to do it."

A slow smile slid over his younger brother's face. "Rikki would try to drown me if I ever turned her over my knee. You should see her out there on the water. She's . . ." He glanced at Reaper, trailed off and then stood up. "I'll let the others know you're here and that you'll be getting in touch as soon as possible."

Viktor nodded but didn't make the mistake of trying to get to his feet. He was absolutely certain Savage was outside and that he had a rifle pointed at Lev's heart. Sometimes it was a pain to have the two men dedicated to keeping him alive. If Blythe turned him down, there wasn't going to be much to live for. Not after taking down Evan.

"Czar." Lev tried out the name. "Blythe is a good woman. The best. We all love her like a sister. I hope things work out for you."

"Be on my side, Lev. Get your woman to be on my side. I'm going to figure out what happened, why none of you got my communications, why she didn't. I left her so many messages. I became obsessed with checking day and night for word. She never left me a single message. None of you did."

"That's not true. Ask the others."

He would, not that he didn't believe Lev, but if they all said the same thing, that they checked messages and there were none from him, that they had left him messages, then he had to figure out what happened and why. Who had managed to mess up his communication with Blythe? With his brothers?

Lev hesitated, then, ignoring Reaper, came to the side of the bed and gripped his brother by the shoulders. "It's good you're here. We all hoped you would come."

Unexpectedly a lump formed in Viktor's throat. He didn't know this man, but he'd known the toddler. The little boy. He'd carried him around and taught him his first words. He'd been so proud of him. He remembered rocking him when he had a fever and his mother was occupied with Ilya. Lev had grown into a good man. A tough one, but a good one.

"Our father would have been proud of you," Viktor told him. It was true. He might not have said so in words, but he would have been proud and he would have showed it. Viktor wasn't so certain his father would think the same of him.

"Thank you. I'll see you soon?" It was a question. A statement.

Viktor noticed Lev didn't look at Reaper. "Yes. We're staying, Lev. I hope that my birth family will integrate with my chosen family. They've had my back, and they got me through hard times." It was an understatement. They'd saved his life numerous times.

Lev glanced at Reaper. Viktor knew what he saw. All of them looked rough. Scarred. Dangerous. Lev was the same, but in a different way. Still, Lev nodded. "I hope so as well. Anyone who helped you has friends in us."

That was sincere, and even Reaper had to hear that. Viktor nodded. "Call if you have need, but don't come close."

"I know the drill."

They all did. Each of his brothers had attended one of Sorbacov's schools. They'd all been brutal, especially the one Gavriil had been sent to, but at least Sorbacov had wanted them to live. The boys and girls sent to the school from hell, the one Viktor had been in, had been expected to die. Sorbacov wanted them dead. He wanted the others to know there was a place worse than the one they were at; one they could be sent to if they didn't cooperate.

Sorbacov had videos made of children being "punished." Torture was more like it. There were even some videos of the pedophiles violating the children, although those weren't authorized and Sorbacov either hadn't known they existed or he thought he could keep them contained. He couldn't afford to have any of those videos surface. It always made everyone in Torpedo Ink uneasy that the videos existed and were floating around in the world of pedophiles. They were old, so hopefully by now, they were corrupted and gone.

Reaper followed Lev to the window and signaled to Savage to let him pass unscathed.

Savage stuck his head into the room after he was gone. "It's a good thing he looks like you. I nearly took him out thinking he was your woman's boyfriend or after you. The light caught him just right and I knew he had to be one of your birth brothers."

Viktor noted that Savage had tacked on the word *birth*. They all referred to one another as *brothers* and *sisters*. In their world, it was true. They were closer than most birth families.

"I appreciate that." He waved at both of them. "I'm going to wait for Blythe to come back. You two take off."

Reaper raised an eyebrow. "You're getting to be an old man, Czar. I don't like repeating myself, but I'll go sit on the roof with Savage so you can figure out in peace what you're going to say to your old lady." He hesitated. "I can fill him in."

Viktor didn't meet his eyes. He nodded, giving Reaper permission to share what he'd heard. Just thinking about his daughter was a body blow. He wanted to be alone to give himself time to grieve. He needed that. He'd all but forgotten how. His world was about survival and survival meant feeling as little as possible, but he was going to allow himself to feel everything. All of it. Just this once. While he was alone and could let himself. Then he'd try to figure out what the hell happened to his messages. After that he'd try to figure out what he was going to say to his woman.

7

"I always love that no matter what time of year it is here at the Drakes', roses are climbing trellises everywhere in bloom and rhododendrons are going wild. You can always count on finding flowers here," Blythe said, trying to put Rikki at ease.

Rikki frowned. "Lexi always has flowers growing everywhere, no matter what time of the year." She looked around as if she could see other homes that might have flowers growing everywhere. "Doesn't everyone on the coast?"

Blythe shook her head, smiling at Rikki's observation. It was very true. Lexi could grow anything anywhere and at any time of the year.

"Blythe, look at these stepping stones." Rikki crouched down to run her palm over one of the ancient symbols carved deep into the stone. "These are cool. And very old."

"Yes, I don't know where they came from, but they've always been here. I used to come visit when I was a little girl."

Rikki straightened. "That's right, the Drakes are your cousins."

Blythe nodded. A six-foot-high, intricate wrought iron gate loomed before them. A collage of creatures mixed with raw power was woven into the gate along with the universal symbols for the Earth elements: water, earth, air, fire and spirit. The inscriptions on the bottom of the gate read in both Italian and Latin *The Seven Become One When United.*

Rikki touched the symbol for water and beneath her fingers it came to life, blazing gold and green, yet was cool to the touch. At once the gates swung open as if accepting her. She looked at Blythe with a small, nervous smile. "That's cool."

"The gate keeps out those who are enemies and welcomes friends." Blythe didn't know any other way of putting it. It was a far too simple explanation, but it was the closest she could come to what was the truth of the Drake property. It always seemed alive on its own.

The porch stairs were as solid as a rock leading up to the wide verandah that wrapped around the house. The space was beautiful and gave off the invitation to sit in the shade and enjoy the view of the sea.

Rikki reached out and clutched Blythe's arm as they went up the steps to the front porch. "Am I doing the right thing, Blythe? I know Lev won't like it. He'll be angry with me for not discussing it first. He always tells me everything up front. He knew when I left to go to your house that something wasn't right between us. I couldn't look at him. He's really good at reading people, especially me."

Rikki was surprisingly strong for being so slender. Blythe smiled down at her. Sometimes Lissa, Airiana and Lexi made her feel as if she were an Amazon woman, but Rikki was of average height and stood very straight. Although she had three or four inches on her, Blythe never felt that way around her. It was the way she carried herself.

"Only you can say that, Rikki. All of us have to make our choices based on what we think is right. If you're worried Lev will take offense at Jackson and make matters worse between Elle, Jackson and all of us, then this might be the best course of action. But you do have to be prepared for some backlash. You'll have to let him be angry."

Rikki nodded several times and let go of Blythe's arm in order to twirl her fingers round and round, a sign of deep agitation. Blythe reached over and gently stilled her whirling fingers. "Take a breath, honey. We can still walk away if we want to." But she knew better. Elle Drake was her cousin. She had inherited all the gifts given to the Drake sisters and she carried the legacy. She would give birth to seven daughters, and each of them would have a gift. It had been going on for generations.

The house would tell Elle that she had visitors and they were on the front porch, and that was without the protection dogs Jackson had, two big German shepherds that went everywhere with Elle. Still, she would remain to talk to Elle and Jackson if Rikki couldn't bring herself to do it. There was so much at stake.

Of course they had discussed having to move. If the Drake sisters and their husbands went against them, Blythe knew their farm wouldn't survive, and that would break Lexi's heart. She couldn't afford any more upheaval. Even now that she had Gavriil, Lexi was still very fragile. And there was Rikki. She had created a life for herself before Lev had come on the scene. She was captain of her own sea urchin boat and she worked hard for a living. She would find it hard to establish herself elsewhere. Blythe was determined to convince Elle and Jackson to allow them to live there in peace.

"I have to do this," Rikki said, her chin up, a sign of stubbornness. "If not for me, then certainly for Lexi. And Airiana's children. The farm is good for them. They're settling in. They need stability as well."

Blythe hid her astonishment. It wasn't that Rikki wasn't brilliant—she was; it was more that no one expected her to take an interest in the children, yet she had Lucia over all the time. Lucia often brought her younger sisters and brother with her. They didn't like to be away from one another too long.

The door opened, and Jackson was there. She wasn't surprised to see him instead of Elle. It hadn't been that long since Elle had been rescued from her captor, only a couple of months, and in that time, she'd gotten married and her husband had taken her to Europe on an extended honeymoon, although they'd cut that short to come home.

Behind Jackson were the two German shepherds, looking all business. She saw Jackson's hand go down to his side and he signaled to them. Instantly both dogs relaxed and even wagged their tails. Jackson took in Rikki's rigid figure and forced a smile. Blythe could see he was wary, that his smile didn't go anywhere near his eyes.

"Blythe. Rikki. Good to see you both. Come on in. Elle's expecting you." He stepped back and waved them inside.

Rikki crossed the threshold, but Blythe hesitated, just for a moment. The house was different. It always had been. It would recognize her blood and judge her. In all the years she'd lived in Sea Haven, she managed to stay out of that house. When she'd volunteered to go with Rikki she hadn't been thinking about having to enter the Drake residence. Now, she had no choice; Rikki couldn't go in there alone.

Rikki was so agitated she didn't notice Blythe's hesitation, but Jackson did. He saw everything. Straightening her shoulders, Blythe stepped inside. There was a tiny instance of disorientation, and then . . . nothing. Just the feeling of coming home. She recognized the feeling; she'd had it before, when as a child she'd gone to visit the Drakes with her mother.

Visits were rare and she looked forward to them. Her mother never drank when she was with her sisters, and those times had been the best. She'd always been leery, afraid Sharon would do something terrible, that the reprieve wouldn't last, but she'd held it together—until they left. Then Blythe would be subjected to hours of how her aunts had tried to spoil her and held up their children as being wonderful while Blythe lacked everything from beauty to manners. The drinking would start, sometimes in the car on the way home, and then the hitting.

The entryway was wide, tiled with a mosaic design,

opening to a huge room. "Blythe." Elle came across the room to wrap her arms around Blythe's waist and hold her close. "It feels like so long since I've seen you." She kissed Blythe on the cheek, her gaze moving quickly over her face to assess how she was.

Touching her, Elle could read her, and Blythe had to work to keep from pulling away. She had too many secrets, and her sorrows were too close. Elle had too many burdens of her own to carry. Jackson would have told her about Viktor. The Drakes didn't believe in hiding much from their husbands.

"I've been good," Blythe said. "And you? How was your honeymoon?"

"Spectacular," Elle admitted with a faint blush, her gaze flicking to Jackson. "I wanted to come home though. I don't like being away anymore."

Blythe felt the tremor running through her cousin, and she automatically hugged her tighter, inhaling, taking her fears and exchanging them with happiness. Elle pulled back, a shocked look on her face. Before she could say anything, Rikki stepped forward quickly, nearly knocking into Blythe.

"I'm Rikki. Rikki Prakenskii." She announced it firmly, sounding almost belligerent, holding out her hand to shake hands.

Rikki hated being touched, especially by those she didn't know. Blythe was proud of her that she was trying to do all the formalities that showed respect.

"Elle Drake. I know I've seen you a few times, but I traveled so much I never got the chance to meet you properly," Elle said, shaking her hand. "Please come in and sit down. Would you care for tea? Or perhaps coffee?"

Blythe wanted to hug her all over again. Her tone was welcoming and very genuine. She stepped back so Rikki could precede her into the warmth of the living room. She remembered that room, the mosaic tiles on the floor, the design and the wood. The artwork on the floor was intricate and gave one gazing at it the feeling of being in another realm. There was a deep blue that was either ocean or sky or perhaps both. Stars flared to life around a silver moon. Some things didn't change, and for some reason they made her feel welcome all over again, as if she was a part of the Drake legacy.

Blythe paused, staring at the mosaic. It seemed to move, darker clouds drifting toward that silvery moon, casting reddish shadows until several rings surrounded the moon, nearly obscuring it with red. In the clouds she could see more red, and she blinked rapidly to clear her vision, feeling the color leech out of her face. Blood. Death. Danger. Viktor was in town, and the last time he'd come, he'd brought death with him.

"Blythe?" Elle asked, her voice like a cool breeze, clearing out the last of the movement on the tiles. She waved her hand toward the chairs.

Rikki took an armchair so Blythe sat in the one nearest her. Jackson waited until Elle was seated and then he raised an eyebrow. "Tea? Coffee?"

"Coffee, black," Rikki said immediately.

"Tea for me, Jackson," Blythe said. "Milk."

"Same for me, babe," Elle said.

"As if I don't know what you like," he responded, walking out of the room.

There was an open archway leading to the large kitchen, so it was easy to see into the rooms from either direction. The floor of the kitchen was also a mosaic tile, the same midnight blue that formed the sky in the pattern on the floor in the great room. A long bank of windows looked out over a garden of herbs and flowers. Blythe could make out the three-tiered fountain in the middle of the courtyard she remembered playing in as a child.

She noticed the hand signal Jackson gave to the shepherds as he left the room. The two dogs immediately lay down on either side of the love seat Elle had chosen.

"I need to talk to you," Rikki blurted out. "*Both* of you."

"I can hear you," Jackson said.

"I'm married to Lev Prakenskii," she continued. "And he doesn't have any idea that I've come to talk to you. It's important though and I will tell him . . . afterward. He'll be upset with me but I just felt you needed to hear me out."

Rikki began to rock back and forth. Blythe reached out to touch her arm just as Elle leaned toward her, pushing air in front of her.

"There's no need to be upset," Elle said. "Of course we'll hear what you have to say. Lev Prakenskii is the man who called himself Sid and was a bodyguard to Stavros," she added helpfully.

Elle said the name of her captor but swallowed hard as she said it. Blythe could see her hands trembled. She folded them neatly in her lap, threading her fingers together. Blythe tried again to soothe her, this time from a distance, reaching out to the air with her fingers only, making them dance in a pattern just above the arm of her chair as if she was playing a song on the piano. It was a song of sorts. Blythe tried to make those around her comfortable. She didn't like them to be upset. Not when it wasn't of their own making, and Elle's distress wasn't from anything she'd ever done.

Blythe had learned, as a child, that she tended to amplify any emotion or energy in a room. She had practiced using that trait only for positive emotions. Her mother's emotions had been so wild and out of control. Blythe could subtly relieve unhappiness, not take it away exactly, but lighten it. As a child she had wanted so much to be able to do that for her mother, but it had never worked on her.

Jackson sauntered in and perched on the arm of the love seat right next to Elle. He threaded his fingers through her hand and pressed it to his thigh. It was impossible to read his thoughts from his carefully blank features, but Blythe was adept at reading energy, and his was *not* happy. Elle was tense, but she was careful to reserve judgment.

Rikki nodded. "He was working undercover to try to get to the top of the human trafficking ring. He told me that he tried to get you off the yacht, but he couldn't, not without blowing his cover. He also said he warned you repeatedly to stay away from Gratsos once he realized the man was obsessed with you."

A muscle ticked in Jackson's jaw. Elle glanced up at him and then began to rub her palm up and down his thigh soothingly. The tension in the room elevated. Both dogs alerted, heads coming up. Blythe could feel the anger coming off Jackson in waves, yet his expression remained the same.

She moved both hands to her lap and began to use her fingers as if playing a keyboard, hoping no one would notice. She wove air with the power of the house itself, sending soothing strains toward Jackson and Elle, not in the hopes of persuading them one way or the other, but to ease them over such a difficult conversation with a woman who couldn't read their building tension or in Jackson's case, anger.

Blythe's gift could be used only if her goal was selfless. She'd learned that as a child; otherwise, the crafting of her song could be twisted and come back to haunt her. Right now, she felt a little sick for Rikki, Elle and Jackson. That often happened, because when she tried to soothe others, she often had to take on their burdens.

"I have a sister—Lexi. She's just beginning to really thrive. Terrible things happened to her and she loves living here. The farm is really doing well." Rikki stumbled over the words, and her rocking began to increase in strength.

Blythe put a gentle, restraining hand on her arm, but Rikki didn't seem to notice. She began twirling her fingers and then lifting them to blow on them. It was an obsessive compulsive action she'd worked hard to stop. Blythe closed her hands over Rikki's, and Rikki startled and then turned red.

"I'm sorry. I'm not used to talking about really important things with people I don't know."

Elle smiled at her. "You don't have to be nervous. I want to hear what you have to say. So does Jackson." She looked up at her husband, her red hair swinging around her face, a trace of amusement there, in spite of the subject matter. It was a blatant lie told to help Rikki through a crisis.

Jackson stood abruptly and hurried into the kitchen as the kettle began to whistle. He glanced back at Elle, who grinned at him. Blythe was fairly certain she'd made the kettle whistle just to get him out of the room for a moment.

"We want to stay here," Rikki blurted out. "I want to stay. All of us do, but if you hate Lev and want to force us out, we'll go."

Blythe wasn't certain that was the truth. The Prakenskii brothers weren't the kind of men to be pushed around. Especially Gavriil. He'd push back hard if he thought anyone was hurting his beloved Lexi. Lev was the same way, only more subtle about it.

"We don't want to move," Rikki added for emphasis. "None of us do, but we don't want a war with you."

Elle sat up straight, looking at Blythe. "A war? Why would we ever have any kind of war?"

"Feud, then," Rikki said. "I'm nervous and not explaining this very well."

"Rikki, I'm cousins with Blythe." She leaned toward them again. "First cousins. I love her. Ilya Prakenskii is married to my sister Joley. I love Ilya. I had hoped, when I returned, to get to know all of you better. I realize, at first, it will be a little awkward for us with Si— Lev." She glanced through the open archway to her husband.

Blythe felt the clash between them. "I imagine, since you were undercover and you understand why someone doesn't break cover, it might be easier for you to forgive him than it will be for Jackson." Bringing the real problem out into the room might make it easier on all of them.

The sound of glass shattering had them all looking into the kitchen. Blythe was fairly certain the teacup had been thrown, not dropped. Elle waved her hand gracefully and the glass leapt into the air, molding itself back together again. The fancy cup floated over to the sink and settled gently on the counter.

Jackson glared at her. "Undercover or not, a man doesn't leave a woman in that situation." It was a declaration. He switched his attention to Rikki. "When I see your man, I'm going to beat the holy hell out of him." His tone remained mild, as if he might have been discussing the weather.

Rikki nodded. "I have to admit, I don't understand men very well, but Jonas hit him and Lev let him. He said you had every right to feel that way because he would if it had been me. If you beat the holy hell out of him—not that I think you can, but if you did—could we stay?"

"You can stay anyway," Jackson said, placing the tray with the teapot, cups, two mugs of coffee and a small pitcher of milk on the little end table between the armchairs. "We wouldn't drive you out. I worry that seeing your husband will bring it all back for my wife, and she doesn't need to have that in her face all the time."

"Your *wife*," Elle bit out between her teeth, "has never forgotten one tiny bit of my time with Stavros, so seeing Lev won't make much of a difference." She waved her hand and the pitcher floated, poured milk into a teacup and settled back down onto the tray. "Rikki, you have no reason to worry that my family will in any way retaliate against your husband. I volunteered to go undercover and I knew what could happen. I accepted the risks. I wanted that ring stopped. In the end, we managed to get Stavros, but from what I understand, the ring is stronger than ever."

Blythe nodded. "Maxim and Airiana rescued the children from one of the ships they use for their special clients. The ship belonged to Stavros's brother Evan. He's impossible to make a case against from everything Maxim told me." She reached for the other teacup and poured milk into it before taking a sip. The tea was perfect, which she thought interesting since Jackson had been the one to make it.

Elle shuddered. "He's a horrible man. Worse than Stavros, if that's possible. He's the one, I think, who was actually running the ring. Kidnapping and training victims.

Stavros provided the transportation in and out of countries as well as ships for clients that enjoyed using and then killing their victims. From what I gleaned, the bodies were dumped at sea. That was definitely Evan's idea."

Jackson put a hand on her shoulder. "Someone else will get him, baby. You don't have to think about that anymore. You're home. You're safe. You're with me."

Elle looked up at him, her hand immediately reaching out to his. "I'm home, safe and with you," she repeated. "I want him caught and held accountable, Blythe, but I can't be the one . . ." She trailed off.

"Of course not," Blythe said. "We didn't come here to bring everything back."

Elle bit down on her lip. "A few weeks aren't anywhere near long enough to recover from what happened. You aren't bringing it back," she reiterated. "It never has faded. So, Rikki, now that we've talked this through, are you feeling better? We're family of sorts, and we'll work it all out. It may take time, but we'll do it."

"*After* I have a little talk, man to man, with your husband," Jackson added.

Rikki breathed an audible sigh of relief. "I do feel better. Thank you for talking it out with me." She ignored Jackson's statement. She'd made it clear she didn't understand men so she wasn't going to argue with him. She didn't believe anyone could beat Lev if he didn't want them to, so she wasn't worried.

"Blythe," Jackson started.

She stiffened. Here came the questions she had no real answer for. She didn't want Viktor in trouble, but she didn't want to let everyone think she was going to stay married to him.

"Yes, Jackson?" She looked him right in the eye.

Elle's hand moved, smoothing down Jackson's thigh, a small brush, exquisitely gentle. There was a surge of power in the room. Immediately Blythe realized they were communicating telepathically. Once or twice when she was with Viktor, she felt a stirring in her mind when she brushed at the little symbol embedded in her palm, and for a moment she'd thought they could do that—talk to each other mind to mind. It had never happened, but she thought maybe with practice they could have done it.

"I thought only the seven daughters of the seventh daughter had psychic talents, but you appear to have a couple of very strong gifts."

Rikki turned toward her, her coffee cup halfway to her mouth.

"We all thought that at first," Blythe said, striving for matter-of-fact and conversational. She never talked about her talent. Her mother was so jealous of her sisters because her talent was not as well developed and over time had faded, probably because of her drinking. Blythe had tried to show her mother one time what she could do and her mother had slapped her, telling her it was blasphemy to lie about something so sacred.

Blythe was *nothing*. Sharon wasn't the seventh daughter, not the favored one, the one everyone loved. She was a throwaway and her daughter was worse—useless, pretending to have a talent she didn't have. Blythe had never brought it up again, nor did she ever show her cousins what she could do. She practiced when she was alone and used it in conjunction with her sisters of the heart.

"Clearly your talent is strong," Elle said.

Blythe smiled and shook her head. "Not really. More like a little parlor trick. I can boost power, but not much more."

Jackson frowned at her. "It's far more than that. You seem able to take whatever energy or power is around you and weave it with emotions surrounding you, and then you must add something else and make it even more powerful. I've never seen that."

"Why didn't you tell me?" Elle said. "When we were children?"

Blythe shrugged, and immediately comprehension was on Elle's face. "Aunt Sharon. She wouldn't let you tell anyone, would she?" There was compassion in her voice.

BOUND TOGETHER 119

In the old days she would have protected her mother no matter what. That had been drilled into her. But she had undergone a lot of therapy, and after what her mother had done, she no longer wanted to protect her. It didn't matter if others believed her or not.

"My mother was a very sick woman. Not only was she an alcoholic, but she was eaten alive with jealousy. She believed she should have inherited all the talents just as the seventh daughter had. She was paranoid and made up fantasies in her head that all of her sisters and parents were against her. What talent I had would simply have set her off more, had she believed in it."

"I'm so sorry, Blythe."

Blythe took a sip of tea in order to maintain her composure. "We were children, Elle. You especially were very young."

"She scared me," Elle said. "The way she looked at me sometimes. I thought she might try to hurt me."

"Had she been drinking, she would have," Blythe admitted. "But she was smart enough never to drink in front of her sisters, and she could maintain for short periods of time."

"Did you ever tell my parents?" Elle asked. "Or any of the aunts?"

Blythe shook her head. "I think children have a need to protect their world, even if it's a terrible one. I didn't dare, although looking back I have no idea why. Misplaced loyalty. I think I thought I could somehow make it all better. I just needed to try harder."

"Of course that wasn't so, but children think that way," Jackson said. "My mother was very ill with cancer. My father was in a motorcycle club—the Swords. They're a notorious club that specializes in everything illegal and treating their women and families like crap." It was the first time Blythe had ever heard an edge to his voice.

Elle continued to stroke his thigh. He covered her hand and leaned down to brush a kiss on top of her head.

"My father would leave us to go off riding with the

club," Jackson continued. "She would just wilt. Sometimes it would take me hours to get her to take her medicine. It was like she only lived to see him again. He had another woman, but it didn't matter to her. I kept thinking I could make it all better, but I couldn't. Children can't."

"I had a really wonderful childhood," Elle said cheerfully. "A fairy-tale childhood, as a matter of fact. What about you, Rikki?"

Rikki frowned. "When my parents were alive, I think I had a really great childhood. My mother helped me a lot. She put me in all kinds of programs and that made me able to be independent. Dad was funny and sweet. He tried, and he really, really loved my mother. They always kissed me good night."

"That's beautiful," Elle said. "My parents always kissed us as well."

"Not so much," Jackson said. "But I get the benefit of your parents always kissing you, Elle. Now you kiss me before you go to bed."

She started laughing, soft and musical, a breath of fresh air circulating the room. The dogs suddenly came to their feet, looking toward the door. It opened, and Jonas Harrington strode in. He stopped abruptly when he saw Rikki and Blythe.

"Sorry. Had no idea you had company. Need coffee now."

"I thought you weren't drinking coffee," Elle said as Jackson rose to go into the kitchen for another mug.

Jonas made a face. "Hannah's on some new kick. No caffeine for either of us. She gets into these healthy bullshit diet things and I suffer. Got anything sugary? Like your cookies?" He inhaled. "That woman of mine can bake up a storm, but does she? No, she's reading all these articles on healthy living, and suddenly it's no coffee or cookies." He waved to Rikki and Blythe and flung himself into a chair opposite them. "Save me, Elle. Talk to her. A man can't live this way."

"Don't be such a baby," Elle said. "She'll settle down in

a month or two. Right now it's all about the baby and making certain the two of you are healthy for him. You have a high-risk job and that has to be making her panic."

"She married me knowing I have a high-risk job," Jonas objected.

"That was before the baby, silly."

Jackson handed him a coffee mug and placed a platter with frosted cookies next to him. He indicated to Blythe and Rikki to have some as well.

"You shouldn't be enabling him," Elle scolded Jackson.

"He should," Jonas said, scooping up a handful. "I knew you'd come through, Jackson. Nice to see you, Rikki. It's been a while."

She narrowed her eyes at him. "You stopped me on the highway."

"But I didn't give you a ticket," Jonas hastily pointed out. "You don't know Hannah very well, do you?"

"I do," Blythe said. "She's my cousin."

"She's nice to me," Rikki said, still glaring.

"*I'm* nice to you," Jonas said, eating half a cookie in one bite. "Sheesh, woman, have a heart. It isn't nice to hold a grudge."

Rikki burst out laughing, startling all of them. She scooped up a couple of cookies and took a bite. "Good. Lev bakes *great* cookies, but I have to admit, these are just as good. Lucia is learning to bake."

"Ah, yes, Lucia," Jonas said. "The mysterious children who are related to the Prakenskiis in some abstract way no one can explain."

"The children Airiana and Maxim are adopting," Blythe said firmly.

She wished she hadn't said anything when Jonas turned his full attention on her. "You got anything to say about what was going on this afternoon?"

Blythe drank the last of her tea and put the cup aside. "Not really."

"That's not an answer, Blythe," Jonas said. "They had

us dead to rights. You know that, don't you? His men had us surrounded. They aren't the kind of men you play games with."

"Thank you for coming to my rescue, but I really would have been fine."

"Since when are you married?" Jonas demanded.

Elle gasped. "What?" She looked up at Jackson. "Did you know about this and you didn't tell me?"

"Baby, I didn't have a chance. I just got home, and you told me we were going to have company," Jackson said.

Elle spun back to gape at her cousin. "Blythe? Is that true? You're married?"

Blythe's first inclination was to deny everything, then to just shrug casually and tell them she was filing for divorce, but for some inexplicable reason, she felt like that was betraying Viktor. She sighed instead. "Yes. It seems I am."

"Tell me everything," Elle demanded.

Blythe sank back in her chair, avoiding both Jackson's and Jonas's eyes. She concentrated on her cousin. "I met him a few years ago. We literally ran into each other while we were both jogging. I would have fallen, but he caught me before I hit the ground. We ended up laughing and then running together."

Jackson made a noise in the back of his throat and looked at Jonas.

"What?" Elle asked, glaring at both of them.

"Classic pickup," Jonas said.

"Absolutely," Jackson agreed.

"So did you use it often?" Elle asked Jackson, the frost in her voice warning him that the answer had better be no.

Blythe noticed Jonas grinning behind his hand as he shoveled in more cookies and took a gulp of black coffee.

"Of course not, Elle," Jackson said. "I just know that some men use that sort of thing."

"Are you implying my cousin's husband wasn't sincerely interested in her?"

"Of course not. Any man would be interested in Blythe.

Well, with the exception of me. Only because I'm interested in you."

"Give it up," Jonas said, shaking his head, still grinning. "You aren't going to win no matter what you say. The Drakes have it down to a science."

"*What* do we have down to a science, Jonas Harrington?" Elle switched her glare from Jackson to Jonas.

"The craziness, that's what," Jonas said. "I don't let it get to me," he informed Jackson. "I grew up with them, and there's nothing to be done but ignore them when they get like this."

Elle waved her hand toward the telephone, and Jonas groaned.

"You little brat. I can't believe you'd rat me out to your sister."

"You *so* deserve it," Elle said.

The phone rang and Jonas was up immediately, snagging two handfuls of cookies, chugging the last of his coffee and heading for the door. "I'm not here. You never saw me."

Rikki nearly fell on the floor laughing. Blythe couldn't help but smile either, although she knew very well that Elle had deliberately saved her from answering any more questions about Viktor. Elle was extremely gifted, and there was no way Blythe could hide that she didn't want to be questioned on the subject. Elle had cleverly saved her by turning the attention onto the men.

Blythe stood up. "We'd better go. We've taken up enough of your evening. Thank you for letting us come tonight."

Rikki stood as well, straight as an arrow, holding out her hand to Jackson and then Elle. "I appreciate you relieving my mind. I'll tell Lexi that we're all safe."

"You're not going to be angry with me when I take a punch at your man?" Jackson asked her.

Rikki shrugged. "You can try, but it won't be fair if you're wearing your uniform."

"I promise I won't be," he assured her solemnly.

She nodded. "I'll let him know what to expect."

Elle followed them to the door, hugging Blythe tightly. "Come see me as soon as you have time," she urged.

Blythe nodded. "I will." It was one promise she wasn't certain she could keep. Elle saw far too much.

8

BLYTHE unlocked her front door and walked inside, not bothering with the lights. She'd taken four steps inside when it hit her. Hard. Mean. A blow that drove her to her knees right there in her entryway. There were some sorrows that were beyond all descriptions, cutting so deep that the wound would never heal. Time might ease the pain but it would always be there, always haunting. It would surface at unexpected times.

That first cut was the worst. It was there in her home. Pain beyond imagining. Sorrow so great it tore at her insides. It was physical. Visceral. She found herself on her hands and knees, fighting for air, silent screams echoing through her head. There was only one time in her life that she'd felt such pain.

She forced her head up and looked toward the stairs. From the moment she'd first seen Viktor in the streets of Sea Haven, she knew she had to tell him. Viktoria had been his daughter as well. She just didn't know how. He'd heard. That was the only possible explanation. He'd heard her tell her sisters about their child.

She pushed back with her hands so she could sink back on her heels, breathing great gulps of air, trying to orient herself. This was *his* pain. Viktor's. He was suffering, living through that first time when it had to sink in that their child was dead. There was no way to save her.

She closed her eyes and tried to absorb some of the wild grief filling her home. It was a large house, two stories with open areas, and that grief had spread to every nook and cranny, every space possible until the air was thick enough to choke on it.

Forcing herself to her feet, Blythe stumbled toward the stairs. He was up there. The grief was too raw, too real, a terrible burn, searing her from the inside out. She had always been an empath, taking on the emotions of those around her. She *had* to soothe people. The impulse was especially strong with the ones she loved, and she loved Viktor Prakenskii— at least the man she'd thought he was. *That* man was the father of her child and she had to get to him.

Her legs felt stiff, yet rubbery, her throat raw. She knew they were his legs, the muscles seizing in protest. His throat, so raw from the silent screams of protest. Grasping the solid oak railing, she dragged herself up to the top of the stairs. There was no sound. None. Yet she felt tears on her face and knew they were his.

Viktor was one of the toughest men she knew. Seeing him in Sea Haven, she knew he was also a dangerous, rough man, but losing his daughter had thrown him. His grief was genuine, terrible and to the core. Instinctively she knew he was in her bedroom. She made her way down the wide hall to stand in the open doorway.

Viktor sat on her bed, head down, his long hair falling around his face. His beautiful, thick hair was disheveled, as if he'd run his hands through it over and over—or tore at it with his fists. The lines of grief were etched deep. He wept, but so silently that if they hadn't been connected, she wouldn't have realized the pain was so deep that he couldn't cry other than the tears tracking down his face. The sobs were trapped in his chest. In his heart. That deep. Bone deep. Soul deep. She knew, because it had been that way with her.

She went to him because there was no other choice. He was suffering, and in that moment, he was *her* Viktor. The man she loved above all things. She wrapped her arms around his head and pulled him into her. He wrapped his arms around her waist and nearly crushed her with his strength. With his grief. She didn't say anything because there wasn't anything that could be said to ease his pain. She knew that from experience.

He felt real. Solid. Hers. She let herself cry because his sorrow was too great to bear without weeping. The death of their daughter was new all over again. For her it had been five years, but for him it had just happened. Tremors ran through him. His muscles were locked tight and tense. She knew that violence ran deep in him and the need was there; she could feel it burning just beneath the surface. Right now, he could barely move, the grief was so overwhelming.

Blythe had no idea of the passing of time, but eventually his hold on her loosened just a little. She stepped back, still in the circle of his arms around her waist, her hands framing his face. "Viktor." She breathed his name. "Honey, I'm sorry. I didn't know how to get ahold of you."

She brushed soothing kisses on top of his head, unable to stop herself. He hurt. Badly. Everything in her needed to take it away. What had gone before didn't matter in that moment. He needed, and she had to help him. For just those moments, he was the man she loved and they were parents grieving together over the loss of a child.

He lifted his eyes to hers, and she could see he'd left off the colored contacts he normally wore. He looked utterly ravaged. Gutted. "I left you the code, Blythe. I left you hundreds of messages. You never once reached out to me. I thought . . ." He closed his eyes.

Her heart clenched hard in her chest. He wasn't lying to her. Right in that moment it would be impossible for him to lie and her to not see it, Prakenskii or not. Trained or not. No one was this good of an actor. Something had gone terribly wrong.

Her heart leapt. Sang. She shut it down fast. She didn't

need or want hope, but the idea that he hadn't simply abandoned her was there whether she wanted it or not.

"I'm going to make you a cup of tea." The universal antidote for everything with her sisters. It gave one time to think, and she needed to. She needed to find balance. To puzzle things out. She needed not to be so close to him.

"Blythe, don't go yet." He refused to let her go even when she stepped back again, putting pressure on his arms. If anything, he tightened his hold. "I need you right now."

She had needed him so many times over the years, but especially when she lost their daughter. For one terrible moment, bitterness welled up and she wanted to strike out at him, hurt him, but there was no hurting him more than he already was feeling. She breathed away the emotion and stood still in his arms, letting him lean into her.

"I'm sorry for not being with you." His voice was muffled against her breast.

She felt the warmth of his breath right through her tank top. Her heart reacted to having him close to her. Remembering what it was like to feel safe with him. Not alone.

"I would have come. I would have come to you if I'd known you were pregnant."

His voice suddenly had gone from gravelly with sorrow to edged with anger. Abruptly, he put her aside and stood up. She was tall but he loomed over her, a giant oak of a man with broad shoulders and ropes of muscle. He looked intimidating and definitely angry. She knew that feeling as well. The horrible, bright need to strike out.

He paced away from her, across the room, his hands in two tight fists. "I was out trying to save other people's children. All those fucking years, Blythe. Risking our marriage, risking *us*. For what? What the fuck did I accomplish? In the end I lost my daughter. Everything has been taken from me. Everything."

He hit the wall hard with his closed fist. "All those children. They killed them, one by one. So damn many. Little girls. Little boys. But first they let the pedophiles loose on them. God, baby, they're sick fucks. I couldn't save them either." He punctuated each sentence with another solid blow to the wall. His voice was strangled, anger and sorrow mixing until her throat burned all over again because his was.

She didn't know if he was aware he had shifted from present to past, talking about things she didn't know. She didn't care about the wall and the fact that he was destroying it. She cared about the fact that his knuckles were torn and bleeding and he showed no signs of stopping. She was a little afraid of him, not that she thought he'd hit her, or do anything to hurt her, but this man wasn't one she knew.

"Stop." She kept her voice soft. Soothing. She didn't know who he was talking about or what he'd seen, but it had been bad. Really, really bad. She knew because she felt that too.

"Don't. Just fucking don't play me that way." He bit out the command, anger stabbing at her.

"I'm not playing you, Viktor," she denied.

He swung around, blood dripping from his hands to the wood floor. His face was a mask of pain, not from the blows to the wall—she would bet anything he hadn't felt those—but from the terrible anguish in his heart. She knew what it felt like when one's heart and soul were ripped out.

"You *are*. Like you do with your sisters. The way you always did with your bitch of a mother. Keeping your voice low, taking on the pain, working overtime so everyone remains calm and happy. Being perfect so no one gets angry. I'm *angry*, baby, fucking pissed. If Sharon were standing in front of me right now, I'd kill her. Beat her to death. Strangle her. If I could revive her, I would, and then do it all over again."

His breath came in angry blasts. His eyes narrowed on her, the color a strange sheen of almost silver. His fists clenched and unclenched. He walked toward her and she forced herself to stand still, not turn and run like her shivering body wanted her to do. She knew that rage; she'd felt it herself. She might not have the exact violent tendencies, but when she woke in the hospital to find there was no hope for her daughter, she wanted to kill Sharon as well.

"Does that scare you?"

"Yes." She whispered the admission. It did scare her, because as much as she had wanted to kill Sharon, she never would have done it. She knew Viktor would have.

"Do *I* scare you?"

She nodded slowly, never taking her eyes from his. Sadly for her, she still wanted to hold him. To comfort him. He'd made that impossible with his blazing eyes, now molten mercury, and his low, whispered words that scared the hell out of her.

"Yes." She refused to step back. "This is the real you, isn't it? You're not the man you pretended to be."

"Don't even start that bullshit. You know what I gave you was genuine. Everything I could, in every way I could, I gave you the real me. This is real too. No one is perfect all the time, Blythe. No one."

In spite of her determination to be understanding, anger was beginning to stir, not a good thing when she had so much of it stored up. "Are you implying that I think I'm perfect?"

"I'm telling you that you need to get used to this side of me. I'm not going away. You're not going to a divorce attorney. We're going to work this out, and that means that you see all of me, not just the parts you want to see."

"That's not fair, Viktor. You never showed me this side of you."

"Bullshit. You felt it each time Ray's name was mentioned or after your mother called and made you cry."

She had. She had ignored the rage she'd known was inside of him, deep, where it was never going to go away. She'd ignored it because it scared her. She'd lived with violence as a child, and she didn't want to think she'd married a man capable of physical aggression. She'd pretended to herself that he was always calm and cool no matter what.

She swallowed the disappointment in herself and nodded. "You're right. I did. I didn't want to see it, but I did." She rubbed her hand down her face, suddenly exhausted. "I have to go downstairs. You need to wash up before you get an infection."

He reached out and shackled her wrist, tugging until she came up against his body. "You're not running away from me. I'm not losing you again. I lived in hell for five years, certain you didn't care enough to contact me even to tell me to go to hell. You lived in a worse hell thinking I didn't give a damn. We're not going to let her win."

"Her?" But she knew. Sharon had somehow managed to tear them apart. It had to be that. Viktor was so adamant that she could contact him. He couldn't fake his grief or the ferocity of his rage.

"Sharon." He spat out the name. Tugging her wrist, he took her with him into the bathroom. "You know she did this to us."

She was very grateful she liked space because Viktor took up lots of it. He seemed to suck up the air around them as he went to the sink. "You got a first aid kit?"

She nodded and reached around him to open the cabinet and pull out the small one she kept upstairs. The big one was downstairs where she could get to it fast if something happened to one of the children or her sisters. "Sit down." She indicated the bench in front of the very large bathtub.

Viktor did what she asked, and that made it easier for her to breathe. The rage was subsiding, and with that the grief it had been holding back rushed to the forefront again. It was impossible to stay angry with him when she felt that.

"You know, Viktor," she said softly as she spread triple antibiotic cream over his smashed knuckles, "I can't help who I am any more than you can help who you are. I feel other people's emotions. That isn't something I can turn off. It doesn't happen when I touch people; it happens when I get near them. You walk into a room and I know how you're feeling. My nature, the empath in me, demands I do something about it. I'm not trying to be perfect. Believe me, I know I'm far from perfect."

She kept her head bent over his hands, fussing more than

necessary so she wouldn't have to look at him. She knew he felt the faint tremor that ran through her body and the slight waver to her voice. He couldn't know how horrible she felt that she hadn't soothed Sharon that day, that she had turned her back, even knowing how vicious her mother could be. She was definitely far from perfect. Had she done the right thing her daughter might still be alive.

"Baby, look at me."

She couldn't. He would see tears burning behind her eyes. She didn't want him to think he'd put them there. "I can't yet. Let's just not say anything for a minute or two."

"I never thought for one minute you think you're perfect. I was being a dick. I can get like that. I'm going to let you know up front, I can be ugly when my temper gets loose." He was silent for a brief moment while she wrapped his knuckles with gauze. "I'm not good when I feel helpless. I fix things. Problems. Messes. I take care of business. It was what I was trained for, in a very ugly way, but the training is all I have. Knowing you needed me—the most important person in my life, and I let you down—that's bad enough, but that our daughter needed me—" He broke off abruptly.

She shifted back on her heels to look down at the raw anguish in his eyes. There was no telling him to leave. To go away. No talking divorce. That was beyond her ability. The only thing she could do was comfort him. Her palm shaped his face and she bent to rub her cheek over the top of his head. He had thick hair, a wild mane, black streaked with silver. She had always liked the silver in his hair and when she'd asked him about it, he had shrugged and said he'd had it from his teenage years.

Her Viktor. So torn. She would see weariness in his face. Lines of grief. She didn't know what happened to him, but if the stories his brothers told were anything to go by, it had been horrific. It was all there for her to see. He was too grief-stricken to hide it from her.

"Honey, everyone can look back and say what they should have done, but that's after, with full knowledge of what occurred." Direct from her many counseling sessions.

She wished she could believe there wasn't guilt for either of them.

"I was coming back. I was, Blythe. I would never have left you."

"But you did." It slipped out before she could stop it and with it the hurt. The betrayal. Five long years of nights with no answers and a lost child. How did one recover from that? "You didn't come back, Viktor."

He rubbed the bridge of his nose, a family trait many of his brothers had. She wondered if their daughter would have had it. "I left you a long letter. Very detailed. How to get in touch with me, the explanation for what I did. My entire history. All of it. I put my birth brothers at risk as well as my brothers and sisters from the school. I gave it all to you. I knew it was going to be bad dealing with Sharon, so I planned to slip back in a couple of days when the heat had died down from the police."

She held herself very still so she wouldn't shatter. A letter. He hadn't just left without an explanation. He'd at least left her a letter. That meant something in spite of her determination not to let him back under her skin. She'd all but worshipped him. She missed him every single day. She ran to get him out of her head. She'd tried to bury him with her daughter, but it hadn't worked. Nothing worked. She'd dated, on and off, but no one even remotely interested her.

She moistened suddenly dry lips with the tip of her tongue, trying not to hope there was an explanation for a five-year absence. She couldn't imagine what it could be, and she saw the woman sitting on the back of his bike. She had to keep perspective. Emotions were raw, and she was so alone all the time. Viktor had always, always been her only. If people had soul mates, he'd been hers.

"You didn't come," she murmured. "Whatever your intentions were, you didn't come."

"I called you two days after. I left four messages at your house. One of my brothers was in trouble. He'd taken a hit and it was bad. He needed medical care and someone to protect him while he mended."

She lifted her chin and looked him right in the eye. "Which brother?" Not a single one of the men she'd come to consider family had said a word about Viktor coming to help them. Not even Gavriil.

"We call him Absinthe. He's here with me if you want to talk to him. He survived, but it took a while. There was no one else, Blythe. He would have died. He was being hunted. We had to lie low because Sorbacov would have had both of us killed. As it was, the hit went out on Absinthe. It was a struggle to smuggle him out of the country and then find a safe place for him to recover."

She had no doubt that Absinthe or any of his other "brothers" would lie for him and look perfectly sincere. Still, she believed that ravaged look on his face. The stunned shock and anger, the grief welling up like a bottomless geyser, ready to consume both of them. She'd lost their daughter and she'd lost him. Still, there was no going back from five long years of emptiness and pain for either of them.

"What happened to him?" She had no idea why she asked. It only took her closer to the abyss. She knew he was the kind of man to sacrifice everything to help someone he cared about—loved. She might as well admit he loved these men he surrounded himself with.

She couldn't let Viktor back into her life. She held herself together by being alone, by trusting only the women who shared a violent past and had shown her she could live in the aftermath. She didn't want to know about his brothers or the woman on the back of his bike, especially if they were hurt in any way. She had too much empathy. Her gift demanded she help others and she couldn't stop herself.

"He was shot five times and left for dead by a band of men who kidnapped, raped and ransomed on a regular basis. They kidnapped the daughter of one of Sorbacov's friends while she was vacationing in South America. Absinthe managed to save her, but then dragged himself into a basement and called me. They were hunting him and he was running out of ammo. I had to get to him as fast as possible."

She hated that she could so easily see the man in her mind, bloody and hurting, waiting in the dark alone to die. Could she fault Viktor for rushing to save his friend? She would have in a heartbeat had it been someone she loved.

"How could he stay alive?" She couldn't imagine.

"You hate enough, baby, you can do anything."

She frowned. "Who do you hate that much?"

Viktor stood up so that she had to step back. He was too close. In spite of the spacious room, he took up too much of the air. Heat radiated off his body, warming her when she felt cold inside.

"Men and women who think they're entitled to fuck up everyone's lives."

It was the edge to his voice that sent icy fingers creeping down her spine. She looked up at his face. She was familiar with his eyes, so unusual, burning hot or cold. The line of his jaw and his nose that had clearly been broken more than once. Every scar on his body, and he had a lot of them.

"I don't really know you at all, do I?"

"You know me. At least one part of me, Blythe, the part no one else has ever had. If you'd read the letter you'd understand me."

"Well, I didn't. And you shouldn't have written me a letter, you should have talked to me. Face to face. After you saved your friend. Why didn't you come then?"

He sighed and ran his hand through his hair, so that the thick mass was more disheveled than ever. "I got the assignment to hunt Evan Shackler-Gratsos. He's the international president of the Swords and runs the largest human trafficking ring in the world. I had to go deep undercover if I was going to take that assignment, and really, when Sorbacov gives you a mission, you have no choice unless you want to be taken out. Still, I could have disappeared. I *despise* men like Shackler. They like hurting people. Children. Speaking of children . . ." He pulled a crumbled piece of paper out of his pocket and handed it to her. "I want you to look into this kid and make certain she's doing okay. If not . . ." He waved his hand.

Blythe frowned and opened the paper as she stepped around him. She needed to get out of the bathroom and back into her huge master bedroom. She was uncomfortable being in any room that had a bed with him, but it was better than inhaling him with every breath she took.

She glanced down at the paper. There was a single name. Darby Henessy. "Who is this?"

"The Swords had her and a few other girls in a training camp. We got them out. Called the local cops, and they took the girls. Most have homes, some are runaways and others just don't have anyone. They're kidnapped or lured in by other kids the Swords use, or promised jobs. She was a fighter. They gang rape these kids, beat the shit out of them and scare them so bad they'll do anything to keep from being hurt again. This one stood up to them. My guess is they would have sent her to one of his snuff ships."

Her stomach lurched. "You want me to find her and make certain she's all right? What did you want me to do if she isn't? She could be in the system already. Foster care, or a ward of the state."

"Then get her. Bring her here. Work your magic. She deserves to have a home with people who care about her."

Blythe sat down in one of the winged armchairs in front of the gas fireplace, because if she didn't sit, she might fall down. She felt a little faint. Viktor had come out of nowhere, telling her they were married and he wasn't going anywhere, heard about their daughter, destroyed her wall and now was asking her to bring a stranger into her home and take care of her.

"How old is this girl?"

He shrugged. "I don't know. She looked really young, but acted older. Her eyes were old. Anywhere from thirteen to seventeen. She wouldn't be of legal age or the chapter wouldn't have taken her. Young girls are more economical."

She flinched. She couldn't help it. It wasn't that she wasn't aware of what went on in the world—they had evidence of it right there on their farm. "Maxim and Airiana were on one of the Shackler-Gratsos ships. They rescued

four children and brought them here. They're adopting
them. One of their little sisters was killed on that ship.
They're all very young. The oldest, Lucia, is fourteen. One
is a boy."

"Pedophiles like both sexes, Blythe." Viktor took the
chair opposite her, sprawling out, his long legs crossed at
the ankles.

"You really want me to bring this child here if she has
no family?"

His silver eyes turned molten and she knew she was seeing the edge of his temper.

"She's not your daughter or anything?" she asked, suddenly suspicious. Why would he think after five years he
could walk back into her life and demand she bring a child
into her home? It didn't make sense. Her fingertip traced
the name over and over.

There was silence. It stretched out so long she lifted her
head and looked at him. Her breath caught in her lungs. His
eyes were alive with temper.

"What. The. Fuck. Why would you ask me that?"

She opened her mouth to tell him to go to hell when his
emotions registered. Yes, he was angry, but more, the pain
of loss was there. It was so raw and new for him. Five years
had helped fade the sorrow so she could breathe again, but
for him, the loss of their daughter was that moment. That
hour. That day. His grief was overwhelming.

"Don't say *fuck*, Viktor. It isn't necessary to swear at me.
I'm just trying to figure things out. Of course I'll check into
this child. It's not like I can just grab her if the state has her
or if she's in foster care. I'm a single . . ." She trailed off
when his eyes went molten again.

Viktor leaned toward her. "You're married. *Married*. To
me. You're my wife. Legally and in every other way." He
caught her hand and turned it over, palm up. The moment
he pressed his thumb into the center, the two rings blazed
to life, coming to the surface, looking like a tattoo. "You're
mine. This says so." He held up his palm and did the same
thing so the two interwoven circles gleamed gold. "I belong

to you. That isn't going away. Not ever, Blythe, so we're going to work this out."

She didn't say anything. What could she say? She didn't think so, not after five years of complete silence. She knew there were unanswered questions and she wanted those answers, but she wasn't so certain she wanted to trust ever again. He'd ripped out her heart. Her soul. She'd been a walking shell until she met the five other women who had banded with her in order to try to live again.

She had built a life for herself here in Sea Haven, on the farm. She liked her life. Viktor was a demanding man, used to dictating, and clearly those around him jumped to do his bidding. Before, when she'd first married him, she'd liked that trait in him, the one that made her feel safe. She'd worked hard on her independence, and she didn't know if it was possible, even if she wanted, to live with a man so intense and such a dictator.

"Some things you can't get past, Viktor. You know that." She smoothed out the paper. "I'll look into this girl for you, and if she needs a place, I'll see if Lev or one of the others can produce some of their impeccable paperwork. Airiana is good with children. So is Lexi."

"You. It has to be you."

She moistened her lips. "I don't think—"

"You." He cut her off. "She needs you. The moment I saw her, I knew she was important and that she needed us."

"Us?" she echoed faintly. It was suddenly hot in the room and she could barely breathe. She was really afraid she might pass out. "For God's sake, Viktor, we aren't together. Not anymore." She held up her hand to stop the protest she could see forming. "Even if we did manage to work things out between us, it would take time and a *lot* of effort. We couldn't possibly foster a child while we were trying to do that."

"You've made up your mind that it isn't going to work before you've had a chance to even hear me out."

"You think?" She folded the paper carefully and slipped it into a pocket of her jeans. "I can hear everything you say and even understand why you did the things that you did, but I still went through an ugly tragedy alone. You can't take that back, and frankly, neither can I. Then there's the little matter of the woman on the back of your bike. You think I don't know what it means when a woman is riding on the back of a biker's motorcycle?"

"She's not my old lady. You are. She's my sister."

"You don't have any sisters."

"I have two of them, and Alena was helping me out, pretending to be my old lady. In the clubs, there are always women who hang around looking to hook up. The other members of the chapter would expect me to sleep with them. I took this assignment, joined the Swords and worked my way up to enforcer because I knew that sooner or later Evan would have to show himself. The one man he hates above all others on this earth is Jackson Deveau. After studying Evan, I knew he'd want to kill him himself."

Something inside Blythe went very still. "Evan Shackler is planning on killing Jackson?"

He nodded. "He sent me and the boys here in order to prepare for the Swords to come en masse in order to provide distractions so he can slip in and kill Deveau."

She took a breath, let it out, hearing a strange roaring in her head. "So you're actually here undercover."

"Exactly. I came ahead of the others, and my brothers are with me, so there's no danger at the moment. You'll have to be very careful to stay away from me as soon as some of the others begin to show up. I can't have them finding any trail that might lead to you. I wouldn't have let you see me, but the first damn sighting I had of you was that fucking lunkhead who was all over you."

Blythe opened and closed her mouth several times. "He wasn't all over me" was what she finally managed to get out when that wasn't at all what she wanted to say. She was still processing.

"He was all over you. The man would have kissed you in another minute."

"All that is beside the point." She struggled to wrap her

head around what he was telling her. "So you're actually here in Sea Haven undercover, on this assignment. The same assignment that kept you away from me for five years."

He nodded. "It was coincidence that my target just happened to be coming to Sea Haven."

Her breath caught in her throat. The blow was hard, a wicked punch to her stomach when it all finally sank in. She'd been so close to believing every word out of his mouth. He was *playing* her. Again. Using her. Again.

"Wait a minute." Blythe stared up at him, a slow burning anger, a very unfamiliar anger, spreading through her, covering the hurt so she didn't have to feel it all over again. "Are you telling me you didn't come here for me? You're here because of a *job*? After all this time, you still didn't come for me?"

There was silence. He slowly sat up straight and blinked. That small movement told her everything she needed to know. She pointed to the stairs. "Get. Out."

"Blythe, be reasonable, baby. I wouldn't risk you like that. I planned to come to you after the job was done."

"Get. Out. I don't care if you need a cover, or a place to stay or just wanted a little change from your female companionship, but I can assure you, you're not getting any of that from me. Get out of my house this instant."

"I'm not going anywhere. We can't get past all of this if you won't even talk to me. I know it isn't easy for you. I have questions too. I'm trying to explain."

"Yes, explanations like the whole sister thing."

"It's true. As long as I had an old lady, no one questioned the fact that I wasn't sleeping with anyone else, and believe me, they would have noticed."

"So now I'm supposed to believe you haven't been with another woman for *five* years. Get. Out."

His eyes narrowed and the gray-blue went to a devastating silver that always took her breath away. "How many men have you been with in five years?"

"That is none of your business," she snapped. He didn't need to know that there was no other man. There never would be another man. She ran instead of having sex. Sometimes she ran half the night.

"I'm making it my business."

"Make it your business all you want, but do it getting out of my house." She hissed it at him, furious that he wouldn't listen. Like she was going to believe one single word he said. "And don't worry, I have no intentions whatsoever of acknowledging your existence while you're doing your *job* here in Sea Haven. Jackson and Jonas can serve you with the divorce papers, because we *are* getting a divorce."

"Over my dead body, and maybe theirs," he snapped, every bit as furious as she was. He stood up. He was so tall, his shoulders so wide he took up a good deal of space, space she needed to breathe when once again her world was falling apart. Stupid. How had she dared to hope? What was wrong with her that after everything that happened, she was so willing to drop right into his lap? And she had been. She wasn't going to kid herself about that. She'd bought into everything he said and all she wanted to do was throw herself into his arms. What an idiot.

He started toward her, and she panicked completely. He couldn't touch her. She'd be lost if he touched her and she'd despise herself. She picked up the nearest object and flung it at him. "Get. Out."

He dodged and kept coming. Behind him, her music box smashed against the wall with a terrible crash. Blythe did the only possible thing she could for self-preservation. She ran to the wall beside her bed and hit the panic button. There would be questions she couldn't answer, but that didn't matter. All that mattered was keeping him away from her.

9

"WHAT the hell did you just do?" Viktor demanded.

Blythe kept her back to the wall, covering the panic button that looked like an ordinary light switch. Her heart thundered in her ears. What had she done? Viktor looked invincible. More, he was, by his birth brothers' own admission, extremely dangerous, more so even than all of them. He certainly had some dangerous-looking men he surrounded himself with. She was very thankful that they weren't present. If they were, she might have started World War III.

"You'd better leave now while you can, Viktor," she said, making every effort to sound reasonable. Just looking at him hurt.

"Tell me what you did, Blythe."

His tone was so scary she felt the color leech from her face. He stepped close and caught at her wrist, tugging until she was propelled forward and into him. One arm locked around her back while he examined the switch. He swore, really filthy words, she was certain, in his native language.

"Tell me now." His voice was low. "I'm not alone, Blythe. Reaper and Savage are out on the roof and the others are close. If my birth brothers are going to show up, someone's going to get hurt. I don't want anyone harmed, but the ones

I brought with me play for keeps. They don't know any other way." He caught her upper arms and held her at arm's length from him. "I have to know now."

She knew immediately he was genuinely worried and that calmed her instantly. She had to protect her family, just as he did. She didn't doubt for one minute that there would be bloodshed if things weren't handled right.

"They'll come. All of them. Lissa probably as well, although she might go with the others to Airiana's to help protect the children there." She wasn't about to tell him how defensible Airiana's home was. She might need to retreat there.

He whistled, a low, one-two note that sounded more like a hunting bird than a man. Immediately a man stuck his head through her open window. She recognized him from the streets earlier.

"We're going to have company very soon, and they'll be out for blood. Stand down and let me handle it. Keep Savage under control. These are my brothers as well, and I don't want them hurt. The one to watch out for is Gavriil. He's a bit like Savage, so we don't want the two of them anywhere near each other."

"What the fuck?"

"Don't say *fuck* in front of my woman. Blythe panicked a little and called them in. She'll talk to them with me and we'll sort it out."

"Not going to stand for anyone trying to search me or remove weapons," Reaper warned. "And I'm calling in the others."

"You make it clear these men are family. No one touches them."

"As long as they don't put a hand on you, Czar, we'll get along."

Blythe closed her eyes tiredly. She really had panicked. What had possessed her to let things get so out of hand? She couldn't be around Viktor without feeling intense emotion. Already her anger was fading, replaced by more familiar hurt. "Can't you just leave? I'm exhausted, Viktor, and I want to go to bed. Alone." She had to make that very clear. "We've talked enough. You said what you had to say and I found out why you're really here, which has nothing at all to do with me. Please go back to your friends—brothers— and your woman and let's just leave it at that."

Reaper's eyebrow went up. He shook his head and ducked back outside.

"Let's get downstairs, babe. We've got to present a united front. They're going to try to get you off alone to make certain I haven't threatened you. Reaper, Savage and the others will stop at nothing to protect me."

"Then leave now."

"No, damn it. Why are you being so fucking unreasonable?"

She decided she must have gone past the point of tired into sheer exhaustion because that made her want to smile. He could use foul language in front of her but his friend couldn't. "Why do you persist in thinking I'm the unreasonable one? You left me for five years. That alone without all the things that happened . . ."

"Things outside my control, and I would have given anything to be with you. I would have come if I'd known."

He pulled her down the hallway, and she went with him because it was clear he wasn't leaving and she didn't want anyone hurt, especially the men she'd called to her aid. She'd come to regard them as family. "But you didn't know and they happened. Then there's the fact that you have another woman regardless of whether or not you want to give me a bullshit story about her protecting you from other women. Like you'd go five years without sex. I know you, you were insatiable. I think we had sex three times a day at least."

"Four, but who's counting," he said, snapping his teeth together as if he might take a bite out of her. "Four, and I wanted more. I remember every single minute of my time with you. At night, when I'm alone, I have my fist around my cock and think of you, the way you looked all sprawled out on the bed for me. In the shower. Your body over the back of the couch. Once on the lawn in the backyard because I couldn't wait one more minute. The night in the car when you . . ."

"Stop. Just stop it," she said desperately, locking her legs so he couldn't drag her.

He wrapped an arm around her waist and lifted her easily, taking her down the stairs fast. "I remember everything, Blythe. Do you think a man can't be faithful to his woman? Or is it only me you have such a low opinion of?"

She began to struggle, and at the end of the stairs he set her on her feet and caught her face between his hands, bending down to put his face inches from her. "Look at me, Blythe. *Look* at me."

At the urgency in his voice she stopped struggling and lifted her gaze to meet his.

"You think you've seen the worst by looking at my birth brothers, at Jackson and Jonas, especially Gavriil. You've seen the hell in their eyes, but, baby, they lived through a picnic in comparison to us. My brothers don't know any other way but to kill. I don't either. That's who we are. It's what we are. They can't be threatened, especially not by my birth brothers, who are all capable as well. Do you understand what I'm saying to you? You *have* to stand with me here. You have to make my birth brothers believe you're not afraid of me." He smoothed back the hair from her face. "I would never under any circumstances harm you. If you pulled out a gun right now and threatened to pull the trigger, I'd let you."

"And the others, your brothers, would come after me."

He fell silent, and she had her answer. The anxiety in him was plain and it was very real. Blythe took a deep breath and forced calm. There was no expression on his face, but there was no way for him to keep emotions from her. Feeling poured out of him, filling the room until she felt anxious as well.

All fight was gone and a calm resolve came over her. She knew, deep down, Viktor wouldn't hurt her; she was being ridiculous fighting him like a child. She also knew that every one of his birth brothers would protect her, and that would be a tragedy. Viktor knew it as well, and he feared for them. He had to know what they were capable of and yet he feared for them—what did that say about the men he traveled with? What did that say about him?

"Blythe? Are you with me?"

She nodded, because she knew the situation was dire and it could quickly get out of hand. He felt so *troubled*. Hurting. The pain of loss beat at him. He was upset that he couldn't get her to understand. All that was right there in the room with them, yet he gave a sigh of relief and straightened.

"Thank you."

That shamed her a little. She had every right to be angry with him, but she knew better than to put others in jeopardy. There was no excuse for it all. "I'm sorry. I did panic, and I don't even know why."

"I scared you, Blythe," he stated. "You were with me every single day we were apart, so it didn't occur to me that you wouldn't be used to the way I move, or look."

That bothered her, because sincerity not only rang in his voice, but filled the room along with the other emotions battering at her. The front door opened without preamble, no knocking, just the door opening, and Gavriil walked in. He filled the doorframe, tall and broad-shouldered, wearing his long black coat that swirled around his ankles. She knew that coat had weapons concealed in it. His face was grim, his eyes cold, taking in both of them.

Again, there was no expression on either man's face, but she felt that sudden stillness as they looked at each other. Two brothers who had been ripped apart when they were children. Now at odds because of her. There was a slight hitch of breath, and such emotion quickly shut down, as if both men had to compartmentalize in order to survive.

"Blythe, come here." Gavriil beckoned her with his hand. He stayed across the room from them, but he'd taken one step to the left so that the open door was no longer at his back.

"Gavriil," Viktor greeted.

"Viktor." Gavriil kept his gaze on his older brother's face, but he beckoned to Blythe a second time.

She crossed the room to him. He took her wrist and very, very gently, guided her around him until she was behind him.

"Are you all right?"

"Yes," she said immediately. "I'm so sorry I hit that panic button. Viktor just surprised me. He's intimidating, and I wasn't expecting it. Him. I hit it before I thought."

"He didn't hurt you." It was a statement, but all of them knew it was a question.

"Of course not. He wouldn't. Not ever." She said that with conviction because they were talking about physical harm, and no way would Viktor ever put his hands on a woman in that way. Even this man she wasn't certain of, the side of him he was showing her now, she knew would never hurt a woman unless it was self-defense or she was responsible for hurting others.

"I'm not alone," Viktor said. "Gavriil, the others with me, they're like me."

She felt the tension rise immediately. "I'm all right, Gavriil. Please tell the others it's safe to come in."

Gavriil still didn't look at her. "Five years. No word."

"I left word for all of you. Hundreds of messages. I wanted Blythe looked after. No one ever answered me."

This time fury shimmered in the room. Blythe realized that rage was a part of Viktor's makeup. How he'd hidden it from her in the months they were together, she'd probably never know, but it was stamped into his bones and impressed on every cell. That fury was directed at Gavriil. He really *had* sent messages, and no one had answered him.

"There were no messages, Viktor. Not for the last five years. Not one."

Blythe clutched the back of Gavriil's coat and held her breath. It seemed as if something had crept into the room and then suddenly sucked all the air out so it was impossible to breathe.

"I can feel that both of you are telling the truth, so how

would that happen?" If Viktor had tried to get to her and asked others to look after her, then at least she could feel as if he'd cared. Maybe it hadn't all been a complete sham on his part.

"That's the question," Viktor said. "If you didn't get my letter and you didn't have the codes and no one else received my messages, then someone else has the codes and deliberately erased them. There's no other explanation."

"How many men you have out there?" Gavriil asked.

"How many did you spot?" Viktor countered.

"Six."

"You missed two. One's probably hanging back deliberately with a bead on whoever you have sitting up with a sniper rifle on me. The other is a woman, and she's lethal. She's already assessed the most vulnerable and marked him, one who might hesitate because she's female. Every one of them has some sort of psychic gift, so you can't depend on your gifts to even the odds. Call them in."

"Blythe? You good?" Gavriil asked.

"Perfectly. I just feel a little silly for causing such a fuss."

Gavriil stepped to the doorway and held up his hand, signaling his brothers. Again, Blythe felt shimmering emotion filling the room—this time it was coming solely from Viktor in anticipation of seeing his birth brothers. She couldn't help herself; she went to him. He needed someone whether or not he knew he did.

He immediately circled her waist with his arm, locking her front to his side. She felt the small tremor move through his body as first Lev entered, and then Stefan. She looked up at Viktor's face. He was utterly still. His features could have been carved from stone.

The emotion in the room was so strong it threatened to drive her to her knees. She had no choice but to cling to Viktor for strength. She recognized that they both were doing the same thing. Holding on to each other. She'd had no one. She'd thought he hadn't either in those days, but now she realized he had an entire life she didn't know about. Brothers and perhaps sisters. And birth brothers. Men she had grown to love. She wasn't alone anymore. She had her sisters, the five women standing with her. She knew them well. They weren't hiding in their homes, cowering; they were somewhere outside, waiting to see if they were needed. Viktor's new family might be lethal killers and they clearly had psychic abilities—he'd said so—but she wasn't helpless and neither were her sisters.

She started to pull away from Viktor and his other arm clamped around her, preventing movement. She glanced up at him again. He wasn't looking at her; he was looking at the two other men entering the house. Maxim and Casimir. Another tremor ran through his body. The emotions in the room ratcheted up another notch. She curled her fingers into his shirt as Ilya Prakenskii walked into her house.

There was a stirring in her mind. A brush along the walls like a caress. *Blythe.* Her name was a whisper in her mind. A shared anguish.

Viktor couldn't show his emotions, maybe he wasn't even feeling them, but they were strong enough to nearly bring her to her knees. Her breath hitched in her throat. She hadn't expected to see Ilya there. Evidently Viktor hadn't either.

It was worth it. I didn't know if it would be, but they're all safe.

Her eyes burned, and then she couldn't see anything because tears swam and spilled over. They were his tears, tears he couldn't shed. It was too much for any one human being. The knowledge of how his daughter died and then seeing six brothers he hadn't seen in thirty years other than from a distance when he'd tried to help them on some impossible assignment.

Blythe rubbed her wet cheek along his shirt. She couldn't have moved even if she wanted to, he was holding her that tight. "Honey, you need to tell your other brothers everyone is safe and they can go home. I know that the women are out there, covering their men. Waiting to see if I'm all right. I'm going to step to the door and let them know everything is good."

No one else had spoken. The seven men faced one another, birth brothers, men who had sacrificed so much for
one another, yet didn't know one another very well and
Viktor not at all.

Viktor swallowed visibly and then he nodded and
stepped with her, holding the lock he had on her. She knew
why. He needed her. She was what was getting him through
this moment. There was so much emotion, he couldn't
allow himself to actually feel it. He compartmentalized.
Instinctively she knew it was the only way he could survive.
Something in him was very, very broken. Very wrong.

Again, it was sheer instinct that had her gripping him
hard and walking in perfect sync with him. His brothers
parted to allow them through, although Lev trailed after
them. She could feel the fierce protective vibe coming off
of him in waves. The other brothers were nearly as fierce,
although it was difficult to read Gavriil. He didn't take his
gaze from Viktor, not even when Maxim moved through
the room, dimming the lights and moving furniture to get
the chairs out of line with the windows.

Viktor gave another call, the distinctive call of an eagle
owl, three hoots, signifying all was well. He lifted his hand
and made a circle, indicating his brothers and sister could
go home for the night. Blythe lifted her hand to her sisters.
She could feel them out there. They could go home and
know she was safe.

"They were a surprise," Viktor said. "I don't know why,
but I thought my brothers would tuck them somewhere safe
and come themselves."

Amusement shifted through her, breaking up the terrible weight of his overwhelming emotions. "Of course you
thought that."

His eyebrows shot up and his entire focus was on her.
His long fingers captured her chin and tilted her face up
toward his. "Why would you think that, baby?" His voice
was low, just between the two of them, and held a warning
caress that slid down her spine like fingers. She shivered
with reaction, her sex clenching.

"Because you belong in a cave half the time."

"Only half?" Now brief amusement cut through all the terrible emotions, and he took a deep breath as he turned her back toward the inside of the house.

She had to nod. "Only half. Sometimes you can be reasonable."

"I'll have to work on that."

She wasn't certain what he was going to work on, being a caveman *all* the time, or trying *not* to be a caveman most of the time. She closed the door while he stood with one arm still locking her to his side. Blythe didn't try to step away from him because she could feel his struggle. He wanted to walk out the door, not allow her to close it.

She was the one who took the first step back into the room filled with his brothers. She was very, very grateful that she had wanted a house built with wide open spaces. The Prakenskii brothers were all tall with broad shoulders and a presence that took up every available space.

"Blythe." Ilya shocked her by putting a hand on her wrist as if he would take her physically from his brother. "Are you all right?"

"Yes. Of course. I'm so sorry I got all of you out of your homes. I just panicked for a moment when I saw Viktor and I just pushed the button. As you can see, I'm fine," she tried to reassure them all. Testosterone was heavy. None of them were going to relax or back down until they believed every single word she said. She felt just a little desperate. Any one of these men could erupt into violence at the slightest provocation, and she didn't want any of them hurt.

"Let go of her." Viktor all but snarled the order. "You don't put your hands on my wife."

"Viktor," Blythe protested. "Ilya is only trying to make certain that I'm all right."

"You don't have to give him explanations, Blythe." Ilya didn't back down for a minute. "He hasn't been here in thirty damned years, he can't just walk in and decide you belong to him."

"Thirty years?" Viktor echoed. "You want to tell me

how difficult your life was, baby brother? In that easy, skate-through-life school straight into Interpol? Yeah, that was a rough fuckin' life, wasn't it? You know who earned you that life? That was me. Thirty years of the worst kind of shit you couldn't even imagine. Did you bother to find out what it was like for me earning you that school and that easy life?"

"Viktor." Gavriil indicated a chair. "No one had it easy. None of us, and we can all acknowledge that you were put in the worst of the worst. We know what you did for us. The point Ilya is making is about Blythe, not about us. She's the innocent here, and yes, she's your wife."

"My mark is on her." Viktor caught her wrist and held up her palm. His thumb slid over the center and the double rings burst to life, etched into her skin like a very perma-nent tattoo. "This mark says she's mine and no one has the right to interfere with us."

Gavriil waved his hand toward the chairs in Blythe's great room. Reluctantly the other brothers sank into the wide armchairs. Viktor led Blythe right past Ilya to the love seat and pulled her down with him. She let him because she wasn't about to be the match setting off the sticks of dynamite. Ilya sat across from them, straddling the arm of a chair.

No one looked comfortable. Blythe struggled for a way to break the ice. They all wanted to—although mostly she felt his brothers' concern for her and for some reason that made her want to cry. She hadn't realized they felt genuine affection for her, although now it came at her in a concen-trated form.

"I could make tea or coffee," she offered.

Viktor's hand tightened involuntarily on her, but then he forced his fingers to let her go, one after another. "That might be a good idea, baby," he said.

It was his most caressing voice, like black velvet rubbing over her skin, the tone that always had disarmed her. It was no different now. Every single cell in her body responded to him. She stood up quickly, looking around, grateful for the reprieve. "Tea? Coffee? Name your preference."

"Coffee." It was decisive. Without their women, their chosen drink would always be what it had been.

"Moscow prefers tea," Viktor said. "Didn't any of you spend time there? And you know how I like my coffee, Blythe."

"I spent a little time in Moscow," Ilya admitted. "But I never picked up the tea habit until I came here and married my wife. Tea is a ritual with the Drakes."

"I understand your wife is pregnant. When is she due?" Viktor said it deliberately so his brothers knew he did his homework. More, that he kept up with them.

"She's a week or so over five months. She's actually with her sister Libby right now. I was visiting Lev when the call came in."

"Why didn't you contact any of us in these last years?" Maxim asked. "I understand deep cover, but no one could have penetrated our code."

"Someone did." Viktor dropped the bomb into the sudden silence that had followed Maxim's blunt accusation. "There's no other explanation. I left you hundreds of messages. I left Blythe messages. No one got them. Someone had to have picked up the messages and then erased them." He looked around the room at his brothers, his gaze touching each of their faces.

"You're not accusing one of us." Stefan made it a statement.

"I don't know any of you." Viktor kept his voice strictly neutral. Someone had severed all of his ties with Blythe. He would have thought Sharon was capable of it, but he had sent messages after her death. By that time, his Torpedo Ink brothers could occasionally get to the States and they reported Sharon's death and that Blythe was happy and living on the farm with five other women in Sea Haven.

"You know us," Gavriil said. "We lived by the oath of our father, even Ilya, although a baby and without any real knowledge of our parents. We kept to the code. If someone destroyed your messages, it wasn't one of us."

The brothers exchanged uneasy looks. The silence was broken by the sounds of Blythe getting mugs down from the cupboard.

"You believe that someone actually read all of our private messages?" Lev asked.

"It's that or I lost my mind and didn't spend nearly every waking minute trying to get word on Blythe. I practically begged the six of you to get to her and make certain she was okay."

Again, in spite of trying, Viktor couldn't quite keep the bite of accusation out of his tone. He hadn't realized until he saw them all together just how emotional he would be, or how angry at them. Blythe had been alone. He couldn't get to her, but at least one of them should have been able to. At least Ilya. He was careful not to look at his youngest brother.

"You disappeared."

Viktor wasn't surprised that Ilya was the one to voice it. He decided the kid was a hothead. He was looking for an excuse to move against Viktor.

"You have a problem with me, kid?"

"I'm not a kid," Ilya said. "And yeah, I've got a problem with you. Thirty years and you never once walked up and introduced yourself."

"I saved your worthless ass on at least seven occasions."

"So what? You didn't so much as say hello."

He hadn't. That much was true. He'd managed to see Gavriil a time or two, and Stefan once, but Ilya he'd watched over as best he could, and he'd interfered when Sorbacov had put his baby brother in situations there was no coming back from. He'd had one of his Torpedo Ink brothers checking constantly. It had been one of them tipping the scales on all but two occasions. It wasn't like he could drop what he was doing and get to Ilya fast enough. Not with hundreds of miles between them most of the time.

He shrugged. He wasn't about to explain himself. Not to any of them. He couldn't help but be conflicted. He'd suffered endless torture for these six men. They hadn't asked him to do it—their father had. He'd kept that promise and they had grown up, served their country and now had families.

He glanced toward the kitchen. To Blythe. She'd saved him. Not only had she saved him, but she'd saved seventeen others as well. His angel. He hadn't believed in angels, but then he'd marked one as prey and she'd turned his world upside down.

Baby, I don't know how to do this. He reached out to her before he could stop himself. He realized he was stroking his thumb back and forth across the center of his palm. It was a bad habit he'd developed since he'd first met her.

"Who are these people you're traveling with?" Ilya asked.

"I'm here on a job." Viktor watched their faces closely. They didn't give anything away, and he hadn't expected them to. They were trained agents.

"Tell us," Gavriil instructed.

"Viktor." Blythe came to the arched entry that was the only break between the great room, dining room and kitchen. "I could use your help carrying all these mugs. Can I borrow you, just for a moment?"

He was on his feet immediately, striding across the room, his arm sweeping around her as he moved with her through the dining room to the kitchen. He noted the archways were wide enough to accommodate both of them. The moment they were inside the room, he stepped away from the open passageway and swept her into his arms, burying his face between her shoulder and neck. Inhaling her. Taking her deep.

She was his safe haven. The only safe haven he'd ever known. She didn't understand that, didn't know just what she was to him, but he made a silent vow that she would.

Tell me what to do.

She held herself away from him at first, a little stiff, but at the question he'd pushed into her mind she melted, her body going soft and pliant. His. All his. It had been far too long since he'd been with a woman, but especially his woman. His body recognized her immediately and made urgent demands of its own. He was a man with iron control and he remembered that feeling of complete and utter exultation, knowing there was a woman who could arouse him naturally.

Just talk to them. Ask them questions about their lives. Just like you started to do with Ilya. Tell them why you're here. Talk to them about your other brothers and sisters and why they're important to you.

He could do that. It didn't seem that difficult. He could talk to anyone in any situation, he was trained and had skills, so it didn't make sense that he was all over the place because they were his birth brothers. Not, he decided, that any of them were doing much better.

"Thanks, baby," he said softly, meaning it.

He looped her ponytail in his fist and pulled back her head, bending to take her mouth. Her lips were soft and tasted of tangerine. Her tongue tangled with his. Danced. Teased. Was provocative. He loved that about her. She couldn't resist him any more than he could resist her.

When he knew he should stop or he wouldn't be able to, he lifted his head and rested his forehead against hers. "Give me a chance, Blythe. That's all I'm asking. Just give me a chance."

She moistened her lips and her long lashes veiled her eyes. Before she could deny him even that much, he turned away from her to pick up the tray with the coffee mugs. She caught up a plate of cookies and followed him out into the great room.

"You were going to tell us about this job of yours," Gavriil encouraged.

Viktor nodded and caught at Blythe and pulled her down next to him before she could escape. "Yes. I've been riding with the Swords for the last five years, working my way up the ranks to enforcer for the New Orleans chapter president. That's Evan Shackler-Gratsos's original chapter. It was also Jackson Deveau's father's chapter. If there's one man on earth Evan hates more than anyone else, it's Jackson. He wants him dead. He might never have done anything about it but Jackson had the bad grace to marry Elle Drake and actually be happy."

He kept his eye on Ilya. The man was reputed to be very close friends with Jackson Deveau, and Elle Drake was his sister-in-law. Viktor stretched one arm along the back of the love seat to curl it around Blythe. He liked her close to him. With his other hand he raised the coffee mug to his lips.

"And?" Maxim said.

"Shackler inherited billions from his brother, but also a huge international shipping company. As international president of the Swords, he had already built his own empire on human trafficking. It's outdoing drugs and he caught on to that very early. With the ships, he can charge an outrageous amount of money to special clients with special needs. They like to kill their victims after or during the time they use them."

Maxim nodded. "I ran into them a few weeks back. Four of the children are with me now. I couldn't save their sister." There was regret, even sorrow in his voice.

"Evan is extremely paranoid. He moves constantly and isn't easily tracked. By the time I get to one hideout, he's already gone. Deveau marrying Elle Drake changed all that. As a member of the Swords club I knew sooner or later I'd get a chance at him; now I'm certain of it. He sent me here, without wearing colors, to set up a camp for more Swords to come in. I'm supposed to find out everything there is to know about the security around Jackson and his wife. From the way it looks to me, he plans on killing Deveau and taking the wife."

There was silence. Ilya pinned him with the same silvery eyes. Their father's eyes. "What are your plans?"

"I'm going to talk to Deveau and Elle Drake. I have to

do it carefully. We just arrived so I need to scout around and make certain Evan didn't send any other scouts ahead. It's like him to put something like that into play. My brothers are on that now."

"What brothers?" Maxim asked. It was asked a little belligerently.

There it was. The question he knew would come. The only person he would ever tell his story to was Blythe. No one else. In the telling he would be revealing things to her about the others, things that were nobody else's business. Still, it was important to him to integrate his two families. On the other hand, he wasn't about to apologize to any of them, not after what he'd done for them.

"There were only eighteen survivors of my school. We formed a family of sorts." A very lethal one. "We watch one another's backs, and they watched yours. When I was given the assignment to go after Evan, they were already disappearing because Sorbacov would put a hit out on one of them after some trumped-up offense. We knew it was a matter of time before he went after all of us. We devised a plan to escape, but once I really looked into Evan, I knew he had to be taken down." Viktor wasn't about to tell them the real reason he took the assignment, not with Ilya in the room.

"One by one they came out of hiding and joined the Swords in order to back me up. When this is over, I plan to live here. It's Blythe's home and she needs to be here with her sisters and all of you. That means I make this my home. And they'll be with us."

He didn't dare look at Blythe's face. Fortunately, he'd chosen well, and she didn't contradict him in front of the others. He would have to thank her for that later. He massaged the tension gathering in the back of her neck.

"You plan on settling here with seventeen other men?" Stefan asked.

"Two of them are women."

Blythe moved, a subtle retreat, but he settled his fingers around the nape of her neck and kept her close.

"We plan to purchase some land and houses. Set up businesses. Go legit. Or as legit as we're able to go. We have our own club with our own colors."

"Bikers," Ilya said. "Outlaws."

"Of sorts." More like assassins, and every single one of his brothers knew that. They weren't all clean, with the exception—maybe—of his baby brother.

10

THERE was a longer silence while his brothers did exactly what Viktor was doing—drinking coffee to give themselves a little time to figure out how to respond to that. Blythe bit her lip to keep from breaking the silence. *Seventeen* others? Good God. Was he crazy? If they all were as scary as his friend Reaper, then she was moving out and leaving the house to all of them. His birth brothers could deal with them.

"So you plan to bring an outlaw biker club with you to settle here. Blythe?" Ilya looked straight at Viktor's wife. "How do you feel about that?"

Viktor's fingers tightened involuntarily on the nape of her neck in warning. She moistened suddenly dry lips, feeling as if she were walking through a minefield with all the Prakenskiis.

"I want Viktor to have a home near his brothers—his family," she hastily added. "If these other men and women mean that to him—that they're family as well—then of course they should be close to him." That was as diplomatic as she could possibly make it. She stumbled a little under every single one of the Prakenskii brothers' eyes. They were weighing her words, watching to see if she was under duress of any kind.

Of course she was under duress with Viktor back and all of them watching her like hawks. She took another deep breath. "And all of you should accept them into the family."

"All of *us*, Blythe?" Gavriil said very gently. He rarely spoke above a low tone, but for some reason, one could always hear and understand him.

A faint tremor went down her back. She'd made a mistake and she could feel it. Although it didn't show on their faces, they knew.

"Blythe, why don't we go get some beer for everyone rather than this coffee," Ilya suggested.

"Why don't you leave my wife the hell alone," Viktor snapped, sitting up straight. Menace poured off of him in waves.

Immediately tension ratcheted up another notch. Blythe despised being the bone of contention, but really? Seventeen members of an outlaw biker club in her home? On the farm? What?

"That's still to be determined," Lev said. "I think I'd like to go with Blythe and Ilya into the other room and talk this out."

"Maybe the two of you can step outside with me and I'll teach you some manners. Whether you like it or not, I'm still the head of this family, and Blythe is most definitely my wife."

"Fuck that," Ilya said crudely. "You don't show up after thirty years of silence and decide we're going to follow your lead. It doesn't work that way, and just for your information, Blythe is *our* family."

Viktor was out of his chair so fast Blythe didn't have time to catch ahold of his arm. Ilya and Lev both leapt up as well.

"Seriously?" Gavriil's voice was calm. He didn't move from his chair. "That's how you plan on handling this situation? Sit down, you two, unless you want him to beat you to a bloody pulp."

"He couldn't," Ilya stated.

"He could," Gavriil said. "What's more, he would. He is

the head of the family whether you want to accept that or not. Blythe is his wife. You wouldn't allow anyone to interfere in your relationship with Joley any more than I would allow it with Lexi."

Ilya shook his head. "He was gone thirty years. He didn't do a fucking thing for me, for any of us. He has his own family and has chosen to become an outlaw biker."

Blythe inhaled sharply. That wasn't true. *All* of them had made bargains with the devil in order to keep their youngest brother as clean as possible. He went to the least brutal school. He worked for Interpol in a legitimate business. She knew they'd all looked after him. Her sisters had told her how much keeping the baby of the family as clean as possible meant to them all.

She expected Viktor to object, but instead, he went absolutely still and then like ice. At least his exterior was like ice. Beneath that glacier was a red-hot volcanic roiling mass that could explode at any time.

"That's enough, Ilya," Gavriil said quietly. "You have no idea what you're talking about."

Viktor paced across the room to the wide stone fireplace, his back to his brothers. He stood staring at the pictures on the mantle, and Blythe found herself standing as well, suddenly terrified for him. There was nothing she could say or do; it was already too late. She knew the exact moment when he saw it. His hand reached out and his body jerked as though someone had punched him hard right in the gut.

She'd framed it in gold filigree. The calligraphy said *Held with love, surrounded by two loving hearts.* Their daughter, Viktoria. She'd lived two days, and a nurse had taken a picture of the tiny infant lying on Blythe's stomach. It was the only picture she had of their child and she'd put the only picture she had of Viktor on the other side, so their child had her mother and father with her in that moment. She'd had the same picture put on canvas for her wall in her sitting room, but for him to see this now . . .

Viktor's finger stroked a gentle caress over the infant as if he could somehow touch her through the glass. Blythe had done the exact same thing so many times she worried she'd wear down the glass. Grief filled the room, so strong, so intense she couldn't stop herself from going to him. For her it was five years. For him, their child had just died. How much more could he take?

She wrapped her arms around him and just held him, feeling the shudders go through his body as he tried to remain upright and unbowed in facing the reality of the death of their child. There was silence in the room. She knew the Prakenskiis were gifted, she just didn't know in what way. She had no way of knowing if they felt his grief. He wouldn't like that. He wouldn't want to appear vulnerable in any way. She desperately wanted to shield him, she just didn't know how.

Blythe knew the others couldn't see the picture, not with Viktor in front of it. She slipped around Viktor until her front was pressed tightly to his side. The position enabled her to reach up to the mantle.

"Gavriil is with Lexi," she said softly, reaching up to touch Lexi's picture. "She's the youngest and a sweetheart. You'll love her immediately, Viktor. No one can help it. Isn't that right, Gavriil?" She'd chosen him because he remembered his brother. He knew what Viktor had gone through, at least part of it. He'd help her defuse the volatile situation and at the same time give Viktor the minutes he needed to recover.

Gavriil stood up as well and came to the fireplace. She thought his approach was interesting. He didn't come up behind them, but rather from an angle, keeping his pace slow and deliberate. His eyes were on the pictures. Not Lexi's, but the one his brother had touched so gently. He reached out as if he would touch Viktor's shoulder.

"Don't." One word from Viktor. A warning. A statement.

Gavriil's hand moved to Lexi's picture. "I'm working on getting her to marry me. She said yes, but we haven't actually gotten to the priest. I'm afraid if I push it, she'll run. She's a beautiful person, inside and out, and she has tremendous patience with me. I can't wait for you to meet her."

There was the smallest of tremors in Viktor's hand when he took the picture from Gavriil. That nearly imperceptible shake made Blythe's heart clench in reaction. She knew Gavriil had to see it because he didn't miss anything. She knew if he looked at her she would shatter. She moved closer to Viktor, if it was at all possible, her fingers curling tightly in the tee that was stretched across his broad chest. At once Viktor's hand covered hers.

"I'd love to meet her. As soon as this mess is over, Gavriil, I'll be more than happy to meet my future sister-in-law. I take it she's the one who works the farm." Viktor's voice was rock steady. He turned Blythe away from the fireplace, wrapping his arms around her as he did so.

She remembered the feeling of being safe and protected from earlier, when they were together. Viktor could do that, wrap her up in his strength. He would fight for her if there were need. He would console her and comfort her. He was the one needing those things, yet the moment she was distressed, he offered them to her.

"I cook," Lev volunteered before anyone else could say anything. "Maybe we should throw a big party."

"Barbecue," Maxim added. "The women can make all those side dishes that are so good. And Lucia makes this dessert that's sheer heaven. I'm putting on weight with that girl's cooking. Airiana and I are adopting Lucia and her sisters and brother. Benito is a mini-me, unfortunately, and determined to keep his sisters from ever coming to harm again. Expect him to come down Blythe's chimney or something."

Blythe was certain they'd read the grief filling the room. They didn't understand it, but several of Viktor's brothers glanced at the framed pictures she kept on the mantle. She knew they were unable to see what had upset their oldest brother, because Viktor had deliberately turned the picture away from their line of sight, but they followed Gavriil's lead in spite of the tension between them all.

"Sounds good," Viktor said. "I want to meet all the wives."

"If you don't mind," Blythe said, "I need a little air." She could barely breathe, Viktor's emotions choking her. She wished she could be stoic like him, an expression of stone, cold eyes and steady hands. Once past the initial moment, that first piercing of his heart, he had stood unbending. She hoped if she got Viktor out of the room, Gavriil would be able to talk his brothers into being kinder. He saw the photograph.

"We'll be right back," Viktor said immediately. He took her hand and, without another glance at his brothers, led her out onto her spacious wraparound covered porch.

Right in front of her stood the man Viktor had called "Reaper." He rested one hip against a tree, eating an apple. Blythe narrowed her eyes at him. "Is that my apple?"

"Yes." Reaper kept eating.

That meant, with all the Prakenskii brothers, including Gavriil, in her living room, Reaper had entered her kitchen undetected. That was a scary thought.

"Is *everyone* still here?"

Reaper paused in the act of taking another bite. He nodded. "Yep."

"Are they *all* eating my apples?"

Reaper nodded again. "Yep."

Blythe couldn't help it. She knew she shouldn't encourage Viktor or his brothers, but Reaper standing there without expression, looking scary with his tattoos and badass persona, eating an apple he'd filched from her kitchen, was too funny. She burst out laughing.

"Have you eaten anything tonight?"

Reaper glanced down at the mostly eaten apple. "This apple."

"You're not going to fix them all food. Get out of here," Viktor snapped before she could offer. "I mean it, Reaper. Take everyone with you."

"Not gonna happen, Czar."

"Do you think my own birth brothers are going to take out a gun and shoot me?"

"Sounded like it," Reaper said. "'Course I would have blown his fuckin' head off first," he added in the same casual tone. "Maybe one or two of the others, but Savage, Storm and Ice would have taken them."

Blythe shivered. For a moment she'd forgotten she was dealing with men who had no compunction about killing. Reaper was so casual, as if he was talking about the weather. These men were trained assassins. She'd thought Gavriil was bad, that the others had done what they needed to do to survive. Yes, they were capable of killing if they had no other choice, but Viktor and Reaper and probably the others would make it their choice. They didn't seem to have a middle ground.

"You don't lay a finger on those boys," Viktor said, his tone low and mean.

"Wasn't plannin' on using my hands, Czar. A bullet would have worked." Reaper sounded as calm as ever.

"Get. The. Fuck. Out."

Blythe threw her hands into the air. "That's it. I'm done. I'm at my absolute limit. Viktor, leave. Take your men with you. All of them. I'm going in and going to bed."

She turned and Viktor's six birth brothers were fanned out behind them, all staring at Reaper with cool eyes.

"And you. All of you. Go home. I'm perfectly fine. *Perfectly* fine. I'm sorry you got called out in the middle of the night, and I thank you for coming, but go home. Ilya and Lev, both of you should be ashamed of yourselves. Your brother comes home and instead of welcoming him you are nasty and mean. I'm ashamed of both of you. I don't care what resentments you harbor, the least you could have done was ask him how he is. Now go. All of you."

She pulled away from Viktor, stomped right through the wall of Prakenskii brothers, slammed her screen and then the door, flipped off the porch light and stormed upstairs.

She was shaking by the time she got to the top of the stairs. Hopefully no one got killed on her front porch. If they did, she was burying them out in the forest and then she was getting in her car and driving away.

Sinking down onto the top stair, she covered her face with her hands and let herself cry. She thought she wouldn't have any more tears, but Viktor had unleashed an entire flood. She didn't even bother to listen to hear if the men came to blows or not. Eventually she made her way up to the master bedroom. Viktor's scent was everywhere. His ragged denim jacket was on the end of her bed.

She should have tossed it out of her room, but she couldn't. Instead, she ignored it completely, took a hot, scented bath in the hopes that her perfume would cover Viktor's outdoorsy, spicy smell, the one she loved, and got ready for bed. In the end she picked up his jacket, held it to her like a favorite blanket, pulled up her covers, turned off her light and went to sleep from sheer exhaustion.

BLYTHE came awake fast, aware she wasn't alone. She took in the air around her to try to determine who was in the room with her and if she was in danger or not.

"Are you awake?"

She recognized the voice. Reaper. Viktor's friend. She immediately sat up, clutching Viktor's jacket to her, thankful she hadn't slept in the nude as she normally did. She'd been a little afraid Viktor might show up, and she didn't want to feel vulnerable. Anxiety gripped her. She pushed back the hair tumbling in her face and looked frantically around for Viktor. Reaper had to be able to hear her heart pounding. She felt like her heart might just come right out of her chest.

"Is something wrong? Did something happen to him?" She pushed back the covers quickly. "Take me to him. I'll call Libby. She's home and she can heal anything." There was no hiding the sudden terror in her voice. Viktor had just come home. Had Evan found out already that he was undercover? Had they shot him? Killed him? Had his birth brothers lost their minds and attacked him?

Reaper shook his head as she dropped both legs to the floor in preparation for finding her clothes. She didn't even have time to be embarrassed about being caught in her thin, racer-back night tee and little boy shorts, or that she had Viktor's jacket held so tightly against her. Only then did she become aware they weren't alone. She turned her head toward the corner where her reading chair was. A woman was curled up there watching her closely—the same woman who had been sitting so casually, as if she belonged, on the back of Viktor's motorcycle.

Blythe took a deep breath when everything inside her felt frozen. Very slowly she set the denim jacket on the bed beside her as if she'd been caught doing something wrong. "What's going on?" Before anything else, she had to know Viktor was alive and well.

"I'd never let anything happen to him," Reaper assured her. "Savage and the others are watching over him, but I wanted to talk to you. We both did."

"I see," Blythe said, but she didn't at all. Now she felt at a distinct disadvantage. The woman in the corner was younger than she was, and really beautiful. She wore makeup while Blythe had carefully washed what little makeup she wore right off.

"We're not here to threaten you in any way," Reaper said.

He had the deadest eyes of any man she'd ever seen. She just managed to keep from shivering looking at him. He was cold, through and through. Yet he was intensely loyal to Viktor, and she could like him for that.

She nodded her head and held on to calm. She had always remained calm in the face of her mother's shrieking temper tantrums. She could apply those childhood lessons here very well. Her fingers crept down and across the sheets to the edge of the jacket. A talisman. Reaper saw, but she didn't care what she was revealing to him. "Do you want something to eat? Drink? I'm sure I could manage to find you both something." She kept her tone friendly, but not too friendly. She didn't want them to see through her façade.

"I'm going to turn on the light," Reaper warned. "I want to show you something."

She wrapped her arms around her middle. Viktor had been the most immodest man she'd ever met. Nudity meant nothing at all to him. He'd been the one to get her to sleep without clothes. He liked to make love to her in their backyard. Once on their front porch in the dead of night. He didn't seem to see anything wrong with touching her no matter where they were, and he liked her to do the same. Once, she'd been very brave and she'd dropped to her knees after skinny-dipping with him in the river and she'd sucked him off, the forbidden of being outdoors in the open adding to the excitement.

Reaper slowly removed his jacket and then pulled up his tee with one hand. She just kept from gasping when she saw his body. Viktor had scars, but nothing like what Reaper's body held. They were everywhere. Burn marks, old knife wounds, bullet scars, at least one kind of whip, other scars she couldn't identify but thought they had been made by worse things she had no idea of.

He turned his back to her. "Alena. Come here. I want you to show her while I explain."

Alena gracefully slid from the chair like a slinky cat, moving with the same fluid ripple of muscle the men surrounding her did. "I'm Alena." She introduced herself as she stepped to the other side of Blythe. "I've wanted to meet you for a very long time."

Blythe forced a small smile. Alena didn't sound like the "other woman." Wouldn't she be there to cut her into little pieces if Viktor was her man? She was more confused than ever. Part of her knew she'd held on to the belief that Alena was Viktor's woman in order to keep him at arm's length. Once again, because she was a little afraid of what they planned, she let her hand slide over Viktor's jacket.

"I want you to take a good look at this tattoo." Reaper's voice was as dead as his eyes. Low. So low it was almost a thread of sound, yet at the same time, it was commanding and cold. There would be no disobeying that voice, not without knowing the consequences would be death.

Blythe willingly obliged him. She stared at the rather gruesome tattoo that took up a good deal of his back.

"It's important for you to know just who and what Viktor really is. Why we ride with him. Why we protect him. You see the tree trunk. That's Viktor. He was thirteen when I came to the school. I was four and my brother was three when we were taken from our parents. There were two hundred eighty-seven students that over the years were brought to that school. Eighteen of us survived. You see the limbs of the trees? There are seventeen of them."

Alena touched each of the branches on Reaper's back.

"Viktor saved all seventeen of us. He didn't just save our lives. He saved our humanity. Or at least he managed to save most of our humanity."

Blythe's gaze jumped to Reaper's face as he looked back at her over his shoulder. She knew he was telling her he had no humanity left in him, and she believed him. Whatever this man had been through had been worse than hell.

"The crows in the trees represent the children we couldn't save. They carry the skulls of the ones we killed to avenge them."

Alena touched the crows almost reverently and then stepped away as Reaper reached for his shirt and yanked it back over his head.

"The skulls on the ground? In the roots?"

"Each of us has a different number. We're assassins. That's what they trained us for and that's what they had us do for the government. Others we killed to survive. Each of us carries the weight of that on our skin."

She raised her eyes to his. There had been piles of skulls in that root system, so many she wasn't certain she could count them all. This was the scariest man she'd ever run across. "You're telling me this because . . ."

"I can't tell you why Viktor fought to save us, only that

he did. He's a good man. They don't come better. He still fights for us. In all the time I've ever known him, the only things he's asked for were to help him keep his birth brothers safe and to watch over you. You're everything to him."

Blythe made an involuntary movement away from him as he turned back around, rejecting what he was telling her. She shook her head, carefully threading her fingers together, Viktor's jacket between them to give her courage. She didn't feel any threat from either of the two; in fact she couldn't feel Reaper's emotions at all. Only Alena's.

"Ink, one of our brothers, began that sketch when we were teenagers. Eventually he perfected it and we took it as our symbol. We call ourselves Torpedo Ink."

Blythe knew that in Russia, sometimes a hit man or assassin was referred to as a torpedo. The *Ink* could be a play on the word *incorporated*. Whatever the reason for their name, no one should take it at face value, least of all her. These were the men and women Viktor expected her to take in along with some unknown teenaged girl. She crushed his jacket in her fist.

"Why a motorcycle club? Won't that get you unwanted attention? All of you have had to be so careful not to draw attention to yourselves."

"We ride because it makes us feel free when we've never been free. Viktor gave us that as well. It was difficult to remove our colors and ride with the Swords, but we'd follow him anywhere."

Alena nodded solemnly. "I'd be dead if it wasn't for Viktor. He figured out a way to keep us alive in that horrible place. We made it through because of him. I know it looked bad, me being on the bike, but the Swords would never have believed him staying away from other women if he didn't have an 'old lady.' It protected both of us to pretend. I swear to you, he's a big brother to me, nothing else."

Blythe didn't know what to say, so she remained silent. She had mixed feelings about them coming to her in the middle of the night on Viktor's behalf, mostly because it made her like them, and she didn't want to feel anything at all for them—especially Reaper. She worried that he was incapable of feeling true emotion, but clearly, he felt something for Viktor.

She cleared her throat. "So you had actually formed a club *before* Viktor rode with the Swords."

Reaper nodded. "We found riding motorcycles and the structure of a family, knowing we had one another's backs at all times, no matter what assignment we took, kept us sane. Well"—he glanced at Alena—"some of us sane."

"You're sane, Reaper," she reprimanded softly. "And we were a brotherhood, a family, long before the club."

Reaper shrugged and turned all his attention back to Blythe. "After Viktor met you, he was different. I thought we'd lose him before that. All of us watched him so carefully."

That brought her head up. "What do you mean, lose him?"

"The deaths of all those other children weighed on him so heavily. He blamed himself for not being able to prevent them," he explained. "Hell, he was ten when he got there. Some of the kids were older than he was. Still, that didn't matter. His sense of responsibility was already so developed that he took on that burden. Sometimes, he just couldn't live with it."

For a moment she couldn't breathe. Just the thought of Viktor killing himself was too much after reliving the death of her daughter with him. Involuntarily she brought the jacket to her face and held it there for a moment, uncaring what either of them thought.

She remembered more than one night waking up to Viktor sitting on the edge of the bed, head in hands, sweat beading his body, his breath coming in ragged pants as if he'd run a marathon. He wouldn't talk to her, so she talked to him in the only way she could; she made love to him, fiercely protective, wholly surrendering to him, giving him everything he demanded and needed. He held her so tightly afterward she thought every bone in her body might break, but she never protested. Eventually he fell asleep, and she would watch over him as if she could prevent whatever terrible nightmares might creep into their world. The idea that Viktor might ever contemplate ending his life was terrifying to her.

"Once he met you, his entire world seemed to change. He was happy. He actually laughed. He was just different. When he had to leave you, he was devastated. He planned to get back to you immediately, but Absinthe was shot all to hell and in the middle of a very bad situation. Viktor was the closest, so he went to try to save him. They had to hole up for a few weeks, and then Sorbacov gave him an assignment."

She realized that Reaper was uncomfortable not only telling her so much, but actually talking. He was stepping out of his usual role to advocate for a man he clearly loved. That made her want to listen when before she'd been reluctant to know anything more about Viktor or his life without her.

"You didn't ever turn down Sorbacov or you found several hit men at your door. More, Sorbacov threatened his brothers. He sent you messages, Blythe. I saw them. He tried to get his birth brothers to check up on you. Eventually we did, but you were here at that time and seemed fine and happy. No one knew why you wouldn't reply back. He could only assume it was because you were angry with him and justifiably so. He thought if he could get here to talk to you he could explain everything."

She knew what he was telling her was the truth. She ached inside for both of them—Viktor and her. "There are things that happened while he was gone," she said softly, trying to explain without telling them. She couldn't go there again, not at night, not when she was alone and Viktor was so close. "Sometimes things happen that make it impossible to go back." She prayed he wouldn't ask because she had the feeling one didn't tell Reaper no when he asked a question. Maybe he already knew. He'd been on the roof when Viktor and she had been talking.

Alena sat on the bed beside her. "You don't have to go back, Blythe," she said gently. "Only forward. Viktor taught us that. Whatever happened to you, and I know it was bad because Viktor was a mess tonight, you have to keep going forward. Hopefully with him. Just give him a chance to talk to you. To really talk to you and you hear what he's saying to you. I know no one will ever love you more or better."

She found herself nodding when everything in her screamed for self-preservation. She moistened suddenly dry lips before she could actually find her voice. "Viktor isn't the kind of man to give up when he wants something."

"That's true," Alena said, "but he likes that you have a good life here, and he doesn't want to mess that up for you. He comes with baggage—with us." She looked at Reaper and then down at her hands.

It was the first time that Alena seemed uncertain, and at first Blythe thought it might be affected, as if she was playing a role to get sympathy. Alena had been trained to appear as anything she wanted to be just as Viktor and Reaper had. The one thing a person couldn't do was fake emotion around her. Blythe felt that uncertainty.

"What are your plans?" she asked gently, because it was in her nature to soothe others in distress.

"We're looking at land in the Caspar area. There's a lot of land and houses for sale there, and we'd need to be able to purchase land that is zoned for businesses as well. We've never actually had a home base. We thought Ink could have a tattoo shop. I'd like a restaurant. I love to cook and for lots of people. Something small, but nice. Keys, Master, Player and Maestro would like to have a small club so they could play regularly, and there's a roadhouse for sale. That would be awesome to have." Enthusiasm poured into her voice. "Transporter and Mechanic would love their own garage where they could build custom cars and bikes and just tinker all day."

Blythe looked up at Reaper's blank features. He could have been carved from stone. The lines in his face cut deep. There weren't going to be any plans for a shop for him. She couldn't imagine how he could possibly integrate back into society. For that matter, she doubted if any of them could.

The Prakenskii brothers hadn't, not really. Stefan did help Judith with the art gallery, and Lev went out with Rikki on the boat to dive for sea urchins. Maxim headed up security for Airiana, who worked for the defense department. Gavriil stayed close to Lexi on the farm, far away from people. Casimir had just returned with Lissa, and Blythe had no idea what his plans were.

"Don't say no to him because of us," Reaper said. It was the first time his voice was a little gruff. It had dropped an octave, causing Blythe to search his face. There was no expression, but something worked behind those cold, cold eyes.

"I wouldn't do that," Blythe said. "Really, my problems with Viktor have nothing to do with any of you."

Just being in the same room with Reaper tore her heart out. She could see why Viktor kept close watch over him. It was heartbreaking to see and feel him. And Alena . . . The woman was young and clearly lethal. Blythe had that built-in radar, her compass when it came to reading people. As a child she had known there was something "off" about her mother. Alena looked like the sweetest innocent, but she felt . . . dangerous.

"But still, you *want* to give him a chance, don't you?"

Those soft words brushed at the walls of her mind and Blythe instantly recoiled. Simultaneously, Reaper let out a low growl. *"Alena.* We agreed. No manipulation. Not on Blythe. She's one of us. She's Viktor's chosen woman. His wife, and that's sacred."

At the reprimand, Alena's eyes swam with tears and her barriers came tumbling down. The force of her fears hit Blythe so hard she reeled under the impact. Alena was terrified. What would Reaper do to her?

"I'm sorry, I'm really, really sorry, Blythe. I did promise Reaper before we came here, but I'm so afraid of losing Viktor."

The relief was tremendous. Alena wasn't afraid of Reaper's retaliation; she was afraid for Viktor. There was no faking that overwhelming fear. With relief came trepidation. If his "family" was so afraid of losing him, it had to be real. Now that she'd seen him, now that she knew something or someone else had prevented him from getting to her, she knew she couldn't live with knowing he wasn't somewhere in the world.

"I'll talk to him, but I can't promise anything. When he shot Ray, dropped the gun and then grabbed me, whispering he'd be back in a couple of days to explain, I barely registered it. Later, when the police confirmed who Ray really was, it was all I could think about. I thought maybe he was a boy Ray had harmed, or his brother had been and it was a revenge thing. I didn't know much about the Prakenskiis until Lev arrived. My cousin Joley is married to Ilya Prakenskii, the youngest brother, but I don't exactly move in their circles so I've never actually talked to Ilya about his brothers."

"Ilya seemed protective of you."

Her gaze once again jumped to Reaper's face. There was no expression and his eyes were back to being dead, but he'd been there in the house somewhere, watching over Viktor. Even the Prakenskiis hadn't known or they wouldn't have allowed it. Not even Gavriil, and he was much like Viktor. Even while it had made her a little uncomfortable that Reaper could be in her house unseen, she was grateful that he was the one dedicated to protecting Viktor.

"All the Prakenskiis have an extremely protective instinct. Joley is my cousin. That makes me family. They also have a huge sense of family."

"We do too," Alena said.

"We'd better go," Reaper said. "Viktor would beat the shit out of me if he knew I was here. And I have to tell him. I still have that to do."

"Alena, just one thing," Blythe said. "So we understand each other. Manipulation doesn't work on me. I feel the energy and emotion when you're using it and it's easy enough to avoid."

Alena's smile was slow in coming, but when it did, it

was full and real. "Good to know." She stood up. "Thanks for listening to us."

"Anytime, but, Reaper, please don't make a habit of midnight visits. I often sleep without clothes."

"Wouldn't bother me."

She sighed. She had the feeling he was telling her the strict truth.

11

VIKTOR studied the surrounding land from where he sat on his bike. The ocean was straight in front of him and today it was acting up as if a storm was brewing. He liked the Northern California coast. The ocean could be wild and quite violent at times and at others, as clear as glass. The various moods suited him.

He lifted his face to catch the wind coming in off the sea. There was quite a bit of land for sale in the small village of Caspar. At one time the town must have thrived, but over the years, the lack of jobs had reduced it to more of a ghost town. He liked the idea of purchasing most of what had been the town along with several houses. They could do a lot with the place. He'd like to make certain each of them had the shop or restaurant that they had long ago dreamt of. It wasn't too late for any of them . . . he hoped. The two he worried the most about, Reaper and Savage, he had no idea what they'd do.

The roar of four Harleys told him the two brothers were on their way back to him with two others. Judging from the sound, Ice and Storm, Alena's birth brothers, were with them. They'd been scouting around for some time. The others were still in the camps they'd set up in a campground with the interesting name of Jughandle. It wasn't a place for the Swords, too many civilians, but it gave Torpedo Ink access to both Sea Haven and Fort Bragg.

It had been too many days—three—since he'd talked to Blythe. She'd disappeared. He knew she hadn't gone back home because he'd spent the last three nights on her bed. She wasn't at any of her "sisters'" homes either. He'd checked. Repeatedly.

He had a job to do, and if he didn't get his mind right soon, it would get him killed. Better that than to try to live without her. He figured his next move was to just ask one of her sisters. They'd probably slam the door in his face, but he'd keep after them until he found her. He'd learned as a child, if he wanted to survive, if he needed anything from food for the other kids to medical supplies or information, to just keep pushing until he got his way.

Reaper and Savage pulled up on one side of him, Ice and Storm on the other. He glanced at them and then back at the ocean. Trouble. He knew it was coming. It had left him alone a little bit too long.

"Tell me."

All four men shut down the motors and stayed, like him, straddling their bikes.

"You were right. That bastard is up to his old games. He sent another team in, but they're watching us, not establishing a campground. They're in Sea Haven right now, acting like fools. Getting rowdy with the locals. Someone is going to call the sheriff, and it's going to turn into a bloodbath. From what I saw of those two, Harrington and Deveau, there's no backup in them," Reaper said.

"Are they watching the farm?" He kept his eyes on the crashing waves, stillness settling in him. He was used to trouble. To action. He needed it, and the Swords were delivering it up to him like sacrificial lambs.

Ice answered. "I followed them. They hung out at the local bar, right there on the main street. I could have done them all when they came out. Loudmouthed. Drawing attention to themselves. They're here for a covert operation but they're making asses out of themselves."

Viktor frowned. "Maybe they're supposed to find us and camp with us, the first wave before the others come." He hoped not. He was restless and edgy. That was always a bad sign with him. He needed the action, the same as Reaper, Savage and the others.

Savage shook his head. "Caught two of them spying on our camp. Spent a bit of time with them, that's what made us go to town looking for the others."

Viktor scowled at him. "You spent time with them?"

"Needed information, Czar," Savage said. "Caught the bastards red-handed ogling Alena while she was showering."

"I'll just bet she stripped nice and slow for them, kept their attention on her while the two of you crept up on them and 'caught them red-handed.'"

"No need for sarcasm. Alena can't help but be beautiful," Ice said. "But no one's going to watch my sister shower when she thinks she's alone."

Fat chance Alena thought she was alone. If Savage caught them, it was because Alena deliberately put on a show to keep their attention. It was the easiest trick in the book and one his family had used even as children. Alena and Lana had both used that technique more than once when they were trapping the worst of the pedophiles in the school.

"I don't want any blowback. Seriously, we're going to establish ourselves here. We can't have bodies turning up," Viktor cautioned. "Especially if they have any marks on them due to a 'talk.'"

Savage shrugged. "Nice thing about this part of the country is lots of places for bodies. No one is going to be finding them."

"Make certain. And make certain nothing can be traced back to you."

Savage didn't bother to answer a second time, nor did Viktor expect him to.

"Are they wearing their colors?"

"No, but they're talking loudly," Storm said. "They want everyone to be afraid of them. It's rather obvious. Deveau or Harrington sees them, for certain there's going to be a confrontation."

"How many?"

"Six in town. The other two don't matter much now," Ice answered.

Viktor sighed. "I want all of you to listen to me. You don't have to stay here and make this our home base. You don't. The only tie you have to this place is me. I have Blythe, and I need her."

He didn't talk feelings with his brothers, it just wasn't done, but someone had to lead the way into another life. None of them would survive if they kept going as they were. "I'm not going to lie to you about that. It's make it or not for me here. We keep doing what we are, sooner or later we'll cross a line we can't come back from. I'm not willing to do that."

"What the fuck, Czar," Reaper snapped. "No one's looking to leave."

"Then we can't make it a practice to kill in our own backyard."

Storm made a sound like he was choking. Viktor turned his head to glare at him, but a part of him couldn't help being a little pleased that Storm found anything he said funny. None of them laughed much. They didn't have much to laugh about. They certainly never showed a humorous side to anyone other than their brothers and sisters.

"What's so funny?"

"'We can't make it a practice to kill in our own backyard.' We *learned* in our own backyard. It's what we did and what we do," Ice answered for his brother. "You think we're suddenly going to be going to church on Sundays?"

Okay, maybe it was a little funny. Viktor kept his face expressionless. "If I say we go to church, we go to church," he declared.

Storm and Ice looked at each other and then at Reaper

and Savage. Reaper let out a sigh. "It's a pun, you morons. We go to church every time we have an official meeting."

Viktor let a smile slip through. "Idiots."

"Very funny. I thought I was totally screwed for a minute there," Storm said. "I was sweating."

Ice shook his head. "You took a few years off my life with that one. You're getting all weird on us, Czar. Maybe you really would want us to go to Sunday school."

"You could use it," Viktor informed him.

"Like we don't get enough sermons from you already," Storm muttered.

Viktor had to reach, but he managed to cuff him on the back of the head. "How many following me?"

"Two," Reaper answered, sounding almost bored.

"Which chapter?"

"They aren't wearing their colors, but my guess is they're out of North Carolina. They have the accents," Ice said.

Viktor started his Harley. The others followed suit. He had to get down to business now, and he hadn't settled things with Blythe. He'd hoped for more time, at least another week to look around, find the perfect place Evan would want for his ambush and yet at the same time make certain civilians could be protected. He needed to talk to his birth brothers again to see if they knew a place he could bring the Swords in that wouldn't alert a paranoid Evan to a possible double-cross.

Mostly, he needed to talk to Blythe. He couldn't keep his mind on his job if he didn't straighten things out between them. More, it nagged at him that none of his messages had gotten through. No one but his birth brothers knew about the message center they had set up for emergencies and to be able to communicate with one another. They rarely used it, and only in code, just in case someone accidentally stumbled across it, but Viktor knew that was next to impossible.

Had one of his brothers betrayed him? If so, which one? Not Gavriil. They'd been the closest, and Gavriil's school hadn't been any picnic. He'd been brought to Viktor's school once in order to scare the brothers into compliance. He knew how bad it could get. Stefan or Maxim? Casimir? He couldn't see that.

He lifted his face to the wind. He loved riding free. He'd been a prisoner so long, locked up down in the basement, sometimes in chains, sometimes not, but living like an animal. Always hungry. Always afraid. There was nothing like the open road. The roar of his bike and the feel of it, solid, part of him, as they moved together like one, man and machine. As he rode he continued to turn the problem over and over in his mind.

Ilya was a hothead. He couldn't really blame the kid, although part of him did—the hurt part of him. Sorbacov brought him pictures of the baby every so many years, to threaten him with bringing the boy to his school. Kids died at an alarming rate there. The last thing he wanted was for his baby brother to be in that terrible place among the criminals and the rats. The things that would be done to him . . .

Even if the kid hated him, he couldn't imagine betrayal. But would Ilya see it that way? He clearly cared for Blythe. Would he wipe out every message from Viktor to Blythe with a misguided belief that he was protecting her? That didn't make sense either. He didn't know Viktor, didn't know what kind of man he was.

He signaled and turned off Highway 1 to take the exit leading to Sea Haven. It was only a few miles from Caspar, where he hoped to settle. Less than five minutes. Ten to the farm if he pushed it a little. It was a good place to try to build a life for his brothers and sisters. There was something healing in the sea air.

He spotted the motorcycles as he turned onto the street leading to the main drag. They were out in front of the local grocery store. Out of habit, they'd left one of their newest members with the bikes. He had to be patched, or he wouldn't have been sent, so there was no discounting him in a fight.

He looked shocked when Viktor rode right up and parked his bike in the space to the left of the row of bikes. The kid swung his head toward the store as if trying to figure out how to warn his fellow Swords. He pulled his cell phone out of his pocket, and as Viktor went past him, Viktor stripped it out of his hands. Reaper stomped on it with his motorcycle boot. Savage, Ice and Storm followed suit.

Viktor yanked open the door to the grocery store. The familiar adrenaline hit, rushing through his veins like a drug. He flexed his fingers inside the leather gloves, needing to hit someone. Hard.

"You have to pay for that." The voice shook a little, but was determined.

An older man stood beside an older woman at the counter. The Sword member was busy pocketing several items. Three others grabbed six-packs of beer, while a fifth shoved a boy who had to be in his late teens or early twenties every time the boy reached to pick up bags of potato chips and rolling cans.

"Let Donny go," a female voice added. "Donny, get out of here now."

"Shut the fuck up or I'll shut you up," snapped the first one, the obvious leader. His gaze went to the boy on the floor that his fellow biker had shoved over with his foot. He grinned as the boy sprawled out on the floor.

It was that grin as the boy landed on his belly, arms and legs splayed wide. The look of fear on the kid's face. The dark rage in the pit of Viktor's belly began to churn. The burn inside grew hotter, searing right through him. The kid looked helpless. How many kids had he seen looking just like that? Maybe they weren't as old as this one, but he wasn't quite right and looked and acted younger.

Still, the boy had courage. It wouldn't do him any good against the kind of men in the store. As he tried to roll over, the biker kicked him again, this time in the ribs. His fellow bikers howled with laughter, as if they were watching a movie, rather than seeing pain spreading across the face of a young man. That rage inside of Viktor erupted into a red river of ferocity calling for violence. The vicious well roiled and seethed while images of dead children shimmered in front of his eyes.

"I'm calling the sheriff," the woman said.

"You do that. He won't walk out of here alive," the leader snapped, leaning across the counter and grabbing her by the neck. He shook her.

"Inez," the older man whispered.

She looked very fragile, her thin body like a rag doll's. He looked at the others, and they all laughed. "He can't do nothin', you old bitch."

"Maybe he can't," Viktor said quietly, "but I can." The rush was on him. The need. "Let her go now." His voice might be low, but it carried unmistakable authority. He'd been Czar since he was ten years old, commanding children older than him, planning battles. He'd learned to fight and then to kill with his bare hands. So long ago. So many dead men since then. It was in his voice. Demons were in his eyes. Need was a living, breathing entity.

Beside him, Reaper, Savage, Ice and Storm spread out, trapping the five Swords between them and the exit. He jerked his head toward the kid on the floor and Ice sauntered over to him, reached down and helped the boy to his feet. Very slowly the leader let go of Inez and turned fully to face him.

Donny scrambled over to the woman, slipping behind the counter to face them. He looked as if he'd been trying not to cry. Clearly the Swords had been pushing him around for some time.

"How much do they owe you, ma'am?" Viktor inquired softly.

"Inez," she mumbled as she rang up the rest of the beer and the cigarettes the leader had indicated. "Everyone calls me Inez."

She was nervous. Her hand was shaking, but both stood their ground even in the face of the five men looking for trouble. He could see bruises already coming up on the woman's thin skin. Her wrist looked as if it was swelling. There were lumps on the boy's face. The evidence of a bully working over a kid and a woman was accelerant on the fire already building inside of him.

"This ain't your business," the leader snarled.

"They knock over the chips and cans I see in the aisles?" Viktor continued, ignoring the Sword leader, his gaze on the woman. He couldn't attack first. He had to make the leader do it, and that had to be very, very clear in the recordings. He'd spotted the cameras the moment he'd entered, although he'd been careful not to look at them. He knew none of his brothers would either; they were too well-trained.

Inez nodded. "They broke the jars of mayonnaise and pickles in the back."

Viktor stepped back and indicated the aisles. "Gentlemen, I suggest you go clean that up. You don't want me to take you out behind the barn and teach you a lesson in manners."

A dull flush of red came over the leader. He had his orders from his chapter president. They weren't to engage with Viktor and the others, just watch them. They weren't supposed to attract attention, but now they were getting dressed down by the very men they were supposed to be watching. They weren't wearing colors, and they'd never met, so the leader had to be thinking maybe Viktor didn't know who he was. On the other hand, it went against everything in him to allow anyone to order him around or embarrass him and his brethren.

"Fuck you," he snapped.

Viktor smiled without much humor, goading him more. "Sorry, only my old lady gets to do that. You, on the other hand, need to pick up the items you or your boys knocked over."

"Or what?"

"Or we're going to be taking this outside and you're going to get your ass kicked. Inez's going to call the sheriff, and he's going to charge you with theft and vandalism. They'll probably lock you up for a while."

Now the leader had a real dilemma. He probably had outstanding warrants and couldn't afford to go to jail for anything petty. He stood for a moment and then stepped into Viktor and swung. A surge of pure, savage joy ripped through

Viktor as he caught him, rolled him around and muscled him right out of the store. Savage, Reaper, Ice and Storm did the same with the others.

Viktor flung the leader into the street, almost into the path of a car. The car screamed to a halt as the man rose with a roar, lowered one shoulder and rushed Viktor, swinging at him. He stepped to the side, delivering a hard, solid blow to the man's face. He heard the satisfying crunch of cheekbone and added two more quick, hard blows, a roundhouse to his temple that rocked him and an uppercut to his gut. They fought like two primitive warriors, although it became clear that Viktor was doing more playing than fighting. Each blow he did deliver was hard enough to rock the man. He even slapped him a few times open-handed, delivering the insults to rile him more.

In the distance the sound of sirens grew louder. The leader heard them after a minute or two and tried to push away, but Viktor refused to allow it. Now he stepped in close and pounded his fists into the man, connecting solidly, feeling the satisfying break of bones and cartilage. Around him, his brothers did the same with the others.

They needed this release, this outlet. Reaper and Savage often fought for money, and they always won. Viktor and the others bet on them because no matter what, they were going to get their money's worth. The two were impossible to beat. They fought viciously; all of them did. They didn't know any other way. They fought because they needed to feel the familiar strike of fist against flesh, raw pain exploding through their bodies, the adrenaline that told them they were alive and not robots designed just to kill.

He detested that this man and his brothers from the club hurt children. They kidnapped women and raped them repeatedly. They beat them, just as they did young boys and girls, in order to make them compliant. It had been nothing to them to harm the older woman and the kid. The dark rage inside him had a good hold so that he saw red, saw the images of the dead children on the floor, their bodies litter, garbage to the ones that killed them. They killed and then went off to drink. He hit and hit, losing himself in the rhythm, trying to get the sight of those children out of his mind.

Viktor. Stop. A soft breeze slipped through the red haze. The lightest of touches. Almost a caress. His name on her lips. God. *God.* He loved her. He wanted her. Right then, high as a kite from fighting. He wanted her with just the sound of her voice whispering through his mind. *Stop, honey, or you're going to kill him.*

He *wanted* to kill him. Wasn't that the point? There were only the targets. That was what he could see. That was what he could feel under his fist as it slammed deep.

Viktor. Stop right now and stop the others. The sheriff is coming.

The worry in her voice broke through and he stepped back, breathing hard, trying to catch his breath, trying to force the rage back into his belly and out of his veins where it rushed like a drug.

The leader staggered and went to his knees, blood dripping from a cut over his eyes and his nose. There was a mouse growing under each eye and his jaw was swelling at an alarming rate. His breath came in ragged, labored pants as he struggled for air. Viktor knew his ribs were caved in and he'd hit hard enough to drive them into his lung.

"Stop." He made it an order, knowing the others were as bad or worse than him when they fought. It was all or nothing. There was no in-between, especially when they had an opportunity to go after any of the Swords. They regarded them as the lowest of the low. To them, that was pedophiles, men and women who brutalized innocent children. "Now."

Just as Blythe's voice could stop him, his command was always obeyed—other than occasionally Reaper—and that was only when Viktor's personal safety was at risk. He looked up, searching the crowd for her. She'd saved him from beating someone to death right in front of a very large crowd. His radar found her immediately and his heart clenched hard in his chest.

She looked beautiful. Gorgeous. *His* woman. He had never looked at another woman the way he did her. He made love to her because his body recognized hers and responded naturally to her. That was a gift. A priceless gift.

You can't look at me or take up for me if the cops arrest me. Walk away, Blythe. This is dangerous. He hoped she understood that he was working and they were all in jeopardy. He'd kill every single one of these men in front of all of Sea Haven if she was in danger and he'd go to prison happily to keep her safe.

She was with another woman, tall, slender, long glossy hair. She looked exotic with her skin and cat's eyes. He recognized her as Judith, the woman married to Stefan, from the photographs in Blythe's home.

The two women crossed the street, giving a wide berth to the bloody, groaning men on the ground. Immediately they both wrapped their arms around Inez and whispered to her. Tears swam in the older woman's eyes but she squared her shoulders. Viktor wanted to kick the living shit out of the man who hurt her. Instead, he carefully stepped back, holding his hands up and out to show they were empty as the sheriff's car screamed up.

"All of you, get your hands out away from your body. Let them do whatever they need to do. We can't afford jail right now," he whispered in a low, carrying tone. "Cooperate."

Jackson Deveau emerged from the sheriff's SUV, taking in the scene, and then his eyes jumped to the sidewalk, searching. Viktor followed his gaze, saw it rested on the older woman who had been inside the store. She stood on the sidewalk, her arm around the boy the Swords had shoved around. She nodded to Deveau, an almost imperceptible movement. That was interesting. She meant something to the sheriff. Viktor stored that information away like he did everything.

"What's going on here?" Jackson asked, surveying the six downed Swords and the five men with their hands in the air.

Viktor took a quick look at his brothers. Maybe they should have done a better job of letting the Sword brethren hit them. Deveau's eyes were sharp and he wouldn't miss the fact that they weren't torn up at all.

Several people began to talk at once, but it was Inez the sheriff listened to, Viktor noted. "Jackson, those men"— she indicated the ones lying moaning in the street—"came into my store, broke things, knocked things over and off the shelves and pushed Donny around and hurt him, then refused to pay. They threatened us, and yes, I want to press charges. If it wasn't for these men"—she marched right up to Viktor as if he was her friend—"they would have done a lot worse damage."

"You all right, Donny?" Deveau asked.

The boy nodded. "Fine. But I have to get inside and clean up the store." He stammered a little when he spoke.

"Not yet, we have to take pictures," Deveau said. "Inez, go stand on the sidewalk. I haven't searched any of these men."

The older woman hesitated but when the cop stared her down, she reluctantly obeyed him.

He turned his attention back to Viktor. "You armed?"

Viktor nodded. He was having real trouble not looking at his wife. He'd never once, in all the years he'd been undercover, had a moment of weakness, but she was right there, breathing the same air. His eyes kept straying toward her and he had to check himself. "Have a concealed weapons permit. All of us do. We have knives on our belts in plain sight as well. Didn't use them. Didn't use any weapon. And they swung first."

"Put your hands down," Jackson said with some disgust. "It seems I get to keep running into you. Does trouble just follow you around?" He held out his hand, and Viktor pulled out his wallet to show his license and concealed weapons permit.

"Nice paperwork." Sarcasm dripped.

The paperwork was impeccable. Viktor had done it himself. He flashed a taunting grin that he knew would earn him lots of questions, but that would work in his favor. He wanted the Swords in jail and calling their president to bail them out. He also wanted it reported that he'd clashed with the cops and they'd given him a hard time. He would be reporting to his own president *after* they took care of the problem lying in the streets.

More cop cars pulled up, uniformed officers emerging with guns drawn. Jackson pointed them toward the men lying on the ground. The leader of the Swords spat blood on the street and moaned loudly. Jackson handed Viktor his license and permit before bending down to pat down a member of Swords. He found several weapons on him and meticulously put them aside.

"I haven't searched the ones standing, but it looks as if they're the good guys in this," Jackson said.

Two of the officers grabbed Reaper roughly and tried to shove him toward the sidewalk. He resisted by simply not moving. At once the two got belligerent with him, taking him down hard to the street. Savage, Ice and Storm all made a move toward them, but Viktor got there first. Just as he caught one by the shoulder and spun him around, Deveau was there, between them.

"What the hell are you two doing? Did you not hear me? They prevented the ones on the ground from hurting anyone. At least treat them with respect."

The youngest officer flushed a dark red and mumbled an apology. The older one looked annoyed. Viktor reached down and offered Reaper his hand, pulling him to his feet. They walked together to the sidewalk. Reaper held up his hands for the search, but remained silent. Savage did the same. Ice and Storm both told their searching officers where their weapons were and that they had permits to carry.

An ambulance arrived, and the men in handcuffs were eventually taken away. Four to the hospital and the other two straight to jail. The jail was in Ukiah, some distance away. As soon as the other Swords members were fixed up they'd be transported as well. That gave Viktor a little time to set things in motion. They needed to find the camp where the Swords were staying and fix a little surprise for them. He wasn't about to have them breathing down his neck while he was trying to sort things out with Blythe.

Still, he had to be careful. The cops would look at him first if something happened to the group. He bet that all of the Swords members had records. The moment their names were run, it was going to come out that they were in the territory of another club without their colors. That wasn't going to go over well and could start a war Evan didn't want. His idea had been to slip the members of his club into the area, hiding them at a campground and staying low-key. Then they'd lure the sheriff to them, and Evan would kill him. Viktor was unaware how Evan thought he'd get his hands on Deveau's wife.

He stood on the sidewalk, waiting to be questioned while the cops and ambulances took the six members of the Sword club away. The older woman marched up to him along with the boy. Up close he could see the kid was probably more like twenty or so. To his absolute dismay, the boy had hero worship in his eyes.

"Thank you," Inez said firmly.

Viktor shrugged. At least the Swords were gone and no one would observe the old lady walking up to him unafraid. He liked her. There was something indomitable about her. Her body was thin and fragile-looking, but her shoulders were straight and she walked with her head up.

"I was very afraid for Donny. He doesn't understand when others bully him, and it was a nice thing for you to do."

Nice thing for him to do. He would have beaten those men to death with his bare hands. He wasn't nice. Nothing about him was nice. What the hell was he trying to do, thinking he could live with people like this woman? His gaze drifted from her face to Blythe. His Blythe. His woman.

She made his heart go crazy and his body as hard as a rock. The things he wanted—no, needed to do to her. She saw him now, the real Viktor. Not just that outer shell where he could be a chameleon and look like others around him. He didn't play in their world. He walked in it, but he saw things they didn't see.

"I'm Inez Nelson, and this is Donny Ruttermyer. Donny helps out at the store and keeps an eye on it for me at night."

What the hell? Why would she tell him that? He couldn't keep his gaze from straying to Blythe. She stood on the sidewalk, trying not to look at him, but she was. Sneaking little glances his way. For a moment their eyes met and the need in him was so terrible he thought he might just push past the woman, walk right up to her, toss her over his shoulder and carry her off.

She'd fight him, but he would win. All he had to do was kiss her. She melted when he kissed her whether she wanted to or not. Her body recognized his the same way his did hers. Damn it all to hell, he wanted her. He couldn't be this close to his own wife and not be with her. It wasn't as fortuitous as he thought it was, his job bringing him there. Already she thought he was just there for work, not for her. Now, how the hell could he ignore her?

He forced himself to look at the kid, trying not to see the eagerness there. He couldn't be mean the way he should, pushing the kid away from him.

"They get out of jail, ma'am, they may come back in the middle of the night and retaliate against you. They won't try to get at me, but they might try to torch your store or hurt the boy—Donny." He gave the kid that much. The moment he said his name, Donny beamed at him, an angelic smile.

"I take care of Miss Inez and Miss Donna," Donny explained, pointing across the street to one of the shops. Above it was obviously a studio apartment.

Great. If the Sword members came back and torched the store, the kid would run out to stop them and get himself killed. He looked directly at the boy. "If they come back, you do *not* go outside. You call the cops and the fire department if it's needed, but whatever you do, don't go outside to confront them."

Viktor switched his gaze to Inez. "Ma'am, you've got to

make that very clear to him. It wouldn't be a good thing if they got ahold of him."

He'd seen what the Swords were capable of doing to children, innocent little boys and girls. It wouldn't matter in the least, age, sex, or whether or not they had disabilities. The Swords didn't see them as human, only whether or not they could make money off of them. There were monsters in the world, and he knew the biggest of them was coming to Sea Haven.

"I'll make it clear. Thank you again. Jackson is glowering at me. I'm probably holding them up."

More likely Jackson didn't want her talking to him. Because he was perverse like that, he stopped her leaving. "The sheriff related to you? Or to the boy?"

Her eyes sharpened. There was nothing stupid about her. She might have aged, but her mind was still working very well. "Jackson is just a friend. He helps Donny out now and then."

Her voice had cooled. Good. She at least recognized that she was talking to the devil. He nodded. "They saw that. Him looking at you and the boy to make certain you were all right. If they want revenge, they can get it easily on all three of you by coming after you." He kept his voice low. "Make certain the cop warns you when they make bail. After that, you and the kid need to lie low until you know for certain they're out of this town." One more reason to make certain none of them returned.

Inez nodded and slipped her arm around Donny. "You know, this is a good town. Lots of tourists, but the people here stick together. You'd like it here."

He shook his head. What the fuck was wrong with her? With people? He knew what he looked like. He knew what he was, pure killer, was plain to see. Still, she was all but inviting him to stay. He glanced helplessly at Reaper. The man shrugged. He didn't understand it either. Reaper's gaze moved behind him, alerting him to the fact that Deveau was coming to question him. The sheriff was light on his feet. Even knowing he was coming, Viktor still couldn't hear him.

He nodded to the woman because clearly something was expected of him, and then he turned to face the sheriff and the questions all of them would be asked.

12

BLYTHE knew Viktor was in her house when she came in from running. There was no motorcycle to give him away, but then there hadn't been the last time he'd been there. She even looked this time, trying to discover his hiding place, her heart pounding in anticipation—and fear—because she didn't want to forgive him. She didn't. That was the sad truth. A part of her had needed to blame him for setting the terrible chain of events in motion.

Intellectually she knew that wasn't fair, nor was he any guiltier than she was. Her mother was solely to blame for her actions, but he hadn't been there when she needed him so desperately. Now he was . . . different. Scary. She didn't want to think that, but he was. She was torn between wanting to take him to bed and then kick him out—or just kick him out, which was much, much safer.

She'd known he'd come. She hadn't been able to stop herself from looking at him no matter how she tried to be strong. He'd been like a primitive savage, conquering an enemy. It had been a brutal display, but she couldn't take her eyes from him. Weirdly, sexual hunger had coursed through her body, bringing her alive. There was no way to sublimate it, even with running—which she'd been doing for five long years.

She went straight to the kitchen and poured water into a glass, drinking it down while she thought about what she was going to do. When she looked up from the sink, he was there, leaning one hip against the counter, looking even more gorgeous and dangerous than she remembered. He'd always done that—come into whatever room she was in, looking lazy and casual, when he wasn't at all.

"You've been gone."

She couldn't read his tone or his expression. She downed the rest of the water and filled her glass again. "I went to see your girl, Darby. It was an interesting meeting."

His eyes lit up. "Thank you, Blythe. Is she okay? Does she have a good family?"

She shook her head slowly. "No. She's in a state-run facility on lockdown at the moment. I produced papers stating I was a relative, a cousin."

Viktor straightened abruptly, going from lazy to a threat in a matter of a single heartbeat. "Damn it. I had a bad feeling."

She didn't want to see his expression, the one that told him he was genuinely worried about the girl. His strange feelings had always been right. She'd learned that over time. She believed he had a gift, mostly because she believed in them. His was very strong.

"Well, you were right. She has two sisters. One, Zoe, was there, in that horrible place you took her out of, and the other, Emily, is in a foster home. Darby wanted to stay with her younger sister, Zoe, because her sister was so traumatized, but they wouldn't let her. She reacted like any sister might under the circumstances, but they locked her up."

Viktor turned away from her, swearing viciously. She winced at his language, but deep down she felt the same way. She couldn't exactly fault him for caring about the girl. "I saw what they did to Zoe," he all but spat. "How old can she be? Eleven? Twelve?"

Blythe nodded slowly, aching for him. Aching for all the

things he'd seen and been put through in his life—things that woke him in the middle of the night. She couldn't make it better for him.

"Darby's highly intelligent, loves her sisters and thinks you can walk on water." She sent him a brief smile, trying to soothe him. "I didn't tell her any different. She's headstrong. A fighter. She'll cause trouble there and will run away the first chance she gets in order to try to get to her sisters, especially Zoe. She's so afraid for her. She hadn't spoken a single word even after the police got there. Darby kept her from looking at the dead bodies, but they'd had time with her. They beat her and repeatedly raped her. Darby had broken ribs from trying to stop them. She'd been raped first by all of the men there, as an 'example.'"

"It wasn't an example."

There was so much rage in his voice that the walls and floor felt as if they shook with it, trying to contain it. She glanced at him sharply. He really couldn't take the things he saw. The things he was expected to participate in being a member of that particular club, yet he'd stayed with them for five years. She needed to understand why. She needed to understand him.

"I know," she admitted, still trying to soothe him. It had been hell to listen to the things Darby had told her. The way the Swords had beaten and raped young girls with no regard for them at all. She couldn't imagine what it would be to actually witness it.

"So what's the plan?"

Of course he would ask that, put it on her shoulders. He'd known if she went there and met Darby, heard her story firsthand, she couldn't walk away.

"I filed papers stating that as their only living relative, the three girls should come live with us on the farm. What else could I do? You knew that too. You knew if I met her, I'd have to help her."

He ignored that. "Is the paperwork going to stand up to scrutiny?"

"I don't know. I wasn't the one handling that. In all honesty, I expect the cops to show up at my door any minute to tell me they're taking me to jail for lying so much. Lev did the paperwork for me. I was lucky that Darby was curious enough to lie as well and say she had a cousin, because of course they asked her."

"Three of them? All girls? That's harsh."

"I said we were a couple, Viktor, but I'm not saying that to you. I don't know if I can do what you want me to."

"Baby." He whispered it. "I want to come home."

She shook her head. "You're a nomad. You take off when you feel like it. You have this club. This huge family. You made your choice, Viktor, and it wasn't me."

"It was always you, Blythe. From the moment I met you, it was always you. I brought my family home so you can work your magic on them. They need you. I need you. It's time you let me back in."

She shook her head again, and then took a step back, putting more distance between them. She even held up her hand as if that could ward him off. "Don't. Don't push this right now. I don't know you. At. All. You ride in here looking scary and you say you're here to do a job, not to be with me, and yet you expect me to just take you back as if everything that happened, didn't. It did happen, and I don't know how to forgive you. I know that makes me a terrible person, but I don't know how."

"Blythe. I want to come home." His voice was low and persuasive.

She felt the notes caressing her skin, sending fingers of desire trailing down her spine. She kept her gaze glued to the kitchen table because if she looked at him she might be lost.

"Baby, I need you to look at me."

He knew. He knew what he did to her when she looked into his eyes. She moistened her lips, shook her head and pushed off the counter. "I have to go take a shower, and then I'll fix us some dinner. I've got chicken and fresh veggies."

"I want to come home."

His voice was so soft, so compelling she felt it move over her bare skin and trail like fingers down her spine. She shivered with wanting him. With needing him. She nodded because she had to acknowledge him. "I don't know if I can get past everything that happened," she admitted, still without looking at him. "You think you can come into my home and start up where we left off, but it doesn't work that way."

"You can forgive me." He said it with complete confidence. "You're soft inside, Blythe. You can't help who you are. I'm a dick. I know that. I'm scary. I know that too. I'm rough, and I know I'm asking a lot from you. A hell of a lot. Taking on my brothers and sisters. The club. The fact that I'm not always a nice guy and that will never change. The three girls. I know what I'm asking of you, but I also know you, baby, and you're that woman. The one I need more than I need air."

She tried not to like what he thought about her. Sincerity rang in his voice, and she didn't want to hear it because she knew he was right. She was that person, but she didn't want to be. "You've been gone a long time. You're obviously not the same person you were five years ago and neither am I." In a way she felt like she was fighting for her life. Her sanity. He'd been her world and then he was gone. She couldn't do that again. Not after what happened. She couldn't.

"Blythe. I want to come home. It's time. It's way past time. I *need* to come home. Let me come home, baby. I swear if you do, I'll spend the rest of my life loving you better than anyone else ever could."

She had no idea how he got from where he'd been standing with his hip against the counter to where she was thinking she was so safe from him, but he was there, a big man moving so fast, so quietly, she barely registered that he'd changed positions. His hands were gentle when he lifted her face, forcing her eyes to meet his.

His eyes. Slate gray. Burning silver. Molten mercury. So beautiful all the time, no matter his mood. He took her breath. Her will.

She took a deep breath, gulped some badly needed air

and nodded and then shook her head, showing her confusion. "Give me some time to get to know you. I need to understand why you made the choices you made."

"Fair enough. That's all I'm asking for, a chance."

That wasn't true and both knew it. He wanted to come home. Home was Blythe. He'd made that clear. He'd always made that clear to her. In those fantasy months before he was gone, when her world was astonishing and perfect— perfect even if they disagreed. She didn't care as long as they were together.

"You're asking for more than a chance," she challenged.

"You're right." He cupped her face in his hands, his thumbs sliding over her cheeks in a slow caress. "I am. I have to. I need you to save me. To save all of us."

She stepped back, rejecting his plea. "Don't. Don't say things like that to me. It isn't fair, and you know it isn't."

He let his hands drop to his sides. "Did you think I would fight fair? You matter more than anything else in my life. You. I'm not about to fight fair to get you back. Just because it isn't fair to tell you doesn't mean it isn't true. We do need you to save us. I need you. Without you, I have no anchor. I'm not really alive. I need you to bridge the space that I can't. The one between me and everyone else."

"Stop. Just don't talk anymore. I'm going to take a shower. Please, please give me a few minutes alone."

She had to get away from him, from his soft, insistent voice that rang with such truth. She did believe him, that was the trouble. Still, he'd chosen his work. He'd left for five long, terrible years. She couldn't just let herself love him all over again. It would kill her if he left her again. She'd come to rely on herself, on her sisters. She had made a life for herself and it had been very difficult.

"I'll start dinner," he agreed and went to the sink to wash his hands. "Go grab a shower. Take up some more water with you."

She'd almost forgotten. She was careful to always stay hydrated with all the running she did, but his presence threw her into some chaotic state where she couldn't think of anything else. She filled her glass a third time and hurried upstairs.

Her house felt different with him in it. *She* felt different. It was the way he looked at her, as if he could devour her any minute. As if he was so hungry for her and thought she was beautiful, even when she'd just come in from running. When she'd been with him before, she thought about him every single minute of the day. It had taken five long years to learn to control her mind so every moment wasn't taken up with worry, with anger, with wondering where he was and what he was doing. Now he was back.

She stepped under the spray of hot water and let it pour over her head and down her back. It felt good on her aching body. She closed her eyes and tried to think about her life again without Viktor. He already was in her head. In her heart. No one else could ever touch her body. But he was different. Very, very different. He didn't want to think so, but he was. Or maybe the man she'd known had been an illusion and didn't exist at all.

She took her time, shampooing her hair and soaping her body with her favorite gel in order to give herself a respite from all the emotions. She told herself she just needed time and closure to get over him, but she knew she never really would. But a biker? Really? Her? That brought her up short. Was she really contemplating taking him back?

Of course she was. But how? She didn't believe in trying to change a man. She didn't want him to change her. You loved a person for who they were, not what you wanted them to become.

The smell of chicken grilling made her very aware she was hungry when she stepped out of the shower to towel off. He'd always done that, cooked meals when she was busy, or late getting home. He didn't mind helping out with housework either. She'd always been a little shocked by that; now that she'd seen him in his more real persona, she was even more so.

Slowly, with some reluctance, she made her way down

the stairs to the kitchen. He was at the stove, grilling two chicken breasts and quite a few vegetables. The food smelled delicious. Her stomach growled. She hadn't eaten much in the last few days. She'd been traveling and then, after meeting Darby and hearing what happened to her and her younger sister, she hadn't felt much like eating.

She opened cupboards and took down her dishes. Instantly the memory of buying them with him came into her mind. It had been a beautiful day. They'd held hands, laughed and shopped for hours. They hadn't needed to—she had kitchenware—but he told her to give it all to Goodwill and they'd buy what they both liked together. She'd loved that he'd thought to donate her nice set and yet cared enough about building a life with her to want to shop for such mundane things as dishes. Now she knew it was because he would be leaving and he'd wanted her to have those memories.

Her hands shook a little as she set the table, careful to place him across from her.

"Babe, what is this pink stuff that should be salt?" Viktor held up the salt shaker.

The look on his face made her laugh in spite of her uneasiness. "It has minerals in it. It's real salt, not processed."

"Does it taste like salt?" He sounded skeptical.

"Yes. You know salt isn't good for you." The moment it slipped out she wished she could take it back. It was a longstanding argument between them and instantly threw her back to being easy and comfortable with him.

"It is. It's a necessary mineral. We all need salt." He grinned at her as he brought the pan with the chicken breasts over to the table and put them on their plates.

He'd said that in response to her reprimand every single time. She knew exactly what would come next.

"Salt controls the way nerves and muscles work, so you need it when you run. It helps control fluid balance." He sounded like a professor giving a lecture.

"Humans eat way too much salt," she said in her

snippiest voice, unable to stop herself from entering into their favorite argument. They had it every time they cooked together, which had been nightly.

"So what you're telling me is this pink stuff has *less* salt in it because they added other minerals to it." He put the pan back on the stove, and picked up the one with vegetables.

She watched him divide them between the two plates. "They don't have to *add* the minerals in, it occurs naturally." She slipped into the chair facing away from the window, knowing he always faced the door or windows. It was habit when he was around to accommodate that in him.

He made a face as he put the salt shaker on the table. "Tell me more about the girls. Did Darby talk much about her parents?"

The knots unraveled a little bit in her belly. She was grateful he wanted to talk about Darby and her sisters instead of them. She wasn't quite ready yet for that conversation. "I think they both had bad drug habits, Viktor. She didn't talk much about them, but I got the impression she'd mothered her two sisters almost from the time they were born. She hasn't had it easy." She raised suspicious eyes to his face. "Did you know? About her parents?"

He shook his head. "We had to get in and out of there fast. Every time we go after one of the Swords' houses and take back the girls they have trained or were training, I'm risking the lives of my brothers and sisters. We've been hitting the Swords' whorehouses pretty hard over the last few years. I worried that someone would connect the strikes against them with some of my brothers joining the club."

"I couldn't help but be sympathetic with her. It reminded me of my childhood, although I didn't have siblings."

"You would have watched over them. You're protective and responsible. You look after others before you do yourself." He reached for the salt shaker.

"Didn't you use salt when you cooked?" She gave him the evil eye.

He snickered. "Baby, you still can't look mean, even

when you try. You'll have to improve if we're taking on three girls."

She stopped chewing and sighed. Chewed, swallowed and shook her head. "We don't know if that's going to happen."

"It's going to happen."

"Why do you say that?"

"Three reasons." He shook salt onto his chicken until she reached across the table and took the shaker out of his hand.

"Tell me, I'm all ears."

"First, you love me. That right there gives me a huge advantage in this fight. Second, you're going to tell me what I need to do and I'll do it. Anything at all. You name it, and I'll make it right. Third, I love you with everything I am. I want to make you happy. I'll devote every minute I have to making that happen."

She shook her head, a small smile stealing up out of nowhere. "You think you'll spend every minute making me happy. What you'll really do is make me crazy. You'll come home and inform me there are ten children that need a home and they're on their way, can I fix dinner for them."

He laughed. "More likely my brothers will be begging for food, and I'll have you feeding them most nights. But I can grill, and so can they. Until we get our clubhouse and their homes built, we'll make certain they're fed."

"You're crazy if you think they're all going to be here."

"They'll be here." He was absolutely confident.

She realized that was one of the things she loved most about him—the way he had utter faith in her. "I need to know things," she said in a low tone, not looking at him.

"I know you do. You're the only one I'd ever tell them to. When I tell you about me, I'm telling you about my brothers and sisters. No one has the right to hear their stories but the person they want to tell."

She was silent a moment, trying to understand. Whatever had happened to Viktor had happened with the men and women he called family. He was asking, without voicing the words, that she not tell anyone else, even her sisters and his blood brothers.

He put down his fork and looked at her. "After, when you know everything, you might be ashamed of me. Of being with me. That's what I'm risking. Having you look at me with shame."

Her heart clenched. It was going to be bad. Worse than she'd anticipated. She raised her chin. "Have more faith in me than that."

"I do." He picked up his fork. "After dinner, I'll tell you everything you want to know, but not while we're eating. Where are you on the paperwork for Darby? Did you explain things to her?"

"I asked her if she would want to live with us. I told her about the farm and Airiana's children. How they were on one of the ships. She'd heard about the ships. They threatened the girls. I told her about the farm and the premise, how my sisters were not birth sisters but sisters of the heart, and we'd gotten together because we'd all attended group counseling for survivors. I told her each of us had someone in our family murdered and we felt responsible. She asked what had happened to me, and I told her. Everything. She deserved to know if she was going to make a decision about her and her sisters."

She looked up at him because she couldn't stop herself. This time the painful memory was shared by another person. By him. Viktor. She saw the grief etched deep into his face and knew it was very real for him, just as it was for her. Somehow in sharing, it helped. She found herself sending him a small, sad smile and reaching out to touch the back of his hand.

"Darby seemed to relax a little more around me. She thought I looked too nice, a do-gooder who would never understand what happened to them or that there would be issues for the rest of their lives. I told her I'm still working through mine."

"So she wants to come here."

His voice was very gruff and she could feel his emotions, so deep, the grief carved inside him, that first cut halfway through his bone. She knew it would stay there, because it was the same for her.

Blythe nodded. "She said she'd feel safe with you. I told her it was very safe on the farm. I didn't want her to get her hopes up that you'd be here."

"I'll be here."

"Viktor . . ." she cautioned.

"Blythe."

She put down her fork and glared at him. "You aren't making this easy. We're supposed to be talking about these children. They're going to be traumatized, even the youngest. She's been in four foster homes already. She may not have been taken by the Swords, but she's been away from her sisters for months. She gets in fights because she wants her family back."

"Then we'll give it to her. You can get them counselors or whatever you think best, but seriously, Blythe, *you're* what's best for them." He chewed and swallowed the last of his chicken. "I knew the moment I saw Darby that she needed you. I didn't want to go there because we had so many things to work out, but I couldn't let go of that thought. I didn't say a thing to her, but I couldn't stop thinking about it. The moment I saw you in the street with the cowardly lunkhead, I knew we had to track her down."

"He's not a cowardly lunkhead." She glared at him.

"Yes he is."

"Anyone would be afraid of you and the mob of badass bikers you had behind you. He called the sheriff."

"Walking away he called the sheriff. He didn't stop to see if you were all right. He left you seven messages, but he didn't apologize for being a fu— A coward."

"You listened to my messages?"

"You left your phone here. I've warned you about that before. You're off running, you need that cell to call 911 in an emergency. Women are attacked on running trails, or parks or on the highway or wherever you've been running."

She sighed. "Cell phone service can be spotty around here."

"You can still call 911."

"Why am I talking to you about this?" She threw her hands up into the air in complete exasperation. "The point is, you can't be listening to my messages. They're private."

"Not when they're from another man. You're married. You can listen to all my messages, whether they're from a woman or a man."

"I forgot how bossy you were," she said, infuriated. Because he always had been bossy. She understood a little better now. If he had all those "brothers and sisters" and he lived in the biker world, it stood to reason that he would be bossy. "I don't like anyone listening to my private messages."

"You never minded before," he pointed out.

That brought her up short. She hadn't minded before. Sometimes she'd ask him to listen to her messages and tell her who called and for what reason. She hadn't thought a thing about it.

"That was when we were together and I trusted you. We aren't and I don't." Abruptly she stood up and carried her plate to the sink to rinse it off. "Let's do this if we're going to. I'm not promising you anything."

He rinsed his plate as well and then opened her refrigerator to take out a beer. She didn't stock beer as a rule, so she knew he'd brought it with him.

"You want one?"

She shook her head and got a glass of water. She rarely drank anymore unless it was with her sisters. She found if she drank, she got depressed, and she couldn't take chances with depression.

"It isn't going to be a pretty story, baby," he warned.

"I realize that." And she did. Whatever had happened to put that blank, emotionless, ice-cold look in Reaper's eyes had to be horrible. She knew Viktor's brothers had all been through hell, but she had a terrible feeling that she was about to hear something worse than hell.

She curled up in one of the wide armchairs opposite from him. He hadn't sat on the love seat or couch. He'd always wanted to be as close to her as possible, but this time he'd deliberately sat first, choosing one of the armchairs. That filled her with trepidation instantly. It was out of character for him.

"This isn't going to be easy telling you. I wrote it down in the letter I left for you, but even then, I was careful, didn't say much, just enough so I'd hoped you'd understand."

She nodded because he looked at her expectantly. She hadn't gotten the letter. Her mother must have and most likely burned it. That would be just like Sharon. She had never wanted Blythe to be with anyone, let alone a man like Viktor who protected her from her mother's ugly outbursts.

"You know Sorbacov had my parents murdered. I was ten. Ilya was an infant, barely a year. Sorbacov knew my father was very respected and Sorbacov feared him, and that made him hate my father. The schools were already established. I was taken to one run by the worst criminal population he could find in Russia. He claimed it was another one of his experiments, but it was far more than that."

"Actual criminals? You mean like murderers?"

He nodded. "Serial killers, armed robbers, pedophiles, rapists, that sort of criminal."

Her heart pounded and she tasted fear. She had a very bad feeling, but she bit her lip and remained silent.

"There were close to a hundred students already there when I arrived. Over the course of the time I was there, two hundred and eighty-seven children were brought there, all various ages. Only eighteen survived."

She gasped. "Eighteen out of two hundred and eighty-seven? Viktor? How could Sorbacov allow such a thing?"

"He had his own secrets to keep. He had a family, and he was very high up and respected in the government, but he had certain proclivities. His appetite ran to children."

No. No. No. Her stomach lurched and she pressed her hand deep. She didn't want to hear this and she had to. "But he sent you after Ray."

"He did send me after Ray. There were films taken.

Videos. He liked watching himself with his victims. Somehow Ray got ahold of them. We don't know how. I found them in his safe. They were copies. I never found the master copies. I'm not certain he had them. If he did, I couldn't find them. Sorbacov wanted the recordings."

She found she was holding her breath, so she forced air through her lungs. "Tell me what happened in that place. How all those children died."

"We didn't live like human beings. We weren't given clothes. Or food. You had to earn food." His tone implied earning food meant cooperating with whatever the inmates demanded. "We had classes, like any other school, because the inmates all had skills. The punishments for the least little infraction were always capital. Beatings weren't the worst. Rapes in front of the class, both boys and girls, were common. Chained in what we referred to as the dungeon was one they particularly loved. They flayed a student, until his or her skin ran with blood, and then chained them down in the dark where the rats were."

She couldn't listen anymore, but she had to. She had to know what happened to him and the others and how they had managed to escape. This was what had shaped Viktor's life. Not only his life, but the men and women he called brothers and sisters. This was the reason he had not come home to her but instead had taken the job Sorbacov had given him.

"That's what happened to your back. All those scars. You were chained down there." In the dark. Alone. With horrible rodents. Her stomach lurched again.

"If that was the worst, baby, I wouldn't be so fucked-up now. The worst was Sorbacov and his buddies. They like to play with children. And the way they played was not pretty. I saw them leave child after child for dead. Sometimes I wanted to die, but his warning was always there."

She raised an eyebrow, and the tension in the room worsened.

"He told me if I didn't survive, neither would my brothers, and that he'd bring them all there, the baby first. I knew he meant it. He was a sadistic bastard. That meant, if I was going to survive and he clearly was going to do his damnedest to make certain my life was a living hell, then I would find a way to turn the tables on them. On all of them."

She could see him as a ten-year-old boy, stoically and silently being used so brutally and enduring it all in silence while he planned and schemed with the other children. She put her fingers to her mouth. "Ilya," she whispered. "The things he said to you. If he knew, he'd be so upset."

"He'll never know," Viktor declared. "I promised my father I'd take care of the others. I gave him my word. And I kept it by staying alive. By killing the men and women in that place." He looked her directly in the eye. "I was raped repeatedly by both men and women and then I systematically killed them any way that I could."

His head wasn't bowed. It was up. Defiant. Waiting for her to pass judgment. She wanted to weep for him, but he held himself still, tension pouring off of him, his eyes filled with a rage she understood. Ten years old. He hadn't been a man. He'd been a little boy, and yet he'd taken on the role of a man.

"I had to find a way to save the others. The older ones were gone over the years, but when Reaper and Savage came, Reaper was more like me, determined to protect his brother. He couldn't of course; he was just a toddler. Four. Savage was three. They had two older sisters who didn't make it. I started developing a plan and recruiting the children as they came into the school. We banded together and fought back."

He looked up at her again, directly into her eyes just as he had before. There was hell there for her to see. Plain. Unashamed. No remorse. "We started killing them. We had a system. Each of us had certain talents, and we used them together."

He went silent and she didn't know what to say to that. It was self-defense; they were children without choices. No one had come to save them so they'd found a way to save themselves. He held her gaze and she didn't blink, didn't look away. The last thing she wanted was for him to think she condemned him for surviving—for finding a way for the other children to survive.

He took a breath, closed his eyes for a brief moment and then looked at her again. She realized he was totally tense, so much that the tension filled the room and pulled the air around them into a tight net that held both of them stationary. He'd expected condemnation.

"Sorbacov liked to make an example out of me." He said it low, as if confessing. "He preferred young boys, but even as I got older, he liked to show off with his friends. I was required to do things. If I didn't, they would beat a child to death in front of me, or rape him or her repeatedly."

She could barely breathe. Part of her horror was the guilt and shame in his voice, as if he should have been able to stop what Sorbacov and the others had done to him.

When she didn't say anything, he continued. "I learned to do as they said, but I retaliated. We all did." He shook his head. "You don't need details, but suffice it to say, it was far worse than you can possibly imagine, and the things we had to do to protect one another made us close. Made us believe in one another."

She nodded. Certainly she could understand why the men and women were considered family by him. He had been the oldest of the survivors and had devised and executed the plan that had kept them all alive. Not safe. There was no safety in their nightmare world, but they lived. He also gave them the ability to retaliate against the men and women who used them for their own sick pleasure.

"Sorbacov didn't just have us killed when he realized we were the ones responsible for killing the criminals. At first, he didn't believe that a bunch of little kids could get away with it, or even have the balls to do it, but then he wanted to catch us at it. The brutes running the place couldn't conceive of any of us retaliating against them. We were too small and helpless. Still, they took Reaper and tortured him.

We could hear him screaming for days. They did all sorts of things to him, and they threatened Savage. Then they took Savage from us."

Sweat beaded on his body. The unrelenting rage was back in his eyes. "I couldn't stop them, and I knew they would really hurt him in order to break Reaper. If Reaper confessed to the killings, we were all done for, but Savage and he both held out. It was worse than anything you can imagine, listening to them, hearing what those brutes were doing to two little boys. I swore if I ever had the chance, I'd wipe them all off the face of the earth."

She was crying because he was. He didn't know he was, or he didn't acknowledge it, but she'd had enough. Viktor Prakenskii had stood for his blood brothers, keeping his word to his father. He'd stood for seventeen other children, keeping his code. It was one of fierce protection for women and children. It was equally one of fierce retaliation for anyone choosing to harm women or children.

She could at least understand his choices. She'd be a monster not to. She was far too empathetic not to feel the reality of his suffering. She wanted to weep a river of tears for him and those other children.

He scrubbed a hand down his face and looked at her. "I want to come home, Blythe. I need you more than anyone else could ever need you. I'll love you better than anyone ever could. I know what I'm asking of you. I do. It's not only me you'll be taking on, but my brothers and sisters, and they're just as fucked-up as I am. I probably will bring home ten more children just as fucked-up. Still, we all need you. We'll all need you, because you're you. You're like a breath of fresh air. You're . . . everything. *Everything.* Let me come home."

13

VIKTOR didn't realize he was holding his breath as he looked at her face. Blythe. Her touch could wipe out the monsters. She took away every nightmare moment and gave him more pleasure than he'd ever imagined in the world. She'd taught him to laugh. He hadn't known humor. He'd forgotten laughter altogether. He'd held too many brutalized children, watching them die in his arms. He'd planned too many deaths and sent children to carry out the sentences. His life was grim and violent and bloody until Blythe.

"I'm not certain that I'm able to do what you think I can, Viktor. I have my own demons. They aren't like yours, but I have them," she replied.

His heart skipped a beat. She wasn't saying no. She'd heard the worst, knew what had happened to him, and she wasn't turning him away. He'd tried not to worry about that. He was a grown man, and he'd told the others that they hadn't been able to stop those attacking them. He'd made it clear the rapes didn't make them less somehow, but sharing that shit with someone you loved, someone you wanted to think you were a man, a protector, was harsh.

"I know you do, baby," he said softly and got up to cross

the distance between them. It was the longest couple of steps he'd ever taken. He watched her closely for signs of rejection, of pulling away from him, but she sat calmly watching his face. He knelt in front of her. "It's because you have those demons that you can have empathy for mine. For my brothers and sisters. For Darby and her sisters. For the women here on this farm. You're a collector, baby, and I'm bringing you an entire collection." He took her face between his hands. "I want to come home, Blythe. Let me come home."

He'd been ten years old when he'd last begged someone for something, and he'd promised himself he'd never do it again, but this was too important. He'd been the one to fuck up. He'd done a royal job of it. She hadn't answered his messages and neither had his birth brothers. He'd convinced himself she didn't want him and neither did they. Pride had kicked in. Hurt. He hadn't investigated the way he should have. She was the most important person in his life. She not only could save him, but he knew her effect would be felt by all the others.

Love me, baby. I need you to love me. He dropped his head onto her lap.

Her hand slid into his hair, her fingers sending pleasure spiraling through him. *I do love you. I've always loved you. I'm just . . . afraid.*

The air left his lungs in a long rush of shock. She still loved him. Five long, empty years, dealing with the death of their daughter and her psycho mother alone, and she still loved him. He recognized instantly that he wasn't out of the woods yet. She hadn't said it aloud. Blythe had never had problems telling him she loved him. He'd been the one to hold back, unfamiliar with being demonstrative. She'd taught him that as well. With her, he felt safe to show her how much he loved her. And he loved her with every single cell in his body, his heart and his soul—if he still had one.

It's a lot to take in. You're . . . programmed to kill. You've been doing it all these years, and so have the others. You've ridden with one of the worst outlaw biker clubs in existence for five years. That had to take its toll on you. You formed your own club with the others. How can you possibly assimilate back into society?

He had to tell her the stark, ugly truth whether he wanted to or not. He could lie to anyone else, but not her. Not Blythe. *We can't.*

There was silence. Long. He wasn't certain he could still breathe, but he had to take a breath. Her hand never stopped moving in his hair. She'd always been like that. Touching him. Loving him with every caress no matter how small. She showed her feelings for him every minute of every day. She'd given him hope when there was none. He wasn't a touchy-feely guy. He was mean and tough and ruthless. But then . . . there was Blythe.

You're bossy. Worse than you were before.

He doubted that. Blythe just never went against him. They'd always gone the same way. Now he was asking her to do things that were frightening to her. It was a massive responsibility. Yeah. Okay. He was bossy. He told others far older than him what to do when he was ten and they did it. He was president of Torpedo Ink and his word was law. He was the boss, but not just to get his own way. It was never about getting his own way. He'd give Blythe the fucking moon if that's what she wanted. He'd figure a way.

The same. I've always been this way.

You don't stop until you get your way.

How did he explain this to her so she'd understand? *We didn't have food, baby, so I found ways to make that happen. When one way didn't work, I tried another and another until it did. When we couldn't stop the rapes, I tried one way and when that didn't work, I kept changing our method until it did. Do you think I would work less hard for the most important person in my life? I can't lose you. I have to find a way to make you understand I'll work that hard for us. There isn't anything I won't do for you.* He meant that too. She just couldn't conceive of all the things he meant.

He felt her take a deep breath. He didn't dare look at her

face. He wanted to kiss her. To not play fair. To use his knowledge of her body. Anything to get her to agree that he could come home to her. He told himself to wait, to give her time; she deserved time.

"Want me, baby, the way I want you."

"I never stopped wanting you," she said softly. "Not for a single minute of the day. Even when I was really, really angry with you, Viktor, I wanted you with me." Her fingers continued a slow, mesmerizing massage on his scalp.

"Can you take me back, Blythe?" He raised his head to look at her face. "I need you to say you can. To mean it. To forgive me for not being here with you when you needed me most."

"Viktor, if I asked you to stop what you were doing right now, walk away from this thing with the Swords, would you be able to do it?"

His heart stopped and then began to pound, an unusual reaction for him. He'd given five years of his life and his own child to get a chance at killing Evan Shackler-Gratsos. The man was hideous. He was the worst trafficker in all countries around the world. For a moment he couldn't breathe. Would he do that for her? Of course. Yes. If that was what it took to make things right between them, but . . .

He knelt back, his eyes meeting hers, searching hers. The Blythe he knew would want Evan gone every bit as much as he did. Her request was out of character. Completely. "Yes. If that was what it took to convince you that you're more important than anything or anyone to me, but, baby, I'd want to know your reasons."

Her gaze stayed steady on his, but she dropped her hands into her lap and twisted her fingers together. "I'm afraid for you." She admitted it in a low tone. "I'm not saying I want you to do it, just asking if you would."

"There's no need to be afraid for me. I've got Reaper, Savage, Ice, Storm and so many others watching my back. I'll have my birth brothers and probably your sisters and you keeping an eye out. I'm good at what I do. I plan things out in meticulous detail. Nothing is left to chance. I've learned how over the years, and I've got a crew that knows what they're doing."

Her tongue touched her bottom lip, drawing his attention. He'd always loved her bottom lip, the fullness of that curve. The softness. He loved biting it and then kissing her all better. He could spend hours kissing her.

"And after? What do you plan to do?"

"We're looking into purchasing large amounts of land in Caspar. That isn't far from here. We'll have our clubhouse, restaurant, bike and car shop, the club, tattoo parlor and of course homes there. I'll stay here with you and the girls."

"What will the club do, Viktor? Will everything be legal?"

He'd asked her to accept so much. Too much. She was doing all the giving and he all the taking. He didn't know how to answer that without lying to her and he wasn't going to do that. He sighed. "Probably not. We go after pedophiles, Blythe. We plan to continue to do the same."

She kept looking at him. He sighed again. "Sometimes, baby, it sucks that you're so intelligent. Other things. We'll take on some bodyguard work. Maybe transporter work. No gun running or drugs. That's not our thing. We saw far too many drugs in the school where we were. Sorbacov and his friends liked to snort cocaine and rape the kids all jacked up. Drugs just aren't in the equation."

That was the best he could do because at this juncture, even though they talked about it, they hadn't firmed up all their rules for the club, what they were willing to take on and what they weren't. The things that hadn't already been agreed on would be put to a vote. In the end, his word was law and he knew it. If he opposed anything, his men would eventually agree with him—even Reaper and Savage.

He took her face in his hands again and tilted her head up to his. "Can you live with that, Blythe? Can you live with us the way we are? Fucked-up. Imperfect, but trying. We want to live as free as possible, but have a home. Have this place. Sea Haven. Caspar. We'll protect it from crime."

"We have cops," she said softly.

Her gaze slid from his, and he knew why. "You know as

well as I do the cops can't always stop certain criminals. We can."

"But *illegally*."

"If Evan is caught by the cops, do you really believe, with all his money, that it would stop him? Even if by some miracle he went to prison, and I can guarantee you he wouldn't, he'd still run the Swords and all his other businesses. You know he would, baby."

"I know. I do," she admitted. "But you can't be the executioner."

"I can. I have been all my life. It's what we do best. It's who we are. You have to think about that and know just who you have in your bed. You have to be able to live with it. I won't make it a habit of telling you what we're doing, but if you ask, I'm going to tell you the truth. Always. I'll tell you." He meant that. Blythe deserved truth and he'd always give it to her—if she asked.

He couldn't stop himself, he brushed his lips over hers. The taste of her was there instantly. Peaches. Cream. She was always so feminine. Girly. He loved that about her too. She ran all the time, but it didn't matter; she still smelled like heaven. One hand curled around her throat. He loved feeling her heart beating in his hand. Feeling her swallow as he brushed his mouth over hers one more time. Even that felt like coming home.

She hadn't turned away from him yet. Not even when he'd told her the worst. "I'm a man who's had things in his life that I never want any other human being to know. Getting raped isn't something men talk about." He lifted her hand, turned it palm up. "Those secrets are here, in your hand."

She closed her fingers tight. "They're safe with me, Viktor."

"I know that. I trust you, Blythe. I've always trusted you. You're not just beautiful on the outside, and believe me, you are. Your hair, so wild and untamed in the bedroom and all cool and put together outside of it. Your skin. Legs that go on forever. Your breasts are perfect, and then that ass, can't stop looking when you walk away from me. I love that I can kiss you just by leaning into you, I don't have to crouch down. But that isn't the best, and seriously, honey, that's all fuc— Great. Perfect."

"What's the best?"

He could see that his compliment affected her. She flushed a beautiful rose, her breathing changed, went ragged, breasts rising and falling with every pant, and she pressed her thighs together. He meant every single word.

"You. Your soul. What's inside you. You shine from the inside out. You're so bright, Blythe. I get close to you and the darkness just recedes. The world I live in slips farther away, and I can see there's hope. You're that hope. Not just for me, but for all of us." He couldn't help pleading his case for the others. They counted on him. He would lose them to the violent world they knew best.

"You think I can somehow save all of them, don't you?"

"I know you can. Right now they don't know any other life than what they were forced to do. To be. I didn't know there was something else until you came along. Fuck, Blythe. You don't even know what you did, do you? What you gave to me. A miracle. Learning to laugh, to look forward to every day. I didn't want to sleep at night because I was afraid I'd miss something with you." He'd known all along his time was running out, that once he'd carried out his assignment and killed her stepfather, she might never look at him again.

She shook her head. "I'm not so different from everyone else."

"You are. To me you're everything. I know absolutely that I'm overwhelming you. I'm trying not to, but I don't know any other way than to push for what I want. For what we all need. I believe I'm what you need. You take care of everyone around you, but who takes care of you? I do."

"Not when you're not here." She pushed back the hair spilling out of her ponytail. It was always a little wild at the end of the day, her sleek look gone just for him to see.

"I'll be here. I don't look at other women, I can support you, I have money . . ."

"Viktor. Really? Do you think I'm looking for a man to support me? I make my own way."

"You said that to me before. When I first met you." He moved back and let his gaze drift over her beloved face. "We have to resolve this. What else? What are the things that concern you the most?"

"Living with these bikers who treat women like slaves, you've learned to tell everyone what to do and expect it to get done. That worries me."

"I've always told everyone what to do and expected it to be done. Don't you remember?" He watched her face carefully. He saw the small flash of amusement as her memories kicked in.

She nodded. "You're worse. Do you think that's really going to work with me?"

"Not all the time, but you're not a woman who sweats the small stuff. You'll do what I ask you to most of the time because it won't matter to you, or you'll see it's for the best. When you disagree, you'll tell me. I trust your judgment, and when I'm not right, you'll let me know and I'll concede immediately. Remember? Think back, Blythe. I was always this way. Pushing. You used to tell me it was both my best and worst trait."

Blythe covered her face with her hands. She needed time to think. Pushing was his best and worst trait. Why was she so afraid to be with him? She loved him. There wasn't another man she'd ever considered being with.

"Baby, don't retreat, we're almost there. We're working things out. Tell me what you need. What to do. I'll do it. I'll make it right for you."

"When you left, I was so devastated. It isn't just about forgiving you for not being here. I understand why. It isn't about not hearing from you. That, I'm still not certain about, but I know something huge went wrong." Her heart pounded so hard she was afraid it might explode. She couldn't let go again. She couldn't trust him again. She had too much to lose. She held herself together with mere threads, so easily snapped.

"Tell me."

She took a breath, let it out and looked into his steely eyes. And let go. "If you left again after I let you in, it would totally destroy me. Totally, Viktor. I would never recover. It isn't your family or Darby or any of the other things you expect or need from me. I can handle those things, it's what I do, but you . . . I can't survive losing you twice."

She saw his face change. He didn't show expression often, mostly when they were alone, but he did now. The love on his face seared right through her. She couldn't take that either, not without feeling the burn of tears. She hadn't had a lot of love in her life until Viktor had come into it. He'd looked at her like that.

She remembered coming in from work and he'd have dinner ready. There was always laughter and impromptu dancing around the kitchen, sometimes out in the yard in the rain. Always he looked at her as if she was the most important person in the world. He looked at her that way now. Something inside her shifted and she bit down hard on her lip. He was slipping back inside, little by little.

"Baby." He said it softly.

She heard the love. Felt it surround her. He could do that. Envelop her in him. Surround her with him. It was frightening how her entire being reacted to him. Body and soul, she was his. She had been from the moment she met him.

"Was it real?" She whispered the question, afraid of the answer. Afraid he'd say no and she'd be devastated. Afraid he'd say yes and she'd be lost all over again.

Viktor pulled her into his arms. "Every minute I was with you was the most real I've ever been."

Blythe heard the ring of sincerity in his voice—the absolute truth—and it was her undoing. There had been far too much to take in. His horrible, horrible life. Him standing in front of her pleading with her, a man who had always stood unbending, never asking for anything from anyone.

"I'm certain there will be times I'll be angry with you all over again for not being here with me when I needed you most. I won't be able to help that."

He nodded. "That's understandable, and when it comes up, we can deal with it."

"Even if I don't speak to you for a day or two?" She made it a challenge, because both of them knew that wasn't Viktor's way.

He brushed his mouth over the top of her head, one of those gestures that was always her undoing. "We'll talk it out, even if you have to hit me."

"I might hit you a lot."

"I'm tough."

He was. He was *so* tough, with everyone but her. Her heart pounded because she already knew it was too late for her. She didn't know how they could work through all the problems, but she knew she had to try. Still, she had to hold tight to herself just to keep from falling apart.

"Why a motorcycle club? That really bothers me. I don't know why. I didn't realize I might be prejudiced, but I think I am. I associate that lifestyle with men and women who have no regard for the law."

He stared at her a moment and then threw his head back and laughed. Real laughter. Genuine. God. It tore through her, taking her heart. So beautiful to see him do that. To know she gave him that.

"Babe. Really? Of course we don't have regard for laws. We make our own. You're going to teach us that, remember?"

She knew he was teasing her, and she melted a little more inside. She remembered that as well, the intimacy of having a man who gently teased her over the hard things.

"Be serious." Although now she didn't really want him to be. She liked him laughing. She liked him gentle. "I don't like the way the clubs treat women."

"Do you like the way I treat women?" Now all hint of laughter was gone. He regarded her steadily. "Do you think because I ride a motorcycle the way I view women would suddenly change?"

She shook her head. "I guess not. It's just that . . . Why motorcycles?"

"You're on the open road with the wind in your face and

the feeling of the bike beneath you. It's freedom, honey. I don't know how to explain it."

"Then show me."

He studied her face as if he couldn't believe what she'd said. "You serious? You'll ride with me?"

"If that's your world and you want me with you, then I have to see if I like it."

She knew, by the look on his face, that he recognized the concession. She still hadn't said no to him. She was taking more and more steps toward *yes*.

"I have to make one phone call, Blythe, and then we'll go. I need to call the Sword chapter president and let him know I was in a fight today. I have to cover myself at all times."

She nodded as he stepped away from her and pulled out his cell phone.

"You can't say a word. Get a jacket. It's cool tonight. We'll make a run along Highway 1, and the wind is coming in off the ocean."

She nodded but made no movement toward the stairs. She'd go up *after* she heard what he had to say to his chapter president. Viktor glanced at her, frowned, but didn't stop punching in the number. Clearly he'd expected obedience. She remembered that about him as well. Anything to do with comfort, health or her safety, he wanted and expected cooperation.

He was in for a surprise. He wasn't going to face Evan alone, not if she was taking him back. There were things she could do, and she wasn't going to listen to him tell her it was too dangerous. If he could be there, she could as well. She knew he'd have a plan. That's what Viktor did. Plan. Right now his plan didn't include her help, but that was going to change.

"Habit. Yeah. Had some trouble today. Nothing big. Few idiots strutting around town pushing old ladies and kids around, talking tough and calling attention to themselves, gave me an opportunity to get in good around here. Beat the hell out of the idiots and even had the cops eating out of my hand. Managed to collect a lot of information on Deveau and his route. I'm scouting areas now on his beat that we can use for a trap. Bad news, Evan can't use a helicopter to come in. It would draw far too much attention. Everyone would know he's here. He'll have to ride in on a bike, but I should have a good place for a large number to camp without anyone knowing. How many?"

Blythe studied his face as he talked. He was entirely different. Totally in the role of the biker badass setting up a sheriff to die. Everything about him changed. He looked hard. Scary. He sounded it, even though his voice was low. A small shiver slid down her spine. He wasn't as cold as Reaper, but close. Very close. Too close.

He suddenly reached out his hand to hers, as if he could guess what she was thinking. She hesitated just enough that he noticed, but his fingers closed around hers and he pulled her beneath his shoulder, locking her against his body, her front to his side. She remembered that as well, the way it made her feel so protected. He seemed to know when she was nervous or scared, especially around her mother, and he always surrounded her with his protection. She'd never felt safer than when she was with him.

"You're shitting me. What the hell? They were Swords? What the fuck are they doing in Sea Haven drawing attention to themselves? They were breaking things in a store, knocking merchandise over, refusing to pay. That alone would have brought the sheriff. In fact, it did. Fucking idiots."

Viktor sounded completely disgusted. He played his role so well. As if he didn't know the men he'd fought were part of the very club he'd been riding with. He listened for a moment, erupted into a storm of really disgusting swearing and then listened more.

"Look, this is a shit assignment for someone like me. I like action, Habit. If you don't trust me to get the job done, then send someone else. I'm not a babysitter. Those fuckers got themselves in trouble and put the entire plan in jeopardy. I can be out of here tonight if Evan has someone else he wants to send."

He listened again, and she could tell whoever was on the other end of the phone was trying to soothe him.

"Does he have anyone else here I should be looking after? Because you know, that's what I live to do. Have my thumb up my ass babysitting idiots." Again silence while he listened. "Find out. And tell whoever is in touch with them to make it clear they don't bring attention to themselves. It was like they were trying to blow the entire operation. Either that or Evan's changed his mind and just wants Deveau taken out. I can do that and then blow this crap town."

He was good, planting that seed. Blythe had to admire him. His chapter president would find out the other Swords were in jail and he'd read the reports. Find out just what they'd done to cause the sheriff to show up.

For one heart-stopping moment she thought that maybe he was playing her again. But then, she could read his emotions, and right now, he was disgusted. Before, when he'd met her, he'd been genuinely interested. She had a bullshit meter that was nearly always accurate.

Viktor got off the phone, pocketed it, turned her to the front of him and took her mouth. She expected wild. She got gentle. So gentle. It turned her heart over. His mouth moved over hers, his tongue tangling with hers, the taste of him filling her up. He poured love into her, love mixed with desire so strong it took her breath. It was a potent mixture that nearly brought her to tears.

He lifted his head, not taking advantage when he could have. She actually chased his mouth, needing more of the taste of him. He brushed his lips across hers several times and then put her gently at his arm's length. "You know we can't go there until you're ready, Blythe, and you aren't ready."

She *felt* ready, at least her body did, but he was right; emotionally she wasn't there. She appreciated that Viktor was a strong man. He might try to overpower her with his relentless pursuit, but he also had a code that prevented him from using her own desires against her.

"You always look at me that way." There was wonder in his voice.

"Which way?" She could barely breathe straight.

"Like I'm your knight. For you, honey, I want to be. I want to be that man you see. When I look in the mirror, I see something dark and twisted. When you look at me, I see myself in your eyes and it's something beautiful."

"Because you are," she said. "No one has your strength. Look at these men and women who follow you. They're strong, and yet they all look to you because they believe in you. They know you're a good man."

"I'm not that, baby, but I'm trying to be. I want to be."

Again she heard the absolute sincerity in his voice. He believed what he was saying, and that made her sad. "How can you not see that you're a good man?"

"It was one thing for me to kill to survive. I had to in order to keep my brothers safe, but I taught the others. It was my plan. I worked it all out. Yes, they're alive, but they don't know any other way of life."

That weighed on him. "Sorbacov is responsible, Viktor," she pointed out gently. "Not you. Let's go for a ride. I'm tired but not sleepy, and I need to get away from all the emotion. I think you do as well."

He took her hand instantly and they went up the wide staircase together. When he was anywhere near her, he wanted to touch her. To hold hands. To put his arms around her. To stand with her back to his front and his arms linked around her chest. Or her front to his side with his arm locked tight around her. That had made her feel protected, precious, important, all the things she'd never had as a child.

They entered the bedroom and she stopped abruptly, surveying the disaster on her bed. It was a big bed. She liked space, and even in her bed, she wanted to know she had room to sprawl out. Right now, her bed looked small. Leather jackets, leather vests and even some ripped denim vests piled in a heap on her bed.

She dropped his hand, put both hands on her hips and glared at him. "What. Is. This?" She enunciated each word carefully.

He grinned at her, looking for a moment like a

mischievous boy. The look was so beautiful and fleeting it
stole her heart. She loved the look on him so she kept her
sternest face, refusing to give in to the need to laugh.

"Don't look cute. Tell me what it is."

"Our colors."

"You just threw them all over my bed?"

"Not me." He held up his hands. "I know better than
that. You taught me to hang up towels, remember?"

It had taken her forever to get him to see why one didn't
just pitch wet towels in the corner of a room. He didn't
mind cooking and he'd actually run the vacuum as if it was
some great toy, but laundry was not ever going to be his
thing. She'd resigned herself to that and the fact that her
man was never going to be Mr. Neat.

"Not you?" She narrowed her eyes and then stalked to
the window. It was wide open. She was certain she'd not
only closed it but locked it before she'd left. She stuck her
head out and glared at the roof. It was dark out and she
couldn't see anyone there, but she knew exactly who was
out there. "Reaper. Next time you throw things around in
my bedroom I'll be escorting you back inside to clean up
the mess."

Viktor made a choking sound, cutting off his laughter,
wrapped his arm around her waist and hauled her back
inside.

"Your woman is a little crazy." Reaper's droll voice
came from outside.

Viktor bunched her ponytail in his fist and pulled her
head back as he leaned down just enough to capture her
mouth with his. There was no resisting him in this mood.
She wrapped both arms around his neck, leaned her body
into his and kissed him back. She gave him everything,
because it was impossible not to, not when it was Viktor.

When he lifted his head, both hands framed her face.
"Thank God you're a little crazy," he whispered. "I'm sorry
he made a mess. I'll straighten them out."

"What are they?" she repeated.

"Our colors. We can't be caught with them and Evan is

paranoid. I wouldn't put it past him to search us, our bikes and gear. We carry our colors. All of us have compartments built into our bikes, ones no one knows about, but it's getting far too dangerous now that we're close to the end of this thing."

She went over to the bed and picked up a leather jacket, touching the upper rocker with her finger. "Torpedo Ink?"

"We thought up the name when we were teenagers. It was cool back then. *Torpedo* is a hit man and *Ink* instead of *incorporated.*"

The patch was the tree, skulls and crows Reaper had inked on his back. There was no bottom rocker to say where they were from. It made her sad that they didn't have a home base. He wanted that so much, not just for him, but for his brothers and sisters. She couldn't help running her finger down the length of that sturdy tree trunk. It looked strong, holding up the seventeen branches. To other people, it was a tree; to his club, it was all about Viktor and the lives they lost—and saved.

Blythe couldn't help but look at the skulls wrapped tightly in the roots of the trees. Most had several but there were a few jackets where the skulls were more than plentiful. Too plentiful. She didn't have to ask whose jackets they were. She knew and felt sad for the little boys they had been. Viktor had deliberately stopped short of telling her anyone else's story, but she knew and it made her sick.

"These mean something to all of you," she said. "Let's get them hung up out of respect." She picked up Reaper's and Savage's jackets and made her way to the large walk-in closet that took up one side of the very large room. "There's plenty of room. I'm not a minimalist, but I don't have a lot of clothes I hang up." She took a hanger from the closet and turned to face Viktor.

He hadn't moved. "Honey? What is it?" The look on his face alarmed her. It was difficult to read. He stared at her as if he wanted to cry, yet his expression was difficult to read.

He swallowed hard. "You know that I love you, right?"

His voice was gruff, as if his throat were rusty, and the declaration came out strangled.

She didn't know how to answer that. She knew. How could she not? She felt it every time they were together. She'd even felt it in the street when he'd looked up and seen her on the sidewalk of Sea Haven. The emotion was strong and always surrounded her until she was cloaked in him. In his love and protection. She didn't know how to answer so she didn't respond; rather she turned and hung the jacket carefully and then did the same with Savage's.

"Thank you, Blythe. You don't know what it means that you understand about our colors. They represent . . ."

"All of you," she finished for him. "Come on, help me. It isn't as if you each don't have more than two. Who sewed all these patches on?"

"Alena, Lana and Code. You haven't met Lana or Code yet, but you will. Never tell Code I told you he helped sew the patches."

She didn't take her eyes from his face when he spoke. She caught the hint of that mischievous boy again and the disparity in his emotions. "You all sewed them," she guessed. "Even big bad Reaper."

He grinned again, a slow, beautiful smile that sent her heart clenching hard and heat pulsing between her legs. She picked up more jackets and took them to the closet. "Hurry up. You promised me a ride." Okay, that wasn't a good thing to say to him. Not in her bedroom. "On your bike," she added hastily.

His laughter made the pulsing turn to pounding.

14

BLYTHE stood beside the large motorcycle trying not to hyperventilate. In all the years she'd been alive, this was something she'd never done. It was dark, but very clear with stars glittering across the sky like diamonds. The moon was mostly a sliver, but a bright silver, shining down on the ocean, sending light spilling across the water.

She could see from the vantage point where he'd left his bike. The place of concealment was some distance from her actual house, in a narrow opening between two of her favorite bushes. He'd rolled it out, and she was a little shocked that the machine was much larger than she envisioned.

"Put this on." He handed her a helmet.

"Very convenient that you have two." That made her sound like a harpy, and she wasn't very happy with herself for sniping at him just because she was afraid.

He didn't say anything, but came over to her, put the helmet carefully on her head and secured it. He took his gloved hand and tucked it under her chin while he looked steadily at her. "Do you think I would ever let anything happen to you?"

She knew better. He wouldn't. His protective gene had to be off the charts. Sighing, she shook her head. She'd asked for this. It had been her idea; now she just couldn't be a baby about it.

"I've been riding a long time. I started in Russia, baby, when I was twenty-one and they released me from the school."

She gasped. "You were there that long?"

He nodded, his face still soft with love, but his eyes had gone molten with a suppressed rage that sometimes—like now—seem to suck all the air out of the atmosphere. "The point is, I'll always take care of you, but you don't have to do this if you don't want to."

Her chin went up. If he could spend all those years in a hellhole, she could get on the back of his motorcycle. "I want to. I really do." She found that was the truth. She wanted to see what drew his brothers and sisters and him to the road.

She thought she understood the need for their club. It was a brotherhood. A family. They'd formed that years earlier in their prison, surrounded by criminals. They'd counted on one another and had one another's back. Essentially, that was what a club was, a family with their own rules and codes. It was the motorcycles . . .

Viktor settled himself on the bike and reached out his hand to her. "Use my shoulder for balance and just step on that and swing on."

Heart beating hard, she did as he told her, settling her body behind his. Close. Very, very close. The engine roared to life and her heart nearly stopped. Straddling the bike with the vibration of the engine between her legs and her body pressed so close to Viktor was *not* a good idea. He reached back, caught her hands and pulled her arms around him, so that her hands were clasped low on his body. Definitely not a good idea. Now she wasn't worried about accidents. She was all too aware of Viktor.

She loved everything about him. His body, so strong and confident. The unexpected laughter. He was so expressionless most of the time that when he laughed, she always felt like it was such a gift. She could spend a lifetime just watching the way he moved. He seemed to flow, and he never made a sound. Like a cat. A great big lazy, dangerous jungle cat, but still that fluid motion always set her blood on fire.

She closed her eyes and put her head against his back, tense and scared, but trying not to show it. She concentrated on how he smelled and the way he felt against her. Her breasts were pressed tight to his back and moved with the motion of the bike, her nipples rubbing along the lace of her bra. She bit her lip. This might be torture.

When nothing bad happened to her, she forced her eyes open so she could look around her. They were already on Highway 1, going south. Moving fast. Her body felt stiff, muscles cramped, and she made an effort to relax. The moment she did, she felt the rhythm of his body and the motorcycle. Hers followed naturally.

She dared to lift her head and look around. She could see everything around her so easily—as if she was right in the middle of it, part of nature. The ocean gleamed like glass, light where the moon turned the water to silver and dark where that beaming light didn't hit directly. Her body moved with the bike and with Viktor as if they were one unit together. The bike felt powerful just as Viktor did. She relaxed completely, giving herself to the experience, just as she did whenever he touched her.

His hand moved over hers, rubbing in a caress, and she wasn't even afraid that he wasn't holding on with both hands. Then he took his hand away and they were flying down the road so smoothly, straightening out the endless curves as if they weren't even there. She didn't ask where they were going because it didn't matter. She didn't want the ride to ever end.

They continued traveling south along Highway 1, going through Elk and then Manchester. It was a long way by car, and she'd traveled it often, but it was a completely different experience on the motorcycle. She did feel free and excited. Definitely turned on. The longer they moved as one, the more she felt part of the bike and Viktor.

She'd always loved Manchester and nearly tapped him on the shoulder to get him to stop. A secret part of her wanted to hike across the dunes, hopefully find the beach deserted and make love to her man. She didn't say anything, mostly because she was having such a good time and didn't want the ride to end.

Riding with Viktor made her feel part of the night. The ocean was on one side and the wild terrain on the other. They went through small towns with few houses and even fewer shops. Point Arena was the biggest, and he barely slowed as they went through it and kept going south.

She knew it took over an hour to get to where they were by car, but it hardly seemed as if time passed at all before they were past Gualala to Sea Ranch and he was slowing the motorcycle to turn onto Annapolis Road. She'd only been out that way once and then just to explore, but the river was close.

Blythe couldn't help herself. The temptation was too much. She dropped her hands lower, sliding them over his hard belly. He'd always had a washboard stomach. She remembered lying in bed with him and just tracing all those delicious muscles. He had never understood her fascination, but he'd never minded. Her hands edged up under his jacket and she caressed his belly through her gloves and his shirt, wishing he wasn't wearing one.

Suddenly all she could think about was Viktor, and the fire building between her legs. Her hands deliberately dropped lower, to cup his cock. She remembered every single detail of his cock. The length and girth of it. How he felt, hot and hard and velvet soft yet like steel. He didn't stop her stroking fingers, but he did speed up just a little, and she knew the powerful engine, the caress of her hand and the press of her breasts into his back were getting to him.

She found herself smiling just for the pure joy of being alive. She hadn't felt that way in a long, long time. Not since Viktor was with her and they spent every minute together just worshipping each other's bodies. "Hurry," she whispered against his back, her hand sliding over his cock, fingers molding to him, dancing and teasing. She really needed him to hurry.

Blythe recognized the river and Iron Bridge when he slowed the bike. Few people were ever there as a rule, and she doubted if anyone would be this time of night. He stopped and they just sat together staring at the river, his hand over hers, pressing her palm tight over the length of his hard cock.

She could barely breathe with wanting him. "Viktor." His name came out with heat and need.

"I know, baby." He tugged at her hand and indicated she get off the bike.

She wasn't certain she could stand. It wasn't just the long time on the back of the motorcycle; it was the need coursing through her veins. Need that had become intense hunger for him. For the taste and feel of him. She'd never forgotten the vivid details of nights and days spent making love for hours on end.

She took off the helmet and shook out her hair, trying to control her breathing. He untied a duffel bag, caught her by the hand and without a word headed down to the river. In the distance she heard the roar of bikes and that brought her up short.

"Did some of the others follow us here?"

"We'll be alone."

Of course they had been followed. He was Viktor—Czar. "They guard you with their lives, don't they?" He kept walking, urgency in his long strides. That told her he was as affected by the ride and her close proximity as she had been with him.

"I'm their president."

"You're more than their president to them." He always would be. She understood why now.

He dropped the bag, went down on one knee and unzipped it, yanking it open. He dragged a thick blanket out, unrolled it and threw it on the ground. "Put your hand on my shoulder, honey."

She did, her heart pounding and her sex clenching. She

needed him. Right. Now. He didn't seem to understand the urgency of the matter, because he was fiddling with her boots. She moaned, looking at his bent head.

"It's been five years for me, Blythe. Haven't touched a woman. My hands are fumbling a little bit."

"It's been five years since I touched a man," she admitted. She held out her hand in front of him. It was shaking. "I don't know if I can do better." She lifted her foot and he yanked off the boot and went to the other one. Somehow he got that off without her falling down. She was shaking so hard she had to hang on to his shoulders with both hands as he removed first one sock and then the other.

He knelt up and caught at the zipper of her jeans. "Take off your jacket, Blythe. Hurry, baby. I might explode before we get started and that would be a major blow to my pride."

She let go of him long enough to rip off the jacket and fling it aside. It landed on her boots. He had her zipper down and caught at the waistband of her jeans, catching her lacy underwear at the same time. He slid the material over her hips, down her thighs to her calves. She had to hold on again to his shoulder while she lifted first one leg and then the other to get out of the offending material.

Her breath came in ragged pants. The burn between her legs had grown until it was a wildfire out of control. She could barely stand when he pushed her thighs apart, wedged himself between them, caught her bottom in his hands and licked up the inside of her thigh.

She gasped. "Viktor." It wasn't a protest. It was a demand.

"Take off your top."

She didn't hesitate. Not for a moment. She didn't even care where his friends were, how close or how far. If they could see or not. She flung her T-shirt after her jacket and without being asked, undid the lacy bra so that her breasts spilled free. She needed the cool breeze on her body.

She *really* needed his mouth on her, but he was doing something slow and lazy with his tongue instead of getting down to business. She caught him by his hair and tugged at his head to bring him closer. *"Viktor."*

"I'm remembering how much I love the taste of you. The feel of your skin. Your scent." His voice was very soft. "Making new memories, baby."

"Make them later," she demanded.

He laughed and blew warm air on her, holding her still while he nuzzled. She tightened her fists in his hair in warning. She *loved* his laughter. Even when he was driving her mad, she loved it. Then his mouth was on her and she lost every sane thought she had. She cried out. Loud. With Viktor there was never a place for inhibitions. He just didn't allow them. Just like that, all her walls came tumbling down, and she was once again just Blythe. All woman. His woman. And that was all that mattered to either of them.

He was relentless, his tongue stabbing deep, teasing, circling, flicking. He knew what he was doing and he did it expertly, but with so much feeling. The rush consumed her faster than she ever thought possible, she was so primed. Then he was driving her right back up, a ruthless demand in his fingers and mouth. Taking her there again before she had caught her breath.

"Viktor." Just his name. Thinking to stop him. There was no stopping him.

He devoured her, taking his time now, slowing his attack so that the terrible sensitivity could ease enough that she could breathe. His mouth was so good. How had she lived without it? Without him? She didn't know. She didn't care now that he was with her. On his knees, holding her up, his mouth eating her as if she was the best treat in the world.

"I can't. It's coming again." It was. A fierce coiling. So tight. A gathering that threatened to take her sanity this time.

"Let go. Give me this, baby."

He whispered against her clit, his tongue stroking, and then he suckled, and she was lost. She screamed as wave after wave of sheer fire blazed through her. The flames raced through her body, up through her belly to her breasts, and down her thighs to her legs and toes. For a moment, spots danced before her eyes. She blinked rapidly, trying to clear her vision while Viktor tore off his jacket and shirt, flinging them on top of her clothes and boots.

Two men rushed down the other side of the road, guns drawn, gravel flying. Both came to an abrupt halt, staring at her through the darkness. Reaper and Savage. Both shook their heads, grinned, gave her a small salute and then turned away. She watched them as they walked back up the road. Neither looked back.

She should have panicked. She should have cared. She was stark naked with a man kneeling between her legs. She was out in the open under a blanket of stars and it was the most decadent thing she could imagine. It only added to the excitement.

"Hurry, Viktor." The fire was building all over again. She didn't know how. He was no longer touching her, pulling off his boots and socks and then reaching for the zipper of his jeans. Still, the relentless pounding of blood in her clit continued. It had been so long. Too long. "I need you inside me right now."

He shoved his jeans down and his cock sprang free. She inhaled sharply at the sight of him, mesmerized. Before she could stop herself she reached out and wrapped her fingers around him, going to her knees in front of him. He'd always told her his body belonged to her alone. She'd believed him the way he responded to her.

Her fist sliding over that velvety steel, she looked at his chest. She'd always loved his chest. So broad and strong, the muscles defined. Right over his heart was her tattoo. It was there, the lock wrapped with chains, razor wire and thorns from a single long-stemmed red rose, the only color on his ink. Her name was written there inside the tangle of wire, chain and thorns.

He sank to the ground on his butt, forcing her to bend forward if she wanted to keep hold of his cock, which she did. So hot. So hard. All hers. Her mouth watered. She needed to taste him. The thought added more heat pounding through her clit. Those small inner muscles clenched as her body wept for him. Was desperate for him.

She bent farther, brushing kisses along his chest, lapping at his left nipple, his belly button, tracing muscles lower leading to his groin.

"You're not making this easy," he said, trying to shed his jeans.

She barely heard him. Her breasts brushed over his thighs, her nipples hard peaks pushing into his skin as she licked up his shaft and her tongue danced along the crown. His cock jerked and pulsed. Pearly liquid dotted the broad head. She licked the drops off and closed her eyes, savoring his taste. She loved his taste. She always had.

His entire body shuddered as she engulfed him, drawing him deep, flicking with her tongue, using it like an exquisite weapon, suckling with strong pulls until he caught her hair in his fist and dragged her head up.

"I'm not going to last long this first time, Blythe. I want to be in you. Hands and knees, baby. I'm going to take you hard and fast and then the second time we'll slow things down and I can look into your eyes and see you get there. I love looking at you when you come."

She was on her hands and knees fast, turning away from him, staring out over the river, feeling the sway of her breasts, her body on fire. He knelt up behind her, his hand moving between her legs to test her readiness, although he had to know she was more than ready. She pushed back, her breath coming in ragged little pants.

"Hurry, honey," she whispered. "You have to hurry."

"I love that you're always ready for me. Always as eager as I am." He circled his shaft with his fist and tore the condom wrapper with his teeth. He rolled it on and then lodged the broad head in her entrance.

Her breath hissed out. He was so hot. She tried to push back and impale herself but he dug his fingers into her hip to hold her still.

"Careful, baby. You haven't done this for a while. I don't

want you hurt. I'm going to go slow until I know you're all right."

"I won't be all right if you don't get on with it. I need you inside me," she instructed, turning her head to look at him over her shoulder.

He pushed in an inch and she gasped. The feeling was so good. He waited a moment for her body to adjust. "You're tight. Scorching hot and so tight you're practically strangling me."

"I can feel your heart beat right through your cock," she said, stumbling a little over the word. He'd taught her that, amused that she'd never used that word. He'd taught her a lot of things, things that at first made her blush, but then gave her so much pleasure she wanted to do them all the time.

He pushed deeper, and she couldn't help the moan that escaped. He was full, stretching her, her tight muscles rippling around him, greedy for him, wanting to pull him deeper, wanting to milk him.

"The second I can, I'll go to a clinic and prove to you that I'm clean and haven't been with anyone, Blythe," he promised, "so I don't have to wear a glove. I know you don't like them."

She didn't. She'd been the one to insist they stop using them when they were married. She wanted to feel every inch of him, just like she did now. He pushed deeper, and then surged forward, burying himself to the hilt. The breath hissed out of her in one long rush. Her body clamped down on his, holding him even tighter.

He groaned and began to move. Slow strokes that sent streaks of fire through her. He'd always hit every single important spot and he did now, so that with each surge into her, he sent ripples of pleasure bursting through her. He began to pick up the pace and she felt a sob of pure joy welling up. Making love with Viktor had always been an adventure, but it was beautiful and perfect and felt so, so good. After all the time without, it felt even better than she remembered—and she'd kept those memories close.

Even after all three times he'd made her orgasm with his mouth, she was close—so close right away. Coiling tight. Panting out demands for more. For harder. He obliged, picking up the pace, sending those fiery streaks radiating out from her center to every part of her body. The cool air kissed her hot skin, adding to her pleasure every time the breeze brushed over her.

His fingers dug into her hips and he pulled her into him as he thrust forward. Again and again. She pushed back, her breath hitching in her lungs. It was heaven. Perfection. It always was with Viktor. He moved in her like he belonged. Like they shared the same skin. Their movements were always perfectly in tune, just like they had been on his bike.

"You close?"

"So close."

"Get there," he demanded, his voice harsh with urgency.

She let go instantly, her muscles coiling tight around him, gripping and milking his cock. His breath slammed out of his lungs and his cock swelled and his balls drew up. Then he was emptying himself into her, filling the condom, his heart pounding right along with hers, his breath ragged and his body beginning that slow glide that she remembered he liked to do when his release was spectacular.

She went down on her elbows because she couldn't keep herself up, but she was smiling. She didn't think she'd ever stop. Her breathing was labored, her lungs burned for air, but nothing could stop her smile. Her body felt great. *Great.*

Behind her, Viktor pulled out of her, the drag over the sensitive bundle of nerves causing another ripple of pure pleasure spreading through her. He sank back, one hand still on her bare cheek, rubbing gently, lovingly. He'd always liked to touch her and apparently that hadn't changed. Removing the condom, he knotted it and tossed it aside.

"Come here, baby," he murmured softly, reaching for her.

They lay on their backs looking up at the sky, breathing hard, neither speaking for a long moment. Viktor moved first, wrapping her hair around his finger and tugging gently. "I love you, Blythe. So much."

She turned her head to look at him. To look into his eyes. "I love you too."

His smile was slow in coming, but this one reached his eyes and melted her heart. "I brought food. Wine. Everything you like."

"When did you pack for a picnic?"

"I brought them with me to your house in the hopes I could talk you into riding with me. I changed my mind when things got intense, and then you asked me to take you on the motorcycle and our picnic was on again."

"I'm glad I did. I loved it. You don't have to use a condom next time. I trust you when you say you haven't been with anyone else. I haven't either, so we're good."

There was relief in his eyes, and satisfaction as well, but he didn't say anything.

"They saw us."

He didn't ask whom. He knew. He grinned at her, reached out and tucked stray strands of hair behind her ear. "I know. We don't have any modesty. I told you that. We were all naked together for years. They couldn't care less. Did it upset you?"

She thought it should have, but the reality was it hadn't. She didn't know why. Because she was with Viktor and they were different together? Because his club was different? "I'd rather not make a habit of it." Truthfully, it was because she was with Viktor and he made her forget everything but pleasure.

"I can't promise that; they're always going to be around." His tone was cautious. "I could ask them . . ."

"Don't worry about it." She wasn't. She didn't think she was an exhibitionist, but truthfully, in the moment, she hadn't even been embarrassed. "I want them to protect you."

"They'll protect you too."

They probably would if they knew she was important to Viktor. She turned her head and pressed a kiss against his neck and then looked back up at the stars. "I loved riding the motorcycle. Thank you for taking me."

"Do you understand now? We were locked up for so

long, sometimes in the dark with no light. The air would get so stifling, so stale, we could barely breathe. We'd lie on the floor if we weren't chained to the wall and listen to one another gasp like fish out of water in the heat, or shivering with cold in the winter. It stank of sweat, urine and feces. There was no bathroom. We had a corner of the room we went in if we could get there. Those chained to the wall couldn't even do that. With the heat, it was unbearable. Add to that injuries, the blood from the floggings and beatings, which drew insects and rats. It was a nightmare world."

Blythe was so horrified she couldn't look at him. She kept staring at the stars, identifying constellations even as she listened to him, her heart beating too hard. He sounded matter-of-fact when he casually told her about pieces of his childhood, but the rage was there, swelling in him and pouring out without him seemingly aware of it.

"The first time I ever tried riding on a motorcycle, I knew I wanted to be on one for the rest of my life. The wind was in my face and I could see the open road in front of me. I'd never experienced anything like it. I was on one of the first weeklong assignments, just twenty-one. I couldn't wait to get back and tell the others. It was the first thing I did when I was able to leave that place—buy my own motorcycle with the money I'd stolen and socked away on each of my assignments."

He turned onto his side in order to cup her breast. His thumb brushed her nipple gently, back and forth in small caresses. He lifted his head and kissed the tattoo just under her left breast. The key. The one that could open the lock over his heart. They'd gotten the tattoos together.

"I dreamt about this. When the nightmares got too bad and I hadn't slept for days," he whispered against the underside of her breast. "I would lie on my bed and think about you. Every inch of you. I pushed my thumb into the center of my palm and I'd build the image of you in my mind. Then I'd start from the top of your head to the bottom of your feet. I'd kiss you, remembering every detail of your mouth. Your lips and tongue. The way you taste."

He lifted his head to kiss her. Long, slow, drugging kisses that started a slow burn. He kept kissing her, cupping her breast in his palm without moving any other part of him. It drove her mad. She wanted more. Heat spread through her veins and went straight like an arrow between her legs.

"Nothing was better than the motorcycle until I met you. You wipe that place out of my head for long periods of time. Your laughter. Your magic. This sweet, sweet body of yours."

His sexy talk was making her burn all over again. He'd always been that way. He could make her want him with one smoldering look, and when he talked, no matter what he said, how crude he was, or where they were, he melted her inside and she craved him.

"I'd get so damned hard I'd have to start pumping my cock. Slow at first while I thought about your breasts. How much I liked sucking on your nipples. Teasing you. Driving you wild. You're so sensitive here."

He took his time lowering his head, his tongue tracing a circle around her left nipple and then her right one. He planted dozens of kisses over the curves of her breasts, drew letters with his tongue, pulled each soft mound into his mouth and then suckled strongly while she gasped and arched her back. The moment she went to cradle his head to her, he pulled back.

"I'd imagine you lying under me, and I'd spread your legs wide." He shifted his body over hers and nudged her thighs apart.

She didn't take her eyes from his face. He looked like carnal sin. So beautiful. Rising above her, his hand on her mound, thumb circling her clit. "What would you imagine?" she whispered, drinking him in.

"My mouth between your legs. Eating you until you screamed for me. I always have loved that you're very vocal about what you want. Your pleasure. That you're always willing to try anything once with me."

"It's never once," she pointed out. "You make everything so good that once is never enough." His fingers were in her now, curling and sweeping, stabbing deep and retreating. She wanted him again with every breath she drew.

"I wonder if those were the nights I couldn't sleep and I'd lie awake under the fan, no clothes, my body burning for yours," Blythe whispered, looking right into his molten eyes. Silver, like the moon. So beautiful. "I'd be so hot and it hurt between my legs, I was so empty without you. I'd push my thumb into my palm and think about you. About your body, your mouth and eyes, all your muscles that you know I love, but mostly about your cock."

He withdrew his fingers, and she took advantage, going up on her knees. "Stand up for me, honey."

"Anything for you, Blythe," he said and obeyed her.

His semihard cock had grown as he'd talked to her into just plain hard. She wrapped her fingers around him. "I have a toy in the drawer by my bed." She licked her lips, her tongue making a slow circle to moisten them in preparation.

"We're going to be using that toy together, Blythe," he warned in a husky growling tone that sent a shiver of desire down her spine.

"I'm okay with that. Just as long as I have you in my mouth while you're playing." She knelt up, caressing his shaft and heavy balls, cupping the velvet spheres and then leaning down to slowly and gently draw first one and then the other into her mouth. She licked along them and under them, and then up his shaft while his breath hissed out.

His hands went to her breasts, cupping them, thumbs gliding over her nipples, but when her mouth took him deep, he shuddered and caught her head in his hands. She never took her eyes from his. She knew what he liked. She knew he wanted to watch her. That he liked not only the feel of her mouth, but the look of her lips stretched around his girth. He always told her how much that turned him on, but more, she felt it. She always felt his response to everything she did to him. He loved it when she did this to him, and she loved doing it just as much.

His hips began to move, gently. He was always gentle

when he was in her mouth; even when he went deep, he took care with her. She was never afraid. In the beginning, before she knew she could trust him absolutely, maybe then she'd panicked once or twice, but not now. Now, she could enjoy what she was doing. The heat. The velvet over steel. The scent and taste of him. How sexy he made her feel. She wondered fleetingly if the men watching over him were watching, and then Viktor groaned and she forgot everything but what she was doing.

"Can't take much more, baby. I've still got that hair trigger from being without you for so long. Your mouth is fucking paradise."

He gently pulled away from her and she couldn't help following, licking at him like an ice-cream cone while his body shuddered with pleasure.

"Lie down. I want you under me."

She went to her back and waited for him to blanket her. Putting her feet flat on the blanket, legs spread wide, she cradled his hips in hers. He didn't need any other invitation. He pushed into her, groaning as her scorching heat surrounded him.

"So fucking tight, Blythe. You feel so good I'm not certain I'm going to survive this time."

She smiled at him and lifted her hips to meet his. Her gaze never left his. He threaded the fingers of one hand through hers and held her arm stretched out above her head while she wrapped her other arm around him. His free arm locked around her hips and he lifted her into him.

They moved together, never taking their eyes from each other. She drank him in. The love on his face brought tears to her eyes. He might not show expression to others, but when they were alone like this, there could be no doubt that he was truly in love with her.

Their breathing mingled with the sound of the river, the frogs and crickets. She didn't turn her head to see her surroundings or look up at the star-studded sky. There was only Viktor filling every one of her senses. She gave herself to him and he gave himself to her. She felt that. Knew that was what he was doing.

"You're safe with me, Blythe," he whispered. "I swear to you, I'm only yours. For good or bad, I'm with you."

He'd said those words to her on the night he'd taken her to the Russian church in San Francisco. He'd meant every word. She felt the absolute sincerity surrounding her. There had been no doubt then. Why hadn't she remembered that moment and actively searched? Asked questions? Tried to figure out what happened, especially after Lev came into their lives and she saw the mark he put on Rikki?

"Don't. We can only go forward. Stay with me right now. Keep looking at me."

She couldn't look away. She didn't want to. She knew it was her commitment to him and he would hold her to it. She wanted him, and if the past came between them sometimes, they'd both have to handle it.

They spent the night on the blanket, making love, sipping red wine. He preferred beer but he'd remembered her favorite wine and brought that instead. He brought fruit, all her favorites. Crackers and cheeses. Even honey to put on the cheese and crackers, a rare but favorite indulgence.

They talked about everything and nothing. Most of the time they made love or slept wrapped in each other's arms.

He woke her before the sun was up. They had to get back before light. He didn't want to chance that Evan might have sent more than one team to watch them. She didn't mind, because she loved the way he woke her up, and she couldn't wait to ride the motorcycle again.

15

"ELLE. Jackson. Thank you both for coming."

Viktor watched from his vantage point where he leaned one hip against the archway leading to the kitchen as Blythe stepped back to allow the couple entry into her home. The moment Jackson stepped inside, his restless eyes took in everything, stopped on Viktor and stayed there. Behind him, his wife, Elle Drake, came in. With her came a surge of unbelievable power.

Viktor was sensitive to energies, and the woman was extremely dangerous. Power crackled, and then she turned her gaze toward him and he saw her draw in her breath and glance at her husband. For support? With that kind of power? She was small with sheets and sheets of bright red hair. She didn't look like she could handle herself, but he knew better by the way she moved and the energy gathered around her.

Elle hugged Blythe hard, her eyes a little wary, but still affectionate. Blythe had called Jackson, not her cousin, to invite them to come over the next evening to talk. She'd told him it was about Evan Shackler-Gratsos and it wasn't great news but extremely important.

Viktor had told her to be very careful what she revealed

in a phone conversation and not to mention him. It was do or die here. The cop was either going to blow Viktor's cover and get him killed or he'd help. Viktor was betting his life that the man would be willing to help in spite of being the law. Once before, when he'd gone up against Evan's brother, Jackson had taken the law into his own hands. Viktor had to hope he'd do the same now. He believed absolutely that Evan was much more dangerous than Stavros Gratsos had ever been.

Jackson nodded to Blythe but kept his gaze on Viktor. All the while his body partially blocked his wife from stepping all the way into the great room until he'd cleared it. Blythe shut the door, walked straight over to Viktor and took his hand, in an effort to show solidarity. Viktor moved slightly to edge her over so he could shield her if things went to hell.

"Come in and sit down. We have beer, coffee, tea and fresh strawberry lemonade," she said, waving toward the inviting chairs.

"Coffee for me," Jackson said.

"The lemonade sounds lovely," Elle added. She looked at Viktor. "I don't believe we've met."

"I'm sorry, Elle," Blythe said. "I should have started with that. I'm a little nervous. This is Viktor Prakenskii, my husband."

"Of course he is," Jackson said. "I looked at that impeccable ID twice and knew it was fake, but couldn't figure out why. Your eyes."

"Ilya's eyes," Elle said.

"I'm his oldest brother, so technically he has my eyes," Viktor corrected with a faint smile. "It's nice to meet you, Elle. Your husband and I have met a couple of times."

Viktor had objected to Elle coming. He knew what happened to her, that Evan's brother had kidnapped her and Evan had taught the man how to "train" her. Jackson and Elle's sisters had rescued her. Evan's brother, Stavros, kept coming after her and eventually he died off the coast of Sea Haven in a mystery scientists were still trying to explain.

Viktor had wanted to talk to Jackson and then let Jackson break the bad news to his wife. Hysterical women weren't his forte, although he could handle them if he needed to. In his school there was no one teaching them the finer arts the way his brothers had learned. His school was more along the line of kill or be killed.

Jackson led his wife to the love seat, which didn't make Viktor happy. He liked the position. It was the best in the house—the most defensible. "I'll get the drinks, baby, you go visit with your cousin." He needed her to settle the two, get them relaxed.

Blythe obliged readily and took a chair opposite them. "How are your sisters, Elle? They're all back from their honeymoons, aren't they?"

Elle nodded. "Actually, they returned before Jackson and me."

She fell silent, and through the open archway, Viktor could see her draw up her legs and curl into Jackson. Few things shocked Viktor, but that did. Jackson immediately put his arm around her and pulled her tighter against him. Elle smiled up at her husband but her hand trembled in her lap as Viktor carried in the tray of drinks. He served her first. She was a woman of power and that need for her husband's reassurance touched him.

"I know this is late, Blythe. Viktor." Elle took a deep breath. "I'm so sorry about your child—your daughter. I've thought about what happened to you and how awful it must have been for you. Both of you."

Blythe looked stricken. Absolutely stricken. She hadn't expected it and she wasn't prepared. Viktor crossed the room, putting his body between her and their visitors. He'd never turned his back on a potential enemy, not without knowing Reaper or Savage had them in their sights. They were somewhere close, but he doubted if they had the deputy in their crosshairs. Then again, knowing Reaper, he probably did.

He bent unnecessarily to put his drink beside Blythe's but the movement allowed him to brush the top of her head with a kiss before turning back to the couple. "Thank you," he said for both of them.

"And also to apologize. Mom and the aunts were so crazy, so afraid for their sister. They wouldn't listen to anyone. I wanted to take back everything that they did and said. I know that was what kept you isolated from all of us," Elle added. "I *hated* what they did. We all tried, every one of us, to stop them, but they were so certain if Aunt Sharon went to rehab she would be better. They didn't think she could be so vicious she would do what she did on purpose."

Blythe had gone ashen. Her fingers dug into the side of the chair. She just sat there frozen, holding her breath in her lungs. In that moment Viktor knew exactly what it had been like for her. Alone. Completely alone. No family to back her up. His heart nearly shattered for her, but she wasn't alone now. He hadn't been there when she needed him. That would never happen again.

He sat on the wide arm of her chair and took her hand, holding it to his chest. Inside he went still. He could read what was happening so easily. Blythe was estranged from her family and had been since the death of their child. He could shut this down immediately and she'd turn only to him, or he could keep the talk going and hope Elle managed to say something that would make Blythe accept her cousin back into her life. The bottom line was, she loved family. She'd made another one for herself, and she was willing to take on his brothers and sisters and Darby and her sisters. But she needed the Drakes. Her cousins.

"What the fuck are you saying?" He was deliberately crude. Rude. Leaning toward Elle aggressively. "Your entire family backed the bitch who murdered our child?" If he could tear out Sharon's heart with his bare hands, he would have.

"It's okay," Blythe murmured. "It's okay. Let's just leave it. It wasn't Elle's fault. The aunts believed my mother. Sharon was their sister and they needed to believe she would never have done such a terrible thing."

He realized she must have said that often, if only to

herself. It wasn't okay, and she was alienated from her family because of something they did or said. "Tell me what happened," he demanded, looking at Elle.

She glanced at her husband, who tightened his arm around her and pulled her beneath his shoulder as if he could shelter her from the grief filling the room. Grief and rage. Viktor couldn't hold either back.

"It was my mother and her sisters who petitioned the court to be lenient and put Aunt Sharon in a rehab," Elle confessed in a low voice. "She had no previous record and there were no documented incidents involving injuries to Blythe. They believed her when she said she blacked out and didn't remember what happened."

Blythe shook her head. "I don't want to talk about this."

"We lost you, and we want you back," Elle said. "You just disappeared out of our lives. You walk past us, smile and wave, but you aren't there. We tried to stop them, to get them to see, we really did. I knew what she was capable of and I told Mom, but she wouldn't listen to me." Her voice rang with sincerity and grief as well. "Blythe, please come back to us."

Viktor understood that the betrayal by her aunts was much worse because he wasn't there to support her. No one was there. He said as much. "Because I couldn't get back, you were completely alone, trying to cope on your own. I'm so sorry, Blythe." More than she would ever know. He hurt for her. Ached for her. He willed her to hear her cousin. To feel his sincerity. To stay with him in spite of not being there for her when she needed him the most.

Blythe held herself very still, as if movement might shatter her. If she broke, Viktor was there to pick up the pieces, but he willed her to be strong—at least until their company left and he could hold her in his arms and comfort her.

Was she at fault?

Blythe looked up at him, and he caught the sheen of tears she hastily blinked away. She shook her head. *I couldn't forgive any of them. It was so terrible and I just held on to my anger.*

You have every right to be upset and angry with me for not being here when you needed me, but it sounds like she tried to see you. To be there.

She nodded her assent.

You have to tell her, baby, he encouraged gently. *She's hurting too.*

Blythe's fingers curled into his tightly and then she lifted her gaze to her cousin's, and he could breathe again. She wasn't shutting him out; she was once again showing him why he had such faith in her.

"I know you tried, Elle. It was so difficult, and I almost didn't make it through. I think about my daughter every single day and wonder what she'd be like. I know it was your mother's decision and she regrets it. She told me." By her tone, Viktor knew she hadn't forgiven the woman and maybe she never would, but Elle was guilty only by association. Not by deed. "I'll do better. I promise."

Elle nodded, tears standing in her eyes.

"Why?" Jackson asked, drawing attention away from his wife. "Why have you been gone all this time, Viktor?"

He was there to tell the cop the truth. Deveau needed to know the events leading up to this moment. This crucial meeting and what it was all about.

"Absinthe, one of my brothers, was shot multiple times on an assignment in South America. He'd gone after one of the key players in a drug cartel there. I had to get to him to save his life. I was closest, and he didn't have much time. That was right after Sharon's husband was killed. When you're shot and left for dead in our business, Sorbacov would send his cleaners after you. Absinthe had to be watched over in order to keep him alive, and then I had to help him disappear."

"No message for her?" Jackson asked. "You couldn't get word to her?"

At the hint of disdain in his voice, Viktor almost told him to go to hell, but something compelled him to tell the truth. "My brothers and I set up a message center for emergencies. I left a letter for Blythe giving her the codes. She could reach me through that route. No one was supposed to have the codes but the seven of us, but I wanted her to know how to reach me if she needed me. I left her hundreds of messages and even more for my brothers to watch over her. Not one person got back to me."

He smoothed caresses gently up and down Blythe's arm and then, when he could still feel her tension, he curled his arm partway around her so he could massage her neck.

"That's crazy," Jackson said, frowning. "What happened?"

"We don't know," Viktor admitted. "My brothers and Blythe never received any messages, and the ones my brothers said they left for me never got to me. Each time I checked the center for messages there were none."

"I didn't get the letter," Blythe said. "I suspect my mother destroyed it. She was taken to my room after Ray died. I didn't even know there was a letter until Viktor told me there had been one."

She was careful not to mention Viktor was the one who pulled the trigger. Jackson wasn't stupid; he had to know that Viktor, being a Prakenskii, had been a hit man for Sorbacov, but she wasn't going to go there and neither, it seemed, was Jackson.

"How did the code work?" Jackson asked.

"We all had the key and knew how to read a message. Once it was read, it was erased so there was no way Sorbacov could track us. We gave one another locations and destinations. Said if we were wounded, that sort of thing. In my case, I needed to know Blythe was all right. I was too far away and they watched me like a hawk in the beginning. After I got Absinthe out of trouble, Sorbacov told me to go after another high-profile target."

"When you had the chance, why didn't you disappear? You have the ability," Jackson asked.

Viktor shook his head. "Ilya was out in the open. Sorbacov would have had him killed. I couldn't take that chance. I went undercover with the Swords motorcycle club, the chapter in Louisiana." He didn't look at Elle or Jackson when he gave them that, but he heard Jackson's swift intake of breath as Jackson recognized the name of his father's club. Instead, he leaned closer to Blythe, trying to give her strength.

"Is it possible Aunt Sharon didn't destroy the letter? That she gave it to someone and they had the ability to destroy your messages?" Elle asked. "She would do that, wouldn't she, Blythe? Just to be spiteful. She hated that you were happy. Even over little things she would be hateful to you."

There was a long silence. Viktor kept his gaze on Blythe's face. She was thinking it over, but eventually she shook her head.

"The key to the code was in that letter along with specific instructions on erasing messages from me." He kept his voice very gentle. His fingers kept working the nape of her neck, trying to ease the tension pouring off of her. She was too still. Worried.

"She didn't have friends. Only her sisters. She drank too much and was too ugly when she drank to keep friends. Especially after Ray. They met in a bar, and once she was with him, she drank even more. They drank together."

"He didn't drink," Viktor corrected. "It was an illusion."

Blythe's teeth tugged at her lower lip and he couldn't help smoothing his thumb over the alluring curve.

"What is it?"

"She just didn't have friends. He only wanted his friends around . . ." She trailed off, her eyes going wide.

"His friends were all pedophiles," he reminded her as gently as possible when his gut tightened into knots and alarms went off in his head. He wanted to swear. Loudly. Crudely. Viktor had put everyone in jeopardy by giving her the code. By sending so many messages. What had he said? About the others? His brothers? Had he mentioned any of the members of his club in any of the messages?

His thinking was always clear. It had to be. He kept panic at bay as a child by reminding himself lives were always at stake, and his brain was his greatest weapon. He had to outthink everyone. He hadn't been thinking when he was sending all those messages to Blythe. He'd been panicked, afraid of losing her. Afraid of what was happening to her when he wasn't there. He'd begged his brothers to look after her. More than once, he'd tried to find legitimate reasons for Habit to allow him to take off for a few days so he could get to her, but the Swords were as paranoid as their president.

The roaring in his ears settled as he breathed away the rage at himself and his many, many mistakes. He'd made them before, and children were killed. He had more sins on his soul than any person alive and that was due to panic, fear and anger. He pushed all emotion down and focused on the woman he loved.

Any conversation about her mother distressed Blythe. Sharon had kept her isolated from family and friends. They'd moved across the country deliberately so Sharon's jealousy and hatred of those she perceived as having more couldn't be seen. Blythe had dealt with her alone. She had dealt with far too much alone. At least he'd eventually had his brothers and sisters.

Baby, we've got this together. Take a breath.

My mother nearly destroyed us, and I allowed it. I was so hurt after you disappeared I couldn't think straight. She had to have given that letter to one of Ray's friends.

He studied her face. She had a good idea just which friend that was, and she didn't like the thought. He wasn't going to push her. She'd had enough. They had brought Elle and Jackson there for a reason.

We'll deal with that when we're alone, honey, he assured her. *Let's see if Deveau is going to cooperate or if he's going to blow my cover.*

He won't, she said staunchly.

"I asked Blythe to call you," he announced, turning back to Jackson. "I took an undercover assignment in order to go after the biggest human trafficking ring in the world. It was a long-term assignment and I had to go deep, to disappear. It was dangerous and that meant losing all ties to family." His hand tightened around Blythe's.

Telling this again meant risking losing her. He'd been out of her life when she'd needed him the most, when she had no family or friends to support her. She'd met the five women she bought the now thriving farm with after the death of their daughter.

Deveau was a patient man and he simply waited. Viktor tightened his hold on Blythe as if that could keep her from pulling away from him.

"Evan Shackler-Gratsos is the most paranoid man I've ever come across, and he doesn't trust anyone."

Elle gasped and looked up at Jackson. Her husband's expression didn't change, but he curved his arm around her and pulled her right into him, almost on his lap. He kept his gaze steady on Viktor's face, watching his eyes. Viktor didn't look away. He wanted Deveau to know just how serious the threat was.

"He rode with the Swords, specifically a chapter in Louisiana."

Immediately comprehension was in the deputy's eyes. He was from Louisiana. His father had been an enforcer with the Swords. When Jackson's mother had gotten so ill with cancer, he'd picked up another woman to ride with him and she had a son named Evan. Yeah. He was getting it and fast. They were all connected.

"I joined the chapter in the hopes that Evan would visit and I could take him out, but he'd grown so paranoid that more than once he killed his own bodyguards and replaced them, certain they were selling him out. Then you got married, Deveau. You got married to the woman his brother wanted and wouldn't let him have. He already hated you, but then you committed the ultimate sin. He has no intention of allowing you to be happy. Either one of you." He included Elle, but he kept his gaze on Deveau. Yeah, the man was smart. He was getting it.

"This is our one shot at getting this bastard. He's got an operation that won't quit and he's running it in nearly every country. The Swords choose a few young boys and girls, lure them or kidnap them, beat and rape them until they submit and then sell them until they get too old or worn out to be of any use. Then they kill them. A select few are put on ships to be sold for top dollar to men and women with particular proclivities. They like to hurt and then kill their victims. Those children are taken to his ships, and the bodies are buried at sea."

Elle drew her knees all the way up and pressed her face against them, making herself very small.

"Keep talking," Jackson demanded when Viktor hesitated.

Viktor hated what he was doing to Blythe's cousin. Her face was very pale. She didn't look away, but she did look fragile. He wished Blythe had listened to him and just asked the deputy to come.

"It's all right," Elle said, her voice surprisingly strong. "Thanks for caring, but I have to hear this. He's coming after us, isn't he?"

Viktor nodded slowly. There was no point in trying to make it easy. Evan Shackler-Gratsos wasn't going to make it easy for any of them. "Yes, I'm afraid he is. The good news is, we'll get a shot at taking him out because he wants to kill Jackson himself. He made that very clear. I was sent down here to scout for a place that the Swords could slip into without anyone noticing a large number of them. They won't be wearing colors, and they aren't supposed to draw attention to themselves."

"Then what the hell was that fiasco in Inez's store?" Jackson demanded.

Inez definitely meant something to him. He hadn't liked that anyone had threatened her. "They were there to watch me. I suspected Evan might send in more than one team. He's that paranoid. They were from another chapter, so it was plausible that I didn't know who they were."

"Your cover still intact?" Jackson asked.

Viktor nodded. "I called my chapter president and reported the incident and then acted outraged that they were Swords and they'd almost blown everything. For all I know he sent watchers to watch them. My men are looking, but we haven't found any others and we're good at what we do."

"I can imagine," Jackson said dryly.

Viktor didn't bother to take the bait. "I've looked at the campgrounds. There are a lot of them that would do, but too many families camp in them. There's no way to guarantee safety. I need a place we can plan an ambush for you and then turn the tables on them without civilians getting hurt."

"You're planning on using me as bait."

Viktor nodded. "Evan plans to kill you. I say, give him his shot. He also wants your woman. She needs to be locked down tight where he doesn't have a possible chance at her."

Elle shook her head. "He doesn't get to scare me."

Viktor frowned at her. "He scares me, and he damn well should you as well. He's not sane. He likes hurting people, especially women. He hates your husband with a passion and wants him to suffer. Hurting you would accomplish that."

"Where would be a good place for Viktor to tell the Swords to come?" Blythe asked Elle before Viktor could say anything else.

He glanced down at her, but she was studiously looking at her cousin and avoiding his gaze. She was up to something and he had a feeling he wasn't going to like it. His feelings were always right.

"I have this friend, Leslee Huber. She walks her mastiffs nearly every day out in an area just off of Highway 20 called Egg Taking Station. It isn't very well marked but it's part of the Jackson State Demo Forest. The Noyo River runs back there. There are campgrounds along the river, a common area, and the roads are all logging roads. It isn't paved, but Leslee said the roads are hard, well packed down. All the logging roads are intact and you can drive all the way on the back roads to Sea Haven from there."

"I know Leslee," Blythe said. "She works as a massage therapist. She's told me about that place. Hardly anyone goes there."

"That's not a good place for a woman alone, even if she has her dogs with her," Jackson erupted, glaring at his wife. "It isn't safe. The people camping there are usually looking to disappear."

"The point," Elle said, "is that it's a perfect place for the Swords to camp. They'll like the fact that the roads give them places to run without being seen. There are ways in and out on the logging roads that would allow them to travel without being seen. Few families would ever camp there."

"It's not a bad idea," Jackson agreed reluctantly. "There are narrow wooden bridges a car couldn't get across, but a bike could. Plenty of escape routes for them. Good place to ambush me. It's on my route, so I'd be the one to answer any calls out there. I think Elle and Blythe are correct, although, Elle, you'll have to warn your friend not to go out there without giving anything away."

"Stavros was afraid of Evan," Elle said in a low tone. She looked at Jackson. "I have tremendous power, but I think Evan has something more, something very scary. Without knowing what that is, it would be foolish to put yourself in jeopardy."

Blythe cleared her throat, but didn't look at Viktor. She waited until she had Elle's full attention. "I can draw power and bind it from any source to any individual. I can boost it as well."

There was silence while Elle all but gawked at her cousin, her mouth open. "You can do what?" she whispered.

"If Evan, or anyone else for that matter, uses power, any kind of psychic power for any purpose, I can steal it from them. Take it. I can direct the energy to another individual such as you or Jackson or Viktor. I do it all the time with my sisters here. The more I've worked with it, the easier it's gotten and the stronger I've gotten."

"Blythe, that's incredible. I can't do that. None of my sisters can either." Elle sounded awed.

Viktor was rather in awe as well, but he knew what was coming and it wasn't good. He tried to stop it by standing up and pacing across the room. He had to move, rid himself of the pounding heart that told him Blythe was going to insist on putting herself in immediate danger. He was too slow.

"You can stop him," Elle said. "Blythe, you can stop him."

"I can definitely keep him from using whatever talent he has. He's counting on the fact that no one knows he has it. The moment he tries to use it, I can stop him."

"How close do you have to be?" Jackson asked. Once again his gaze was on Viktor, even as he asked the question. He knew Viktor wasn't happy when both women seemed totally oblivious.

"Close enough to feel the energy start to gather," Blythe said. "But that shouldn't be a problem. I can take one of the campsites . . ."

"No." Viktor used his hardest, scariest voice, the one that stopped even Reaper.

"How many Swords do you think Evan is going to bring in?" Blythe asked in a very quiet voice.

He knew that voice, and it meant it didn't matter what he said, she was going to do what she thought was right. He knew that side of her from their earlier relationship. Blythe was as sweet a woman as she could be, giving in to him most of the time because if it mattered to him and didn't to her, she saw no reason to argue, but when she made up her mind about something, there was no stopping her. At least he hadn't found a way yet, and he'd tried everything.

"Viktor?" She insisted on an answer.

"At least thirty. Maybe more. He likes a show of force. It would be like him to kill Jackson and then send his men in to tear up Sea Haven. He'd want to burn down the Drake house, and he definitely wants his hands on Elle." He had made up his mind to tell her the truth so he couldn't lie to her, but he knew he was digging his own grave with that information.

"Then you need your own army to stop them," Blythe said.

"We'll talk about it later," he said. She didn't understand

the level of violence the Swords were capable of. The cruelty and vile behavior toward women. They *enjoyed* what they did, breaking the young girls and boys. Evan recruited men like himself. That thought led back to Ray and the fact that he had started a pedophile Internet site that attracted men and women like him.

Viktor needed somewhere to breathe clean air. That somewhere was wherever Blythe was. He'd lived too long wading in slime—so long he wasn't certain he could ever find clean again until he saw her. Until he kissed her and she took him away from it all. He wasn't about to chance those men getting their hands on her. She'd been hurt enough thanks to his mistakes.

Viktor. The walls are turning red. Your anger is spilling out and it's gathering there. We'll talk about it later.

He didn't respond but he did take a breath. He didn't dare allow rage loose in her home. Not around her. Not ever.

Look at me.

He couldn't. He didn't deserve her. He couldn't change what he was—a fucking killing machine—but he wanted to be something different. He wanted all of them to be something different. But if he had to give her up in order to protect her, then he would. He wouldn't survive it, but then there wouldn't be much point in surviving without her.

Viktor. Look at me.

She was in his mind. Her clean, fresh spirit pushing through all the ugly muck threatening to pull him under. He smelled her, the faint peaches-and-cream scent she favored. He had to turn his head and look at her because he couldn't deny Blythe anything, other than allowing her to put herself at risk.

She had to see the pain in his eyes. The fear of losing her. She had to feel it because he could and he rarely allowed himself to feel.

"I love you, Viktor," she said gently. Meaning it.

He could see she meant it, but the terrible lump in his throat making it impossible to draw breath stayed until his lungs were raw, burning for air.

"I don't care if anyone else ever knows or sees what a good man you are. I know. I see, and I'm proud to be your wife. Stop thinking you're going to lose me. I let my mother take you away from me once, but it won't happen again."

"Baby, I can't give you this. I told you I'd give you anything, but I can't give you this."

"It isn't your decision. It's mine. We're partners and we're good together, Viktor. What I can do can tip the scales in our favor. That keeps the lives of your brothers and sisters safe. Your birth brothers as well, because they're going to help you. Elle and Jackson because they have to do this too. I'm a huge asset, and you know it."

He kept shaking his head. She made sense. It all made sense, but he kept shaking his head. He couldn't stop the visceral reaction to the thought of her being in danger from Evan or the Swords. He hated that she was right. He hated it more that she wouldn't argue with him and he knew she wouldn't. Blythe went her own way when she believed she was right. She not only believed it, but she knew it this time.

"If Elle and Blythe are going to be there, we'll have to make certain we have plans in place to keep them safe," Jackson said.

Viktor recognized that the deputy was trying to help him out. Help him understand he couldn't order his woman to do as she was told. There were some rules to the biker world he could embrace right about now, and getting his woman under his control was one of them.

"How many men do you have with you?" Jackson asked.

"Seven riding with me now and Alena. She's every bit as good in a fight as my men. I have eight more coming, and Lana. Like Alena, she's lethal. The others will be riding in with Habit, the chapter president from Louisiana."

"Eighteen of you?" Jackson said thoughtfully. "You certain you can count on them?"

"Absolutely."

"I've got your birth brothers and their wives," Jackson said. "Don't know about Jonas. I've asked him to do some things that just aren't in his comfort zone. I don't know if he's going to be up for this one. Probably."

Viktor shook his head. "Unless you know, don't risk it. If he talks and decides to try to take him alive, no one is going to be safe." Jackson had to know that and it was his wife at risk. "And I don't know about the women. When you think of outlaw clubs, you're not looking at anything like these men. They're the worst."

"We're going to be dealing with psychic energy," Elle said. "He's powerful. Even with Blythe there to tip the scales for us, we don't know what we'll need to counteract him. Some of my sisters are expecting. I can't risk them right now, so we'll need Blythe's sisters to help us. They're used to working with her."

It was getting out of hand. "Evan is bringing a fucking army, Jackson. He wants to tear the town apart. You think he's going to act nice around these women?"

Honey, your protective gene is off the charts and it's showing. You know you can't go in there naked, without all of us. Your brothers have talent. You do. You know exactly what we'll be facing. Do you think I love you less than you love me? I want you safe. It's within my power to help keep you that way. If it were beyond my abilities, I wouldn't put you in a position of having to look after me. I wouldn't, Viktor. I love you and I would never do that to you.

He both hated and loved that his woman was intelligent. The hating it was stronger right then than the loving it. He was going to tell the others to make certain their women were on the dumber side and "yes, anything you say is law" women.

They talked for several hours. Jackson mapped out the various logging roads for him out at Egg Taking Station. He and the others would take their bikes there and ride, seeing how fast street motorcycles could travel through. Jackson would do the same with trucks just to be prepared.

Blythe wanted to go with him, but he was concerned it was too dangerous. Still, she had to see the area. All the women would have to. Elle thought it would be a good idea to arrange an outing with all of them. He managed not to roll his eyes, but he did exchange an exasperated look with Jackson, who just shrugged. Clearly, he had been around them all a lot longer. Still, if Blythe was going, he and his men wouldn't be far behind. They would be keeping an eye on her. She'd have to get used to having protection from the club whether she liked it or not.

16

"LESLEE told me about this place," Elle said as the four-wheel-drive truck bounced a few times on the pitted road. "But I've never come out here. When we were kids, this was one of the places Dad didn't want us going. He didn't forbid us much so, although it was tempting, I didn't rebel to that extent. Joley might have. She was a hellion growing up. Then I forgot all about it."

"You didn't mention to Joley what was going on?" Blythe asked, surprised.

The Drakes tended to do everything together. The sisters were best friends. She understood that concept now, because she'd found that with her sisters of the heart. She felt better when they were with her. Right now, only Rikki, Lexi and Lissa had accompanied Elle and her to the Egg Taking Station to explore.

They needed to know the roads every bit as much as the men did. They'd brought food with them, and Gavriil's dogs. They were big Black Russian Terriers and very protective, particularly of Lexi. Where Lexi went, Gavriil went.

Blythe hadn't seen Gavriil, but he'd insisted Lexi take the dogs, and he'd made it clear he'd be close just in case anyone tried to bother them. That made her want to laugh.

It wasn't as if the women weren't forces to be reckoned with, especially when they were together.

She hadn't spotted Viktor or any of his brothers, but she knew they were also following or already ahead of them somewhere on the grounds. She thought it was a bit ironic that they were exploring a place that normally only a few people went to, but this day, it would be populated with all sorts of individuals.

"There's the entrance," Rikki pointed out. "Road 350. Camp One. Jackson Demonstration State Forest. The sign is so small it's no wonder people don't know it's back here."

They could easily have missed the sign. They made the narrow turn off of Highway 20 and stayed to the right on the dirt road. Hundreds of acres had been logged since the early 1800s and there was a network of old logging roads riddling the park.

Blythe was silent as they continued down the dirt road. It was hard, scraped, kept in good condition, but she didn't like the idea of Viktor or any of the others riding Harleys fast on that bare ground. There was spotty, if any, cell service. No way to keep in contact that way.

"There's the river," Rikki said, her voice eager. She was often hesitant and refused to look at people until she was around water, and then she changed entirely. She was a strong water element and around rivers, lakes and especially the ocean, she blossomed.

"It's beautiful back in here," Elle said. "I know Joley knows about this place, and she never told any of us, that rat."

Blythe held her breath for a moment, her fingers tightening around the camera she carried. "You didn't tell your sisters what was going on, did you?" It was Viktor's life on the line. Viktor's and his brothers' and Alena's. The more people who knew, the more chances there were to have his cover blown. And Jonas Harrington was a huge question mark. He was the sheriff and he definitely went by the book—she was certain of it. He and Ilya were best friends. Jonas was married to Hannah Drake and Ilya to Joley.

She realized just what a risk Viktor took warning

Jackson and bringing him in on his mission. She was suddenly so anxious she was afraid she might throw up. He could have just allowed the Swords to call for help. Jackson would have shown up, drawing Evan out into the open. Viktor could have killed him and then he and his brothers and sisters would have fought their way out. Probably successfully. By telling Jackson the truth he'd risked his life. If the Swords found out he was undercover and planning to kill their international president, the entire club would be after him.

"Of course I didn't," Elle said. "Although Sarah was suspicious. She came over right before I was leaving, and you know Sarah, she just knows things. She questioned me and I said I was going on a picnic with some friends."

Sarah. Blythe's heart really began to pound. She bit at her thumb, trying to think what to do. She should have warned Viktor not to say a word. The Drakes were special. Gifted. They each had talent. It wasn't the same as her sisters there on the farm. They were elements, bound to earth, water, fire and air, but the Drakes just could do things, know things . . .

If Viktor hadn't warned Jackson she would have been upset with him, but now that he had, and she knew the very real risk he took, she was even more distressed. She realized he would have gone to Jackson no matter what. That was who he was. He would have protected the deputy and Elle. He had assumed that role when he was ten years old and he continued it. He would always continue it. Others might not know or ever realize, but she did and she would stand with him.

"Breathe, Blythe," Lissa reminded softly. "We're here to help. We're strong when we're together, you know that."

"Gavriil and the others are going to help him too," Lexi reminded. Her voice was gentle and serious. So Lexi.

Blythe found herself smiling in spite of her worries, and her stomach settled at the sound of Lexi's voice. Her chosen sisters. They were there for her. No matter what was going on in their lives, they were there for her.

"He's a good man," she murmured aloud. Needing them to know.

"If you love him, then we know he's a good man," Lissa said. "We'll fight for him too. Just know all the Praken-skii brothers are blockheads. You're going to have to deal with that."

"Hey," Elle said, her fingers tight on the wheel as they bumped along the road. "Jackson's a blockhead too."

They all burst out laughing. Blythe couldn't help laughing with them. "Of course he is. No Drake would marry anything *but* a blockhead."

They drove up and down the roads that were open and many that had gates across them. Elle was very adept at unlocking gates without touching them. The campsites on either side of the river were perfect. Viktor had already inspected them and had made his report to Habit, so any day, the Swords would be arriving in small groups. The plan was, they'd set up their campsites and familiarize themselves with the old logging roads while they planned out the ambush.

"It really is beautiful here," Blythe said. "It's funny that we've lived here this long and didn't realize it was here."

"I knew it was," Elle said. "But Dad made it seem like every outlaw since the Wild West camped out here. Some of the kids from school came out here during ditch day, but not often. Leslee's husband's family own property out here and he's very familiar with all this. I talked to her last night and told her I was asking tons of questions because Kate needed it for research for a book she was writing."

Blythe twisted her fingers together and held herself very tight. Kate Drake was another of Elle's sisters—a best-selling author married to a former Army Ranger. Talking to Leslee and using Kate's name just added one more complication. She knew her cousins. The least little hint and they ferreted out exactly what was going on.

"We'll need a back road in," Lissa said. "We have to be above them with no one behind us so we have a clear escape route."

"They could hear or possibly see any vehicle coming in on these old logging roads. At night sound would carry, and during the day the dust rising would give the location away," Lexi said. "I could minimize the dust, but sound . . ."

"I could take away the sound, but if they have scouts," Elle ventured, "we would still be seen."

"We could hike in from the other side," Rikki said. "That's what we did when we——" She broke off abruptly, glancing at Elle from under her lashes, her fingers twisting and whirling.

"That's not a bad idea. We just need to find the right road," Blythe agreed, laying her hand gently over Rikki's.

"Let's go back to the common area," Elle suggested. "We can eat and decide the best way to do this. Once we have a plan, the men won't be so crazy and expect us to stay home."

"Like that will happen," Lissa said. "Not that I'm going to be that much help out here. Fire can get loose fast and there's too much danger of a forest fire if I try to manipulate it too much. On the other hand, if they have campfires going already, I can wreak a little havoc and maybe upset any plans they have."

"You have to remember that Evan has a major talent or talents," Elle reminded. "The moment any of you use power he'll be able to zero in on you fast."

Blythe bit her lower lip hard. She was dragging her sisters into this mess in order to protect Viktor. There was a note of fear in Elle's voice, and Elle Drake had never been afraid of anyone. Fingers of dread sent chills down her spine. Still, she held on to the fact that she had a gift. A talent. Her mother hadn't believed her and she'd only used it for the farm, when it was needed to boost Rikki and Lexi and Judith.

She knew her sisters believed it was mostly Judith, but she was the one binding them together and amping up the power Judith created. She had learned to stay in the background and it never bothered her that others didn't realize she had a gift. She really could only use it around others gifted. She just took the energy they gathered and boosted or directed it.

Blythe glanced at Elle's set face. Elle really was afraid of Evan, and that told her to be very careful around the man. "It's all right, Elle. I can take his power and redirect it to one or all of you. We'll come up with a plan. I'm starving." She wasn't, but she didn't like seeing her cousin afraid. Elle, when they were young, was never afraid. To see her almost fragile was disconcerting.

Elle maneuvered the big truck down the logging road following along the river back toward the common area. There were a few picnic tables there and they could eat, drink and toss around ideas.

"Oh no," Elle said as she rounded the last curve to get to the main road. "We have company."

Blythe sat up straighter. She recognized the four-wheel-drive RAV4 parked just outside the common area. Airiana and Judith sat on the picnic table, Airiana swinging her foot back and forth and leaning back to look up at the sky. Judith laughed at something she said. At the sound of the truck, they both sat up straighter and watched Elle park.

Lexi jumped out and let the two big dogs out. Both ran to Airiana and Judith to say hello. "Hey, you two," she greeted. "You decide to have a picnic?"

"Yep," Judith said. "Right here at the good old Egg Taking Station no one told us about. I see you came prepared for a picnic too. Great minds evidently think alike. Hi, Elle. Nice to have you back."

"You didn't invite the two pregnant ladies," Airiana added, petting Kiss, the female Black Russian Terrier. "So we talked it over and decided something was up."

"Not to mention," Judith added, scooting over so Rikki could put their picnic basket next to Judith's, "our men are acting like idiots. You know, those late-night consultations with one another. Even Ilya's been hanging around. We aren't stupid you know, just pregnant."

Blythe heard the hurt in her voice. This was *so* getting out of hand. "No one thinks you're stupid, Judith," she said gently. "Just pregnant. No one wanted to risk you."

"It's Viktor, isn't it?" Airiana guessed shrewdly. "He's in some kind of trouble, and all of you are trying to help him out."

Blythe nodded, avoiding looking at Elle. Very few people knew the true details of her cousin's kidnapping. "It's dangerous and I didn't want either one of you hurt. Any of you," she added, sweeping her hand to include the other women. "But we can't take chances with babies." She ducked her head. "Especially unborn babies."

Airiana's eyes filled with tears and she hopped off the picnic table to rush to Blythe. She threw her arms around her and hugged her hard. "Of course we won't take any chances. We'd just like to know what's going on and see if there's a way we could help." Blythe started to pull back, stiffening, and Airiana hugged her harder. "From a distance," she added. "Away from any danger."

"We just thought maybe your man was a male chauvinist or something," Judith explained with a small smile, obviously hoping to lighten the mood.

"Well, he's something," Blythe admitted, trying for humor when she wanted to cry. This could be a disaster.

"We don't talk about family business to anyone," Judith added, sobering again. "We're family. If Viktor is your choice, he's family. He's my husband's brother. He fights like a machine, so I'm putting my money on him."

Blythe shook her head as Airiana slipped her arm through hers. "It's too dangerous. I know you'd want to help, if only to make certain the boys don't get into trouble, but both of you are—" She broke off, shook her head again and forced command into her voice. "It's too dangerous."

"Let's sit down and see what we have in the way of food," Elle said. "We can all think better with clear heads."

Blythe's head was clear. Totally clear. Any pregnant woman was *not* participating in the coming war with the Swords club and Evan Shackler-Gratsos. The panic was so strong she had to turn away from the women she called sisters. They were there for her, but it wasn't right. She couldn't live with herself if anything happened to the un-born babies.

Without thinking, she pressed her thumb into the center of her palm. She had done that so many times over the last few years when she was distressed that it had become a habit. She hadn't understood why it comforted her.

Take a breath and tell me what's happening. Viktor's voice in her mind confirmed her belief that he was close.

They're pregnant. They'll insist on helping. She closed her eyes briefly. *Great. Now's your opportunity to tell me you don't want me here, but I'm still here and I don't have the right to stop them. Go ahead and say it.*

They're pregnant. I understand, Blythe.

She breathed a sigh of relief that he wasn't going to lecture her. She didn't think she could take it. Around her, they were spreading out a checkered tablecloth as if they picnicked there every day of their lives. Laughter and the murmur of conversation swirled around her, but she couldn't do any-thing but hear the roaring in her ears and see the black spots that told her she'd better try to outrun what was coming.

Baby, breathe. Seriously. You're going to pass out.

Will you ask your brothers to forbid them to help?

I can do that. No problem, but do you believe they'll lis-ten? You don't listen to your man. You're their sister. They love you. They're loyal to you. They want to help. We need another solution.

Like what? You have to tell me what. They couldn't lose their babies. She couldn't take it. She'd barely lived through the loss of hers, but if it happened again to one of her sis-ters, especially because of her, she wouldn't survive. She just wouldn't.

We'll need eyes and ears in town. Evan isn't going to be happy unless he sends men to burn that store. To burn the Drake house. To hurt as many ways as possible. He also will use that as a diversion so that only Deveau will come here and all other law enforcement personnel will head

*into Sea Haven. Once Jackson has turned onto the entry
road, they'll start trouble in town so he won't have backup.
From what he's told me they're spread pretty thin over here.*

Okay. Okay. She could deal with that. Maybe. *How
much danger would they actually be in?*

*Very little. Evan isn't going to send his best men into
town to wreak havoc. Those he sends will be the pawns. His
expendable ones. He won't care if they make it out or not.*

*Maybe it would be a good idea for Lissa to go with them
as well. She's a fire element. If they're working with fire,
she can do all sorts of scary things with that. At the same
time, she can protect them.* The idea sounded good to her.
Airiana and Judith would be safe if Lissa was watching
over them.

"Blythe. Come sit down with us," Elle said. "He's going
to be all right. He knows what he's doing or he wouldn't
have gotten this far. I've been undercover. No one here will
blow it for him. If he worked his way up through the club
to get to a position of trust, then he's that good."

"Evan still sent a group of men from another chapter to
watch over him."

"Because he's paranoid." Elle patted the bench. "Fried
chicken. The real deal. And we've got pie. Come on, we've
got a lot to discuss."

*It's going to be okay, baby. I promise. I've had a lot of
time to figure this out.*

Viktor's voice was so reassuring. So gentle. But mostly,
it was strong. She remembered the way it felt to walk with
him down a street. He seemed invincible. Now she knew
why. *I love them all.* She did. She needed to tell him that.
He had to know that these women were family. If he was
with her, then they were his family as well and that meant
under his protection. That was his code.

I get you, baby. Now go have a little fun.

His voice was comforting to her. She felt for a moment as if he'd wrapped her up in his arms and just held her
to him.

"I'm all about fried chicken," she said, when she wasn't. She didn't eat fried foods as a rule, but with Viktor in the house, that just might change. She'd always been extremely disciplined, to the point that she didn't really know how to have fun. When he came into her life, that had changed. She'd been the one to initiate the things she'd always wanted to try but had been afraid to. He'd been the one to show her things she'd never thought of. Together, they'd made a good pair.

Elle scooted over to make room for her. "You were talking to him, weren't you?"

Blythe nodded. All of them were looking at her and she found herself blushing for no reason at all. "He was just giving me more details about what would happen and how, when we're discussing our strategy, we have to account for those as well."

That was a good way to lead into it. She wasn't leaving anyone out. They could help, and it was important to protect the townspeople and the Drake house, although it was rumored the Drake house protected itself.

"Uh-oh," Lissa said. "We're about to have company."

Blythe turned her head toward the sound of the vehicles. Two trucks came up the road slowly. Her heart sank. Of course. No Drake sister would ever get away with telling a sister a lie. Even a small one. Especially to Sarah, the oldest sister. She just knew things.

"Quick, look like you're eating," Elle said to Blythe. She handed her a plate of chicken and potato salad and a glass of lemonade.

Blythe sighed and took the plate. Her sisters were studiously eating and trying not to laugh. If it weren't such a serious situation, she'd be laughing as well. What else was there to do?

She watched as Sarah parked the truck next to Judith's RAV4. Kate and Abigail got out. Abigail was a marine biologist and married to a man named Aleksandr Volstov. Ilya had known Aleksandr in Russia. Both had worked for Interpol at one time. Sarah was married to a man working for the defense department, Damon Wilder, who worked with Airiana quite frequently. Kate carried the picnic basket. She and Abigail looked innocent. Sarah didn't bother to try.

To Blythe's horror, Hannah and Joley Drake got out of their sister Libby's truck. Hannah had just had a baby, and worse, she was married to Jonas Harrington, the local sheriff. Joley was pregnant, married to Ilya Prakenskii, Viktor's brother. Libby jumped out of the driver's seat and waved at them, all smiles. She was a doctor and married to a medical researcher, Tyson Derrick.

"Who's with the baby?" Elle asked, waving at her sisters.

"Jonas. His exact words were, 'Go find out what that jackass Jackson is up to. It's probably illegal and he's going to get himself in trouble without me to figure out just how to get away with the crime he's about to commit.' That's what he said, so here I am. We brought tons of food, even if you didn't bother to invite us," Hannah said.

"We weren't invited either," Airiana informed her. "But we brought food too."

"Jackson isn't a jackass," Elle protested.

"Jonas said you'd say that, and he said to tell you right now, both of you are jackasses. Your judgment is impaired so how would you know?" Hannah continued with a sweet smile.

"I have to agree with him," Sarah said. "What is going on?" She glared at her youngest sister and then turned to Blythe. "I didn't expect to see you here, but then I should have. It all makes sense. You're usually so level-headed I didn't see that you could be part of one of my sister's harebrained schemes."

Elle tossed her head and gave a little sniff, completely undismayed by her older sister's assessment. "No fried chicken for you."

"I get some," Joley said. "At least two pieces. Hey, Blythe. Good to see you. So you weren't invited either, Airiana?"

"Nope. Neither was Judith. We're both pregnant, so Blythe gave us the big boot out of the sisterhood of dubious deeds."

"She was letting us back in until you came along," Judith added, passing out plates.

Sarah, Libby, Abigail and Lissa carried a second picnic table over to make one long one. They spread out a table-cloth and put their picnic baskets down.

This is the reason men want to be in motorcycle clubs, Viktor said. *Women are nuts.*

Maybe nuts, but we have the food and you're out there somewhere without any because I bet you didn't think to bring any with you.

Only because I know you'll feed me tonight.

Blythe glared in every direction. *Go away. You're annoying me.* Because he was absolutely right; she would feed him.

She had the impression of laughter and then he was gone out of her head. She found her cousins and sisters all staring at her, Sarah with one eyebrow up.

"So you're telepathic."

"Not necessarily," Blythe denied, pushing her thumb into her palm under the table. "Just with him."

"With Viktor Prakenskii."

"Word travels fast."

"It's a small town," Sarah said.

"Are you certain, Blythe?" Hannah asked. "Because Jonas says he's bad news."

"Jonas thinks everyone is bad news," Libby said, putting potato salad on her plate. "Even Ty, and he's so sweet."

"He thought Lev was bad news," Rikki added. "He even got in a fistfight with him, but Lev is cuddly and sweet and wonderful and he cooks."

"There you have it, Sarah," Blythe said, studiously wiping her fingers on a napkin to avoid her cousin's eyes. "Jonas doesn't know what he's talking about. You can tell him I said that, Hannah."

"You can tell us what's going on, Elle," Sarah said, still looking at Blythe. "I mean, like right now."

Elle squirmed. She glanced at Blythe and then set down

her plate. "I can't. I'm sorry. Really. It's just that it's not mine to tell."

Viktor. They know something's wrong.

Just tell them. It's out of hand anyway. If I get shot, you can go after all of them for me.

Blythe sighed. "Don't be all over Elle, Sarah. I asked her not to say anything. Viktor's life is at stake. More." She pinned Hannah with her gaze. "If Jonas objects to what we're trying to do, he could put a lot of us in jail."

"Including Jackson and me," Elle said.

Sarah sighed. "Maybe you'd better just tell us what's going on and we can decide for ourselves if anyone needs to go to jail."

Blythe shook her head. "I'm not willing to put Viktor's life on the line just so all of you can have your explanation. It doesn't work that way."

"You can't expect us to just give our word when we don't know what you're going to say," Sarah objected.

Elle lifted her chin. "Either you trust us or you don't, Sarah. I'm in this with Blythe. All the way in it. You're with me or you're not."

"We've always chosen one another," Kate said softly. "We always will."

Blythe frowned over that. It sounded too much like the explanation her aunts had given her when she found out they'd petitioned the judge for leniency and rehab for her mother. She was asking for blind faith, and so was Elle. Blind faith wasn't always the best thing.

Blythe forced air through her lungs and listened to the birds in the trees. The squirrels rustling through leaves and pine needles looking for food to store for the coming winter. Insects droned. A frog down by the river croaked.

She loved that the Drake sisters were so close. She'd always envied them that. They had one another's back through everything, where she'd been entirely alone. Each of their mothers had what they had. The belief in one another. The knowledge that they'd always be there when needed. Still, that didn't account for one of them taking a wrong turn as her mother had.

"Blythe?" Sarah turned to her.

She moistened her lips and then told them. "Evan Shackler-Gratsos is coming after Jackson and Elle."

She said it softly, afraid the birds might hear and carry the message to Evan, wherever he was. For all any of them knew, he could be sitting in the hotel in Sea Haven right at that moment surrounded by a dozen spies.

She knew she'd dropped a bomb on them. Hannah actually went white and reached out to take Elle's hand. "Honey, why wouldn't you want Jonas to know? He would do anything to protect you. He has already, you know that."

"It wasn't on our soil, in his jurisdiction," Elle pointed out. "This is different. It's right here on his home turf. I didn't want him touched by any of this. Jackson has no choice, because he's the main target, but Jonas can stay clear of it and clean. Especially if he has no knowledge of it."

"Jonas knows when there's trouble," Hannah said. "He has gifts of his own. No way can you hide something like this from him. You and Jackson need to come over tonight and sit down with him and explain the plan. You do have a plan, don't you?"

"We're putting together what we can do to help the men," Elle explained.

"I take it Viktor has been working undercover to try to get to Evan?" Abigail asked.

Blythe nodded. "He was sent here with some others as a forward scout to get Jackson's routes and find a place to ambush him. Elle remembered Leslee, her friend from high school, talking about taking her mastiffs here. Jackson said it was perfect, and he and the others are figuring out how they're going to handle it. We need an entry where we can come in above the campgrounds without the Swords knowing. That's Evan's motorcycle club. They'll be coming in a few at a time without colors. Viktor's sent word about this place."

"You could go in on the side where the railroad tracks are," Joley suggested. "It's a little bit of a hike, but you'll come out on one of the roads above the campgrounds. There are all sorts of unmarked logging roads, but I can show you the entrance and the right road."

"That would be great, Joley, but there's more. Evan intends to destroy the Drake house, to burn it to the ground," Blythe said. "He also will go after Inez's store and possibly other businesses in town. He'll have as many people hurt as possible. That will be happening simultaneously with what's going on out here. I would like you and anyone else pregnant or having children to stay in town and cope with that. Jonas can be there with some others to help you. That way, Jonas isn't doing anything against the law, and with your help, he'll be safe. So will Sea Haven."

"But you and Elle will be out here," Joley protested. "Ilya would never allow his brothers in a fight like this one without helping them."

"I couldn't take it knowing you and the others were in danger," Blythe said. "I really couldn't, Joley. I can ask Viktor to try to get Ilya to stay in town with all of you. You'll need a couple more people unless Jonas can arrange for extra law enforcement to help him, but that's a risk. None of them can come out here when the call comes in that there's a problem. Only Jackson can come."

She couldn't stop any of them, but she hoped they understood and cared enough to give her that much.

"You really need someone in the village?" Airiana said. "You're not just saying that?"

Blythe shook her head. "I wish I was making it up. No, there's a real danger. I think especially to Inez. She identified the members of the Swords as the ones causing a scene, and when they were taken to jail, they all had records and outstanding warrants. The club is very angry with Inez, and Viktor says she and her store will be targeted."

"Naturally we want everyone as safe as possible," Elle said. "With all of you working together, you should be able to control things there."

"I thought you might stay with them, Lissa," Blythe ventured, hoping her sister got her silent plea. Lissa was lethal and she could protect the others if there was a problem. "They'll use fire and you can stop that . . ." She trailed off.

Lissa nodded. "Hannah and Airiana are the best with wind and weather. Judith can boost power to them."

"Inez will cooperate," Elle said. "She acts like she's Jackson's mom half the time. She'll do anything to keep him safe."

Blythe groaned. "You can't tell Inez."

"We have to," Joley pointed out. "She can't just be bait. Only her. Jonas and Jackson can figure out what to say to her, and she'll keep her mouth shut. She always does when it's needed. She loves Jackson. And the bonus, Blythe, is that Viktor will be a hero in her eyes and she'll get everyone else to view him that way."

It was true that the village of Sea Haven followed Inez's lead in most things. Still, Viktor was bringing in a motorcycle club to reside in Caspar, which was only a few miles from Sea Haven. It was all getting out of hand. She couldn't keep her man safe, no matter how hard she tried.

"Blythe." Elle put her hand over her cousin's. "The Prakenskiis and the Drakes together with you and your sisters will stop them. Viktor is going to be safe."

"I know." But she didn't. She wasn't counting on the Prakenskiis or the Drakes. She wasn't even counting on her sisters, and she knew what all of them could do. She was counting on Viktor's brothers and sisters from his club. Reaper and Savage. Ice and Storm. Alena. Transporter, Absinthe and Mechanic. The men Viktor talked about to her. The others who weren't yet in Sea Haven but would be coming with Habit and his crew of Swords. The last nine would be riding with him, deep undercover, ready to protect Viktor and follow his lead anywhere. She was counting on all of them.

"When's he coming?" Sarah asked. "Evan. When can we expect him? How much time do we have?"

"Viktor reported to Habit last night. He's spreading the word to the other chapters to come to the Egg Taking

Station via Highway 20. He told them to avoid Sea Haven and come prepared to camp rough. There are only outhouses here, not that the club is going to mind that, but no showers either. Who knows, maybe they don't care about bathing," Blythe added.

"Will Evan be on a motorcycle? Can they take him out before he gets here?" Abigail asked.

Blythe shook her head. "He's totally paranoid and doesn't trust anyone. No one will know ahead of time how he'll get here, but he'll have to meet with Viktor to get the information he wants and formulate a plan to ambush Jackson." She tried to close her mind to the fact that Evan had killed his bodyguards for no apparent reason.

"Then we'll have to wait for the word," Sarah said. "We may as well eat, and Joley can explain to all of us how she knows all about those unmarked roads and how to hike into them when Dad specifically told her not to ever go there."

Joley took a bite of her chicken and looked up into the sky. "I might point out," she said when she swallowed, "that everyone here is planning on coming here and I'll be in town behaving myself." She used her most innocent, self-righteous voice.

Even Blythe couldn't help but laugh.

17

"IT'S going to rain tonight," Blythe said, watching Viktor spread out a thick ground blanket in the backyard.

Vines grew up trellises and the wrought iron fence she'd put in more for looks than for anything else. The backyard was actually more of a courtyard, with wings of the house coming out on either side to form a U-shape.

"We won't melt," Viktor said. "In fact, we might need cooling off a little."

She couldn't help the smile. He did that. Made her smile when he said absolute nonsense. He preferred being outside. He always had, even in their early days. He'd talk her into sleeping in the garden or on the front porch rather than in the house. Now she knew why.

"Fortunately, it should be a light rain. I can feel the mist in the air already."

"It's always misty here," he corrected. "You're wearing too many clothes."

"It's not quite dark."

"It doesn't have to be dark. In fact, I prefer to see you." He flashed a grin. "We've got everything. Your wine. My beer. Cheese. Honey. Crackers. Whipped cream. A bucket of ice. Ice cream."

"That's going to melt. What in the world are you planning to do with all that?"

"Get naked, woman, and I'll show you."

It was a growl. He'd done that many, many times, and that particular tone always sent a frisson of desire creeping down her spine. He was already stripping, uncaring that the sun was sinking, that it was more orange-red across the sky than dark. She deliberately backed away from him. She was still fully clothed, was a good runner, fast, with long, ground-eating strides. She had good stamina. He was naked and barefoot already, and she knew he occasionally snuck a cigarette even though he knew he shouldn't.

She turned and sprinted for the house. He was on her in seconds. She'd barely made the steps leading up to the wraparound porch. She didn't hear him, but then his hands were on her and he tossed her easily over his shoulder so that she hung upside down, staring at his very fine backside.

Viktor took her to the blanket and set her on her feet. She was laughing so hard she almost couldn't stand upright. "Clothes, woman. Or they'll be gone."

"Gone?" She tried to be serious. He *looked* serious, and that wasn't always a good thing. He had something in mind.

"Gone," he said firmly.

"It's still daylight. Anyone could walk up." She knew they wouldn't. She had five acres to herself, with her house in the center of the acreage, but she wanted to tease him a little more. She liked playing and Viktor was always willing to play—with her.

One moment she was standing in her blouse and the next he caught the front of it and jerked, splitting the material in two. He dropped the pieces on the ground and caught at her skirt.

"Not the skirt. I love this skirt," she protested hastily. Her hands dropped to cover his. "I really, really love this skirt."

He yanked it down and she let it fall, kicking it aside. Her bra was gone the same way her shirt had along with the scrap of lace she called panties.

"You're so crazy."

"About you." He pulled her into his arms. "I love the way you feel. All that soft skin, Blythe."

"You just like me naked."

"No, baby, I *love* you naked." He tipped her face up so he could take her mouth.

Her breath caught in her lungs. When he kissed her the world receded until there was only the two of them. The wind touched her body, cooling her skin when inside, her temperature soared. She wrapped her arms around his neck, pressing her breasts into him, fitting her naked mound tight against him so that he could feel every inch of her. He reached down and caught her leg behind her knee, lifting it to wrap it around his waist, opening her up to him.

It felt decadent. Sexy. Perfect. He kissed her over and over. These weren't his gentle, beautiful kisses that brought tears to her eyes. His mouth was aggressive, demanding, his tongue dueling with hers, stroking and teasing, his hands sliding over her body to take in as much skin as possible.

She did the same, unable to stop touching him, needing him closer, every single cell in her body alive and demanding. She wanted him right there. Right that moment. Her hand dropped to his cock, fisted the heavy girth and began to pump. He broke the kiss and took her down to the blanket in one breathless move. How he did it without hurting her, she didn't know. He was always so smooth.

"Spread your legs for me, Blythe," he whispered, his mouth traveling from hers down her throat to her breast. "And put your hands over your head and leave them there."

"I want to touch you."

"I know you do, baby, but I want to have a little fun first. My turn and then yours."

She pretended to glare at him. "It has been my experience that it never gets around to my turn when you're in this mood." Already her nipples peaked and she went damp at the idea of Viktor playing with her body. He was inventive and she always managed to get the better end of the deal.

His teeth nipped the curve of her breast and then his

tongue bathed the sting. "But I always make it worth your while, don't I?"

If she was honest he made it more than worth her while, so she did as he said, but slowly, lifting her arms above her head in a stretch, so that her breasts jutted out at him. Very slowly she began to slide her legs apart. Wide. Giving him free access.

"I decided since you like clothes so much, I'm going to paint you."

His mouth kept working her breast until she was squirming, but she didn't move her hands or legs. A shiver of anticipation went through her. Warm liquid pulsed between her legs. When Viktor was in the mood to play, her body welcomed every single thing he did to her.

"You've always been so artistic," she acknowledged, wide-eyed.

"Are you being sarcastic?" His lips closed over her nipple and tugged.

She felt the streak of fire race straight to her sex. Her gaze jumped to his, but he was busy with the bucket of ice. He pulled out a small pint of Neapolitan ice cream.

"I've only got three colors, but I think I can give you some really nice clothes," he murmured as he opened the lid.

All the while he stared down at her body as if he might devour her any moment. He looked like sin itself. His eyes were dark with lust. Lines were cut deep in his face, a carnal expression that sent chills of excited anticipation through her. He was so beautiful. Like a fallen angel intent on her downfall.

He lifted a small brush a man might use for shaving cream, swirled it in the ice cream and then brushed a curving stroke over the top of her breast. She nearly jumped out of her skin. The combination of cold and the soft bristles riding over her skin sent another streak of fire straight to her sex.

"Chocolate for your bra."

"Honey," she said, her voice a breathy moan. He hadn't even gotten started and she was afraid she'd come apart.

"The canvas can't talk, and don't breathe so hard. I might mess up." He added more chocolate ice cream over her breasts, lavishing it over both heaving mounds. He swirled the brush, so that the bristles teased her skin, making her so sensitive that by the time he began to lap up the drips running down the sides of her, she cried out with each stroke of his tongue.

He took his time, which was Viktor's way. He never rushed when he was worshipping her his way. Just when she thought she couldn't stand it a minute longer, when her hips were bucking because she needed him inside her so desperately, he began to paint again.

"Vanilla for your shirt." The brush stroked along each rib and then down the center between her breasts all the way to her belly button. He put a scoop in the little indentation and lifted his head to study his work. "Hold still."

"I'm trying." She wasn't. She couldn't stop moving her hips. She really couldn't. His tongue was wicked, moving over her skin, lapping and teasing. Flicking and dancing until she thought she might scream with need.

"I want some ice cream," she groused.

He looked up from swirling his tongue around her belly button. "If I give you some, will you behave? You have to eat everything I give you without making a mess."

"I will." She loved when he looked at her that way. So dark and dangerous. So completely sinful. She needed the reprieve. Her body was on fire, coiling tighter and tighter until she thought she might go insane with need for him.

"Which flavor?"

"Strawberry," she said promptly, expecting him to take a mouthful and kiss her.

He dipped the brush in the strawberry and began painting his cock and balls. He was as meticulous with his own body as he had been with hers, putting a thick coat of the ice cream over him and then crawling up her body. He positioned his groin over her mouth.

She licked up his balls and shaft in long strokes, her tongue dancing along the underside of the crown and then swirling over the top of it. She licked frantically as the ice cream melted quickly from the heat of his body.

"Open." He growled the command. "And keep your arms above your head."

Obediently she opened her mouth, feeling vulnerable without her hands, but she knew him and trusted him. He was gentle as he pushed inside her mouth, and she closed her lips around his thick cock. She suckled strongly, her tongue flicking and swiping to find every drop of ice cream. He groaned and pushed forward with his hips, several shallow strokes, going deeper with each.

She loved the feel of him, that hard, hot length of him. He tasted of ice cream, man and his particular brand of aphrodisiac. He thrust gently several more times and then pulled out of her mouth.

"Now behave yourself. I gave you what you wanted. Let me do what I want."

"That's hardly fair," she pointed out. "I just got a small taste. You're eating the entire pint."

"You're lucky I gave you any," he said, using the brush, this time on her mound. "If you had agreed to stay home like a good girl, you might have gotten more ice cream, but you were very, very bad defying me like that. Now all those other women are involved and I have to put up with their bullshit."

He carefully painted up the inside of her thighs and then the brush was on her clit. She cried out, gripping the blanket to keep from coming apart. He laughed softly and pressed a glob of ice cream right into her burning entrance. At once his mouth was clamped over her, his tongue stabbing deep.

She nearly came apart. She actually thought she saw stars. She couldn't help thrashing around, and then she reached down to try to use her own hand. He caught her hand as he lifted his head inches from her pulsing clit to annunciate each word.

"Don't. You. Dare. Come. You wait for me," he warned. "We'll be at this all night."

He bent his head again and flicked at her clit. It felt like a lash of pure fire. Deep inside that coiling tightened until she thought she'd go insane. He licked and suckled and flicked at her until the rush threatened to overtake her. He seemed to know just when to stop before she could get there. She moaned and reached her hand between her legs again when he started a third time, desperately needing the orgasm.

Viktor lifted his head that fast, rolled her over before she could catch her breath, his hand coming down in a loud smack on her left cheek. "Are you supposed to be coming?"

"I thought you were finished." She tried not to laugh, even though her body was in total overdrive. She *needed* the release.

The flat of his hand sent scorching heat spreading like a wildfire through her already overheated center.

"Well, I'm not. Hold still, you little liar. Your clothes can't just be on one side of your body. Spread your legs again and this time keep your arms wide out from your body and over your head."

"You're torturing me." Her breath was going in ragged little sobs now. There was no way to still her hips, not with the cool breeze on her bare bottom.

He was already painting her with ice cream, down her spine, radiating out along her ribs and in the small indentations at the curve of her spine. He spent time lapping up the ice cream and then he popped open a can of beer and poured it over the remains dripping down her back.

The ice cold of the beer after the heat of his tongue was nearly her undoing. She cried out and nearly came.

"Don't. You don't get to come yet. You have to wait for me." He left a second handprint on her skin, this one on her right buttocks. He bent to lap at the beer. "Hold still while I paint my hands on you." He used the chocolate to brush ice cream over the two handprints. "I think we should tattoo those there."

"It won't happen, so get over that one," she whispered, turning her head to the side to try to look at him over her shoulder. It was impossible. She could barely breathe. He was using the brush all over her bottom, meticulous in coating her with the ice cream. He added beer, and then his tongue was all over her, lapping it up, licking and sucking. His teeth nipped. He didn't miss anywhere, making certain he claimed every inch of her body. She knew that was what he was doing and she closed her eyes and just let him. His fingers went between her legs, pressing deep and then disappearing.

"Honey, I can't take much more," she said. She couldn't. She was going to go up in flames. She knew him. If she did, if she didn't hold back, he'd start all over. He could keep it up all night.

He must have heard the raw need in her voice because he caught her hips and pulled back until she was on her hands and knees. He didn't wait, but surged into her hard, driving her forward so that she fell to her elbows, her breath coming in ragged pants as she pushed back for more.

He took her hard and fast. Over and over. She screamed as her orgasm overtook her in a scorching rush she couldn't stop. It was powerful, ripping through her body, spreading up to her belly and breasts, and down her thighs all the way to her toes. He didn't stop, powering through the strong ripples, the tight muscles clamping down on him. He drove her up fast again. "You're not done," he bit out between clenched teeth. "More. Give me more."

She did. She couldn't have stopped the force of it if she'd wanted to. It overtook her fast, with the force of a tsunami, wave after wave and still he continued to thrust into her like a piston, hard and hot and dragging over sensitive nerves. Her muscles gripped and milked at his cock. She could feel his heartbeat right through his shaft and up through her own muscles.

"Again."

"Honey." Her voice was a sob. It was too good. "Too high."

"Fall for me."

"Catch me."

"I've got you."

She let go, and this time he went with her, his hot seed splashing her sensitive inner walls so that the ripples rocked them both. She gasped and fought for breath as she was thrown into a whirling vortex of sheer pleasure. The powerful quakes kept coming and she screamed, letting it take her, letting it throw her into subspace where she seemed to float endlessly in pure bliss.

"Oh for God's sake, Czar, do you know what a fuckin' bed is for?" Reaper's voice brought her out of her floaty, perfect wonderland.

He stood in the shadows, Savage about five feet from him, both with guns drawn. She gasped and went down once again on her elbows as Viktor wrapped both arms around her, covering her nearly completely with his larger frame.

"Get the fuck out of here, you pervert." There was no menace in Viktor's voice, more amusement than anything.

"She screamed."

"Women scream. She's a screamer. Can't you tell the difference between a woman screaming because she's in trouble and one screaming because her man is all over her?" Viktor demanded. "Of course you can't. You don't know the first thing about women."

"I learned that when I was eight, you moron," Reaper snapped back.

Blythe closed her eyes and jammed her fist into her mouth. They were arguing. She was on her hands and knees with Viktor's cock buried deep inside her, her body sticky with ice cream and beer and still pulsing, her inner muscles tightening rhythmically around Viktor's shaft, with the men arguing back and forth.

"Then what the hell, man? I'm going to shoot your ass the next time you barge in when I'm with Blythe."

"You're the one with the ass in the air," Savage pointed out.

"And you're not technically 'in' anywhere. You're outside, *not* in the bed," Reaper added.

"Um. Technically he is 'in' somewhere," Savage corrected.

It was either laugh or cry. These men had no idea how

inappropriate they were. Viktor had told her about their childhood, but she had the idea they'd been given the same kinds of instructions the rest of his birth brothers had been given. That they'd all be suave and charming with women. They'd know the right thing to say and do in every circumstance. These men didn't know the first thing about etiquette or how to behave properly in society. They were raised without clothes and had sex in front of one another without batting an eyelash.

Tears burned behind her eyes, but she refused to shed them. They held their heads up, and she could learn to live with their ways—although maybe not this. They had to live in a world they probably didn't understand and most likely, even with gentle help, they probably would never quite get society's rules. They'd had their own rules, developed from their horrific childhood. Clearly modesty and private time was not part of that.

"What the hell, Savage? This is not the time to joke," Viktor snapped.

She started to laugh. She couldn't help it. It wasn't the time to argue either, but he was doing it. It was an impossible situation, and she wasn't about to be the one embarrassed when clearly they weren't. "Go away," she said, although her muffled laughter made it impossible for any of them to understand her.

"What?" Savage asked.

"Go away," she repeated. Viktor's weight was threatening to break her in half.

"Stop screaming," Reaper told her.

"She likes to scream, she can scream. Besides, I like her screaming. Learn the difference," Viktor snarled.

"Go away," Blythe said again.

She let her body collapse, Viktor sprawling on top of her. She had no idea how he did it, but his arms locked around her hips, pulling her bottom back into him so that his cock was still buried deep. It was only then she realized he was still as hard as a rock. He wasn't finished.

"Get the fuck out of here," Viktor ordered, his voice this time one of pure command. He was moving again, a slow glide that sent streaks of fire spreading through her body. How he could do that when she was somewhere between laughter at the absurdity of their situation and tears for the men and women who had suffered at the hands of vile, brutish criminals, she had no idea. Only that he could. Viktor could make every situation better.

Reaper and Savage shook their heads, turned and walked away, Reaper muttering to himself.

She turned her head to one side and let him take her back to that place where it was just the two of them in their own world. He was gentle, his hands moving over her body, claiming her for his own.

"I can never get enough of you," he whispered. "Never. I dreamt of you every night. I thought about you every day. I don't believe in God, but I found myself praying you would wait for me, that you were everything I remembered." He whispered the confession as he moved in her body, keeping that connection between them.

It was so good. It was always good, but when he was like this, so gentle and sweet, he took her heart along with her body.

"I spent hours of every day thinking of all the things you like. How to get them for you. How to make things right for you." His mouth whispered down her back, returned to the nape of her neck and pressed kisses there. "I want to give you the world, Blythe. Everything."

"You give me you," she said. "That's enough for me." It was. He was.

He fell silent, letting his body speak for him. She heard the love there. She felt it. This time when he brought her to the very edge, she bit her lip and made certain she didn't make a single sound. That didn't matter. Sound or no sound, it was perfection.

Viktor collapsed over top of her and then slowly, reluctantly, pulled out of her body. The movement sent another ripple of pleasure shooting through her body. They were silent, both trying to catch their breath, and then he rolled over to lie beside her on his back.

"Thanks."

She turned her head just enough to look at him, her eyebrow raised.

"For being you. Not freaking out when they showed up. They really aren't perverts," he said, staring up at the sky, his hands locked behind his head.

"They might be," she pointed out, amusement in her voice. "That's twice." She waited a heartbeat and then took a chance. "So you know that's entirely inappropriate."

He turned his head to look at her, frowning. "I just knew you were uncomfortable. I can read your body language like a book. You're uncomfortable, then it doesn't happen."

"But it doesn't bother you that they walk right in when we're making love?"

"I love you. Totally. With everything in me. I'm proud of you. Taking your body is just that, loving you. Claiming you. Having you claim me."

"But I'm naked."

"It isn't anything they haven't seen since they were babies. But bottom line, Blythe, you don't like something, it isn't done. I'll talk to them," he promised. "I'm sorry. They just won't listen when it comes to my personal safety."

"I suppose we're going to have to add a few more bedrooms on to the house, or maybe a wing just for them," she ventured, amusement returning.

"That won't be necessary. They aren't living with us. They can get their own damn homes. If they want to hang around, they can sit out on the roof and play with their guns."

She didn't point out that they'd be right outside their bedroom. What would be the point?

"And I like you to make noise when I'm inside you, baby. Screw Reaper. Make as much noise as you want. It sounds like fuc— music to me."

"I will." She wouldn't.

"Promise me, babe." He turned on his side, his arm

curving around her waist and pulling her closer into his body. "I'll talk to them. Seriously. It matters to me that you can relax and be you when I'm inside you."

"I'll try, but if they come rushing into the bedroom when I'm right in the middle of coming, I might shoot them myself."

He laughed and rubbed his chin along her jaw. "I knew you'd be like this about them."

"Like what?"

"You don't get angry with them—or me. Give us time. I swear we'll get it figured out."

He bent his head and his hair brushed along her sensitive skin, sending a shiver down her spine and peaking her nipples as he kissed the curve of her breast. She had been completely sated, bordering on exhaustion, but with just one touch, her body was alive all over again.

"I know you will." Because it mattered to him. *She* mattered to him and what she wanted or needed mattered. She knew it in her heart. He really would work to fix whatever was wrong. Still, he believed in her—had faith that she wouldn't judge them or be angry over the way they'd lived and would most likely continue to live. "We're a mess. We're sticky with ice cream and beer."

"It's going to rain soon. It'll wash us off."

He was complacent. He meant it. The rain didn't bother him any more than Reaper and Savage running into the yard with weapons drawn. He didn't sweat the small stuff because his life was filled with big things to worry about.

"Where are we with Darby?"

We. She had to fight the smile that wanted to come. He meant her. What had she done to expedite Darby and her sisters getting to their home? He wasn't moved in. His undercover mission wasn't finished. He was surrounded by danger and could be killed any moment, but what mattered to him were three homeless children, two of whom had been victims of human trafficking.

It was always going to be that way. Viktor would request something and turn it over to her, having faith it would get done. She could live with that. It was in her nature to take care of the details.

"The paperwork is going through. Lev and Maxim seem to be the best at falsifying documents. I can't believe I just said that." She burst out laughing. "The six of you have changed our lives."

"Seven. Baby brother is part of us whether he wants to be or not," Viktor corrected. "He'll always have our protection."

"I know." That made her love him even more.

"What's the holdup with our girls? I heard it in your voice that there is one."

"It's just taking a little longer. The latest foster parents for the youngest girl—her name is Emily and she's six—have decided they want to fight for her."

"What the fuck? I thought she keeps running away."

"She does, which my attorney has pointed out to the court."

"I can get a few of the boys and we'll go pay them a little visit," Viktor said.

"No, you won't," Blythe said, glaring at him. "I mean it, Viktor. On this, we're going to do everything by the book."

"Like falsifying documents?" Now his voice was tinged with amusement.

"Everything else."

He laughed. "I'll go along with you, babe, unless they continue to make trouble. I've gone through the house a few times to familiarize myself with escape routes and the layout. It's nice. Big rooms. I like the bedrooms downstairs and the master suite upstairs, but we're going to have to get alarms on the windows and doors. Keep those kids in and everyone else out."

The wind picked up, blowing leaves into wild little eddies, cooling the heat of her body. The cool breeze and fine mist felt good on her skin. Darkness had fallen, and she felt braver talking about a subject she abhorred.

"Viktor, I'm pretty certain I know what happened to your messages."

"I'm listening, baby." He brushed little kisses over the curve of her breast again, this time for her bravery.

"If Sharon didn't destroy the letter—and now, I don't think she did if it contained a way to reach you, or a way for you to reach me. She hated me having you. She used to say you'd cheat on me, that a man like you would never settle for someone so boring."

He made a sound in his throat as if he were strangling, but he refrained from speaking. His hand cupped her breast, his thumb stroking along the velvet soft curve. It was just distracting enough to keep the bile from rising. Just the thought of her mother sickened her.

"She was so jealous of me having you. She was always jealous of other women and me in particular. Having you meant escaping her. If there was a code, she never would have figured it out on her own."

"There was a code."

His thumb kept moving, a mesmerizing glide that helped anchor her when her chest felt too tight and her breath kept catching in her lungs.

"She wouldn't have been able to have the discipline needed to figure it out and then check the message center for any message you sent to me. She would have given the letter to Ray's partner. She thought he was so smart. He came to her house often and she'd drink herself into a stupor, and then the two men would disappear together. I thought, at first, that Ray cheated on her with women."

"He was a pedophile, Blythe. There were no other women."

"I understand that now, but then I didn't know. Walter Sandlin was an oily creep. I couldn't stand to be in the same room with him. He was definitely Ray's partner, though. They worked on a site on the Internet together."

"It was a worldwide site for pedophiles to gather, share their videos and sell the kids they were tired of, and a place to acquire more when they wanted. Ray actually envisioned conventions and meeting places."

"They. Walter definitely was every bit as involved, and

Ray always referred to him as his business partner. Once I asked what business and if it made any money, because Ray never left the house to go to work. Walter laughed his head off and said it was very, very lucrative."

"Walter Sandlin?"

She nodded. "He's about sixty, a retired attorney out of LA. He owns a house out in Occidental. Viktor, he's got very powerful friends. His family has money, and he backed the DA as well as the sheriff in that location. He's friends with law enforcement and holds parties all the time. Ray and my mother used to go there quite often."

"All right, baby, I've got it," he said softly, brushing more kisses up to her throat. "You don't have to think about that anymore. Never again, you understand me? That's mine. I'll take that little problem and figure it out, and you keep on the girls. You need me for that, you say the word and I'll be all over it." He tipped her chin up. "Tell me you understand."

She nodded. "It's your problem. I don't want to think about it ever again."

"And one more thing. I know Elle is your cousin, but your aunts, baby. I'm never going to like them or get along with them. You have to be okay with that. I don't give a damn who likes me or who doesn't."

She knew that from his meeting with his brothers. He was unbending. Unapologetic.

"You want me to be around them, I'll be polite, because you ask me, but they left you out in the cold. That's never going to be acceptable to me. Part of that might be guilt, that I wasn't here for you, but damn it, they're your family and they should have been protecting you and standing for you. That's all I've got to say on that."

There was finality in his voice and she knew she was hearing Czar, not Viktor. Both men were hers and she could understand because, honestly, she felt the same way. She nodded to let him know it was okay.

He nibbled on her chin. "I want to dance with you."

"Dance?" His mouth was distracting her. On some level she knew he was doing it deliberately, but she didn't care.

"Dance," he said decisively. "I brought music."

"Music and ice cream. What woman could ask for anything more?"

He reached back with a lazy arm and turned on an iPod. For some reason the thought of Viktor owning an iPod seemed totally out of character, and then the music started. She laughed. "That's my iPod."

"Yep. Your music too." He stood up and pulled her to her feet. "The mist is finally turning to rain." He turned his head up so the light drops could wash over his face. "I love the way the raindrops feel on my skin. I used to think, when I was a kid, that it would wash all the ugliness and shame away. That it would take the blood from my hands. It never did, but I held out hope." He smiled down at her, but the smile didn't reach his eyes. "Maybe I still have hope."

She circled his neck with her arms, locking her fingers at his nape. His long hair fell around his face, giving him that sinful, fallen-angel look. She pressed her body close against his. "If the rain can't do it, I will," she said, looking into his eyes. Meaning it.

He moved with her, small steps, taking her around the blanket and then onto the grass. The rain fell on their bodies, until what was left of the ice cream and beer ran off them in small little rivulets. They danced for three songs. Laughed through another one. Then he was lifting her and she circled his hips with her long legs and he was inside her.

It was good. It was perfect. It was all Viktor. She threw her head back and let the rain hit her face, laughing as her orgasm rushed over her. She was going to scream, and she didn't much care if Reaper and Savage heard or came running. She was just too happy with her man.

18

THE roar of Harleys, as they smoothed out every curve in the road, seemed loud in the gathering night. The sun had set, first plunging the world into gold and orange, and then into a silverish sheen that reflected on the leaves of the trees as they passed under them.

Viktor lifted his fist, signaling they were coming up on the road leading to Walter Sandlin's house. They needed to stop and park their rides. He slowed until he found a small trail leading off the main road. He pulled over and shut off the engine, looking up at the sky through the branches.

Bats wheeled and dipped, catching insects, and a few lone stars shone through. A fog bank moved steadily toward them from the coast. Sandlin lived outside of Occidental, along an older, well-maintained road. His private road branched off from the older one. Houses had been few and far between. One ranch had several mournful-looking cows, and another had a herd of sheep kept watch over by a very large Great Pyrenees who kept a wary eye on them as they passed by.

"Alena, you stay with the bikes," he ordered.

She rolled her eyes. "Seriously? Why me? Because I'm the girl?"

"That's right. You don't need to be doing this shit anymore." His tone brooked no argument.

"Maybe I want to do it," she muttered rebelliously, but she turned back to yank a blanket out of her pack and throw it down by the line of motorcycles.

"Babe." Viktor waited until she looked up. "None of us should want to be doing this kind of thing. We're turning over a new leaf."

"I call bullshit," she snapped back. "Just because we're going all official, don't think you can relegate Lana and me to the position of old lady."

His jaw hardened. A muscle ticked there. The silence stretched out. "Are you in any way putting my woman down?" There was menace in his tone and he felt rage rising, the berserker rage he strove to keep under control when it was with one of his brothers or sisters.

Alena shook her head quickly. "Of course not. I didn't mean it like that. We formed Torpedo Ink together, Czar. All of us. Lana and me as well. We were as much a part of that as all of you, and now suddenly, I'm not wanted in on the action."

"Do you think I want any of you torturing or killing someone?" He all but snarled it. "I've been working my ass off trying to get us to a place where we have a choice in what we do. All of us, but yes, you and Lana especially. We have two sisters left out of how many? Every time your life is on the line all of us hold our fuckin' breath. We survive because you did. You might not value your life or think it's important, but to us, it is. I'm not putting you in harm's way if I don't have to, you get me?"

She nodded. "Yes, but we need some damn prospects the minute we're settled because I don't want to sit around twiddling my thumbs watching your bikes."

He caught her by the nape of her neck and hauled her to him. "You get that you're important, right?"

She hesitated but then nodded. "I get it, Czar."

"Watch sharp. We don't know what setup this bastard has. My guess is he's paranoid as hell. Worried the cops are going to come nosing around or some of his other friends he's probably blackmailing. Code looked at that site and it's set up to gather all kinds of information. Their little friends they've invited to join from all around the world are probably getting blackmailed. That makes him doubly dangerous. He might have patrols this far out."

She nodded again. "I have no problem with that. Might be entertaining since I didn't bring my book."

Ice snorted. She glared at her brother. "You implying I can't read?" she snapped.

Ice held up both hands in mock surrender. "Just saying, baby sister, you can read, you just don't." He smirked at her.

Alena flipped him off and threw herself on the blanket. The men moved into the heavier brush, spacing about five feet from one another, slipping into their normal personas. They were phantoms. Ghosts. Assassins. This was what they'd been shaped into all those years ago and the fit was perfect, settling into their skins easily.

They didn't speak because they didn't need to. They'd perfected their skills as a team when they were children, some as young as two and three. They might have been sent out as adults individually to do Sorbacov's dirty work, but they were essentially a team and always would be.

A dog barked in the distance. Viktor held up a fist and pointed to the thickest tree. Transporter went up it fast, climbing with speed that always astonished Viktor. In another life, Transporter would have made it big. He devoured books and retained everything he read. He could actually learn languages in a few hours. His hand-eye coordination and reflexes were astonishing, making it easy for him to drive at high speed. More, he was a human GPS, mostly, Viktor was certain, because of the maps he devoured in his spare time, but also because he just was.

The hoot of an owl sounded from above them, out of the higher limbs, four times. Viktor wanted to swear. Four dogs patrolled with their handlers. They didn't like killing animals if they could help it. The dogs were just doing their jobs. It wasn't their fault they worked for one of the biggest networks of pedophiles in the world.

He circled in the air with his finger and pointed to Reaper. The man had a gift—one that allowed him to move through impossible situations, including dogs. Once in a while, whatever trick he used didn't work, and it was left to Savage to keep his brother alive by whatever means necessary.

Savage was quick and deadly, just like his older brother. Neither talked much to outsiders and both meant what they said. No one laid a hand on them unless it was one of the brothers—and only then if they wanted a beating. Reaper and Savage came into the school together along with two older sisters. All four children were from a privileged family, doted on by loving parents. The children had seen their family brutally murdered right in front of them.

Savage and Reaper had been targeted by two of the cruelest, most brutal pedophiles in the school. Their sisters had tried to protect them, and both had paid the ultimate price, but only after being raped, beaten and tortured in front of the two little boys. Viktor had been fourteen by then and when the bodies of the two girls had been left in the "dungeon" with the boys, drawing rats and flies, he had stepped in. He couldn't let things go on as they were. He made up his mind to stop those running the school—and for the most part, over time, he'd managed to do just that. But that beginning had taken a toll on the two brothers.

He watched over them carefully now, uncertain what kind of life either could lead. Every single survivor was fucked-up, but in their world, Savage and Reaper were the question marks. The two played for keeps. They often fought in underground fights. At first it had been for quick money, but Code had taken care of all the money problems. He had cleaned out more than one criminal nest with no way to trace the devastation back to them. Torpedo Ink had more than enough money to give them all a good life. Now, Viktor knew, Reaper and Savage fought because they had to. They needed to feel fists hitting solidly into flesh. To feel those fists hitting them. It wasn't something Viktor could stop so he didn't try.

They continued to inch closer to the large, ornate wrought iron fence surrounding the property. Viktor spotted the first of the four dog handlers with a big Doberman. The dog was a big brute, a "Warlock," one much larger than the normal breed. Dog and handler were outside the fence and moving in a clockwise circle around the property, but delving into the woods, going along well-worn trails. They seemed to be headed straight toward the spot where Viktor knew Reaper was concealed.

Suddenly the wind changed direction, picking up speed, moving fast toward the house and away from Reaper. Ice and Storm were doing their jobs, keeping their brother safe. The dog couldn't possibly catch a scent with all of them now downwind.

The dog was a beautiful animal, and Viktor knew it only had minutes to live if they kept on course. Savage would kill it first and then the handler. Whatever gift or talent Reaper had to make people and animals look the other way, now was the time to employ it. He waited, his body still, his heart rate normal. This was a world he lived in most of the time and he was used to the danger. He was cautious, but everything was very familiar to him.

The handler suddenly changed course, looking toward the west, away from Reaper, moving quickly in that direction. Viktor sighed with relief. Savage would have killed both before they got to his brother, but still, there was always a chance the guard might shoot first.

He joined the two men. Reaper shook his head. "They have more than four dogs, Czar. The place is totally wired, cameras, mics everywhere. Sandlin is definitely paranoid and he's into electronics big-time."

His men gathered around him. Reaper, Savage, Ice, Storm, Mechanic, Transporter and Absinthe, the ones who generally ran any mission with him. The vice president of their club, Steele, ran the missions with the other eight members. They were used to working with one another and performed like a finely tuned machine. Each had their gifts and particular skill set.

"I can take them out, Czar," Savage offered, his tone strictly neutral.

Viktor glanced at him. The man was young, but his eyes looked old. There was no expression on his face. He would do it, kill the dogs and men if Czar asked him to, but the scars were there. Viktor shook his head. He wasn't adding more, not now when he had them all perched right on the edge of their goal. So close. He could give them a life. Blythe was there to help him. To show him what he needed to do.

Already he'd seen the shift in them. They had included her in their circle. She was his, and that meant she was theirs. Just that acceptance of another human being into their family was miraculous. None of them trusted an outsider. They kept to themselves and looked to one another for backup.

"We've got Mechanic," Viktor pointed out. "We'll do it the way we used to at the school. It's good practice for us."

"I mess up his cameras he's going to hard alert," Mechanic said, confident that he could.

With his brother Transporter, Mechanic worked on all their bikes. He was just as good with cars. Viktor had seen his drawings of custom cars and bikes, and they were really good. The hope was a shop where Transporter and Mechanic could do what they loved in peace. Mechanic could mess with anything electronic. Something in his body radiated enough energy to disrupt any electrical signal.

"Not if we provide him with good reasons," Viktor said. "Ice and Storm can do their thing, bring a limb or two down on power lines. Start picking up the wind, bring it in just enough to beat at his windows and drive his outer guards closer to shelter."

"You got it," Storm said.

Ice just nodded. He had three teardrops tattooed on his left side, as if he were crying. He'd done it because he never cried. He couldn't cry. He rarely, if ever smiled, but then, smiling or laughing wasn't that common. Mostly with one another. It was never real with outsiders.

Viktor and the others moved deeper into the woods, getting off the path the guard dogs and their handlers took. As they walked, he put his hand on Savage's shoulder, something rare. He felt Savage's body stiffen and then shudder under the gentle pressure, as if just being touched hurt. Still, Viktor did it, trying to get the man used to it.

"Didn't want to kill those dogs," Savage muttered.

"Me either," Viktor confirmed.

"Would have done it, if you needed me to," Savage added.

"I know, but it wasn't necessary." Viktor removed his hand casually, wishing Blythe could give him some advice on how to handle the nightmares and the effects of the trauma that continued even now when they were all supposedly free.

He believed in her—had the utmost faith in her—and that hadn't been misplaced. Five long years without a single word from him and she had taken him back when most women, after what she'd gone through, wouldn't have even considered it. There wasn't another woman like her. He worshipped the ground she walked on. He loved and admired everything about her. He knew she'd take in traumatized children without so much as batting an eyelash. That was Blythe. His Blythe.

"You're thinking about her," Savage said, startling him.

He nodded tersely. He had to be more careful. Protect her. He never wanted an outsider to be able to read his feelings for his woman.

"How did you know she was the one for you?"

Viktor shrugged, wishing he had magic words to make the world right for all of them. He knew the others were listening. They wanted to know as well. Already, Blythe had given them hope that maybe there were other women out there who would accept them with all their flaws and issues. "The moment I laid eyes on her, heard her laughter, saw the way she treated others, I just knew. It felt like something hit me hard, I mean really hard, right in the chest." He grinned at them. "You know how we control our cocks? We decide if we want to fuck someone. That went right out the window with her. I see her and my cock is ready. Not just ready, it's fighting for all the attention. There's no controlling that."

Laughter erupted, but it was muffled. They were very cognizant of being in a danger zone. A few of them looked a little skeptical, and he couldn't blame them. One of the most difficult and disturbing lessons they'd learned was control of their bodies at all times no matter what was being done to them—and a lot had been done to them.

He glanced over at Ice and Storm. They spread out, putting a good ten feet between them. Both had stopped, were completely motionless. He knew they were communicating telepathically. They could use the weather, harness the power of storms for their own purposes. It was all about energy and projecting that energy where they wanted or needed it.

Both looked up, searching the power lines and the trees. Storm nodded, and Ice moved out of the center of the woods and the heavier brush concealing them to the wider hiking trail. Immediately, Absinthe slipped around to the other side, guarding his back.

Reaper, Savage, Transporter and Mechanic waited with Viktor to be in position as close to the fence as possible, waiting for Ice and Storm to take out the electricity. The two brothers had chosen the tree limbs they wanted to bring down. Now it was a matter of doing so as naturally as possible. The wind shrieked, tearing through the trees straight toward the Gothic-looking mansion.

Sandlin wanted nobility so he'd had a castle built out in the woods at the end of his long private drive off a road with few neighbors. The house was a monster, with gargoyles staring out along the rooftops and round turrets. There were few lights on, but the ones that shone through the windows were a yellowish-green, like the eyes of a predatory cat.

Viktor stiffened. The house had been built for secrecy

and to make anyone entering uneasy. More, out in the middle of nowhere, in a house that large, Sandlin could do anything he wanted. He could entertain in his living room, even have a dinner party and hold a child prisoner downstairs in the basement and no one would ever know. He was perverse enough to enjoy that kind of thing. Viktor knew because he had studied his online persona. Sandlin was the one encouraging others to take sexual advantage of children, declaring the children loved it and society refused to recognize their needs.

A gust of wind battered at the house, rattling the windows, shrieking to get inside. Dogs and guards moved inside the gate, out of the woods, knowing it was dangerous in a storm to be where branches could fall on them. Sensitive to the energy hurtling through the air toward the house, the dogs roared and leapt to the end of their leashes, barking ferociously. Their handlers reprimanded them and yanked them away from the fence back toward the shelter of their kennels.

The wind retreated and was quiet a moment, as if taking a deep breath, and then once again it rushed the house, howling with rage, throwing twigs, leaves and debris at the sides and windows. The lights flickered, went brown and then glowed again a garish yellow.

Sorry, buddy, Viktor whispered in his mind to the child he was certain was being held in the basement. He'd been in a similar situation for years, and he knew what it was like when the lights went off and it was pitch-black. The rats came out—human and otherwise.

He shuddered and turned his head to look up at the chosen tree. It swayed and rocked with the force of the winds. The wind rose to a shriek of glee as it tore the limb from the tree and hurled it into the power line. The lights flickered a second time, went off and then came back on.

"He'll have a generator," Mechanic warned.

Viktor nodded. "One thing at a time. We'll be able to locate it easier by the sound. Ice and Storm can keep this up and the dogs and handlers won't be able to be out. We'll be in position the moment we know they've knocked out the cameras. We'll only have a few seconds."

The team was already moving to the woods just outside the fence. The patrols had a good six to eight feet of bare ground between the woods and the fence, but Sandlin had wanted to keep the forest close. It protected him as much as it was a threat.

The buildup of electricity in the air was shocking in its intensity. He hoped Ice and Storm were careful of starting a fire. The sound of lightning cracking across the sky and a tree splintering simultaneously was loud. At once the lights were off. Viktor and the others ran to the fence, were up and over it, counting seconds as they ran. They'd already chosen their places of concealment and were in them before the generator began to power up.

The estate had extensive gardens. Sandlin believed in every luxury. He also relied heavily on his cameras and sound equipment. The generator began to hum and then the noise was very loud. Right next to Viktor. At first he didn't see the cement pad artfully hidden by the lacy bushes surrounding it. The generator was on the pad, encased in a wooden housing. Viktor shook his head. Sandlin had spared no expense on his elaborate house, but something as important as a generator he'd skimped on. He was from the city and probably didn't think too much about it when locals told him he'd need a generator, and then he simply hadn't bothered to upgrade. Good for them, bad for him.

The wind shifted minutely, giving the house a brief respite. An owl hooted. Just once. That meant the generator was located close to Czar. Absinthe answered him from the woods. Message received. Mechanic had to move without being spotted.

The buildup of electricity had the hair on Viktor's body standing on end. Cursing, he went down to his belly and lay flat in the heavy foliage. Lightning cracked across the sky and thunder roared almost simultaneously. Side lightning and forks split the night sky, lighting up the grounds as the bolts rained down. He knew it was necessary to keep the guards and dogs inside until the others were over the fence. No one could move around in such a dangerous storm—including them.

Thunder cracked and shook the ground as the lightning receded from the main house, moving east toward the barracks. As soon as it did, Mechanic made his way through the garden on his belly, using elbows and toes, utilizing the plants for coverage. He sent a quick grin to Viktor as he eased up beside the generator.

Viktor hooted twice to ensure Ice, Storm and Absinthe were moving into position in the woods just outside the fence. The moment Mechanic stopped the generator, they would be up and over the fence, joining them. He watched as the man crouched beside the large box and studied it, mapping it out in his mind.

Viktor had always admired Mechanic's ability with anything that had moving parts. The generator droned steadily and creaked repeatedly. Metal ground against metal. There was a loud, ominous crack and the strong smell of oil. Mechanic sat back and waited. The generator sputtered. Black smoke rose around it. The grinding got worse and then, abruptly, it shut down.

The lights in both the house and the barracks went off. Storm, Ice and Absinthe were up and over the fence in seconds, all three running to join the others. Ice turned back toward the barracks, directing the powerful energy around that house, to ensure the guards stayed inside.

He could feel the anger in the storm and knew it reflected the rage hidden in all of them. When the brothers had first discovered they could utilize the energy weather provided, they had been very weak at it and then out of control. This storm felt that way—out of control. Viktor didn't want the barracks burned to the ground.

The feeling in his gut that they had it right, this was their target, grew with everything he saw. Sandlin was definitely a viper, a snake poised to strike at any unwary child he could get his hands on. He might not be part of Evan's human trafficking ring, but he had one of his own going. He was almost positive that it was this man who had destroyed his messages to Blythe. Why he would do that for Sharon, he didn't know, but he was going to find out.

Lightning and thunder crashed together, rattling the gutters in the barracks. Viktor's heart clenched hard in his chest. Little beads of sweat dotted his forehead and ran down his face and chest. He remembered storms vividly. Being in the "dungeon" without lights. The things they did to him in the dark by candlelight, telling him he was lucky he wasn't alone. Storms always brought the nightmare of memories.

"Pull back," Viktor hissed, afraid for the kid in the basement, because now he was certain there was a child down there. Enduring. Sometimes the lightning would go after the water pipes and those would connect in the basement.

Storm blew into the air, a long rush of warm breath, and the lightning receded as if on his command, leaving the sky dark. A few heartbeats later, it started up again, striking the ground near the barracks where the guards had retreated with the dogs.

His brothers gathered around him. "He may have people working for him inside. Housekeepers, maids, that sort of thing, but they'll know what's going on so they won't be innocent. Still"—he looked straight at Savage—"until we know who is guilty and who is innocent, we aren't going to wipe them out."

His word was law when it came to that sort of thing so he didn't wait for an acknowledgment. Still, a part of him wanted confirmation. Savage worried him. They all did, but Savage had it nearly as rough as Reaper and definitely from a younger age.

Reaper went with Viktor. He always did. He'd appointed himself Viktor's personal bodyguard back when he was six years old and Viktor was fourteen, over twice his age. Viktor went up the side of the house while his men scattered in pairs, going in from every direction. He entered through a second-story window. It had an alarm, but that was hard-wired into the electricity and failed when the backup generator went down.

He moved in silence, going quickly through the upper-story rooms, clearing them. No one appeared to live in any of them. There was a thin layer of dust on the bureau, but otherwise the place was clean, telling him the man had a cleaning crew that came in regularly, but not daily. He didn't want to think about where the kid was put when the cleaners came.

Downstairs he found the master bedroom. It was quite large, very decadent with mirrors from floor to ceiling on the two walls on either side of the bed and also on the ceiling above it. There were manacles attached to the foot of the bed and also at the head. Obscene pictures of Sandlin with a young boy decorated the walls not covered in mirrors.

Sandlin wasn't there. Viktor didn't find a foot patrol or even a security room in the house. The cameras were monitored from the barracks housing his guards. Clearly Sandlin didn't trust anyone to know what he was doing. As he blackmailed others like him, he had to fear that someone would discover his secret and blackmail him.

"Coffeepot is hot in the kitchen," Transporter reported. "Ice and Storm are keeping the storm heavy to keep the guards indoors. They can't keep up the lightning forever though. We've got to find him."

"Pretty certain I know where he is," Viktor said grimly. "He'll be downstairs. With the kid."

The tension in the room rose to a dangerous level. Viktor felt scary dangerous himself. This time he wasn't going to tell them to be cautious. He hoped he was wrong about what they were going to find, but he knew he wasn't.

Reaper and Savage turned first but Viktor held up his hand. "We go in careful."

He led the way, Reaper in step behind him, as they hunted through the downstairs for the door leading to the basement. It was just off the kitchen, looking as if it was a closet. Viktor pushed open the door very slowly. There was a creak. He stopped and glanced back at Savage. The man stepped forward and nodded for Viktor to open the door. The sound was muffled, so that the door was silent as it swung inward.

It should have been pitch-black beyond the door, but a flickering light danced on the walls. Candles. Sweat broke out on Viktor's skin. He remembered candles vividly, flickering in the darkness, the hot wax on his skin, the burn of cigarettes, Sorbacov's cruel laughter as he rutted and then turned him over to the vilest of the prisoners running the school. Bile rose, burning Viktor's throat.

He forced air into his lungs and kept moving forward. They crept down the narrow crude staircase, Savage muffling any noise they made. He smelled blood. The disturbing scent of Sandlin's perverted arousal.

"You should be happy I love you so much," Sandlin crooned. "I didn't want you all alone down here. I know how much you hate the dark."

The sound of the boy's breathing was a harsh, painful rasp with each brutal jerk of Sandlin's body. The sound of flesh slapping flesh was loud, echoing through the room. Viktor's mind went from total clarity to complete meltdown. He actually saw red. The rage in the pit of his stomach welled up like a volcano, ready to erupt.

He didn't wait. He couldn't. He was across the floor, uncaring whether or not Savage could mask his presence. It didn't matter now. He wasn't that helpless child, unable to get out of the manacles and kill his attacker. He was free. Dangerous.

He caught Sandlin by his bare shoulders and literally ripped him off the boy and threw him halfway across the room. The man landed with a thud on his naked buttocks, howling as he hit hard. The boy sagged across the back of the bed, his arms outstretched, his wrists bleeding. There were bloody stripes and welts on his back, buttocks and legs.

Viktor had to turn away from the disgusting sight of

the sputtering, naked Sandlin. "Where does he keep the keys?" he asked. "Just give me a minute and I'll get you washed up."

The boy didn't respond. He kept his head down and turned away from Viktor, but not before Viktor saw the wax coating the front of his body. Viktor wasn't shocked in the least that the teen didn't respond. More than once, in the early days of his captivity, Sorbacov thought it was funny to send "rescuers" to "free" him, but they were friends of Sorbacov playing their role, and the sport that followed had been painful and cruel. He didn't bother with platitudes either. The boy wasn't going to believe a single word he said. Actions were necessary, not words.

He stalked across the room to where Sandlin was sprawled on the floor, trying to cover his flaccid cock with both hands. He stared up at them with horrified eyes. "Where're the keys, you son of a bitch? You got three seconds and then we start working you over with a broken bottle." He poured enough rage into his voice that Sandlin couldn't do anything but believe him.

"The wall by the staircase."

Viktor stepped over the bloody condom and stalked to the wall, shining the penlight hanging from his key chain along it until he found the nail with the key hanging from it. The others had spread out, one poking through a box until he found a shirt and jeans that had to belong to the boy. At least he had clothes. For many, many years, Sorbacov hadn't bothered to cover any of them.

He was gentle as he unlocked the manacles. "You got a bathroom around here, to wash up in?"

He'd seen the doorless hellhole Sandlin had given the kid, but it did have a sink. The boy didn't move. Not even to pull his arms back to him. He'd retreated from reality to distance himself from what Sandlin was doing to him. Viktor had seen plenty of children crawl into their own minds to stay sane.

"Czar," Transporter said softly. "Let me take care of the kid. We don't have a lot of time before those guards come looking for their boss to make certain he's all right. We have to be gone."

Viktor hated that he was right. They needed to get their business done and get out of there as quickly as possible. He turned away from the boy who was far too much like all of them. Distant from everyone. Ashamed of what he couldn't stop. Living in his head to survive. Suppressing a rage that could consume the world. He stalked over to Sandlin. Absinthe crouched down.

"Sharon gave you the code and you erased every one of Viktor Prakenskii's messages to Blythe." Absinthe made it a statement.

Reaper made a show of pulling his knife from the sheath on his belt. Sandlin's gaze was all over the place, darting in every direction, but Viktor's brothers had spread out, surrounding him, looking grim. Merciless. Sweat poured down the naked body. Sandlin kept himself fit, needing strength to keep his prisoners under control, but right now, he was only trying to think of a way out. Like most true pedophiles they'd run across, he was a wimp, weak and scared when confronted.

Viktor held his hand up and Reaper put the knife in it. In one motion, Viktor turned his hand over and stabbed down hard, sinking the blade right into the man's upper thigh. "Answer him or I'm going to cut off body parts."

Sandlin screamed and screamed.

"It's a good thing he soundproofed down here, isn't it, Czar?" Ice asked.

"I did. I did. She wanted it done and she didn't know how."

"You kept doing it after she died," Absinthe pointed out. His voice dropped an octave. "I would like you to tell me why."

Absinthe had studied law by devouring all the books available to him. He was the one to negotiate all deals. He had a voice that could hypnotize, allowing him to force his will on others.

Sandlin shook his head several times, but he couldn't stop himself from blurting out an answer. "I told an old

friend about it. He's in Russia, and he knew Viktor as a
child. He sent me tapes. So many wonderful tapes. I had
them put on DVD so I could watch them over and over. He
has the master tapes. Kenny watched with me." He indicated the boy Transporter was washing the blood off of.
"My nephew. He's attracted to older men. Begs me to let
my friends come down here and play with him. I'll let
you . . . Tell me who you are, what you want. Anything. I've
got money . . ."

Viktor slammed the knife right through the other thigh
and blood erupted in a geyser. "Whoops."

Sandlin shrieked. "I'll sell him to you. My nephew. No
one will ever come looking for him. I paid a doctor to sign
his death certificate. He doesn't exist. See? You can take him
and do anything you want with him. Just take him and go."

"Who is this man in Russia?" Absinthe pressed.

The knife sliced down and across the groin before Viktor could stop himself. Sandlin screamed and screamed, his
eyes rolling back in his head. Ice shook him.

Absinthe smiled. "Come on, Sandlin. Man up. You don't
want to look weak in front of the boy, do you? You want to
tell me who this man is."

Sandlin shook his head over and over while the blood
sprayed. Ice let go of him, and he fell backward. Drool
trickled from his mouth and he began babbling.

"He's done," Absinthe stated. "Shit. Sorry, Czar. We
need to know where those tapes are, and he's bleeding out."

Viktor rose slowly, suddenly tired. No matter what he
did, how hard he worked, he couldn't seem to stop men like
Sandlin. He didn't want to think about what could be on
those tapes. He especially didn't want to think about the
hell the boy went through. "If he made the kid look at them,
then they're probably in this room somewhere."

Absinthe went to the bed where Transporter was pulling
a shirt over the teenager's head. "You know where the
DVDs are kept?"

For the first time the kid seemed to come out of his mind
with a little start. He jerked his head toward the wall be-

hind him. At once Mechanic was there, feeling along the wall for a safe. Kenny looked over his shoulder at Sandlin, a fleeting expression of satisfaction on his face.

"Don't look at him, kid," Viktor snapped, cleaning the knife on Sandlin's discarded clothes. He handed the knife back to Reaper. "That's not something you want to see."

"I want to see it," Kenny muttered. "I *need* to see it."

Transporter handed him his trousers. "Get these on."

"We're out of here, kid. Call it in. You tell them we killed the bastard."

"I'm not sticking around. He has friends. Powerful friends. They were down here often with him, and they have a lot to lose. I'm out of here."

"Where you going to go, kid?" Transporter asked.

Kenny shrugged. "Don't know, don't care." He looked at them defiantly, taking in their scars, their tattoos. Their scary appearance. "Maybe I'll go with you."

"Like hell," Viktor said. "Call the cops as soon as we're gone."

"He's gotta come with us, Czar," Storm said.

The others nodded.

Viktor scowled at them. "What the fuck are we going to do with him? Drag him along when the Swords try to blow our brains out?"

Mechanic had the safe open. There were dozens of DVDs and piles of cash as well as notebooks and photographs. "It's packed full."

"Take everything," Viktor said. "He probably has his entire blackmailing operation in there and we can get the names of his friends."

Mechanic jerked the pillow out of the case and scooped everything into the pillowcase. It looked heavy.

"I can fight," Kenny decreed.

"Take him to Blythe," Reaper said.

"Great. She barely took me back, and now you want me to bring her home another mouthy, seriously fucked-up kid. Like she doesn't have enough problems with all of you."

"I'm not mouthy, but I am fucked-up," Kenny said.

"Don't you say *fuck* in front of Blythe," Reaper snapped. "She doesn't like it."

"He's dead," Storm announced, keeping a distance from the body so the blood didn't touch him. "Let's get out of here."

"He can say *fuck* all he likes, I'm not bringing him home to her," Viktor said. "She's taking on three girls who all are going to have major issues."

They were on the move, hurrying to get out of the house now that they had the tapes and Sandlin was dead. Kenny followed them. Viktor swore in his native language, but ignored the kid, halting abruptly in the thick gardens while Ice and Storm built the wind again and brought with it the rumble of thunder to keep the guards inside long enough for them to leave.

They jogged back to the bikes, and Viktor had to give it to the boy; he kept up when he clearly was hurting and out of shape. He was thin, every bone sticking out. His arms looked like sticks and there were red circles around his wrist, old scars on top of new ones. Viktor didn't want to look at him. Didn't want to see himself, that ten-year-old boy so helpless still there inside of him. A victim. No one to stand for him. But damn it all, he couldn't ask Blythe for one more thing. Not one. She'd taken him back. She'd accepted his family.

Alena stood up when they came into view. She looked them all over and relief lit her face. She lifted an eyebrow when she saw the boy and looked to Viktor for an explanation. He shook his head.

Instantly, Ice went to his bike and rummaged through a bag. "I keep an extra helmet for Alena," he said and tossed it to Kenny. "Put that on."

Kenny held the helmet to his chest, looking up at the sky and around the trees. He reached out to touch Viktor's Harley.

"Don't, kid," Viktor cautioned. "You don't touch another man's bike without permission. Not ever."

Kenny drew his hand back and then just stood there as

if he didn't know what to do. Absinthe took the helmet and put it on the boy.

Viktor shook his head and straddled his Harley. "I don't know what you're going to do with him, but I'm not taking him home to Blythe."

"He'd make an excellent prospect," Alena said, pulling a jacket from Storm's pack. "I've got this extra one. It's not terribly warm, but it will work for you."

"What's a prospect?" Kenny asked, taking the jacket.

The kid couldn't stop shivering. Probably from a combination of shock, cold and fear. Viktor sighed. "When was the last time you were out of that house?"

"When I was nine. I went to live with him when I was nine, and he took me down to the basement. I was fourteen when he took me up to his bedroom. That was two years ago. Mostly I stayed down in the basement."

Viktor cursed under his breath. What the *hell* was he going to do with the kid? The boy couldn't fend for himself. He didn't know the first thing about life outside that basement.

"What's a prospect?" Kenny insisted.

"Someone wanting in the club," Mechanic answered.

"They watch the bikes when we're all doing something and make certain no one touches them," Alena added.

"I could do that," Kenny said.

"He's sixteen years old, damn it. He's not going to be a prospect," Viktor declared. He turned the engine over, so his Harley roared to life.

"Get on the back of my bike, kid," Transporter said.

Kenny stood there staring. Alena patted his shoulder. "Watch me." She put her hand on Viktor's shoulder and swung up behind him.

Viktor shook his head. The kid needed a doctor. Counselors. An education. Parents who could deal with trauma. Understand what had happened to him and guide him through the pitfalls of shame, guilt, depression and terrible, terrible rage. He didn't have their training. He didn't know the things they at least had been taught. He was vulnerable, and he'd be acting out a lot.

Everyone was looking at him as if he could save the world. Including the kid.

"I'm not asking her," he declared and got out of there.

19

"BABY, wake up," Viktor whispered softly. "You got any weapons in here?"

Blythe blinked sleepily and shook her head at the same time, even as she pushed aside the blanket and sat up. The room was dark and Viktor sat on the edge of the bed, fully clothed. "What is it? You should be in bed with me." She made it an invitation.

She'd slept naked, and it had taken her a long time to fall asleep. She'd thought so much about him, her body refused to stop burning, so she'd resorted to using her favorite toy. It barely had helped. In the end, she'd washed it and left it out on the small table beside the bed in the hopes that Viktor would get inventive.

She leaned toward him, letting her breasts brush his chest and her hand drop to his lap. As usual the moment she touched him, she felt his growing cock, hard and hot and perfect. "I'm so glad you're home, honey."

"Babe," Viktor started, drawing back just a little, reaching for her hand.

"Nice tits," Transporter observed.

Mechanic kicked him. "Nice rack," he corrected.

Gasping, mortified, Blythe looked around her bedroom. Shadowy figures occupied the space. Eight of them.

Grabbing the blanket, she dragged it up and over her breasts. Her gaze found Transporter. "Thanks," she managed. "Do you happen to have a gun?"

"We can't let you shoot him," Reaper said.

"I wasn't planning to shoot him. I was thinking shooting myself might be much more appropriate under the circumstances."

"Sorry, ma'am. We can't let you do that either. He's in a much better mood when he gets laid regularly," Absinthe said.

"Is there a reason you're all here, or do you just need a place to sleep?"

"We've got something to ask you," Ice said.

"Something important," Storm added.

Alena shoved to the front. "Blockheads. It's about the boy. Our newest prospect."

"He's not a prospect," Viktor denied, clenching his teeth. "Blythe, he isn't a prospect."

"I am," called a defiant voice from the hallway.

"Shut the fuck up," Viktor snapped. "You're a kid. A fu— just a kid. You can't be a prospect."

"He's old enough to guard the bikes," Alena muttered rebelliously.

Blythe didn't know whether to laugh or cry. She was beyond mortified. There was a point when embarrassment didn't matter anymore, and she was there. They were all so crazy and her man was the craziest of all.

Viktor snapped on the lamp beside the bed, giving the room a soft glow. "You can say no, baby, it's all right."

"Oh. My. God. Seriously, Viktor?" Blythe threw her hands in the air. The blanket slipped and she grabbed at it, jerking it back over her breasts. "It's the middle of the night. This couldn't have waited until morning?" They had a boy, a *child* waiting in the hallway for her verdict. She could give him a bed or throw him out. Were they all crazy?

"Not really," Absinthe said. "It's kind of an emergency situation."

"Just where did you find him?"

No one answered. The room fell silent. Strangely, she only heard herself breathing. Storm shifted restlessly, moving closer to her end table. He reached down and picked up her toy. Her mouth opened to say something, but nothing came out. Not one word.

"Sweet," he said.

"Do you people not have rooms where you're staying? Somewhere other than my bedroom to sleep?" she finally managed, because there was nothing to say to the nonexistent smirks on their faces. They might not *show* their shared amusement, but she *felt* it. Even Viktor, who had started out reluctant and upset, was a little amused, although too wise to show it.

Alena snatched the toy from her brother's hand and looked it over with avid interest. Blythe was certain by now her entire body was glowing a bright crimson red along with her face, but she refused to acknowledge what was happening another moment.

"Wow. Who knew? Does it work?" Alena asked. "I've never seen one like this, but Lana told me about them."

Ice and Storm groaned. Storm shoved his sister. "That's so wrong on every level."

That was wrong, but not coming into her bedroom in the middle of the night when she was naked? Blythe glared at him, hoping he might get the idea to leave, but none of them seemed inclined to do anything but stay right there, with her naked in her bed.

Viktor grabbed the toy out of Alena's hand, opened the end table drawer and tossed it in. "What do you want them to do with the kid?" he asked.

Blythe looked around the room at their faces. Again, they were expressionless, but she felt the wave of hope. Of faith in her. In Viktor. Whoever this "kid" was, they didn't want him thrown out.

"How old is he?"

"Kenny." Transporter raised his voice. "How old are you?"

"Just turned sixteen," a voice answered from the hall.

"Is he wanted by the cops? His parents, guardian or foster care?" Blythe asked.

"No cops, no parents, guardian or foster care," Absinthe answered immediately. "Come on, Blythe, you know you want—"

Viktor surged to his feet and shoved Absinthe hard in the chest, knocking him back halfway across the room. "Don't you fucking *ever* try that on her," he hissed. "You won't live through what I'll do to you."

The atmosphere in the room changed from hopeful and amused to instantly tense. No one made a move to get between Viktor and Absinthe.

"Honey, stop," Blythe said.

Absinthe had frozen where he was, hands at his sides out in surrender. He didn't make a sound. Viktor hadn't backed off, not even when she asked him to. His body language screamed hostility and rage poured off of him.

All right then. There was nothing else for it. She snagged her robe from the end of the bed, dropped the covers and stood without looking at any of them while she donned her kimono. It was short, but it would have to do. They'd already seen her, so she wasn't about to be so embarrassed she wouldn't stop Viktor from unnecessarily protecting her.

She wrapped her arm around his waist, slipping under the arm that was outstretched, his fist in Absinthe's shirt. "Honey. I asked you to stop."

"You don't know what he just did."

"Viktor." She looked up at his face. The hard lines were there, danger carved deep. He was furious with Absinthe. She waited until his eyes met hers. The fury there shook her, but she forced calm into her voice. "Honey. I'm an empath. I feel everything, from the amusement you all conceal to fear and anger. I also feel energy the moment it's released or used. I felt it and simply directed it away from me."

She didn't see how the others took her announcement, because she was keeping all her attention on Viktor, but she felt the shock running through them all. They relied on their talents and to have someone be able to keep them from using their gifts was disconcerting to say the least. She understood that, but at the moment, the important thing was soothing the man defending her when she didn't need it.

"He didn't know that, did you, Absinthe?" Viktor bit out.

Absinthe shook his head. "I apologize."

"Say it to her," Viktor insisted. "You treat her like she's one of us, because she is. If she isn't, neither am I." He let go of Absinthe's shirt and turned to face them all, his arm sweeping Blythe close. "All of you need to understand this. She's one of us. She's my other half. The best part of who I am. If you can't accept that, say so now and I'll walk away. You can appoint another president and . . ."

"Don't be an ass," Reaper said. "We get it. We all get it."

"The agreement was, we never use our gifts on one another. If Blythe is family, that includes her." Viktor refused to let up.

Absinthe nodded. "I totally fucked up. I'm sorry, Blythe. We don't know what to do with the kid, and we can't take him to the camp, we can't leave him out in the cold, so we brought him here, figuring you'd know what to do."

Instantly the tension drained out of Viktor and the rage subsided. Blythe let her breath out, feeling the relief in the room. Once again the atmosphere changed. Evidently when one of them apologized, the incident, no matter how bad, was clearly considered over.

"No problem," she said, because she could tell they were waiting for her acknowledgment.

Blythe went across the room, pulling the kimono tighter to make certain she was fully covered. When she opened the door, the boy nearly fell inside. He'd been listening, his ear to the wood. Stumbling, very pale, he threw out his stick-like arms for balance and caught at her. She steadied him.

She'd never seen anyone so thin. Every bone seemed to be protruding. He had scars, especially around his wrists. The moment she saw him, saw the marks on his wrists and the look on his face, she knew exactly what kind of situation Viktor and the others had found him in.

"Are you hungry?" Boys were always hungry, and this one looked starved.

Kenny nodded.

"Can any of you cook?" Blythe asked.

"Alena." They all said her name simultaneously.

Blythe smiled at her. "I take it you're a good cook."

Alena tried to keep all expression from her face, but she was pleased. She shrugged. "I can manage."

"Would you mind fixing him something to eat while I make up the bed in one of the other rooms?"

"How much food do you have in the house?" Mechanic asked hopefully.

She couldn't help but smile. They'd gone through a gamut of emotions and now they were all hungry and hoping for one of Alena's meals. "Plenty."

The boy straightened his shoulders. "Are you going to let me stay?"

Instantly they were all still. Waiting. She took a deep breath. "For the night, and then we'll talk in the morning. You might not want to stay here."

"I want to be wherever he is." Kenny jerked his thumb toward Viktor.

Viktor had saved him. Viktor had saved all of them. She could feel the way they all viewed her man, and she knew they were crushing him with the weight of their needs. She slipped her arm around Viktor's waist and indicated the door.

"Go eat. The room downstairs at the end of the hall would be perfect for you, Kenny. Viktor and I will discuss this."

"Where are the sheets and blankets, Blythe?" Absinthe asked. "I can make up the bed for him."

She knew he was trying to make up for his earlier blunder. "In the closet. I keep blankets and sheets in the closets of each bedroom. Thanks, I appreciate it."

He flashed her a smile. "No problem."

His smile didn't reach his eyes either. It was rare that they smiled and even rarer for it to be genuine. That made her sad, but more, she realized just what Viktor was facing. The Torpedo Ink club members were lost, wandering through a world they didn't fit into. They needed direction. Maybe a little guidance. They were grown-ups and they'd seen the worst the world had to offer. The very worst.

Her childhood hadn't been easy, but by comparison— there was no comparison. She was bringing three girls into her home, two of whom had been victims of human trafficking, brutal rape and beatings. Now a boy. Clearly the same thing had happened to him. She closed the door quietly and turned to face Viktor.

"I'm not a counselor. I'm not. I want to help with your cause, but I don't know the first thing about how to make these children better."

Viktor reached out to take her hand, threading his fingers through hers to tug her over to the bed. "You can't make them better. They're never going to be the same. Never. Their childhood was ripped from them in the worst possible way and there's no way to get it back."

She sank down onto the bed, shaking her head. "What do you all expect me to do? I have no training in this. That child needs things I can't hope to give him."

"He needs a home. A family. Someone to teach him that hatred and rage has a place but not a destructive one." He cleared his throat. "Maybe even someone who can give him a little love, teach him there are better things in the world waiting for him."

She just looked up at him a little helplessly. She didn't know what to say.

"I did that to you." He indicated the hallway. "I swear to God, baby, I never meant to. I just didn't think."

"What did you do to me?" she asked as gently as possible.

"The way they look to you. That you're going to take the boy for them. That you're going to make it all better. I think that about you. That you're magic. All the stories I told them about you. How you laugh. How you make things right. How you're the best in the world. No one better. They

made fun of me, but they believed it. Deep down, it got to
them and they believed it. Now they expect you to save the
world because I expected you to save them."

Viktor shook his head. "I'm so sorry, Blythe. I didn't
mean to come here and put these burdens on you." He
frowned. "Well. I did. That's the worst of it. I did. I saved
their lives, but I can't save my own soul so I brought them
here with me hoping you could do it. Now it's just . . .
more."

"Honey." She didn't know how to take seeing herself
through his eyes. He had her up on a pedestal, larger than
life, giving her an impossible status to live up to. "Your soul
isn't in jeopardy, and neither are theirs. I think, with your
childhood, you all get a pass. As for me being magic . . ."

"You *are*. Look at you sitting there. Calm. Composed.
Worried about me. About them. About the kid. You don't
know the first thing about him, but you have compassion for
him. They were here, invading your sanctuary, our bedroom,
and yet you didn't get hysterical or scream at all of them."

She wasn't the hysterical type and she didn't scream . . .
Well . . . unless she was having sex and she really, really
had to stop that. She bit her lip to keep from saying so. Viktor looked so . . . desolate. She kept quiet because clearly he
wanted or needed to say more and it was difficult for him.
He wasn't used to talking, explaining or getting emotions
out. She waited, her hands folded in her lap so she could
twist her fingers together tightly, knowing whatever was
coming would be difficult to hear.

"I have things to tell you, Blythe," he started, and then
began pacing back and forth across the room. "I know some
men wouldn't say a word to their old lady. It's club business,
but not you. You have to know. I told you I'd tell you the
truth no matter how ugly it is." He turned to face her.

Blythe held her breath. His face was—ravaged.

"Sandlin had a video made thirty years ago. Several of
them. They were of me, Blythe. The rapes and beatings. I
haven't looked at them yet, but I suspect the others are on
there as well. Someone has the master tape."

She didn't know what to say or do, so she just looked at him, her heart breaking for him. It seemed his nightmare was never going to end.

"My guess is those tapes are going to haunt us until the day we die. They'll be put on the Internet and distributed among hardcore sadistic pedophiles who like that kind of shit. You have to know that could happen. One of your friends might hear . . ."

"Stop, honey. Stop that."

He shook his head. "You have to know. It's bad. What they would see is bad."

"First, a friend wouldn't be looking at that kind of thing, and if they did, I wouldn't want them for my friend. And I would never, under any circumstances be ashamed of you because of what happened to you when you were a child. I'm proud of you, proud to be with you. And in any case, babe, you're a grown man now. Nobody is going to recognize the boy you were thirty years ago."

"I killed a man tonight." He said it abruptly, his eyes on her face. Watching her. Watching her reaction.

He dropped the bomb and she felt it strike like a punch to her stomach. Hard and mean. She even hunched, her breath leaving her lungs in an explosive rush. For a moment she closed her eyes. The worst. This wasn't what she was expecting, but she kept quiet, silently urging him to give her the facts and praying he had reason to do what he did.

"Me. Not the others. I did that. We were questioning him . . ."

"Who? Questioning whom?" she whispered. Her voice wouldn't come out any stronger than that.

"Sandlin. That prick, Sandlin. We were questioning him and he said things about the boy. Things that made me crazy."

"What kinds of things?" Already some of the tension left her. Sandlin had been Ray's partner. He'd helped create the largest pedophile site on the Internet. She had the feeling the conversation would give her more insight to Viktor than he realized.

"That he wanted it. He liked what Sandlin did to him. That's the kind of shit they say, Blythe, to justify what they're doing. He had paid a doctor to make out a death certificate so no one would ever come looking for the kid. He told us we could take him and do whatever we wanted with him."

"Honey." She said it softly, her gaze on his face. She knew he wasn't the grown man looking back at her. He was that ten-year-old, unprotected boy thrown to the predators.

"Sandlin took that kid when his mother died and should have protected him, but he didn't. Did you hear what I said? He paid some scumbag doctor to pronounce him dead. Legally. So he could keep him and do whatever he wanted. It made me . . ." He trailed off. "I lost it. We needed answers, and I lost it. I'm supposed to be their example. I tell them it's wrong and we need to live differently and then I just . . ." He turned away from her, swearing.

Her man. He was breaking her heart. She loved him so much. So much. Someone had to and she knew that someone would always be her. He'd looked at Kenny and he'd seen himself.

"I told them they couldn't bring him here. I'd already asked too much of you, but the kid followed us and I couldn't leave him out there alone. He's vulnerable. He said if he called the cops, some powerful people were involved with Sandlin and he was afraid. I didn't know what to do."

"Will they find him here? Do you know who they are?"

"We took the contents of the safe, and Sandlin was into blackmail. Hopefully we'll find out, but they might come after the boy. If they do . . ."

He'd come to her because he didn't know what to do. She took a deep breath. "We'll figure it out, Viktor. Certainly we can protect him here, but he might not be happy living with me. I'd insist on things like him seeing a counselor. Going to a doctor. Having rules. You don't have rules."

"We have rules," he defended. "A code we live by."

She wasn't touching that. "He's still a child. What about school?"

Viktor sank onto the bed beside her. "Baby, that's all a little ways off. First, the kid needs sleep, and so do you. You can talk to him in the morning and then you decide. I'll abide by your decision."

"What decision? If we don't take him, where will he go? He'll run and just end up on the street again. Or if you're right and he knows faces and names of men in powerful positions, they could try to harm him."

Viktor shook his head. "We wouldn't abandon him. He can stay with the club. When this is over, we'll have places in Caspar. He can stay there with Mechanic and Transporter. Or Absinthe. We'll build him his own room. Something."

That was hardly a choice, but she wasn't going to say that. He was sincere. He thought he was giving her an out, but the last thing she wanted to do was leave the boy with the club members without supervision. As far as she was concerned, they all needed supervision, let alone giving them a young, angry, in shock, traumatized boy.

"Do you want to take him in?" She looked him straight in the eye. He hadn't been afraid to ask—no, tell her— about Darby and her sisters, but maybe he didn't want the boy for some reason she wasn't aware of yet.

Viktor hesitated.

"Honey, we have to be able to talk to each other. If you don't want this boy for some reason you need to tell me why."

He shook his head. "I don't want to influence you one way or the other. It's your decision."

"Viktor, it's *our* decision. We're in this together. We're going to raise Darby, Zoe and Emily . . ."

"That's on me. I didn't exactly ask you," he muttered.

So he did know that he'd all but ordered her. "I would have said no if I didn't want to do it, Viktor. I'm not a retiring violet. I speak my mind, and I'm not afraid to tell you to go to hell if I don't like something you say."

He sent her a faint smile. Blythe couldn't help reaching out and smoothing the hard line of his jaw with her palm.

"I want the boy. Someone has to help him, and we understand what he's been through. The club. Me. You. The girls will too. Maxim's children will understand. I know it won't be easy, but I swear, you won't be raising them on your own. I'll be with you every step of the way."

"Even if I insist on rules?"

"We'll talk about the rules, but yeah, kids need structure and rules."

"School?"

"They'll have a difficult time going into a regular school, but education is important."

"Airiana and Maxim homeschool their children right now. We can help them with that and send ours."

He nodded. "I can live with that."

"And a counselor? That's nonnegotiable," Blythe said firmly.

He raised an eyebrow. "Can we do that? Say something is nonnegotiable?" He didn't sound in the least bit upset by it.

She knew a trap when she saw it. "Only I get to say that."

"Yeah?" He raised an eyebrow and then leaned close to rub his lips over hers. He kissed the corner of her mouth and then down to her chin. He nibbled on her chin with his teeth. "You sayin' yes? We'll take him?"

"If someone can do the proper paperwork *and* . . ." She pinned him with what she hoped was a steely gaze. "If he wants to stay with us." Already he was melting her, turning her soft inside. Love welled up, a fierce, protective emotion that was stronger than anything she'd ever experienced.

"He'll stay." He was decisive.

"We'll talk to him in the morning. I want to lay it out for him, rules and all, before he makes a decision. Handling a sixteen-year-old trauma victim isn't going to be easy."

"No, but you'll have me and the entire club helping."

She groaned. "That doesn't make me want to jump up and down with joy."

"I might have to think of things that will make you want to do that." Viktor leaned across her to open the drawer beside the bed. He took out the toy she'd used earlier, holding it in front of her, speculation in his eyes. His face had gone soft, and that dark, sinful, very wicked look was on his face. "Looks interesting. You plan for a fun evening tonight?"

She glared at him, but her heart jumped and deep inside her sex clenched. Heat rushed. Pooled. Her veins began to grow warm, a slow burn that boded ill for her.

"Alone or with me?" he prompted.

She reached up, took it out of his hand, tossed it in the drawer and slammed the drawer closed. "You are cut off. Maybe for days. Weeks even. I want you in a terrible mood, and I hope you take it out on your brothers and sisters, because they *so* deserve it." She was condemning herself to bad moods, but someone had to do something about the entire lot of them.

A slow grin eased the lines in his face. "You're cuttin' me off?"

"Absolutely I'm cutting you off. Go sleep outside on the rooftop. Or with the boy. Or down in the camp with your monster children." She did her best to sound tough and not laugh. She refused to let that mischievous, bad-boy look on his face melt her heart more than it already was melted.

One hand slipped inside the lapel of her robe. His fingers traced the curve of her breast and then his knuckles swept along the underside, sending streaks of fire arrowing straight to her sex. Her nipples hardened into tight buds and a shiver slid down her spine. That fast. She was that responsive to him. The slightest little touch and he owned her.

"You're certain, baby?" he murmured, his voice low. Persuasive.

"Positive." But she shook her head at the same time. She couldn't help herself.

"Did you use that toy on yourself tonight?"

Her chin went up. "Yes. That's why I don't need you. I'm perfectly fine."

"That's too bad, because I need you." He unzipped his jeans and curved her palm over his cock. "Feel that. I'm burning up for you, baby."

"You should have thought about that before you brought your crazy brothers and Alena with you into our bedroom." Her hand stroked the hard thickness of his shaft. Her voice dropped an octave, was deliberately sultry. "I had such plans for you tonight. But now . . ." She shrugged her shoulders even as her thumb slid along the crown of his cock, smearing the pearly drops all over.

His body shuddered with pleasure. He undid the knot of her sash and pushed the robe open. "Spread your legs, Blythe."

He already knew she was lying to him about sending him away. Still, she made a show of reluctance. "That toy is very satisfactory."

"Does it make you scream the way I do?"

"No, but that's a good thing."

"It's never a good thing if you don't scream, baby. A woman like you deserves a man who can make her scream." His hand slipped between her thighs and he moved her legs apart, one slow push at a time.

Instantly the cool air fanned her hot body. A rush of liquid greeted his palm when he pressed it over her entrance. "I think your toy just made you want me more."

"I'll get over it."

His thumb brushed her clit, sending a spray of hot sparks showering her skin and peppering the inside of her body. Air left her lungs in a rush of heat.

"At least tell me what you were thinking about when you pushed that toy inside you and turned it on."

His voice was an aphrodisiac, so much so that she didn't notice when he pushed the kimono from her shoulders so it fell in a silken pool around her hips. Not until his thumb stroked her left nipple in time to the one stroking her clit. Then his mouth was on her breast, drawing it into a scorching hot cauldron, so that every thought left and there was only Viktor and his hands, mouth, tongue and teeth.

"Tell me, baby," he insisted, switching to lavish attention on the other breast.

She found herself cradling his head, arching her back to

give him more, to feel the sensual brush of his hair over her sensitized skin. It was difficult to think when his mouth was on her, pulling at her breast, tongue flicking her nipple and teeth scraping gently. His thumb between her legs kept up a rhythm that was going to kill her.

She forced air into her lungs.

"You mean like wanting my mouth around your cock? Pushing you down on the bed and straddling you so I could ride you? Hard."

His cock jerked under her hand and she wrapped her fist around the hard flesh tightly. Her hand began a slow glide, pumping him.

"Did you burn for me, baby? Is that why you brought out your toy?"

His mouth was pure sin. His voice wicked. His hands were everywhere, all over her body, making her burn all over again. She couldn't think with wanting him.

"You're wearing too many clothes, Viktor," she complained.

With one hand he caught the hem of his T-shirt and yanked it over his head, tossing it aside. She pulled at his jeans as he stood, stripping him. The material caught on his motorcycle boots and hung there. She pushed him back on the bed. He caught the back of her head and brought her down to his groin, and then began to work to get his boots off. She took him deep, loving the feel of him, so hot and hard in her mouth.

She heard the heavy boots hit the floor and then his hands were on her bottom, kneading and stroking, then in her hair, gripping, his groan loud in the room as she sucked, her tongue flicking and dancing up and down his shaft, working him.

Then his hands were tugging at her. "Enough, or it will be too late. I want you straddling me." His hands went to her waist and he was lifting her.

Blythe obliged, guiding his cock into her as she settled over him. Gasping as he filled her, letting the burn take her. It was so good. Perfection. It always was with him, no matter who was doing what. She moved her body, picking a slow rhythm, one she knew would drive them both insane. She rose up and then spiraled down, tightening her inner muscles so the friction was exquisite.

She threw her head back and let the feeling take her. So good. His hands went to her breasts, her nipples pushing into his palm. Every movement sent heat crashing through her. The slow burn had turned scorching hot. His breath coming in ragged gasps added to the beauty of the movement.

"Baby, faster."

"So impatient." She could barely get the words out, grinding down, spiraling up. He stretched her to an almost burning point, but that added to the pleasure coursing through her body. Impossibly, his cock grew in size, in girth, pushing against her sensitive walls, sending more flames spreading like a wildfire out of control.

His hands went to her waist and he physically lifted her and slammed her back down over him. Flames sizzled, burned through her. So good. The best. She followed the urging of his body, riding him fast and hard, her breasts bouncing, her hair spilling down her back, watching his face—his beloved face—and what she was doing to him.

Then his thumb was on her clit and her head fell back as the fire consumed her completely, unexpectedly, taking her over with such force she couldn't do anything but go with it, screaming as it threw her into the atmosphere. His body surged up as his hands brought her down even harder and faster. The ripples kept coming, building again to a fierce tidal wave of pleasure.

Viktor's cock swelled, jerked, then jet after jet of hot seed splashed deep inside her, coating her sensitive walls, causing more explosions. His hands were back on her breasts, fingers tugging at her nipples, determined to extend her orgasm as long as humanly possible.

The door burst open and the room filled with men with guns. Blythe froze, but her body didn't seem to be aware of the men or the guns and neither did Viktor's. He emptied himself into her as she leaned into his hands, exhausted. Sated. Embarrassed. *Embarrassed.* She closed her eyes.

"Get out," she hissed, but she had no air and it didn't come out very strong.

"What the hell, Czar?" Mechanic said.

Reaper's voice came from down the hall. "Forgot to tell you, she's a screamer. Come on, kid, we can get to the dessert before anyone else."

"Bastard," Transporter snapped. "There wasn't that much ice cream. He's probably eating the entire carton."

Guns disappeared and the room quickly emptied and the last one out closed the door. Blythe put her forehead on Viktor's chest. His entire body was shaking. She lifted her head to glare at him, but the sight of him laughing was too beautiful to bother with a reprimand. She joined in. He caught her around the waist and rolled, trapping her body under his while his mouth came down on hers in a long, slow kiss. When he lifted his head, he rubbed his mouth along her chin.

"I love you," he whispered. "With everything in me."

"You make me forget everything around me," she whispered when he lifted his head so they both could breathe.

"You wipe out every bad thing that ever happened to me," he confided, and kissed her again.

Long. Wet. Demanding. She gave herself up to him. Gave herself to him. Let him take her to that place where no one existed but the two of them. She loved that he thought she could take away his childhood nightmares, even if just for a short while. His hands were perfection, each stroke of his fingers. He knew her body so well. Their time apart hadn't faded his memories one bit.

"With all the children living here, I'm going to have to learn not to be so vocal," she said. Her hands slid down his back, loving the long, muscular length of him.

"No you don't. I like you screaming. Tells me I'm doing something right. We're going to soundproof the room."

She laughed.

He pushed up with his hands on either side of her head.

"I mean it. I'll have the club soundproof this room the minute we're free."

She could see he meant it. "I'm fine with that, but, honey,
get locks on the door. And window. Maybe three or four
locks. It might slow them down when they try to pick the
locks to get in for some silly reason, like they need to know
if we'll take the ten children they found living under a boat
on the beach."

He burst out laughing and collapsed back over top of
her. "That could happen, you know."

She did know. She *so* knew it was entirely possible and
the funny thing was—she was all right with it.

20

THE wind blew in off the ocean, carrying the scent of the sea and bringing with it fingers of misty, silvery fog. Hannah Drake Harrington walked the widow's walk as she had since she was a child, looking, not out toward the sea, but back toward the little village of Sea Haven. In the dark, the lights from the houses looked like distant twinkling stars of all colors. The village was built on the edge of a bluff and stretched back toward the Pacific Coastal Highway, Highway 1.

In the distance, coming from the north, from the Fort Bragg area, came the loud roar of several motorcycles. She glanced over at Airiana Prakenskii. Airiana smiled at her and stood up slowly. She was pregnant, but not yet showing. Her smile was calm. Serene, even. She nodded her head to Hannah.

"We've got this."

"I know. I'm not worried about us, although I have to admit, I'd give anything to see Damon with my baby right now."

"So would I," Airiana admitted. She worked with Damon, Sarah Drake's husband. He was brilliant, but she didn't see him as a man to rock a crying baby to sleep. "Aren't Kate and Joley with him?"

The Drake house was silent and dark, with only one light on showing through the downstairs' great room window. Damon, Joley and Kate were in the house together with Hannah's baby. The house looked peaceful, as if Elle Drake was in residence, waiting for her husband to return from his shift.

"Kate and Joley are being really mean to Damon, making him hold the baby. He doesn't know it yet, but he's going to be a father. They're just giving him the chance at some experience," Hannah said, amusement in her voice.

"Why hasn't Sarah told him?"

"She just found out tonight for certain, and she didn't want him worrying. She'll be in the truck with Jackson," Hannah replied. "It was too late to change the plans." She kept her eyes glued to the distant lights of Sea Haven and raised her arms to send the wind to her husband. *They're coming.*

The 911 call went out and Jackson was dispatched to the Egg Taking Station a few minutes ago, Jonas reported.

Any sign of trouble there? she asked. She told herself Jonas could handle trouble; he'd been doing it forever, but still, she detested that she wasn't closer to him.

Not yet, but I feel uneasy. It's coming.

The roar of the Harleys was getting louder. Hannah and Airiana went to the wide, curved bannister of the widow's walk on the street side and looked down. Six men wearing Swords colors parked their bikes off the road, under the trees, just down from the house. The two women looked at each other. They'd expected four men, maybe even three, to try to burn down the Drake house. Not six.

Tyson Derrick, Libby's husband, and Matt Granite, Kate's husband, were outside. Matt was a former Army Ranger and no doubt could take care of himself in a firefight, but Tyson was with fire rescue and worked mainly in medical research. Neither could do anything to protect the house until the Swords actually made an attack on them.

"You ready?" Hannah asked. "Ilya wanted Joley inside. She can't move as fast as she might need to out here, but she'll help us." Airiana seemed as if she wasn't so advanced in her pregnancy that it might hinder her, but one never knew.

Airiana smiled. "No worries. I feel great. They aren't going to get to the house."

It was Hannah's turn to smile. "The house will protect itself against any threat to it. Joley, Kate, Damon and the baby are much safer than we are out here."

They were in the open, but up very high. If the Swords spotted them on the widow's walk, they might try to shoot them, but they'd have to be a sharpshooter, and she controlled the wind.

She watched as the group paused just down from the Drake house. They appeared to be waiting for something.

"You have a cool house, we just have a massive alarm system. Lexi talks to the earth. She can get the ground to do just about anything, and it tells us if someone is on the farm that isn't family."

Hannah raised her eyebrow. She knew the women living on the farm were elements, all of them, with the exception of Blythe, but Elle assured her Blythe had gifts as well. "When Lexi is around, you can feel the power emanating from her." She cleared her throat, looking down at the Swords. "What's Gavriil like? He looks intimidating."

"He is. Absolutely he is. He scared everyone when he first arrived, everyone but Lexi, that is. He doesn't look at anyone else. I'm not sure he sees anyone else. He's good for her," Airiana said.

A white van drove up and parked just off the road, just down from the entrance to the drive leading to the Drake house. Hannah's heart plunged. The Swords ran up to the van. Clearly they'd been waiting for it. The back doors opened and two more men wearing the distinctive Swords colors leapt out. The men began pulling out bottles that looked like alcohol.

"They're going to try to throw them," Airiana said.

She sounded unfazed, and Hannah glanced at her. "There's more of them than I thought Evan would send.

Why so many?" If she told Jonas he might try to get to her, and that would leave the team in Sea Haven vulnerable.

Airiana shrugged. "We can handle it."

The men were already running up the drive toward the house. Two of the Swords fell behind, both with long, thick, blond hair, but they kept coming. Hannah boosted the wind coming off the ocean and sent it toward them, a small test. The gust hit the men in the chest and they paused for a moment, the force of the breeze catching them off guard.

Along the drive the vines stirred ominously, moving against the wind. The first six coming toward the house didn't appear to notice, but the two in the back slowed to a halt and looked around them. They split up, moving closer to the vines, but on opposite sides of the drive.

One of the men with blond, almost platinum hair ripped his jacket from his body and tossed it aside, right into the vines. The vines caught the jacket as if they were alive, pulling the Swords colors into the thick mass of dark green leaves until it disappeared. The other blond did the same. Simultaneously the two men pulled on another jacket, these bearing the colors of Torpedo Ink. Both continued up the drive behind the other club members.

The air suddenly charged with electricity, a fast buildup that shocked the two women on the widow's walk. Small flurries Hannah had been using to slowly build the wind were suddenly towering clouds exploding from sea to sky. She turned her head to look at Airiana, who was looking at her.

"Not me," Airiana denied.

The gate had been deliberately left open as if overlooked, and the first four Sword members lit rags and stuffed them in the bottles as they ran through it toward the house. The men flung the bottles, but the wind caught them in midair, hurling them right back at the club members. The bottles, with deadly aim, hit all four in the chest hard enough to break the glass and explode the liquid all over them. The flames licked out and all four screamed. The other two Swords flung their bottles at the house without real aim, rushing to the aid of their companions.

The wind caught the bottles, spun them in a wild display of flames and smoke, and then launched them back at the men who threw them. One hit the man squarely in the face, breaking, spraying alcohol over him along with shattered glass. He went down hard, but rolled, coming up with his gun. He began firing blindly as if his finger was stuck on the trigger.

The second bottle hit the man's shoulder and careened off. He drew out a weapon as well. The driver of the van leapt out. He was carrying an automatic rifle. The blond with the lightest hair turned and fired a single bullet. The driver went over backward, sprawling out on the drive.

Three of the four men on fire had dropped and rolled in an attempt to put out the flames. The fourth ran straight into the vines, shrieking in a high-pitched voice. The vines opened around him and then enfolded him with twisted, dark stick-like arms, dragging him into their midst. The flames didn't appear to affect the green leaves in the least. There was no withering or shrinking from the heat. Vines began to wrap around the man's neck like a noose, other vines encircling him like a mummy. The shrieks were cut off, and then he was deep inside the thick maze of vines, with no part of him showing, not even a shoe.

One of the Swords on fire was consumed with flames and lay still. The ground beneath his body opened and he was slowly dragged beneath the earth. Two of the men had stripped off shirts and thrown them, and were now firing steadily. Bullets flew, mostly aimed at the house. The bullets didn't seem able to penetrate the howling wind, stopping in midflight. Just hanging there in the air.

They turned back, as if to leave, saw the two blonds and immediately opened fire on them. Both blonds already had weapons out and were also firing. One winced, and went down on his knee. The wind faltered even as the two men who had shot at them went down hard.

The second blond rushed to cover the first. Matt came out of the vines, firing his weapon at the other men, covering the two blond men. Matt's bullets took down two of the remaining three, and the big blond shot the last one. Tyson came out of the brush to kick away weapons.

Matt went up to the two blonds, his weapon not quite aiming at either of them, but somewhere between them. "You Viktor's boys?"

The one standing nodded. He reached down and helped his brother up. "I'm Storm. This is Ice."

Blood spread across Ice's shirt, down low, in the region of his ribs.

"We've got to go. Evan brought in far more men than any of us expected. You might get into town and see if you can help out the sheriff. He's going to need it," Storm continued.

"Let the girls take a look at that wound," Tyson advised. "You're not going to be of any help if you go down, and it won't take long."

Ice shook his head, his face pale and little drops of sweat beading on his forehead. Storm ignored him. "Get them out here fast."

Tyson glanced up at the two women on the widow's walk, but both faced the village of Sea Haven, already in position to help out the sheriff. He jogged up the drive, yanked open the door and called for Kate and Joley.

JONAS Harrington watched through binoculars as a swarm of men wearing Swords colors roared into town. They drove straight down the street toward the ocean, their bikes loud, announcing their presence. He counted them from his vantage point on the roof of Inez's grocery store. A good twenty coming at them, and he was certain he'd heard more coming from another direction.

He should have felt better now that he knew Hannah and the others were safe at the Drake house. Hannah had sent the wind to him and he'd breathed a sigh of relief, but that nagging feeling in the pit of his stomach just wouldn't let him go. Not even now, when he knew what he faced.

He didn't like that Jackson was relying on strangers to keep him alive, but he couldn't be in two places at one time and he understood that Jackson and Elle were trying to protect him, to keep him from having to do anything illegal. He understood—but he didn't have to like it. Right now, his gut told him something wasn't right.

An explosion coming from behind him and toward the ocean rocked the entire building. He knew the gas station had blown. He glanced to see the towering columns of orange-red flames and black smoke. A diversion to keep law enforcement and firefighters concentrated there while the others did their jobs.

He adjusted the binoculars and watched as a small redheaded woman walked down the main street of Sea Haven, her hands in the air as if she were surrendering to the four men who had just blown up the gas station. He wasn't as sorry to see the gas station go as he should have been— they'd been price gouging for years.

Lissa Prakenskii was a fire element, he knew. He'd never seen one and didn't know exactly what they could do, but the flames seemed to be responding to her direction, staying contained in a single long column rising toward the clouds like a fiery tower. The flames didn't spread, but kept rising, fed by the fuel tanks in the ground.

The four men watching the flames seemed to become aware of Lissa, turning one by one, first heads and then bodies. One began to laugh. Another smiled. All four went for their weapons. Lissa's hands moved, a blur of speed. She drew a gun from her waistband and fired twice, dropping two of them.

A second gun fired twice and the remaining men went down. Jonas recognized the woman joining Lissa. Viktor referred to her as Alena. A third woman, tall with glossy dark hair, joined them and they checked the bodies before turning and sprinting toward the street where the sound of motorcycles had come to a halt. Both Alena and the new woman wore Torpedo Ink colors. He knew the other woman had to be Lana. Viktor had said to watch for her. Both women were trained assassins just like the other members of their club—something he wasn't happy about but right now was an asset.

He turned his attention back to the members of the Swords club. They weren't local and just coming into this territory could start a war, but Evan didn't care if he sacrificed his members in order to get his revenge on Jackson and Elle.

Jonas felt the light touch of the wind on his face and his heart gave him that funny melting sensation it always did when his wife brushed her fingertips over his skin. A light caress, and he knew that was his woman alone, just for him. Then the tug of the wind grew stronger and he felt Airiana merge with her.

The kick nearly blew him off the roof. The two women together were lethal. He watched as the men parked their bikes across from the store. The wind blew across their bodies, but it wasn't a gust, more like a long rush of air testing them. He felt the buildup coming in from the sea. The moisture in the air. Then receding as if the wind had been called back and went out over the ocean.

He found himself holding his breath as Kate kicked in power. He'd grown up with the Drake sisters and he knew each one and how they felt when they joined together. He didn't understand how the Swords, now swaggering across the street, didn't feel the swelling power. Then Joley joined with Hannah, Kate and Airiana. Out at sea, waves leapt into the air and crashed against the bluff and cliffs, breaking over high-towering stacks and rocks, foaming white against the darkness.

Another woman joined the other four, Judith Prakenskii. He knew her as well, but had no idea she was so powerful. The five women were joined and woven together so tightly, he couldn't feel them separately. The wind shrieked as it rose off the surface of the ocean and raced toward shore. It didn't slow as it hit the first street of Sea Haven, rattling windows and tearing at the signs.

Jonas saw Lissa grab both women and they raced for the alleyway. Ducking inside, they crouched low and held on to the fence. He braced himself, dropping the binoculars and gripping the wooden strip in front of him. Howling, the wind roared straight up the street. The powerful force tore up everything in its path, papers off the bulletin board on the fence, where it had been for years. The awning off the coffee shop. The sign above one of the clothing shops.

The men turned as it hit them, knocking them into one another, as if the wind was an actual physical blow. Their bikes, parked in a single long row, went over one at a time like dominos. That had to be his wife's touch. He smiled in spite of himself.

"This is the sheriff. Put down your weapons and get your hands in the air," he shouted, without any hope that they would obey. The Swords were a club back east, and they were reputed to be brutal and bloody, one very high up on the FBI's watch list. He'd bet his last dollar that every man down there had a rap sheet a mile long and probably was wanted. He knew they wouldn't surrender, but he was the law, and the law required him to try.

A hail of bullets thudded into the building, some breaking glass and some tearing into the wood around him. He glared toward the Drake house, but kept his head down.

Lissa, Alena and Lana ran behind the ferocious wind, spreading out, each picking a building. They climbed easily and ran along the rooftops, Lissa coming in on the other side of the street. Alena and Lana chose the building next to the store on the same side of the street. Lana, crouched low, swept past him, blowing him a kiss as she jumped to the next rooftop.

Lissa returned fire, choosing a man holding a grenade in his hand. He went down, and the Swords member next to him kicked at the grenade. The wind slammed down between the club members and the store, providing an invisible barrier, at the same time throwing everything back at the men in the street.

They scattered, diving for cover, running to get away from the blast. The grenade exploded, shredding the metal into flying shrapnel. The metal fragments were about a quarter of an inch thick, the size of a thumbnail, very jagged and sharp. Most of the Swords were able to get clear, but two were just inside the target range, the shards ripping into them, penetrating deep and tearing flesh.

The explosion sounded a little louder than a twelve-gauge shotgun going off close to them. Ears rang. Smoke rose, and when it cleared there was an inch-deep chip in the asphalt with a circumference of about six inches. The concussion wave was fairly mild and broke out the windows in the store across the street from the market. The wave hit the Harleys already down on the street, lifting two into the air and slamming them back down hard onto the others.

The screams of the two injured Swords were loud. Two of their buddies dragged them behind the relative cover of the roof sheltering the sidewalk under the building where Jonas was.

Cursing, they fired upwards, as if that could possibly hit the sheriff. Lissa shot the two men, and then, as the others tried to bolt around the corner of the building, she shot them as well.

Most of the Swords fired at Jonas, trying to take out the sheriff before he could call for backup. He chose his targets carefully and methodically, taking his time, squeezing the trigger, making every bullet count. The wind continued to protect the store from any assault on it, but there was no way to shield him completely from the rain of bullets.

Jonas felt the kiss of one bullet along his bicep and another skimmed the top of his shoulder. The bite was hot and fierce, but he ignored it and kept firing, as did Lissa. She was good, picking her targets the way he was.

Alena climbed down from the roof on the far side, away

from the gunfire. She was better moving fast through the targets, rather than sitting up on a rooftop picking them off one by one. She could fire a weapon and hit what she was aiming at, but she'd never been the best marksman. She jumped the last few feet, landing lightly, knowing Lana was doing the same.

Lana was the younger birth sister of one of the other men in Torpedo Ink, Kashmir. They called him Preacher. They'd lost two older siblings to the school. Lana was nicknamed "Widow," not because she was one, but because she made them. She was lethal with her tall, curvy body and shiny black hair. She attracted men easily and they fell all over her, never knowing she was a very dangerous woman.

Alena always felt that, next to Lana, she looked pale and washed out. She had glossy platinum hair like her brothers, thick and wild, her eyes the same icy blue, but she was not short and not tall, just average. Easy to overlook. Underestimate.

She had loathed being with the Swords, even though Viktor protected her by declaring she was off-limits because she was his old lady. That hadn't stopped her from hearing the disgusting way they talked about women, especially the ones they trafficked in. They told horrible, vile stories of gang rape, laughing when they talked about the girls being virgins and so young, but how they "wanted it." Most treated their old ladies, if they had them, with disrespect and often used them to run drugs or guns.

She'd had to relive her childhood over and over. She had tried to put those memories in a closet in her mind. She had to work to keep the door shut on them, but the Swords' treatment of women and children sickened her and the nightmares had come back in full force. She'd recognized three of the worst offenders, men who were sadistic and cruel and enjoyed the damage they inflicted on young children, boys and girls alike. They had no idea what was about to be unleashed on them.

She moved with the wind, a silent, deadly predator, sliding through the darkness like a wraith. Bypassing two of the club members shooting toward the sheriff, she slipped up behind the third one. He and two of his friends always worked together, taking women in the clubhouse and hurting them, laughing when they did. They leered at her, made suggestive remarks, but they were afraid of Viktor and they'd never touched her. They should have been afraid of her.

"Harold," she said softly, standing right behind him. Close. Close so that her breath was warm against his ear. "You're a sick bastard and I'm going to kill you." She didn't do it cleanly. She sliced through arteries as she spoke, the burn of the blade cutting through flesh. Her knife was so sharp he hardly felt the deep cuts to first his gut, and then both thighs.

Alena stepped back as he spun around, his gun still in his hand. He had a shocked expression on his face as she disarmed him, the weapon flying toward the street. "You're dead," she explained softly. "Just like all those women you hurt." She left him bleeding out and faded into the night.

Twice more she repeated the ritual, dispatching two of the worst Swords members in the Louisiana chapter. Code was taking Evan's empire apart, starting with the club's finances and moving on to Evan's personal ones. Torpedo Ink was benefiting from his creative hacking, but it didn't seem to slow the club from trafficking. She wanted it stopped as much as Viktor and the others did.

She slipped back into the shadows as two more men joined Jonas Harrington in the firefight. One was a sharpshooter. She heard the difference in his rifle. The club members began to try to ease back with too many of their brethren lying in the street dead.

In the distance she heard the wail of sirens. Evan had been right in his thinking. Creating this diversion would send all law enforcement converging on Sea Haven, leaving Jackson Deveau completely alone—except he had Torpedo Ink to protect him. The other nine members had ridden in with Habit and were there to back up Viktor as they always did.

Alena crept through the darkened street toward her next

target, Ben Higgler, a particularly nasty individual. She had to admire the Torpedo Ink members. They'd all managed to be so useful to Habit that he'd surrounded himself with them when Evan had commanded Habit to send several of his men with representatives of the other chapters.

The Swords hitting Sea Haven had thought to tear up a sleepy town with no way to defend itself. They hadn't come with the big guns Evan had brought with him to the various camps at Egg Taking Station. There were so many she was terrified for her brothers in Torpedo Ink. She'd grown up since infancy with all of them. Ice and Storm were her birth brothers, sharing her blood, but all of the others were just as much her siblings. She loved them and she had wanted to be with them when she saw the enormity of their task.

One didn't disobey Viktor. His plans always worked if you had faith and didn't deviate. They'd all learned that from hard experience. In the school, if one diverted, or in any way changed details, even when the mission was fluid, loss of life had always been the result. Most times, it hadn't been one's own life, but one of the other children. Living with that guilt and sin was nearly impossible.

She went into the small space between the two buildings, staying low, moving very cautiously. She knew Ben had wedged himself in there, staying quiet. She'd watched him go in. She half expected that he'd run for it, leaving his club brethren to fight without him. He was that kind of snake. Still, he was the kind of man who was utterly dangerous because he was that low. It would be like cornering a wounded animal.

Between the two buildings it was very dark. She paused to listen for heavy breathing. There was none. She waited until her eyes adjusted to the lack of light and then she crept forward, a few inches at a time. She couldn't tell if he was there, but it didn't feel as if he was. She regretted not climbing to the roof, but she would have been exposed to the gunfire.

The sounds of the battle, which had been hot and heavy, were now more sporadic as the Swords crew had been caught in a crossfire between Jonas and Lissa. Lana had been busy taking several out just as she had. They were picking off the men around the edges, trying to keep them contained so none escaped and returned to the camp.

Viktor and the others in Torpedo Ink had enough to contend with. Now, two more men had joined Jonas, and she heard the unmistakable blast of a shotgun as one of the Swords tried to get into one of the buildings. The townspeople were helping their sheriff. Any moment now, any stragglers would break and run for it. It was Alena and Lana's job to stop them.

She got to the end of the building. It opened up into a yard of some kind. Picnic tables were set out under trees for employees to enjoy breaks and eat lunches. The yard was enclosed with a high wooden fence. The gate on the other side was open a few inches. She stayed very still as she inspected the entire yard. There wasn't anywhere for even a child to hide, let alone a big man like Ben.

Satisfied he had to have gone out the gate, she moved along the fence, careful not to make any noise. She had hunted the worst kinds of human beings, and she knew she was now. Men didn't join the Swords unless they were particularly vicious, and if they were borderline, they were soon corrupted into thinking it was perfectly okay to rape young men and women. To sell them. To run drugs and guns, the guns going to terrorists. Evan found them in every country.

Ben hadn't needed to be corrupted. He'd killed a girl he was dating in high school because she had tried to break up with him. He and a friend went on a spree across the country finding young women, beating, raping and leaving them for dead. They'd both found a home in the Swords.

She eased the gate wider with her foot, staying low. The wind moved grass and leaves, but there was no sound. Still, the adrenaline kicked in. He was close. She reached with every one of her senses. He was there. She smelled sweat. Fear. He was only about five feet from her, crouched low in the bush just past the open gate.

Alena took a breath, gripped the knife she was accustomed to using and somersaulted straight into the bush, her blade slashing deep across his stomach and ripping through both thighs in a wide *X* pattern. She was on him and then gone before he could react.

He bellowed his hatred as, with one hand, he tried to stop the pumping blood. With the other, he fired his automatic, spraying the entire area with as many bullets as he could before his arms wouldn't cooperate.

Alena had rolled away, coming right up against the fence and belly-crawling until she was behind him. His body shuddered; he dropped his weapon and then toppled, hitting the ground hard enough that she felt the small tremor. Taking a breath, she stood and moved back out into the open.

Ben's partner Charles loomed right in front of her. She nearly ran him over, walking toward Ben. She felt the bite of his knife as it sank deep, not once but three times. She had hers in him as well, slashing sideways, ripping through flesh to the bone, seeking arteries. A shot rang out and Charles's body jerked. A second one and he was down, going over backward.

Alena went to her knees, her body suddenly weak. She looked down at the stab wounds. It was bad. She'd seen enough wounds to know she was already dead. It was just a matter of time. A very little time. In a way, she was glad it was over and she'd gone out fighting the kind of men who had robbed her of a childhood.

Lana sprinted across the yard to her, wrapping her arm around her and easing her to the ground, calling out for help. Alena wanted to laugh. Who was going to help them? The only two female survivors of a vicious school made up of criminals, run by a cruel, sadistic pedophile.

Their brothers, the only people they mattered to, were off fighting a war that would probably get a few of them killed.

Lana called out again, her hands pressing deep into the wounds. "Honey, don't do this. Stay with me."

"It's all right."

"No, it isn't. Don't do this. I need you here. We all need you here."

She was so tired. She tried to keep looking at Lana. She loved Lana. They'd grown up like twin sisters, the same age, both knowing the world they lived in was violent and scary. They'd relied on each other.

"No, Alena," Lana whispered, tears in her eyes. "Don't. Don't go. You can't leave us. You can't leave *me*."

"I'm so tired," Alena said. She wanted to sleep. Not wake up. She was tired of what she was. She'd never have normal. Never have her own family. A man. It wasn't possible.

"I can't do this without you," Lana insisted. "Open your eyes, honey. For me, open your eyes."

Alena tried. She struggled to lift her lashes, but her eyelids were too heavy. She tried to move her hand to touch Lana. They'd been sisters since they were infants. She should have told her she loved her. Funny that she never had. She'd never told her brothers either. They didn't do that. Any of them.

"Never have a life," she murmured, wanting Lana to understand.

"We have Blythe now, Alena. She'll help us. You saw her, isn't she just what he said? Viktor is right, she's magic. We didn't think anyone like her existed, but she's with us. Ours."

Alena wanted to laugh. Lana had never seen Blythe. Even if the others told her about the woman, she was just using any means possible to keep her there. Still, Lana was right about Blythe—there was a kind of magic about her. They believed she could change their lives, or maybe they wanted it so badly they were willing to believe. And they all believed in Viktor. If he believed in Blythe, then she was for real.

There was a stirring behind them. Lana whirled around, her weapon up. Lissa was there with another woman. The woman smiled at them. "I'm Libby Drake-Derrick. I'm a doctor—a healer. Let me help."

Was Lana crying? They'd all learned not to cry. Alena wanted to tell her she had to keep silent or the sound would draw attention to her. That could be fatal. Then there was warmth. A blue light behind her eyes. It burned in the wounds. She closed her eyes and let herself slide into darkness. She'd lived there for so long, it was an old friend. She could hear Lana weeping openly now, but she couldn't open her eyes.

"She's going to live," Libby said softly. "But it's going to take a while to heal completely. I've got to get to Jonas. He was hit as well. It's not serious, but bad enough he needs attention. An ambulance is coming. She'll need a hospital stay and then a place to recover."

"Blythe has a big house," Lana volunteered instantly. "We can take care of her there, no problem."

Even sliding into darkness with burning wounds, Alena found humor in that. Blythe would be taking on another wild child.

21

IN spite of being surrounded by women of power, elements that could call on water and earth, Blythe was terrified. She'd hiked into Jackson Demonstration Forest using one of the old logging roads that would bring them out above the various campgrounds by the river. Viktor had said the Swords had slipped in a few at a time, taking over the campgrounds along the Noyo River and radiating out from there. They were a hundred strong.

No way had any of them expected Evan to bring that kind of firepower with him. Ordinarily, a club respected territories of other clubs, and the Swords claimed the East Coast mainly. They had chapters in various states and countries, but they stayed off the West Coast as far as she knew. She hadn't heard about any clashes or wars going on between clubs recently. Of course the Swords hadn't been wearing their colors when they arrived in the campgrounds a few days earlier.

Jackson and Jonas had made certain the gates leading to the upper campgrounds were locked and the Swords members confined themselves to the lower ones, leaving the higher vantage points to Viktor's birth brothers and the women. He'd assured Blythe that the rest of Torpedo Ink had arrived, coming in with Habit and the chapter from Louisiana, the one Jackson's father had ridden with.

She peered down at the men moving through the woods, preparing to ambush the deputy. There were so many they reminded her of ants marching through the jungle, taking everything in their path. Her heart pounded so hard she feared she might have a heart attack. They looked . . . invincible.

Elle took her hand. "I've never seen you like this."

Blythe glanced down at her. Jackson was her husband and the target, yet she was calm and seemed to have faith. She didn't even know Viktor, but she was putting her trust in him, his birth brothers and the members of Torpedo Ink.

"I lost him once," Blythe said, "and it terrifies me that it could happen again. He isn't always careful. He just goes in like a kamikaze and wreaks havoc." Even as she stated her fear, she knew it wasn't true. Viktor always had a plan. He was meticulous about every detail. So much so that he had a backup plan for every contingency. She shook her head. "I shouldn't have said that. He's fearless and that's not always a good thing, but he plans and he's a good strategist."

"I hope when this is all over, you and Viktor will come visit us and allow us to visit with you," Elle ventured in a cautious tone. "I know Mom would love to see you as well."

Blythe shook her head automatically. She hadn't talked to her aunts since the trial, not even at her mother's funeral. She hadn't gone. They'd buried her and she let them. She hadn't wanted anything to do with her mother, even after she died. She'd taken her child, her beautiful daughter from her, and Blythe just couldn't find it in her heart to forgive her.

"I don't know, Elle." She tried to be honest. "Viktor knows me so well, and if I'm the least bit uncomfortable—" She broke off and then tried again. "He isn't a man to care what others think. He might say something the aunts wouldn't like."

"That's their consequences," Elle said. "You're family. He's family. He has the right to express his opinion and to protect you if he feels you need it. Jackson certainly does. He's not quiet if he doesn't like something. Neither is Ilya or Alek or Jonas. Just think about it. I'd like to stay part of your life."

Blythe found herself smiling. She wanted to be part of Elle's life as well. She'd loved her cousins, envied the way the siblings stuck together, and had always wanted to be one of them. "I hope all of you give Viktor a chance. He's rough, but he's a good man."

"Who was the boy on your front porch?" Lexi asked, catching up with them as they hiked along a narrow game trail. "He was terribly thin."

"That's Kenny. He'll be living with us," Blythe said.

They'd had an interesting talk in the morning after Kenny had arrived, especially after she'd insisted a doctor examine him. Kenny had insisted he was going to stay with Viktor and Torpedo Ink, and Viktor had insisted he was going to live there on the farm and do what kids do. In the end she'd had to make peace between them. Kenny didn't want to back down, and Viktor resorted to physical threats. She realized that was the way his "brothers" handled things between them. She'd had to make it very clear that wasn't going to be the way problems with the children were going to be handled.

"I thought you said you were taking in girls," Lexi said, puzzled.

Elle shot her a quick glance. "Girls? Plural?"

Blythe was resigned to the reaction. "Yes," she admitted. "We're taking in three girls. They're sisters, and two of them were victims of human trafficking."

"Like Airiana's children," Elle said softly. "Ilya thinks she's amazing. How are they doing?"

"They still prefer to sleep in Airiana and Max's bedroom, but they're getting better," Lexi reported. "Airiana was worried they wouldn't be happy when they learned she was expecting, but they're all very excited. She told them Blythe was going to have three girls for them to play and study with."

"Three girls, Blythe?" Elle repeated.

Blythe shrugged. "They need a home and I can give them one. The farm has a way of helping to heal. It's been good for all of us, and I think it will be for them as well."

"And the boy?" Elle prompted.

They were nearly to their destination and began to move much more cautiously. Lexi made certain brush and leaves didn't give them away as the group made their way to the knoll overlooking the Noyo River.

"He was a victim as well," Blythe said, hesitating. She knew that sympathy always ran high with female victims, but not so much with males. Sometimes even parents, especially fathers, could blame the child. She was already very protective of Kenny.

Lexi shook her head and moved ahead of them, but not before Blythe caught the sheen of tears in her eyes. She wanted to put her arms around her youngest "sister." Lexi had a huge heart and she'd gone through so much it was easy for her to understand and sympathize with the children living on the farm.

"You don't seem in the least bit nervous," Blythe pointed out to Elle, needing to change the subject. She didn't know what she'd do if Viktor didn't survive, or how she could possibly cope alone with four traumatized children, two of whom were teens.

"Sarah's with Jackson," Elle said. "She has precog and she'll know when one of the men is in trouble. Ilya's in the truck with the camper shell, along with Lev and Alek, Abigail's husband. He attended the same school with Ilya and worked for Interpol too. I think Maxim and Stefan are also with them. The vehicle has armor plating and bulletproof glass. I've rested for the last month and, although I have to be careful still, I can feel power returning."

Blythe felt the familiar tightening in her belly that signaled trouble was coming. Looking down at the activity below them, she was certain of it.

Viktor?

I'm here. Safe. You stay above that gate and keep to the

*heavier brush. Evan is a dangerous psychopath. Seriously,
Blythe.*

Now that she knew she could touch his mind with hers,
she could breathe easier. Beside her, Elle suddenly tensed.

*Jackson just drove past the checkpoint. There are seven
Swords hidden on the main road watching for him. They
just radioed Evan. They will have him surrounded when
they make their move. Those seven are blocking the way
back out. More will join them when he gets in the pocket.*

"He's here," Elle whispered. "Blythe, are you absolutely
certain you can keep Evan from using whatever talent
he has?"

"Yes." Blythe said it firmly. "Tell Jackson there are
seven club members coming in behind him and the plan
is to surround him and then block him in so he has nowhere to go."

Already she could feel the air charging with energy, and
that allowed her to pinpoint Evan. He was in the middle of
a swarm of men, at least thirty with him in the center. She
found it interesting how men like Evan gave orders to kidnap, torture and kill, but they surrounded themselves with
bodyguards in order to stay alive. He certainly wasn't taking any chances.

Evan was down in one of the hollows by the river, a bad
position for him, but he had no way of knowing that. He
thought he was safe with his psychic gifts, his club members and bodyguards.

*They have heavy artillery. He sells guns, so he has ac-
cess to all kinds of them. All kinds. He's given the order
that Jackson can be wounded but not killed. He actually
said he'd kill anyone who disobeys him. That gives Jackson
some breathing room. No one is going to want to go up
against Evan, so they'll hang back and try to keep him
pinned down.*

Viktor's voice in her mind steadied her and she noticed
that Elle had settled as well with Jackson reassuring her
telepathically. Still, there was no ignoring that tightness in

her belly that signaled trouble. Viktor was down there in the worst of it.

Be safe, she whispered to him, pouring everything she felt for him into his mind. He had to know that she needed him that much. That she wanted him that much. That he was forever her choice.

I love you more than life, Blythe. You don't come down from there for any reason. You have to be safe. You understand me? I've been doing this all my life and I'm damned good at it. But you . . .

Blythe glanced behind her. Lexi had settled into the small depression they'd made days earlier, before any of the Swords had arrived. They'd had a couple of days to plan out their strategies. Viktor and his birth brothers had gone over the area where the women would be concealed many times, placing each of their positions carefully.

Lexi put her hands in the soil and Blythe felt, even through the soles of her shoes, the way the earth responded, and the shimmer of power that rushed around them. Leaves on the trees rustled of their own accord without the presence of the wind.

Rikki and Abigail were closer to the river. They'd found a small two-inch steady stream of water leading down to the river. The entire area was wet, moss growing everywhere, and that moisture was all Rikki needed. Abigail had positioned herself where she could direct insects and small animals.

Blythe was mostly worried about Elle Drake. She was a powerhouse when it came to psychic energy, but she'd almost destroyed her abilities just a short month or so earlier. Using psychic energy was risky for her, and Blythe had overheard Jackson cautioning her—strongly—that she couldn't overdo it. He wanted her only to use her abilities when they were desperately needed. He'd constructed a blind for her, much like a sniper might use, one that concealed her completely.

We're in position, she reported to Viktor.

* * *

EVAN had positioned his club members in a loose circle around the road. It hadn't been difficult. All the campgrounds were off the main road, either down on the river or up above it. He had the various members simply remain in their camps as if they were staying there. It was a simple plan. Draw the sheriff into the middle of the net and then close it around him. The thing was—it could work.

The road made it impossible to travel at high speeds. The terrain was rough. There were narrow wooden bridges a motorcycle could get across, but a vehicle couldn't. The odds were stacked against Jackson, for certain. There were so many Swords, far more than Viktor had ever conceived the man would bring with him. Evan was putting his motorcycle club at risk with this venture, but apparently his hatred of Jackson and need for revenge far outweighed his love of the club.

I'm passing the point of no return, Jackson said, using the bridge Elle created between the other members of their group and Torpedo Ink.

Keep coming. They'll have a truck fall in behind you, Viktor said. *My boys will take care of that. Steele? Savage? You on that?*

Savage and Steele, both wearing Sword colors, stepped out on either side of the road as the truck carrying the six men Evan had sent to watch for Jackson's arrival came up the road. It slowed and came to a stop when they approached.

"Need a ride. Habit sent us to back you up," Steele said as he approached. "We'll climb in the back."

The driver nodded. Steele had already picked his three targets. He didn't bother to confirm with Savage. Knowing him, the man was going to take them all. Steele put his hand on the door, smiling amicably, and shot the driver in the head, and then turned the gun on the two closest Swords in the back of the pickup. Savage had dropped all three of his targets before Steele finished squeezing the trigger.

We'll be coming up behind him, Czar, Steele reported.

The truck is ours, just ignore it as if you think they're campers. You feelin' a little like the turkey at a turkey shoot yet?

Not my favorite person right now, Viktor, Jackson said. *Don't expect anything under the tree at Christmas from me.*

I should be, Viktor said. *My boys are going to save your ass.*

Viktor, Blythe broke in, *I'm not close enough. I can feel tendrils of energy coming from the source and I can't tap into it and take it until I get the entire stream.*

Viktor's heart jerked hard. *Stay where you are.*

I have to move a little closer. I won't be able to stop Evan when he resorts to using a psychic power.

He could tell she was already on the move. He shot a glance in her direction. Evidently the others were masking her presence, because there was no telltale sign of dirt rising or even the movement of the trees or brush. He breathed a sigh of relief.

Jackson's truck was nearly to the ambush site. A beat-up ancient-looking camper was sitting just ahead in the road with a man dressed in old blue jeans and a plaid shirt standing beside it waving a cell phone.

That's Ronnie, one of Evan's hand-picked soldiers, armed to the teeth, and the camper shell houses four others, Viktor informed him. *Come up on his left, away from the river. Angle your truck so you're closer to that ditch.*

Jackson drove to within several feet of the camper, but did as Viktor instructed. *I want you to know, you don't keep my ass alive, my woman is going to roast you.*

Not my job. My job is to kill that son of a bitch. My boys have the job of making sure your ass is still alive at the end of all this. You hearing this, Elle? Viktor questioned.

Jackson. His name was breathed into their minds. Soft. A caress. So intimate it was difficult to hear.

I'm alive, baby, Jackson assured her. *You know I've been in worse spots.*

Ink, we need that map now. We need to know where each of us is all the time. Keys, the moment he gives it to you, light us up. Good guys blue, bad guys red. Got that, everyone? Bad guys red. Don't shoot one another, Viktor cautioned.

Almost done, Ink said. Using the vision from the birds and animals surrounding them, he was able to map out the location of every Sword member and pass the information on to another Torpedo Ink member, Keys.

Keys immediately projected the laser-like red dots on their targets and then the blue on everyone left. *Check to make certain you're wearing the correct colored dot, and if I missed someone, shout out.*

Pretty certain you missed me, Jackson said.

You have the biggest targets all over you, Viktor said. *You just can't see them yet.* He felt Elle's reaction and wished he hadn't joked with the man. His woman was having a difficult time with her husband being a sitting duck.

Jackson deliberately sat in his truck as if he was listening to his dispatcher. He spoke into the radio and then opened his door. Casual. Confident. Viktor liked the man for that. Most would be sweating.

Lexi, get the ground prepared for him. All hell could break loose at any time.

She's on it, Blythe said.

He heard the strain in her voice and wished, for the millionth time, he had forbidden her to participate. He found himself torn in two directions. After five years of living with slime, he wanted to kill Evan Shackler-Gratsos and rid the world of someone so vile. On the other hand, he wanted to throw his woman over his shoulder and get her to safety.

The moment Jackson set his foot on the ground, Viktor felt small vibrations traveling up his leg. Lexi, he knew, was communicating with the earth, sending it orders. He hoped she was as good as Gavriil and the others had said. She'd need to be.

Jackson slid out of his truck, his thumb sliding the safety off his weapon as he approached the camper.

Don't go past that bumper for any reason, Viktor cautioned.

Jackson stopped abruptly just short of rounding the hood. "You call? I've got another call I have to go to. Tell me what's going on, but make it fast."

As he spoke the Swords stepped out of the tree line on three sides of him, all wearing their colors. A good hundred strong, making an arc, coming out of every campground or rising up out of the brush. Jackson pulled his weapon from his holster and laid it against his thigh as he looked around. "You invited me to the party? How nice. Haven't been to one of these in years."

Ronnie shook his head. "Not my party, but you were invited."

He stepped back, and a group of men walked forward together as a tight-knit unit just as a truck closed in behind the sheriff's truck, effectively blocking him in. Jackson kept his eyes glued to the man in the center he caught glimpses of.

That's Evan. He's surrounded by bodyguards and they're keeping close to him. They're all wearing body armor, Jackson reported to Viktor.

Viktor slipped back out of the crowd of Swords where he'd been stationed with Habit and the Louisiana chapter. As he'd expected, Evan wanted them close. They were to the right of Jackson. He didn't have a good angle for a kill shot. *I have to get into position. Reaper, Mechanic, Absinthe, Transporter, Casimir and Preacher, get into position to take out the guards.*

Moving now. Within moments each man had checked in to say they were in position.

Viktor still couldn't get a clear shot, but the angle was better and he was certain once he had the guards cleared away he could kill Evan. The moment the guards fell, or the sound of gunshots rang out, all hell would break loose. Jackson's safety was paramount and he was in a dangerous position.

"Are you going to hide in your little protective circle like a coward or come out and face me?" Jackson said. "Clearly you arranged the reception." He gestured with one hand, keeping the other, holding his gun, down by his thigh. "I'm feeling very honored that you thought so much of me you had to bring an army with you."

The air shimmered. Grew hot. Around the bodyguards a visual shield of translucent, iridescent waves appeared. Evan Shackler-Gratsos stepped to the front. He wasn't tall, and his once stocky frame was thin. His nose was slightly hooked and his cheeks hollow. His skin looked sallow but his eyes were alive with hatred and glee.

"I see you sample your own products," Jackson continued matter-of-factly. "Not a good idea, but then you never were very smart. Evan Shackler, the whiny kid who followed my father around everywhere. I remember you. You looked better when you were fifteen."

Do you feel his power? My God, he's nearly filling the entire campground and he's not even generating much actual energy. Elle's voice shook.

You've got this, baby, Jackson assured.

The moment he responded, little sparks of red and orange zipped through the air around Jackson, landing on his skin like tiny fireflies, burning him.

Evan looked around. "Is that little bitch of yours here? Good. My men are going to party hard with her tonight. She was hard to train, not one of the bright ones, but in the end she did what she was born for."

I'm moving closer. Blythe was firm. *Jackson, don't answer us no matter what. He's concentrating on you.*

Damn it, Blythe, you stay put. Viktor didn't want her anywhere near Evan. That bad feeling nagging at him kept growing. That wall of transparency shimmering between Evan, his bodyguards and everyone else meant no bullets would penetrate. *Just get down his protection so I can take the shot.*

I have to be closer to do it. He's very powerful. It's going to take a minute, so be ready. Lexi, you need to be ready just in case. Rikki, you and Abbey too. This entire forest could go up in flames if he gets a chance to retaliate.

That didn't make Viktor feel better about her moving

from the pocket of safety they'd created for the women. He risked a glance up toward the road where the women were concealed. The gate was closed and locked, but that didn't mean bullets couldn't reach them or any of the Swords rushing up the road to get to them.

Player, you're nearest to Blythe, make your way closer. Do it slow so no one notices you changing position.

"I killed your father," Evan said. "And then I killed my mother. I shot him six times and drowned her. Everyone thought a rival club killed him and my brother drowned my mother. It's easy to manipulate people into believing anything I want them to. I kept my eye on you, but I couldn't get to you, but then my brother took your woman. I tried to get her from him, but he wouldn't let me have her." Evan grinned. "He was such an idiot I had to show him how to train her. He enjoyed it, but learned he did too late."

Jackson just watched him. He didn't move a muscle.

"Put the gun down. You're surrounded in case you hadn't noticed."

"I'll keep it, thanks." Jackson deliberately took a slow look around the circle of grim faces. "You really must think I'm a badass to bring so many of your little friends."

Evan shrugged. "They need to witness what I do to my enemies. It keeps them in line. Put the gun down."

Jackson slowly shook his head. Evan raised his hand. The tension in the air became so heavy it felt like a gathering tornado. He pushed the air toward Jackson. Fire crackled. Flames snapped toward him like a great whip. The crack was loud. The whip of flames never touched Jackson.

The moment Evan created it and the long sizzling whip of fire rushed toward Jackson, a powerful vacuum sucked it away from him. The shimmer around Evan tumbled down.

Under the truck. Now, Jackson, Viktor commanded as he took the shot.

Evan dove to the ground as his bodyguards began to shoot at Jackson and the camper with automatic weapons. They'd lined the inside of the camper with protective bulletproof armor, but it was taking a tremendous hit. Jackson was already rolling under the truck into the depression Lexi had created for him. He hunkered down as deep as the long depression allowed while hundreds of bullets hit his vehicle.

The moment the first shot was fired, the world turned to hell with the Swords shooting at everything and nothing. The noise was loud and chaos reigned. A wall of flames rushed toward the truck and leapt to surrounding trees. Men rushed between Viktor and his target but he was relentless, stalking the man, trusting his brothers to take out the bodyguards.

It was impossible to see for a moment as Lexi and Elle created some kind of dirt barrier between the truck and the wall of rushing flames.

Go, go. Blythe said. *Get out of there, he's very powerful.*

Jackson rolled to his left, down into the deeper ditch. Ilya, Sarah and Alek burst out of the truck with Maxim and Stefan as a wall of flame rushed over it. They leapt for the ditch. The flames followed and hit a solid wall of dirt and water.

Lexi, Rikki, Abbey, I've got this now. Ilya said. *I can defend us here. You and Elle let Blythe feed you power and take out the rest of them.*

Steele and Savage joined Jackson and the others in the ditch. They went back to back as did Sarah and Ilya and Jackson and Alek.

Reaper fired and one of the bodyguards went down, giving Viktor another glimpse of Evan, just his leg, but it was a target. He took the shot and the man screamed. One of the bodyguards reached down and dragged him up and into the center of them. Evan disappeared, but the battle began for supremacy.

The Egg Taking Station campground became an instant battleground. The Swords members stepped toward the truck from all directions, pouring bullets from every type of weapon from handguns and shotguns to automatic rifles. Torpedo Ink and the Prakenskii brothers shot their targets methodically, kill shots as they'd been trained from the time they were children. As the Swords went down, they became aware that Jackson and his small band of defenders weren't the only enemy. The club members rushed for cover or hit the ground. A few ran toward the bikes.

The fight in those few seconds was hot, not just from the wild gun battle, but from the flames Evan threw in every direction in order to cover his retreat. Viktor had to fight through the bodies and skirmishers, the smoke and flames, to try to keep track of the bodyguards and Evan abandoning the field.

Viktor felt the exact moment when Blythe took control. It was impossible *not* to feel it. Everyone felt it. For one moment guns fell silent. Power became a living, breathing entity, so strong the force of it shook the earth beneath their feet, the trees and bushes swaying. The flames froze so they appeared as long towers of flickering orange and red.

Evan's scream pierced the stillness. It was the wounded cry of an animal, and then he was yelling for his men to get the bitch on the hillside. "Get her. Get her now. Kill her. One million to the man who brings me her fucking head."

Viktor's heart nearly stopped. He turned his head to see his worst nightmare. Blythe was in plain sight, her face a mask of concentration.

Get down. Get down. Viktor yelled the command into her mind, willing her to obey him. Blythe wasn't the kind of woman who jumped at a man's directive but he poured every ounce of who and what he'd been made into inside that order. His heart thudded wildly and he could taste fear in his mouth.

As Evan screamed, she dropped to the ground and dirt and leaves geysered up in front of her like a massive fountain, a wall between her and the barrage of bullets coming her way. He vowed to remember to find a way to thank Lexi later. Rikki was taking the energy Blythe wove and bound to the women's powerful gifts and she doused the flames licking through the grass and trees. At the same time, the river rose, sweeping several of the Swords away with the sudden force of power in the water.

Gavriil, Lev and Master, one of the Torpedo Ink members, ran toward the locked gate, firing at the ten club members who had peeled off to obey Evan. Gavriil was fearless, firing on the run as he leapt over the gate, and then ran backward, using two weapons, blocking the road between the club members and the women. Master went to his knee just in front of the gate and Lev to the side of it.

The ground trembled and then shook, knocking the four remaining club members down on top of their brethren Lev, Gavriil and Master had killed. The moment the four men went down, Lev and Master were standing above them, firing the kill shots before any of the men could recover.

Mechanic followed the group of bodyguards surrounding Viktor. He moved carefully through the Swords, his weapon out, trying to look as if he were part of the battle. He sighted on the calf of one of the bodyguards, squeezed the trigger and brought him down. While the man lay writhing on the ground, the group kept running, dragging Evan between them. They were angling up toward the back logging roads headed back toward the railroad tracks. Mechanic shot the bodyguard in the head as he lifted his automatic toward the bluff where Blythe was.

To Viktor, it looked as if every Sword member was looking to collect the one million dollars Evan had promised for Blythe's head. They turned away from Jackson and began to try to work their way up through the campgrounds and trees toward the road where the women were stationed.

Get out of there. All of you.

We can't. We move and Evan will take over again. I've got his power. He can't use it. You have to kill him, Viktor. Blythe said. *We'll hold them back until you get the job done.*

There isn't holding back a hundred men, Blythe. The woman made him crazy. *Can't you do one damned thing I tell you to do?*

Not if it means you and the others could die.

She was firm on that. There was not going to be any budging her so Viktor didn't argue. The Sword members looked like locusts swarming, but Torpedo Ink and his blood brothers were whittling them down. He saw Player and Maestro take out six with just six quick shots and then they ran to protect Blythe, still firing, picking off two more on the edge of the road. Code fired methodically, bringing down a good number by himself.

Absinthe went to one knee between two Sword members, but he wasn't looking toward Blythe, but to the left of her. He fired and one of the bodyguards jerked and then fell, tumbling down through the grass. He immediately turned right and then left, firing at nearly point-blank range on the two Sword members on either side of him.

Evan turned toward the battle and raised his arms, gathering power. Viktor took a shot at him, but was at an odd angle and just winged him in the shoulder. Cursing, Evan dropped to the ground, the two bodyguards putting their bodies in front of him. As they did, Preacher and Casimir fired simultaneously and both toppled. Evan wasn't there.

Viktor raced toward the spot where Evan had been. When he reached the two bodies on the ground, he realized just how close to the women Evan had gotten. He was parallel to Blythe and over to the left by about thirty feet. Club members were still firing weapons, trying to get to her, trying to be the one to collect the reward.

Where'd he go, Blythe? I can't see him.

He's hidden in the grove of trees just above where you are. Be careful, Viktor, he's up to something.

Viktor was still wearing Sword colors, relying on the identifying mark Keys had put on him. He began to make his way up toward Evan, hoping the Sword president wanted more company than just the one bodyguard remaining.

He actually felt the small tremor in the earth and thought it was Lexi, but then dirt trickled and burst like a fountain right under Blythe. His heart stopped. Out of the corner of his eye, he saw Evan rise with his bodyguard shielding him. Blythe tumbled with the dirt toward the men below.

Transporter fired and the bodyguard went down. Viktor

was already running toward Blythe. No one was more important. It didn't matter if Evan got away, even after five years and all the sacrifices. Blythe was everything and he wasn't about to lose her. He sprinted toward his woman as she rolled almost to the feet of three of the Swords. The men lifted their guns to empty them into her and Viktor shot while he ran. Three rapid squeezes of the trigger, with blurring speed, sending the men falling on top of her.

She didn't make a sound, not even when four other club members began shooting at her and the bullets thunked into the bodies of the dead men protecting her. Maxim and Stefan had worked their way through the Swords to get to Blythe and killed two of the shooters and Viktor the others. The three were there, forming a solid wall of protection while Lexi, Abigail and Rikki threw up a barrier.

Evan turned and ran up the logging road, his heart pounding, his belief in his superiority still safe. He was legend, a man impossible to defeat. It didn't matter that others had psychic gifts or an army against him. He would win. He always won.

A small figure slid out of the trees just in front of him. The wind whipped through the trees, blowing her red hair around her like a cloak.

He skidded to a halt. Fate always favored him. Always. He had fought his way up and this was his reward. A fortune that kept him safe. A club he'd taken by force, killing the members in his way. The largest human trafficking ring in the world and growing every day. And now, his greatest enemy's woman. Elle Drake.

She was still damaged. Burned out. He'd paid a fortune for that information and then he'd killed the source, a man from Sea Haven who had spent time in the grocery store, listening for any gossip or small tidbit of information he could pass on to Evan. Evan had pieced it all together.

He waited for her opening move. He would counter it and bring her to her knees in front of him before he destroyed her. He wanted Jackson to find her that way. He wished he had time to drag her out of there. Jackson would suffer more thinking she was in his hands. He could have sold her to the Arabs. The possibilities were endless.

She glanced toward the general direction of the Drake house and the wind touched her face. Her eyes never left him. He didn't have time to dick around; he had to kill her and get out of there before someone came looking. He lifted his hands and realized that stupid bitch diverting his power might have fallen, but she hadn't released her hold on the energy flowing. In fact, it had increased. She'd gathered the energy from the battle and from him and bound it together with the women and men there. She'd taken it from the wind and the women standing on the widow's walk at the Drake house.

The power crackled in the air surrounding Elle Drake. She lifted her arms and countered his weak push. Fire raced around him. Water bubbled up from the earth beneath his feet, turning the ground to mush. He began to sink. The first tree toppled, landing close, the branches whipping around him, knocking him to the muddy ground. The earth seemed to rise, dirt and mud covering him as vines and the branches of the tree reached for him.

She was going to bury him like a worm in the ground. He couldn't have that. Evan screamed. This couldn't happen. A woman. A damaged woman at that. She was nothing, a body to use; this couldn't be happening. He fought to get away from the vines and the rising water turning the ground to quicksand. The vines slithered along the top of the ground and then over his body, wrapping him up, holding him still. Roots burst from the ground like terrible spears, penetrating his flesh everywhere.

He kept his eyes on Elle Drake. She hadn't moved other than her arms. She looked calm. Serene. There was no brain bleed to end her life. The power the others offered up and the way that woman bound the energy together, Elle didn't have to use much of her own. She simply took what was offered. He died hard, the pain excruciating, all the while looking at the woman who didn't so much as flinch.

Behind her two men wearing Torpedo Ink colors skidded

to a halt. One held a hand to his bloody shirt, low on his left side. Ice and Storm watched as the body sank beneath the mud and dirt and eventually disappeared.

"Nice work," Ice told Elle. "Your man's causing a ruckus. Wouldn't want to be in your shoes when he finds you."

She smiled tiredly and touched his wound. At once warmth flowed into him. "How many wounded?"

"Quite a few, but none dead on our side. That's a plus," Storm said.

"Are my sisters here yet? I'll need them to help with the wounded."

"Not yet, but I imagine word was sent for them. They're still mopping up, making certain we have all the Sword members. A few got away and hopefully they're long gone."

"Won't they come after you and the others?"

Ice shrugged. "Maybe. Let them come. We don't mind enemies. We wouldn't know what to do without them."

22

"BLYTHE, did you hide the salt again?" Kenny demanded.

Darby gave him a look of pure disdain from under the crescent of feathery, dark lashes. "Salt isn't good for you."

Blythe glanced at Viktor, who grinned at her. "Darby's right, Kenny, I salt the food when I'm cooking it. There's plenty on there."

Kenny muttered something under his breath Blythe ignored. She was fairly certain he wanted the salt because Viktor did. Anything Viktor did, Kenny did.

Emily giggled and even Zoe, the eleven-year-old, gave a faint smile. Darby caught it and glanced at Blythe to make certain she'd seen it. Zoe rarely spoke and never smiled. She was very traumatized by what had happened to her. A doctor had declared that all of the children were free of disease and neither girl was pregnant, but Zoe's and Darby's bruises were just now fading.

Emily was still uncertain about her new home. She was terrified she'd be separated from her sisters again. Blythe knew it was going to be a long road ahead for all of them to integrate into one family, but at least all the children wanted to be there, and that was a start.

Alena nudged Kenny and handed him something under

the table. She was pale and couldn't be up for more than a few minutes without getting tired, but she was recovering.

Kenny scowled when Blythe held out her hand, but he put the salt shaker in her open palm. "It's pink anyway," he declared. "Who wants to use pink salt?"

The door opened and Reaper and Savage walked in. "Hey, Blythe. Sorry we're late. Had to escort that kid back home. He's taken to trying to sneak up on us."

Blythe laughed. "Benito is a handful. He's trying to follow in Maxim's footsteps."

"He's pretty good," Savage commented, and dragged a chair out from the table with the toe of his motorcycle boot. He winked at Emily. "You up for a ride today?"

Blythe loved that all the members of the club were good with the children. They seemed to have an affinity for them. Emily shook her head, but Blythe noticed she smiled again. The smiles were coming a little more often.

"I'm ready for a ride," Kenny declared. "I want to learn to ride a motorcycle."

"You do your schoolwork?" Viktor asked.

Kenny kept his head down, forking eggs into his mouth.

"Yeah, that's what I thought. No schoolwork, no motorcycle," Viktor said. "We made a deal. In this family, we have a code of honor, Kenny. You get me?"

Kenny looked up at his hero, gave a brief nod and went back to eating. Reaper wedged himself between Blythe and Darby and helped himself to eggs and bacon out of the warmer. The door opened and Ice and Storm came in. Both nodded at everyone at the table, drew up chairs and reached for plates off the stack Blythe had resigned herself to keeping on the sideboard along with extra silverware and napkins.

Club members never knocked, they just walked in. They treated the children and her as family. They had a strict code they lived by, but they didn't have many rules. Blythe hadn't had the best family life, so she was willing to change some of her beliefs when it came to rules within a family. That meant the members walking into her home and treating it like their own was part of that.

Her refrigerator was always full with groceries because if they came, they always brought food and drink with them—and they came every day. She sat back as Transporter and Mechanic came in, followed by two of the newer-to-her club members, Steele and Code. The first week after the battle, the club had brought in a second long table. Blythe had realized why immediately.

"Savage has contraband," Darby declared.

"You little snitch," Savage said, scowling at her. "See if I give you a ride to school."

"We don't have school today," Darby said, her nose in the air, but laughter in her eyes. "In any case, I can walk. It's just at Airiana and Maxim's house."

"Give it, Savage," Blythe demanded, holding her hand out.

"Come on, Viktor, control your woman," Savage said.

Blythe snapped her fingers. "Hand it over right now."

Savage glared at Viktor, who shrugged. "Don't want to get cut off because you can't eat your eggs without pouring salt on them."

"Oh. My. God. That is *so* inappropriate," Blythe said, switching her attention to her husband. "You can't say things like that in front of the children."

"Why not?" every member of Torpedo Ink sitting at the table asked simultaneously.

"What can't you say?" Absinthe, Master and Ink asked, walking in. Behind them came Preacher, Maestro and Keys, followed by Lana.

"Czar wants to get laid," Transporter supplied.

"Did Blythe cut you off?" Absinthe asked. "Reaper says the two of you go at it like rabbits."

"Viktor, stop them right now," Blythe demanded, and snatched the salt shaker away from Savage, who had liberally doused his eggs and was passing it to Kenny.

"Babe."

It was Viktor's word for everything. The rest of Torpedo Ink pulled out the chairs around the second table, and Lana grabbed the food warmers to put them out while Maestro and Keys plopped the plates and silverware on the table.

"Got coffee, Blythe?" Master asked.

"In the other room, a full pot," she said.

She'd learned that coffee was essential. It seemed to be in its own food group. She had also learned that the club was big and noisy, but treated one another as family with a great deal of respect—and her most of all.

She opened her mouth to try to tell them about children, but then closed it because a small sound escaped from Darby's throat. Her eyes were filled with tears. Instantly she had the attention of everyone at both tables. She jerked her chin in the direction of her little sister, who was watching Ice and Storm and her bottom lip had definitely curled into a very small smile.

Zoe was smiling. It wasn't big. It wasn't a laugh. It barely reached her eyes or lit her face, but she was smiling. It was a first, and Blythe felt like crying right along with Darby. Instead she followed Zoe's gaze to the two brothers who, like everyone else, had stopped moving. Ice's hands were wrapped around a salt shaker and he was just handing it to his brother.

Blythe cleared her throat. "More contraband? Seriously? Hand it over right this minute." She beckoned with her fingers. "What is it with all of you and salt?"

"Catsup too," Alena said with some disgust. "I told them I wouldn't ever cook again for them if they poured that stuff on my fine cuisine. They are food morons."

"You're a food snob," Storm said, grabbing the salt shaker and dousing his eggs. "But the best cook ever, so you're allowed." He hastily tacked his assessment of Alena's skills on at the end of his sentence because if he didn't he feared she wouldn't cook them another meal.

"Where are we with the money for the land and houses we're purchasing, Code?" Viktor asked.

"We're set. I sent every dirty detail about each of the chapters in every country or city to the cops not listed in the books I discovered. Every chapter kept their own books, and they were required to keep perfect records for Evan.

Good for us, bad for them," Code answered. "The Sword club is officially bankrupt, as is the Shackler-Gratsos estate. All the freighters and ships were confiscated. Most of their money disappeared as if Evan never had it. Again, too bad for his estate and good for us. In other words, we've got enough to never worry for several lifetimes."

Blythe closed her eyes. She wasn't certain talking about club business at the breakfast table, particularly stealing money even if it was a criminal's money, in front of the kids was a good idea. She'd argued with Viktor but he pointed out they didn't have a clubhouse yet, so their home was the only place. In any case, he insisted, the children would grow up with the club and had to know they didn't ever talk about anything they heard to anyone.

She just hoped that what Code said was over Zoe's and Emily's heads.

"A couple of your brothers want in," Steele said. "Gavriil and Casimir. I told them we'd talk it over and put it to a vote."

"I want in," Kenny said.

"School." The word reverberated through the dining room as all eighteen members said it simultaneously.

Kenny groaned, rolled his eyes and looked at Darby. She smiled at him in sympathy.

Viktor nodded. "We'll take care of that later. There might be concerns."

Blythe was fairly certain he meant Gavriil and Casimir knowing they were still doing things that could be construed as illegal. Gavriil, for certain, wouldn't care. She didn't know Casimir well enough to know if he would.

"What about the permits? You get what we need, Absinthe?"

Blythe's breath caught in her throat. "Did you . . ."

"Babe."

Of course Absinthe had used his psychic gift to get the permits they needed for building. He made the deals for the club and he could persuade anyone—with the exception of those at the table—to do just about anything he wanted.

Blythe sighed. She loved that they were working for a common goal. They wanted homes and businesses. They wanted a clubhouse. They wanted to put down roots. She'd wanted a family of her own. Looking around the table, she knew she had it.

She felt her husband's eyes on her and she looked up at his face. She could see love there. It was in every line, in his eyes, in the curve of his mouth.

"Blythe and I are headed out on the bike today. She needs a little downtime and I want the day with her. Ice, Storm, you're on duty here with the kids. The rest of you get our bedroom finished."

He'd promised to soundproof it and he hadn't been joking. The first thing the club members had done was arrive with a truckload of material and tools. She'd been worried that they'd tear her bedroom up and it would look awful, but she could see they were taking great care to keep it the same as it was before they added the soundproofing.

She loved that whenever any of the club members were asked—or ordered by Viktor—to watch the children, they never protested. Not ever. Alena made it clear she would always prefer watching them over keeping an eye on the bikes. She even worked with Kenny on his school papers to try to tutor him so he would catch up faster, but she didn't encourage him to be a prospect until he'd finished school.

"You finished, baby?" Viktor asked, standing and pushing back his chair. He reached over and removed his plate.

That was another thing. They cleaned up after themselves. She loved that too.

"I am." She stood up with him. "Darby? Zoe? Emily? You girls good with me leaving?" She always asked because she wanted them to feel comfortable with the club members. At first they'd said no. She hadn't left. Now, they all three nodded, even Zoe, the most reluctant to be alone with the men.

"Kenny?" she asked.

"Yeah, I've got lots of schoolwork," he said.

"I can help you," Alena volunteered.

"Kenny, please make certain Alena rests," Blythe said.

Kenny looked important and nodded curtly, using the exact same gesture Viktor often used.

Hiding a smile, Blythe grabbed her plate and followed Viktor into the kitchen. The moment the plate was rinsed and in the dishwasher, he wrapped his arm around her waist and drew her into him.

"I love you, Mrs. Prakenskii," he said.

"I love you, Mr. Prakenskii," she whispered.

He kissed her. She melted. He deepened the kiss and she pressed into him.

"Let's get out of here. I found a couple of places I'm pretty certain we can be alone," he said, lifting his head. "I really, really want to be alone with you."

She smiled up at him because she could hear the scraping of chairs in the other room. Savage and Reaper came in to rinse their plates and put them in the dishwasher.

"Just remember, you two, I'm going to do a lot of screaming. Stay away," she warned. She even managed to say it without turning bright red—until they laughed.

Keep reading for an excerpt from the next
Shadow Rider novel by Christine Feehan

SHADOW REAPER

Available soon from Piatkus

RICCO Ferraro wanted to punch something. Hard. No, he *needed* to punch something, or someone—preferably his brother. It would be satisfying to feel the crunch of his knuckles splitting open flesh. Cracking bone. Yeah. He could get behind that if his brother didn't shut the hell up. They were in a hospital with doctors and nurses all around. If he really went to town and made it real, Stefano wouldn't suffer for too long. Of course, it might not be such a good idea when he could barely stand . . .

"Ricco," Stefano hissed again, using his low, annoying, big-brother tone that made Ricco feel crazier than he already was feeling. "Are you even listening to me? This has got to stop. The next time you might not make it. You were in surgery for hours. *Hours.*"

Considering the fact that Stefano had been lecturing him for the last ten minutes, Ricco figured no one could listen that long, let alone him. He didn't have the patience. He knew damn well how close he'd come. They'd replaced every drop of blood he had in his body not once, but twice on the operating table. He'd hit the wall at over two hundred miles an hour, but he knew he hadn't driven into it. Something broke and the suspension went, driving pieces of metal through his body like shrapnel. He'd lived it. He still felt it. Every muscle and bone in his body hurt like hell.

"I'll listen when you make sense, Stefano," Ricco snapped and finished buttoning up his shirt. It wasn't easy. The pain was excruciating when he made the slightest movement, but he was getting out whether the doctor signed the release papers or not. Six, almost seven weeks in the hospital was enough for him. All he could stand. Even though he'd spent three of those weeks in a coma and wasn't aware, it still counted. He'd had enough of all of them—doctors, nurses, surgeons, the neuro doc, but especially his older brother.

He turned to face them, his five brothers and one sister, with their faces looking concerned. Grim. But there was Francesca, Stefano's wife. He focused on her and the compassion in her eyes. She had nudged Stefano several times to get him to stop. It had worked both times, but only for a moment or two.

"I'm going to say this one more time and then never again. You don't have to believe me." He spoke to Francesca because, surprisingly, it was Francesca who believed him. They all should have. They could hear lies. That gave him pause. *He* could hear lies. If no one believed him, it was because he had to be lying to them—and to himself.

He turned his back on them. Just that little motion hurt. His body protested the slightest thing he did. "At least wait until you get the report on the car before you jump to conclusions. I didn't have control. The car's system just shut down." That much he was certain of. He drove at speeds of over two hundred miles per hour and had no trouble; his hand-eye coordination and his reflexes never failed him. The car had failed. He knew that with absolute certainty, so why couldn't he convince his brothers and sister that he hadn't tried to end his life? Why couldn't he convince himself?

It took everything he had to stand there, trying not to sway when his body broke out in a sweat and he could count his heartbeats through the pain swamping his muscles. What had he done to try to save himself? Nothing.

He'd done nothing. He'd let fate decide, closing his eyes and giving himself up to the judgment of the universe. He'd woken up in the hospital with needles in his arm and pain in every single muscle and organ in his body in spite of the painkillers.

His room was filled with flowers. There were boxes of cards, all from the people in Ferraro territory, the blocks considered off-limits to any criminal. Their people, all good and decent. He hadn't looked at the cards, but he wanted to keep them. He didn't deserve those cards any more than he deserved the concern on his brothers' and sister's faces, or the compassion Francesca showed. Still, he was alive and he had to continue.

"Something went wrong with the car, Stefano," he repeated, turning back to look his brother in the eye.

"We're checking the car," Vittorio assured. He was always the peacemaker in the family and Ricco appreciated him. "We immediately towed it to our personal garage and it's been under guard. Only our trusted people are working on it."

Ricco flicked his brother a quick glance that was meant to serve as a thank-you. He didn't say it aloud, not with Stefano breathing down his neck.

"You almost died," Stefano said, and this time the anger was gone from his voice and there was strain. Apprehension. Caring.

That was Ricco's undoing. It was impossible to see or hear the stoic Stefano torn up. He was the acknowledged head of the family for a reason. Ricco didn't deserve for them all to care so much. There were too many secrets, too many omissions. He'd put them all in jeopardy and they had no idea. Worse, he couldn't tell them. He just had to watch over them night and day, a duty he took very seriously.

He shook his head, sighing. "I know, Stefano. I'm sorry. I lost control of the car." That was true. He had. He remembered very little of the aftermath, but in that moment when he realized the car wasn't an extension of him anymore, that it was a beast roaring for supremacy, separate from him, he had felt relief that it was over. If he had died, it all would have been over and the danger to his family would be gone.

"Are you convincing me? Or yourself?" Stefano asked quietly. "We're taking you out of here, but you have to pull yourself together. Enough with the craziness, Ricco, or I'll have no choice but to pull you off rotation even after you're physically cleared for work—which, by the way, won't be for some time."

Gasps went up from his brothers and Emmanuelle, his sister. Francesca uttered a soft *no* and shook her head. Ricco's heart nearly seized. He was a rider. A shadow rider. It was who he was. What he was. A rider had no choice but to do what he'd been trained for from the age of two—even before that. It was in his bones, in his blood; he couldn't live without it.

Stefano stepped directly in front of him, close, so they were eye to eye. "Understand me, Ricco. I won't lose another brother. I'll do *anything* to save you. Anything. Give anything, including my life. I'll use every weapon in my arsenal to protect you from yourself and any enemy that comes your way. You do something about this, whatever it takes, and that includes counseling. But there aren't going to be any more accidents. You get me, brother? There will be no more accidents."

Ricco nodded his head. What else could he do? When Stefano laid down the law he meant every word he said. It wasn't often that Stefano spoke like this to them, but no one would ever defy him, including Ricco. He loved his brother. His family. He'd sacrificed most of his life for them gladly, but Stefano was more than a brother. He was Mom, Dad, big brother, protector, all rolled into one.

It was Stefano who had always been there for him. His own mother hadn't even come to the hospital to visit him after the accident, but Stefano had barely left even to eat. He looked haggard and worn. Every time the pain had awakened Ricco from his semiconscious state, Stefano and his brothers and Emmanuelle had been right there with him. They'd stuck by him throughout those long six weeks. That solidarity only reinforced his decision to keep them safe. They were everything to him.

"I get you," he assured softly.

"It's done, then. You don't train any more than the regular training hours, and that's after you've done your physical therapy and the doctors okay you for training again. You sleep even if you have to take something to get you to sleep. You stop drinking so fucking much and you talk to me if you are having trouble doing those things."

His heart was pounding overtime now. He couldn't promise Stefano that he would stop with his extra training hours once he was cleared. He had to make certain he was in top form. That he didn't—couldn't—ever make a mistake again. That was part of him as well. But how did he explain that to his brother when he couldn't explain why? He just nodded, remaining silent so no one could hear his lie.

He drank sometimes to put himself to sleep; he could stop drinking with no problem, he just wouldn't be able to sleep. He wasn't about to say anything more to Stefano. It was impossible to lie to him and he didn't want his brother to worry any more than he already was.

Staring into the mirror as he finished buttoning his dove gray shirt, he looked at the vicious bruises and the swelling, at the side of his head that felt as if it had nearly been caved in, causing the severe concussion. Beneath the shirt his muscles rippled with every movement, a testimony to his strength—and he was unbelievably strong. According to the surgeon, a miracle and his superb physical condition had saved him from certain death. His frame was deceptive in that his roped muscles weren't so obvious the way his cousins' were, but they were there beneath the skin of his wide shoulders and powerful arms.

He reached for his suit jacket. The Ferraro family of riders always wore a pinstriped suit. Always. It was their signature. Even Emmanuelle wore the suit, fitted and making her look like a million bucks, but then she could wear anything and look beautiful. He sent his sister a reassuring smile because she looked as if she might cry. He knew he looked rough. He felt worse than rough, but his sister didn't have to know that.

"I'm fine, Emme," he reassured softly. He wasn't, but then, he hadn't been for a long, long time.

"Of course you are," she said briskly, but she looked strained. "Walking away from a crash like that is easy for a Ferraro."

He hadn't exactly walked away from it, but he was standing now, and that was what counted. He forced himself not to wince as he donned his jacket. Once the material settled over his arms and shoulders, he looked the way his brothers looked—a fit male, intimidating, imposing even. No one could see the bruises and internal injuries, or inside his head where someone was taking a jackhammer to it.

There was a rustle at the door. His brothers Giovanni and Taviano moved aside to allow the doctor and nurse to enter. The doctor glared at all of them. The nurse kept her eyes on the floor. He noted her hands were shaking. She didn't want to confront the Ferraros, but had no choice when the surgeon insisted on saying his piece.

"You shouldn't be up, Mr. Ferraro," Dr. Townsend said. "You were in a coma for three weeks and your operation took hours to repair all the damage to your organs. You need rest and extensive physical therapy."

"I've done nothing but rest for the past six weeks."

"You're going to have headaches, blurred vision, dizziness on and off for a while. You need care."

"I'm fine," Ricco assured. "And very grateful to you." That had to be said whether or not it was a lie. And it was a complete lie. He had the headache from hell, was dizzy and his vision was blurred, but he was leaving.

"I refuse to release you. You could have blood clots, an aneurysm, any number of complications," the doctor continued.

"I won't," Ricco said, giving them the look every Ferraro had perfected before their tenth birthday. His eyes were cold and flat and hard. Both the doctor and nurse immediately moved back. That, at least, was satisfying. He took another step toward them and they parted to allow him through. He might look like hell, and feel worse, but he was still formidable.

"I want the boxes of cards, but you can distribute the flowers to other hospital patients," Ricco continued, ignoring Stefano's frown. He knew what that meant. Stefano would want to talk to his doctor. A shadow rider could hear lies and compel truth—even from someone in the medical field. He kept walking, knowing his brother would never let him walk out to face the reporters alone.

"You're leaving against medical advice," the doctor reiterated.

Ricco didn't slow down. Immediately, his brothers and Emmanuelle fell into step around him. Surrounding him. Shoulder to shoulder. Solidarity. The moment he was one step outside his hospital room, his cousins, Emilio and Enzo Gallo, moved in front of them. Tomas and Cosimo Abatangelo, also first cousins, dropped in behind. The cousins always acted as bodyguards for the Ferraros, and Ricco knew he needed them. He might say he was ready to leave the hospital, but he wasn't. His body needed rest desperately, as well as time to heal. He just couldn't do it there.

The press had been all over the accident, trying to sneak into the hospital and get photographs of him covered in bandages. One nurse had been suspended while they investigated the allegation that she'd taken numerous pictures of Ricco unconscious and sold them to the tabloids. There had been several other attempts by orderlies and a janitor. Anyone getting a picture of playboy billionaire Ricco Ferraro after he crashed his race car in a fiery display stood to make hundreds of thousands of dollars.

"Did Eloisa come to visit you?" Stefano asked, walking in perfect step with him.

Ricco glanced at him, one eyebrow raised. "I crashed, Stefano. Not perfect. Why would you think our mother would ever come to visit me when I showed the world I was less than perfect?" Stefano had raised them, not Eloisa.

Stefano glanced at Francesca. "I thought she was attempting to turn over a new leaf. Guess I was wrong."

Ricco didn't answer. He knew Francesca, Stefano's wife, had been trying to make peace with Eloisa, but his mother didn't seem to have one maternal instinct in her body. He couldn't care less. They'd had Stefano while growing up and he'd watched out for them—just as he was doing now. His eldest brother might be annoying, but he loved his siblings. A. Lot. And he looked after them. It was something they all counted on.

Ricco hated that he'd caused his brothers and sister so much concern. He knew he had to change his life around. It was time. He just didn't know how.

"Ready?" Stefano asked as they approached the double doors leading to the parking lot. No one broke stride, all moving with the same confident step. The town car had already been brought to the entrance. It was only a few feet, but the paparazzi, several rows deep, already had flashes going off.

"Yeah," Ricco said. He wasn't. He could barely walk upright. Every single step jarred his body and reminded him he was human.

The doctors had told him that if he hadn't been in such good shape physically, he wouldn't have survived. That was both a blessing and a curse. He knew more sweat dotted his forehead even before he could reach the privacy of the car, but he kept walking. He had to get out of the hospital before he lost his mind. He'd had his own private wing paid for by the Ferraros, complete with bodyguards, but that hadn't stopped the madness of the press and the fear that they'd catch him at his most vulnerable.

Stefano and the rest of his siblings had stayed the three weeks he was kept unconscious; at least that was what Francesca had whispered to him. They only left if a job was imperative. Once he was awake, it was mainly Stefano with him while the others took care of work. He felt their love, and in that moment, facing the paparazzi with his siblings surrounding him, he knew it had all been worth every sacrifice he'd made to protect them. He'd do it all over again in a heartbeat.

Ricco kept his head up as they moved as a single unit to the town car with its tinted windows. Emilio and Enzo cleared a path through the reporters. None of the Ferraros even looked at them. Ordinarily they were friendly with the paparazzi. They needed the reporters and photographers to provide alibis for them. Today, the family just wanted to get Ricco home.

To his dismay, Stefano slid into the car with him. Ricco sighed and shook his head as Tomas shut the door on the frantic cameras and shouted questions. Enzo slipped behind the wheel.

"Stefano." God, he was tired. He lifted a hand to wipe at the beads of sweat dotting his forehead. "You don't have to escort me home."

"I wanted a private word with you."

Evidently the fact that Enzo was driving the vehicle and Emilio was in the front seat with him didn't matter.

Ricco laid his head against the cool leather. "I'm listening."

"I've been patient since you returned from Japan. More than patient. You've not been the same since Japan and I've waited for you to tell me what the hell happened to change you, but you pretend it's all good. It isn't, Ricco."

Ricco stiffened in spite of all of his training. It was the last thing he expected Stefano to bring up. He was barely fourteen when he'd been sent to Japan and had just had his sixteenth birthday when he returned. It seemed a lifetime ago. He'd tried to bury those memories, but nightmares refused to go away. They haunted him no matter how much liquor he consumed.

"You have to talk to someone about what went on there. It's colored your life. You're the best rider we have, Ricco, but you're too reckless. You don't care about your own life, and that's something I won't allow you to risk. You've gotten worse, not better."

He couldn't deny that. "I've never once failed a mission. Not one single time, Stefano." Ricco could barely breathe when he told that truth that wasn't the entire truth. The thought of having his legacy—what he'd been born to do— taken from him was enough to kill him. He wouldn't survive. Doing his job kept him alive. His brother couldn't possibly be saying what Ricco thought he was.

"No, but you don't give a damn about whether you live or die."

It was the fucking truth, and if he opened his mouth, Stefano would hear it. He forced air through his lungs and stared out the window at the buildings as they drove through the streets of Chicago. Outwardly, he looked calm. Confident. There was one truth he could give his brother. He turned back to face him. "There is no surviving without being a shadow rider. You take that away from me and I've got nothing to hang on to."

Swift anger crossed Stefano's face. "That's fucking bullshit, Ricco. You have us. Your family. How do you think I will do without you? Or Emme? The rest of them? You're important to us. Do you even give a damn about us?"

He loved his brother and sister fiercely. Protectively. He'd alienated himself from them—for them. Fury burst through him, that rage that sometimes threatened to consume him. "What does that mean? You think I would do this if I had a choice . . . ?" He broke off. That was a mistake, and shadow riders didn't make mistakes. He couldn't afford to have Stefano launch an investigation. It was the painkillers, loosening his tongue when he knew better.

Stefano fell silent. That was a really bad sign. He was highly intelligent and little got by him. Ricco tried desperately to think of something that might distract his brother, but nothing came to mind. He hurt too much. Every muscle. Every bone.

Most people didn't realize how physically demanding it was to race a car for as long as a race took, let alone wrecking at such a high speed. Even with all the safety measures built into the car, the jolting and spinning on one's body was incredible. Add an actual crash into a wall of thick concrete and metal, and his body felt as if it had been beaten by an assembly line of strong men with baseball bats—or run over by several very large trucks.

"I get what you're saying to me, Stefano, and I'll do something about it. I have to be a rider. You won't have to replace me in the rotation. As soon as I'm healed, I'll be back to work." He poured truth into his voice, knowing his brother could hear him.

That wasn't going to be enough and he knew it. He made a show of sighing, so it would be more believable when he caved. "I need to change my life." There was nothing truer than that. "I can't wait for a woman to walk down our streets throwing shadows out like Francesca did. I have to find someone now. I've been giving it some thought, but I had decided it wouldn't be fair to find someone, allow them to fall in love with me, and then have to give them up to marry a rider so I can produce children."

All riders were expected to marry another capable of producing riders, even if that meant an arranged marriage. Emme had it the worst because she was a woman, and if she didn't find her man by the time she was thirty, her marriage would be arranged. The men had a few more years before they were forced into an arranged marriage, but there was no falling in love and getting married to just anyone.

Stefano's dark gaze never left his, and Ricco forced himself to continue. "I've thought a lot about this. I'm an artist. I know I need physical therapy before I'm ready for work again, so I think now would be a good time to work on my art. I've continued studying Shibari, and I love the artistic elements, but the only place to actually display or practice my art is in one of the clubs."

Stefano blinked, his only reaction.

Ricco nodded. "I know what I do can't be protected in the kinds of clubs I'd have to frequent. Sooner or later the paparazzi would find out and it would be in every magazine from here to hell and back. But if I find a good rope model, one I can work with in the privacy of my home, I can photograph my art. I've always wanted to do that. I have my own darkroom and can develop the photographs myself.

Eventually I can put them on canvas or in book form. I just have to find the right model. I'm hoping if I do, I'll feel a strong connection with her."

Stefano rubbed the bridge of his nose as the car slowed and then turned through the heavy throng of paparazzi standing on the sidewalk and nearly blocking the drive up to Ricco's home. Both men ignored them as Enzo inched the car through the crowd to the high iron gates protecting Ricco's home. "It's a risk, Ricco. Not the art. The woman."

Ricco nodded. "I'm aware of that. I want to find someone I can connect with on a more intimate level. Someone who could love me and maybe understand if I have to be with another woman."

"That's highly unlikely."

"I know. I know that. I just can't live like this anymore." Staying up all night, drinking himself into a stupor, or partying with multiple women at the same time until the sun came up. Never feeling anything. He watched as the gates swung open to allow them inside. He didn't realize he was holding his breath until they closed behind him, locking out the paparazzi.

"Someone threatened us, didn't they?"

Stefano asked it quietly—so quietly Ricco almost missed it and almost asked what he meant. Stefano said it like he already knew, that he was just confirming. Of course he would figure it out. Stefano had been the head of the family for years, since he was a teenager. He'd taken care of them all when he was even younger than that. He would know. He'd probably considered that possibility all along.

"I can't talk about it." That was confirmation and it wasn't.

Stefano swore, a long tirade of Italian. He kept his voice low, vicious, and Ricco heard the promise of retaliation there.

He shook his head. "Just let it go."

"Let it go?" Stefano looked at him as if he had grown two

heads. "They threaten my brother, a fellow rider, and you want me to let it go? We have an international council . . ."

"Don't. I mean it, Stefano. Let it go. There are reasons."

"There are never reasons for one family of riders to threaten another family."

"It was a long time ago. I'm asking you to let it go." Ricco didn't allow desperation to show on his face, no matter that he was feeling it. Stefano would go to war in a heartbeat over him, but there was no way to know how many families in Japan would unite against them. Ricco wasn't willing to risk his brothers, sister or cousins.

Ricco had remained silent for years. They'd been long, hard years, always looking over his shoulder and training harder than ever. Often, when he couldn't sleep, he'd go to one of his family's homes and watch over them, paranoid that something might happen to them. After several years had gone by, he was certain they were safe, and he didn't want his brother to stir up trouble, but he still checked on them throughout the night.

"I think finding a partner for your art is a positive move, Ricco. Looking for a woman to be your partner when you know you'll have to walk away later is something else altogether."

Ricco already knew that, but he was losing too much of himself. Going too wild in a desperate attempt to feel something. Anything. He was already too far gone and didn't know if there was anyone who could bring him back. He'd deliberately separated himself from his family, spending less time in public with them and more time racing, or partying in the hopes that others would think he didn't care about them. He must have done a good job for Stefano to ask him if he cared.

Ricco dropped his hand to the door, needing to escape. Stefano shifted in his seat as if he might follow him. "I need to lie down," Ricco said, knowing his brother would hear the ring of truth. He did need a bed, and fast, or he was going to topple right over.

Stefano backed down. "Angelina Laconi is going to

come check on you, and don't give me any trouble over it. She's a nurse."

"She makes eyes at me." Now she'd have excuses to touch him. Life sucked. He wasn't going to get out of having a nurse drop by; he could tell by Stefano's expression.

"Live with it. Emmanuelle made certain your fridge is stocked and Francesca made several meals for you. They're in the freezer. One's in the fridge."

"Please thank them for me." Ricco shoved open the door and forced his legs to work. It wasn't easy, but he had discipline in abundance, a trait every rider needed. He was very, very aware of Stefano's eyes on him as he made his way up to the door.

"FRANCESCA." Ricco bent his head to brush a kiss along his sister-in-law's cheek. The weeks of healing had helped. Pain didn't crash through him every time he took a step, and he'd begun training again, although Stefano watched him closely. His older brother was still unaware of the training hall Ricco had installed in his home a few years earlier. Most gatherings were in Stefano's penthouse in the Ferraro Hotel.

"Ricco." She flashed her amused smile, the one that mocked him a little for his greeting.

He rarely said hello or good-bye. He said her name and she responded by saying his. He loved that about her. He loved everything about her, mainly that she loved his brother more than anything or anyone.

He'd never really learned the art of relaxing. He could play his part out in public, but at home, with his brothers and sister, he had always been the one to pace around; to help Taviano, his youngest brother, in the kitchen; or to find his way to the training room and work out while the others conversed. Since the accident, he'd made attempts at being better.

"Smells good."

"I hope it tastes good. I've been working with a few new

recipes for the artichoke sauce you said you liked and I think I've got it for you now. I'm serving homemade pasta with artichoke sauce, zucchini flan, guinea fowl and fried stuffed flowers. Oh, and for dessert, tiramisu."

"Nice. I've never had anything you've ever cooked that I didn't like." It was the truth. He wasn't into flattery, but Francesca was truly the nicest woman he'd ever met and she cooked like a dream. She loved and accepted all of them right along with her demanding husband. "Where's the boss?"

She laughed. "He only *thinks* he's the boss. I still have my job at the deli, don't I? You know how much he hates me working."

"Here's a little newsflash for you, honey," Ricco said. "We all hate you working. We've got enemies."

"I don't."

They'd taken care of her enemy. Permanently. "They can get to us through you," he pointed out. It was an old argument, and one he was certain Stefano had tried many times. Francesca might be the sweetest woman he knew, but she was no pushover.

The fact that Francesca still had her job surprised him about his eldest brother. He couldn't imagine allowing his woman to put herself in danger, and Stefano had no trouble bossing all of his siblings around.

Ricco shrugged out of his jacket and let her take it to hang up along with his tie. "Just us tonight?" He was already unbuttoning the top three buttons of his shirt.

"Yes." She made a face at him. "Family business."

He found himself relaxing. He was good at family business. Francesca would have told him if Eloisa was present. As a rule, his mother didn't show up for family events at Stefano's—which meant she was almost never present.

Taviano had come to him three weeks earlier with his findings. A casing had cracked on the shock absorber. The family had put out the word to other teams to stay away from that particular company for their casings. Stefano had yet to talk to him about it, so he was fairly certain that was what this night was all about. He didn't really care what it was that brought the family together, only that they were together.

"Stefano told me you're advertising for a rope model again," Francesca continued. "How's that coming?"

"There's a lot of fucked-up women in the world," he said.

She laughed. "You're just finding that out?"

"Since meeting you, I had high hopes." That was partly true, but mostly he was teasing her. Something new for him with an outsider, although he'd never considered her that. Francesca fit right in with his brothers and Emmanuelle. She was family, and every one of them would lay down their lives for her.

She gave him another smile. She really was a beautiful woman. Stefano was lucky to find her. Not only was she sweet, intelligent and beautiful, but she also could have been a rider had she been found and trained from the time she was a child. She was rare. Very rare. She had accepted their way of life, shrouded in secrecy and living outside the accepted laws of the land.

Ricco sighed. He'd secretly hoped that by advertising for a rope model, the woman of his dreams would appear. She would be tall and blond, because he liked that look, with lots of curves, and she'd be very willing to accept him as the focus of her life. More, she would be an untrained rider, one who could give him children so his family would be happy. So far he'd gotten every body type, every hair color and a variety of curves, a lot of women willing to do kink and more who wanted money. A lot of money. He hadn't connected with any of them, not even physically—and that was a first for him.

He hadn't conducted the interviews, but he'd been there, in the shadows, watching where they couldn't see him. Trying to find one woman who aroused him at least emotionally, if not physically. But nothing happened. It was depressing.

He'd always liked women, especially when he came out

of the tunnels after a job, but really all the time. He never connected with them on any level but physical. He never wanted to spend any time with them outside of having sex. He was adventurous sexually and surrounded himself with women who were the same way, but he played and he left. He always made that clear. He wasn't a man who stayed. Lately, even that was fading. He played with the Lacey twins occasionally, but he wasn't into it any longer, and hadn't been for some time.

Ricco envied Stefano his ability to have a relationship. He wasn't certain he could do it. Now that he'd been in on the interviews with the various women applying to be a rope model, he was fairly positive he would never be that man. He wanted it, but he just felt indifference or annoyance. None of the women knew who the rope master was, but they'd tried to find out, and several suspected it was a Ferraro—specifically Ricco, as more than once in magazines his love of rope art had been written up. He'd been careful to have Emilio conduct the interviews in a neutral location—the conference room of the Ferraro Hotel, where many interviews for various businesses took place.

"It's going to happen for you, Ricco," Francesca said, walking with him through the enormous open room toward the kitchen where the family usually gathered. "I know you don't think it will, but I feel it. She's close."

He glanced at her sharply. Francesca wasn't given to fantasy. He shook his head in denial. He'd given up that dream a long time ago. "Done too many things in my life to ever have a decent woman throw in with me."

"I'm a decent woman and I love you," Francesca said.

"Yeah, but you're my sister."

"I love you too." Emmanuelle joined them, slipping her arm around his waist as well. "But then, I'm your sister too, and it's well known by the lot of you that I have no sense."

Ricco couldn't help but laugh. Emmanuelle could always make him smile, no matter how bad his nights had been. She was a ray of sunshine to all of them.

Emmanuelle turned her face up to his, her eyes moving over his features, seeing things he didn't want her to see. At once the smile disappeared. "You aren't sleeping."

He shrugged, trying to look casual. "Never been good at sleeping, honey. Tell me what's happening in our neighborhood. I've been out of the loop for a while." Isolating himself as much as Stefano would allow it. He wanted to be with his family but had always considered that it could be dangerous for them.

"Francesca knows far more than any of us. Working at Masci's, she hears everything, don't you?"

Francesca went to the stove where Taviano was turning the guinea fowl in the frying pan. Using olive oil, he'd sautéed garlic and scallions and then placed the fowl skin-side down before adding sage. He glanced up and winked at Ricco. "She was just going to let this burn."

"She never burns anything," Giovanni objected. He mixed the homemade pasta noodles with the artichoke sauce. "Stefano scored big-time with this one. He just needs a few bambinos running around, with her pregnant and barefoot, and the man will be happy."

"He's already happy," Francesca said smugly.

"Well, I'd be happy," Giovanni clarified.

Francesca blew him a kiss and sat up on the bar stool between her brothers-in-law. "Lucia and Amos are having the time of their lives with their new daughter, Nicoletta. Extremely happy." Lucia and Amos Fausti owned Lucia's Treasures, a small boutique that Francesca and Emmanuelle often frequented.

"Is Nicoletta going to a regular school yet?" Stefano asked, coming up behind his wife and circling her around the waist with his arms.

Ricco had noticed Stefano couldn't get near Francesca without touching her. He envied his brother that and wanted it for himself. He just wanted to feel for someone. Connect with someone.

"She's smart," Vittorio said. He stabbed his fork into the pasta and took a bite, then held up his thumb, indicating it was good. "But she doesn't want to go to a regular school. Amos asked me to talk to her. I did, but I don't think she was impressed. She didn't say much, just looked at me. I don't envy them. The girl is gorgeous. Every young man from here to hell and back is going to be knocking at their door."

"Why do you all want her in a regular school?" Taviano asked. "More trouble, if you ask me. All those horny bastards leering at her. Do we really want that kind of problem? One of us would have to go scare the crap out of them, and then she'd be embarrassed or pissed and we'd get the blame. Keep her home. Locked up. It's for her own good."

"It's her last year of high school," Francesca said. "She deserves to have fun."

Ricco wasn't positive Francesca was right about sending the girl to the local high school. Nicoletta had come from New York from a terrible situation. She'd been brutally abused—physically, sexually and emotionally—by her three uncles, men belonging to the notorious Demons, one of New York's bloodiest gangs. Stefano and Taviano had rescued her, but the damage had been done and it had been severe. Ricco knew the girl, like him, didn't sleep. He knew because he often pulled guard duty.

Nicoletta was one of the rare potential riders, her shadow throwing out feeler tubes to connect with the other shadows around her. The riders all took turns watching over her. He took the night shift because it suited him, and she went out her bedroom window and sat on the rooftop listening to music. He kept watch, but he didn't interfere. She looked so young and alone, and he knew he'd just scare her if he suddenly appeared beside her.

"She likes being with Lucia and Amos," Stefano said. "I've talked to her often and she wants to stay with them."

"Who wouldn't want to be with them?" Taviano asked. "They'll spoil her rotten. She's good for them as well."

"It was a cracked casing, Ricco," Stefano said abruptly. "On the shock absorber. Not you, a cracked casing. The wrong metal alloy was used and passed off to us as the real deal. I've already informed the other racing teams and they are boycotting the company."

Ricco didn't look at his brother. That was the most Stefano was going to give him, when both knew that everything else that had been said between them still stood. He just nodded and sank down into the chair at the table beside Emmanuelle. It wasn't exactly news anyway. Taviano had come to him immediately a good three weeks earlier and told him. Taviano preferred to race Indy cars, and he was the one, along with Vittorio and Emmanuelle, who designed their engines. Stefano had been pulling extra jobs, taking Ricco's place in the rotation, and the family had been very, very busy.

"How are you coming along on your hunt for a partner?" Vittorio asked, sliding into a chair at the long table.

Ricco shrugged. "I guess I've got to choose someone soon. I'm doing one more round of interviews and then I'll have to pick someone."

"Or not," Francesca said. "Seriously, hon, don't hook up with just anyone. It won't work."

He knew that, but he was determined to try. He had to if he was going to survive.